The Great Deception

JOY CHAMBERS

headline
review

Copyright © 2012 Joy Chambers

The right of Joy Chambers to be identified as the Author of
the Work has been asserted by her in accordance with the
Copyright, Designs and Patents Act 1988.

First published in Great Britain in 2012 by HEADLINE REVIEW
An imprint of HEADLINE PUBLISHING GROUP

First published in paperback in Great Britain in 2013 by HEADLINE REVIEW
An imprint of HEADLINE PUBLISHING GROUP

2

Cataloguing in Publication Data is available from the British Library

ISBN 978 0 7553 5266 1

Typeset in Centaur MT Std by Palimpsest Book Production Limited,
Falkirk, Stirlingshire

Printed and bound in Great Britain by
CPI Group (UK) Ltd, Croydon CR0 4YY

Headline's policy is to use papers that are natural, renewable and recyclable products and
made from wood grown in sustainable forests. The logging and manufacturing processes are
expected to conform to the environmental regulations of the country of origin.

HEADLINE PUBLISHING GROUP
An Hachette UK Company
338 Euston Road
London NW1 3BH

www.headline.co.uk
www.hachette.co.uk

To the two Renaissance men in my life: my darling husband
Reg Grundy AC OBE PhD Hons, creator and visionary;
and my father, Alan Chambers, philosopher,
soldier and champion of the needy.

Your advice and guidance abide with me always.

Thanks

To my brother Dr John H Chambers and to our dedicated
personal staff who made it possible for me to complete
The Great Deception.

A Tribute

To my mother Evelyn May Chambers, who, like Shelly Longford, waited behind in Queensland, Australia and worked for the war effort while the man she loved was fighting for freedom overseas.

THE PEACE

Chapter One

New South Wales, Australia: October 1947. Two years and two months after the end of World War Two.

'In one hundred years? Mr Churchill, yes, they'll probably remember him. But the others like Montgomery, Brooke and MacArthur, well, military historians will know of them, but the rank and file? No, they won't. Mr Roosevelt? He has a chance of being known, but I'd say only in America – unless, again, you're a military historian. Now, Hitler? And Stalin? Yes, I'd think they'll be remembered. Monsters like that stand beside Attila the Hun and we've heard of him. Mussolini? I doubt even the Italians will recognise his name. It's a tricky business, fame . . . or infamy.'

Shelly Wareing was remembering her husband's words from the previous night. She was in the south field looking down the gentle slope past the dam and around her the bush smelt clean, the subtle scent of eucalyptus trailing on the morning air. In all the time Cole had been back from the war he had spoken so rarely of it that she was surprised when he had brought it up and began to talk about the leaders and the generals of the Allies and the Axis. She had agreed with him, there in the big kitchen

3

with the wood stove burning and the pleasant spring breeze urging her floral curtains to billow in from the open window. Fame was fleeting in the main. She had gently referred to his time in the prisoner-of-war camp but he soon deflected any more talk of that kind with the words, 'Let's not speak of it any more, darling. How about some supper?'

She had smiled and acquiesced. She understood. She supposed all the boys who had been prisoners were fragile emotionally. He had been wounded too; another thing he would not talk about. He had scars on his ribs and knee and two on his face and another on his throat. Every now and then, just for a few seconds, he limped. Shelly put that down to his knee hurting, even though he had never admitted it.

The comforting sensation of the sun stealing down her spine gave her a mellow feeling. The breeze swirled eucalyptus leaves across the paddock where the overnight dew lay on the grass and soft circular imprints from the hooves of the dairy cows indented the blades, their lowing in the field beyond drifting through the wind-break of pines. She could hear lizards scuttling at the base of the tall silver gums near where she stood, her sandalled feet planted in the brown earth by the barbed-wire fence.

Shelly closed her eyes and savoured the moments. Cole had caught the 07.40 express train north to Sydney. He was doing farm business in the city and she had waved to him from their wide front verandah as he rolled down the drive of pin oak trees in their old sedan to head into the township of Bowral in the cool of early morning.

In the year on this farm she had grown to love the place: the brilliance of the daffodils and camellias, the masses of blue hydrangeas near their front steps, the verdant trees, the evening mist that swept in from the coast to blanket the landscape with a sense of mystery. The crispness in the night air instead of the soporific warmth of evening she had grown up with in the old colonial house in the sprawling suburb of One Mile across the creek outside Ipswich in southern Queensland over five hundred miles away. Though she had loved that house too with its extensive verandahs and avenue of cedars — instead of pin oaks as there were here — leading up to the house.

They called this farm *Apple Gate* after the single apple tree which grew at the entry gate to the property.

As she stood in thought, the day Cole returned from the war stole into her mind.

He stepped down from the train silhouetted against the grey steam gushing from the snorting engine on to the concrete platform behind him. The sun glinted on the buttons of his uniform as he looked around. His face was gaunt and he was thinner than before the war, and she was shocked by the scars on his temple and near his mouth, but his blue eyes found her and she felt the impact of them as she always had. He stood looking at her as she hurried towards him. It was Cole, home at last. Drawing to a halt a yard from him, her uncertainty was obvious. They gazed silently at each other.

In 1940, his RAAF squadron had been sent to North Africa and from there he had been transferred to an RAF squadron in England. She had written to him regularly and for almost two years he had replied. It was early in 1942 that the worrying letter from him had arrived. He told her he was releasing her from any obligation to him:

> *Perhaps it's better if you forget about me; in war anything can happen and it is not fair of me to expect you to wait.*

That had broken her heart — as if she could forget the man she loved. She had continued to write to him but he had not replied. So she had faced up to reality and thrown her energies into the war effort. But when the telegram had arrived from Sydney informing her of his return, there was no doubt that it made her heart leap again.

> If you have a mind to meet me, please do. Realise how much I've missed you. Demobbed yesterday. Arrive South Brisbane Station Thursday 1100.

She travelled by rail from Ipswich into Brisbane elated, but the longer she had waited for Cole's train to arrive, the more doubt had risen in her mind.

And here he was . . .

His gaze rested on her, his expression enigmatic. Was he truly glad to see her? She gave him a diffident smile and then, abruptly, he stepped forward and caught her to him.

He held Shelly close to his heart, her face pressed into the shoulder of his uniform. His fingers ran through her hair. Suddenly she was consumed by the miracle of his return, standing there holding him. How badly she had missed him. She could admit it now after years of being strong. She was back in his arms.

And at that moment the miracle happened. 'Will you marry me?' he asked.

Shelly sighed and opened her eyes and was about to turn and walk back down the pin oak drive to the stables when she caught a movement in the periphery of her vision and swung her head towards it.

A man was entering the property through the open gateway and coming along by the outer dam, striding towards her. Apple Gate Farm stood at the end of a dirt track and was the only habitation in this direction. They rarely received visitors they did not know. But there was no sign of recognition in Shelly's eyes as the tall figure approached. At six yards' distance he halted and took off his hat with his right hand, revealing in the sunlight a smooth-shaven, lean face under fair hair, a stray wisp of which clung to his high forehead.

She noticed his eyes in the morning light: they were trained upon her as if he examined her and did not merely look at her. They were blue, but a fascinating sky-blue, not the deep indigo of her husband's eyes. His features were not symmetrical: his forehead was high, his nose was aquiline with a slightly prominent bridge, and there were faint hollows in his cheeks which emphasised his cheekbones and defined his jaw and yet the sum of the whole was very good indeed to look upon. She felt she had seen him before, but she could not place him.

'I believe I'm at the property owned by Group Captain Wareing?' It was an American accent, educated with a muted, hardly perceptible, Southern sound – very easy on the ear. She recognised it immediately because so many American servicemen had been in Australia during the war.

'Yes.'

He looked beyond her to the roof tops of the sheds in the distance as he moved closer. 'Is he at home?'

'No.'

Swinging his gaze back, he studied her. 'Are you related to him?'

'I am.'

'Not . . . his wife?' He appeared to weigh his words.

'Yes, and who are you?'

He did not answer immediately but lifted his right hand to shade his eyes and view her more closely. It was in that instant she recognised him. Of course! She had never met him, but she had seen his picture. In fact, she had kept a studio photograph of him and Cole on the mantelpiece for years during the war.

'I know you,' she said, 'you're Cole's friend, the one from Carolina – aren't you?'

The expression altered in his pastel eyes, a wariness appeared, just for an instant, before he blinked in the sunlight. 'Why yes . . . that's right. I'm surprised you know me.'

'I should do, I had a photograph of the two of you in our lounge room at home for most of the war.'

He frowned. 'Really?'

'*Tudor*, that's your name. Tudor Harrington.' She gave him a sympathetic look. 'Originally you were his navigator in the Lancaster Bomber when he was transferred to the RAF squadron. You came over from America to England and volunteered in 1940. Before the Japs bombed Pearl Harbor and the USA came into the war. Cole doesn't talk about all that now. But I understand.'

He made no comment as he shifted his weight from one foot to the other.

'Cole sent the photograph to me when you were stationed in Essex. The one you had taken in your uniforms . . . just after Cole had been made a wing commander.'

His gaze remained fixed on her. 'Ah . . . yes . . . that photograph, of course.' He gave an affirmative grunt, his eyes lifting skywards in recollection. 'I think I remember the day the picture was taken.'

She nodded. 'It had "Bury St Edmunds, Suffolk 1941" printed on the back of it.'

'Did it? Then yes, that's right.' He seemed to speak almost to himself, '1941 it was.'

Unconsciously he lifted his right elbow and rested it on the fence post near him and now she noticed that his left arm hung limply at his side and his hand was folded into a fist. She guessed he had been wounded too, like Cole, and felt a rush of sympathy for him.

Momentarily they both fell silent, listening to the sound of the Friesian cows on the far side of the pine trees. He continued to study her. 'He . . . Cole . . . posted the photograph to you, did he?'

'Yes, it was a really good likeness of both of you.'

'Was?'

She shrugged. 'It's gone. When we moved here it got lost. But I recognised you.'

'Indeed, so you did.' He squinted in the bright sunshine. Fleetingly there was something in his expression which she thought might have been pity; it was difficult to analyse, for it departed as swiftly as it had come. His voice altered as he spoke again in a confidential tone: 'Are you the girl who likes evening walks?'

'My goodness.' She nodded. 'So, he actually spoke about me, then?'

'Only once or twice.'

She tried not to be deflated by that as he went on, 'Some of us talked about home a lot; others rarely did.' He glanced around. 'Where is he?'

'In Sydney, up there on business.'

His brows drew together and she thought he was disappointed, so she said, 'But he'll be back this evening.'

He hesitated and glanced around again. 'Right, then I'll come back another time. Tonight, tomorrow, sometime.'

'Oh, no need to go.' She gave him a warm smile. 'Why don't you stay and wait for him now? After all, you're his friend and you've come all the way here. He'd want you to wait, I'm sure of it. I can give you lunch.'

Tudor Harrington stepped some paces backwards, shaking his head. 'No, thanks, I can't wait now. Just tell him I was here . . . and . . . that I'm coming back.'

'Did you walk from town?'

'Yes.'

It was a five-mile walk, and her answer was spontaneous. 'Good heavens! Then I'll drive you back, just wait here and I'll get the farm ute.'

His voice rose determinedly and the southern accent became more pronounced. 'No, not necessary at all. I like to walk. It's good for me.'

'But . . .' She was about to protest and insist that she take him; but she did not, for he gave her an abrupt nod, replaced his hat, spun on his heel and strode away.

Her voice rose as she called out, 'You might see Cole get off the evening train . . .' He did not look back but lifted his good arm, signalling he had heard.

Shaking her head she watched him walk away. He had come all the way from Bowral on foot and now was walking all the way back, a ten-mile round trip! How strange! Yet she supposed all the ex-servicemen, especially those who had been prisoners of war, did odd things. Months ago she had read an article in the *Bulletin* magazine about the psychological effects of being a POW and returning to 'civvy street' as the ex-servicemen called it. Yet Cole was not like that. She was so lucky. He was just himself — well, except for not wanting to talk about his imprisonment. He was delicate where that was concerned . . . so, in fact, there had been some sort of psychological effect on him.

Watching Tudor depart from her, his limp arm hanging at his side, she thought what a shame it was. Yet, in a perverse way, it somehow heightened his appeal, gave him an enigmatic air. She wondered just how it had been damaged as her eyes followed him until he rounded the dam, exited the gate and, half a minute later, disappeared behind the stand of eucalyptus trees on the side of the narrow dirt road.

She felt quite odd. As if somehow she had been interrogated, but why she felt that way she could not say.

Chapter Two

Cole leapt down from the slowing train on to the platform of the Bowral railway station. He ran along the concrete under the awning past the waiting room and ticket office, through the wooden exit gate and across the street to the ancient dark green Austin parked opposite. Soon he was over the level crossing down Station Street and in low gear climbing Oxley Hill, named after the English explorer John Oxley. Behind him in the pine trees opposite the station Tudor turned his gaze to the muscular but wiry man who stood beside him. 'We'll wait till after midnight, Felix.'

'Sure, I'm ready any time.'

Cole drove the car through the gateway of the farm, into the property. He slipped out of the driver's seat and latched and locked the gate in his ritual sun-down procedure.

His gaze caught a movement on the barbed-wire fence and he bent to look more closely. A lizard was entangled and trying to escape. He helped it by pushing it through the wire but it left its tail behind as it fell to the ground. Abruptly his eyes glazed over; locked in a stare at the barbed wire. He did not see the cows returning from the dairy to the near paddock nor the sun dipping to the horizon. He did not feel the gentle tableland breeze at his back. What he felt was the chill of a damp morning settling upon his shoulders and what he saw was the barbed wire in the distance and prison guards and prowling Alsatian dogs. And what he heard were shouts and the screams at hand and in front of him the little innocent human face staring at him from the cattle transport carriage before the door slid across and slammed closed like the jaws of hell shutting.

His stomach turned as the screaming altered to screeching and a flock of rosella parrots swooped by towards a roost for the night and he rose and shook his head, erasing the stark mind-numbing memory. Climbing back into the old jalopy, he accelerated down the track through the vista of pin oaks where he saw his wife coming down the front steps to greet him, her cotton skirt swirling around her legs and her smile warm and inviting.

He swung open the car door to her query, 'How did it go?'

'Pretty good. I ordered everything.'

She entered his arms and hugged him and they stood for a few moments watching the myriad shades of pink and gold daubing the far western sky above the trees.

She leant her head on his shoulder as his hand rested on her waist; her voice was mellow. 'I love this place.'

They slowly turned together and he hugged her closer into his side and kissed her golden hair. 'You've helped me in ways I can't explain.'

She turned her head to him. 'What do you mean? Why can't you explain?'

'Oh, darling, it's just you, your beautiful nature, your quiet strength, just being here with you – the way you look after me, accept my oddities, my idiosyncrasies . . .'

She gave a gentle laugh. 'Now now, Group Captain, you aren't all that odd – difficult, eccentric, sometimes gruff and occasionally overbearing, but odd? Oh no, never odd.'

They both burst into laughter and she threw her arms around him and hugged him again and he looked keenly at her before he kissed her tenderly on the mouth, feeling the womanly curves of her body nestling into his. 'Are you happy?' he murmured into her hair.

She drew her head back and looked into his eyes. 'Happy? I'm wonderfully, amazingly happy. I'm in your arms, aren't I?'

'Then that's all that matters.' He kissed her once more and she clung to him another moment before she moved out of his grasp and his fingers slipped reluctantly from the cotton of her dress as he asked, 'Did you repot the canna lilies?'

Shelly answered as she moved forward to the stairs. 'Yes. Just finished not long before you came home.'

As he watched her he gave a small smile. They had been here well-nigh a year now and recently he had begun to feel almost calm. He was actually starting to enjoy the physical work and the life of a farmer.

He was watching his wife's back as she mounted the steps and half turned and spoke lightly, throwing the words over her shoulder. 'Oh, your American friend who was with you in the RAF came today. Tudor Harrington. Wonder how he found us? Anyway, he said he'll come back another time.'

If she had faced him to deliver her words she would have been astounded. Cole flinched and his face tightened. He stood stock-still; not a muscle moved except for his eyes as they widened and flicked back and forth.

Shelly had reached the verandah and now she turned to see him remaining still at the bottom of the flight of stairs. 'Cole? Did you hear me? Your friend Tudor from the air force came today.'

He took a deep breath and suddenly laughed – alien and unreal as it sounded to his own ears. He could feel his heart beating. He was glad of that because he reckoned it had stopped back there for a few seconds. He forced himself to take a step. 'Yes, Shell, I heard you.' He tried as hard as he could to sound normal. 'When did he say he'd come back?'

'Oh, this evening or tomorrow. He said sometime; he wasn't specific.'

Of course he wouldn't be. 'Did he say where he was staying?' He turned completely around, facing back along the pin oaks, his gaze searching the distance in 180 degrees, scrutinising each yard before he rounded back to the steps and, lifting his foot, slowly began climbing them.

Shelly answered as he moved. 'No. He said he'd walked out from Bowral, all that way. Can you believe it? He wouldn't let me drive him back even though I wanted to. And funny, but I thought I heard a vehicle start over in the distance after he left here.'

'What else did he say?' He reached the verandah and did not come to her side; instead he halted, turning to grasp the railing and to look out across the landscape again. Gaining time before he had to meet her eyes.

'We didn't talk about much for he wasn't here long. I met him down near the dam. I recognised him, you see, from the photo. You know? The one we lost when we moved here last year?'

Cole coughed and remained clasping the railing. 'Yes, right, that was a shame.' He concentrated on making his voice sound casual. 'Did you talk about anything else?'

15

'I said you were in the city.'

'Yes . . . of course you would.'

'He was wounded in the escape from the prisoner-of-war camp too, was he?'

Jesus.

'Yes.'

'Shame. He's such a good-looking man to have lost the use of his arm.'

So he's got a bad arm.

When Cole did not comment, Shelly went on, 'Anyway, he said he'd come again, so you can have a long chin-wag when he does.' She moved over to him and slid her hand to the inside of his arm. 'Look, if he doesn't come back tonight you should drive into Bowral tomorrow and see him. He's probably staying at the Grand. Everybody does. Now . . . what about some chicken stew?'

He cast a last look down the drive and around the fading landscape. 'Yes . . . sure. Let's eat.'

As they walked inside he slid the bolt and she stood on tiptoes and kissed him.

'With all your scars you are still the handsomest man I've ever seen.'

'You're biased. So? How about that stew?'

Shelly smiled and hurried down the hall ahead of him.

Tudor? So he's using his real name . . .

Chapter Three

Oh Jesus, what can I do?

Sounds like dozens of them.

That's Von Bremen's voice. He's here. Dogs! God, they've got Alsatians with them! Is that Cohen over there with a rifle?

Run . . . Run . . . where am I? Must get away . . . start this car.

Clouds everywhere, that's Letta's voice I can hear . . . No, it's Shelly . . . why is she screaming? I can't see anything. I'm in a cockpit . . . all clouds.

Where did this piece of paper come from? It just appeared in my hand.

Who's that yelling out my name? Isn't that Tudor?

What's this written on the paper?

I'll get you, Cole. There will be nowhere on earth you can hide.

Cole woke. But he did not move. Perspiration dotted his temples. He took deep, slow breaths as he lay still, listening to the sound of Shelly's measured breathing. The same old nightmare! The same cold ache in his chest, how many times had this happened? And always he had managed to hide it from Shelly. But now everything had changed. Tudor had been here!

He knew he was just as good as Tudor, just as good at everything, so there was no need to be alarmed. *Calm, stay calm.* He must remember he had expected this and prepared for it.

Quietly and with care he slipped out of bed and stood watching his wife. She appeared to be still fast asleep, thank God. He moved across the rug over the planks of the floorboards and walked to the window. Opening it he felt the chill of the Southern Tablelands night and gingerly looked right and left and up at the clear sky. He could feel the wood beneath the soles of his feet and he was aware of the breeze on the hot skin of his arms and face: the caress of the cool air brought composure.

He gave a wry smile looking up at the waning moon. The day had arrived. The one he had to admit he had feared.

He had tried to convince himself that Tudor wouldn't go through with his threat. That in any case no one would be able to find him here, secreted away in the country. Yet, he supposed that all along he had known better.

He must take Shelly and get out of here first thing in the morning.

But how in hell could he explain that to her? Getting her here in the first place had been a minor miracle. He had originally thought to change his name as well but he could never have justified that to Shelly.

He turned to the left to look along the side of the house and as he did so, a gush of air brushed his cheek. He flinched as the thud beside his ear resounded on the night air.

He spun back, eyes wide, to see the metal glinting in the pallid night light. The smatchet had missed his cheek by a hair's breadth. The double-edged commando knife was embedded in the wood of the window frame, its blade gleaming ominously.

Ah! Felix is here too! So, they recruited him? They won't have come all this way to take chances: that means Mako is out there as well.

With a deftness and speed Shelly would have been amazed to see, he snatched the knife and brought his body inside and closed the window.

His eyes flicked back and forth. *Shelly?* Was she still asleep? He moved with haste and care back to the bedroom door and looked in: she was in the same position. She had not woken.

His mind raced. They were outside. The house was sealed. They could not get in without breaking a lock or a window. He had been meticulous about the hinges and the locks, making them strong, much to Shelly's surprise, but she had accepted it as an eccentricity of a returned prisoner of war. *They aren't interested in Shell. All they want is me. She will wake and be terrified. I've got to get out right now.*

The trousers he had worn to Sydney hung over a chair and with silent speed he dressed, taking a clean shirt and jacket from the wardrobe. He tied the laces of his business shoes together and hung them round his neck before he reached into the back of the bedside cabinet and took out his long-unused, felt climbing slippers. His eyes were on Shelly as he put them on, but she did not stir. With continuing haste he passed down the hall to his study where moonlight threw an anaemic strip of clarity across his desk while he reached for his pad and pencil and scribbled a message.

He opened the drawer of his desk and took out his cheque book, slipping it into his inside pocket and leaving the bank book with their savings for Shelly. Holding the knife which had nearly killed him, he studied it a second or so, recognising it as a versatile throwing knife designed by Majors Fairburn and Sykes and it was obviously Felix's, by the holes cut in the handle for speed and accuracy against wind. Felix had altered many of his knives this way. In a neat, rapid move he buckled a belt from the drawer around his waist and slipped the smatchet in the attached sheaf. Removing a key from the back of his desk drawer he openend a walnut box and took out a Walther P38 double-action 9mm parabellum pistol, a black belt holster and two full ten-shot magazines. There were loose bullets lying in the bottom of the box and he grabbed them and stuffed them into his jacket pockets along with the pistol, a lead pencil and his wallet.

He returned to the bedroom and even though speed was now of the essence, he placed the sheet of paper with infinite care on his pillow so that his wife would see it. His mind raced. Tudor and Felix would be outside. They would have reconnoitred the entire property and probably Mako would be waiting on the track down towards the farm gate. But they did not know what he knew: though no doubt they would have searched for it.

Hastening through to the kitchen he took the stairs to the loft.

If they had discovered his escape route, then it was possible that Felix could be up on the roof, but Cole had chosen his way out painstakingly and he truly believed they would not have found it. In fact, he had made a trapdoor and concealed it at the rear of the house near a trench that led away to the sheds. He reckoned that, after a pretty thorough search, they *would* find the trapdoor, and in doing so, he hoped like hell that they would believe that this false lead was his route out.

There were four windows in the roof of the loft; innocent, normal push-out windows, and by the first of these lay an eight-foot pole, which he picked up and took with him as he opened the glass and climbed through. Crouching, he looked around. The world was black except for the mean gleam from the quarter-moon and the stars, but it showed enough for him to realise he was alone up here. *You beauty! They fell for the trapdoor as my way out.*

Seven great oaks grew in a line away from the northern side of the house. Along with the avenue of pin oak trees this had been a feature of the farm which had impressed him. The nearest mighty oak did not touch the roof – that would have been asking his visitors to look more closely at it – and down the roof he slid towards it. He looked over the edge of the roof line. A shadow moved across an open space to the back of the house towards the trapdoor. Oh yes, he knew that shape: Tudor! *Looks like you're expecting me out that way pretty soon, boys. Good! Just wait there for me.*

Yet Cole was aware they would not wait long. When he did not appear they would find entry so he had to move swiftly. He took a deep breath and leant out with the pole to the spot in the oak's foliage where he knew the length of rope was hanging. He caught it and brought it to his hands. It was attached to a massive bough and would allow him to swing into the tree and take the course out which he had planned a year ago when they first came here. He had maintained the rope and whenever Shelly had been away from home, he kept the leaves cut away from certain branches which allowed free access into the tree. Placing the pole in the gutter of the roof he swung out over the open space into the vegetation and up to where his feet met a wide, smooth bough.

The action had been virtually noiseless except for a rustle of leaves and a gentle creaking of the tree limb taking his weight.

With cat-like agility he passed along the branch to the trunk and across to meet the next tree and so he continued, from bough to bough in the black night, and from tree to tree, until he reached the last trunk, and now, over ninety yards from the house, he slid down the mammoth bole and entered the barn.

He could barely see in the moody haze within the barn but he knew exactly where to go and his hands were on the bicycle and he was outside and mounted and riding away, within twelve seconds more. At three hundred yards from the barn he rang the bell of the bike with a determined action. The ring carried loudly on the night air.

Good, now they'll follow me! That should get them away from the house and Shelly.

The heads of the two men hidden outside the trapdoor jolted upwards. 'He's getting away. Bugger, we've missed him.' Felix spun in the direction of the sound. 'It's to take us away from the woman, that's why he's made the racket. We'll have to rely on Mako down near the farm gate.'

Tudor's Southern tones were cold, like the night. 'Goddam, now I see it . . . He's not going to the farm gate. He'll have another way out. He's fooled us with this trapdoor, it was a trick.' He reached out and touched the shoulder of the shorter man. 'Pity you missed him, buddy.'

'Yeah. If he hadn't turned his head just at the critical moment I'd have had him! So? Do we go in and get the skirt?'

Tudor shook his head. 'She knows nothing. I saw that today. She's a pawn in this game. The only thing we'll do by talking to her, is scare her to death and I've seen enough terrified women to last me ten lifetimes.'

'Yeah. Reckon you're right.' Felix shook his head disconsolately. 'After coming all this bloody way to Australia and searching for months.'

Tudor exhaled a long noisy breath and pulled the collar of his coat up. 'So I guess it's round one to Cole Wareing or should I say Lucien Bayer? Round two is another matter.'

Chapter Four

'Cole?' Shelly opened her eyes. Something had woken her. She did not know what, but she felt odd; a foreboding feeling. She sat up in bed.

'Cole?' Reaching out to an empty space she could hear sounds outside: voices, she was sure. *What on earth is he doing outside?*

She left the bed and threw her dressing gown around her shoulders. For some reason she did not switch on the electric light and she hurried down the hall in darkness calling, 'Cole? Where are you?' Into the empty kitchen she ran and, crossing to the window beside the stove, peered out.

Two ebony shapes walked away from the house towards the dairy. Her heart accelerated as she opened the window and called, 'Cole? Is that you?' But there was no reply as the figures hastily disappeared. Now she was really frightened but she closed the window and, still without switching on the light, searched for and found the metal torch which resided on a shelf near the back door.

Cautiously sliding the locks she opened the door and moved hesitantly out on to the landing which ran the length of the kitchen to the front of the house. Her eyes were now accustomed to the darkness and as she reached the front verandah she saw movement near the entry to the pin oak drive.

When she clicked on the torch, the beam revealed a couple of men on bicycles riding away. 'Cole!' Yet even as she shouted his name to the departing black wraiths, she knew Cole was not one of them.

She remained on the verandah, bewildered and mystified; her mind refusing to work, a sick feeling in her chest. Where was her husband? Had those men done something to him? *Oh Lord God, what if he is dead? Why am I thinking that?*

She forced herself to walk down the front steps, even though she trembled as she flashed the ray of light to right and left and crossed to the dairy.

Why had those men ridden bicycles? Only one answer came to her – to come and go in silence!

The dairy was empty. Abruptly she recalled that Cole kept his bicycle in the barn beyond the great oaks. Fear told her to return to the house, but her need to know what was happening was stronger and it took her down to the barn where she saw Cole's bike was missing.

She exited the barn and started as the call of an owl lifted on the night air. Crossing to the house, her foot was on the bottom step when, suddenly breaking the silence, clearly and unmistakably, carried the sound of a truck engine revving up in the distance. She paused and turned towards it. It came from outside the farm on the dirt road.

Those men on the bikes, whoever they were – it will be their truck; they will have left it on the trail and ridden in on their bikes. Now they're leaving.

She shook as an overwhelming terror came over her again. Cole, where was Cole?

Taking the steps two by two Shelly hurried back down the verandah to the kitchen door and entered the house. This time she switched on the light and closing the door behind her, locked it.

She had no idea what to do and with a dragging step she returned down the hall to the bedroom. Turning on the lamp she glanced to the bed and saw the note on Cole's pillow. Her heart thumped again as she lifted it and read in a scribbled hand:

Darling Shell,
Please understand I have to leave. I'll come back, no matter how long. Trust
me, sweetheart.
Cole

It did not help her state of mind, but even through the blur that substituted for her thought processes, she realised that Cole must have known those men were here to harm him. Where had he gone? And why were the men after him?

She sat down on the bed feeling impotent and defeated. Finally a tear broke over her eyelid and she began to cry. What did it all mean? And as she wept she began to comprehend the significance of the visit from Tudor Harrington. It had something to do with this. She was remembering Cole's reaction to the news that his friend had been here. It had not been the joyous response she expected when an old RAF friend he had been a POW with had appeared out of the blue. She thought of how he had seemed almost unsettled. He had been quiet and had only asked when Tudor was coming back and what was said. And, now that she was thinking about it, Cole remained taciturn last night, and she had seen him check the locks on the doors more than once.

And now he was gone! He had slipped away in the night without telling her anything or warning her of anything. How could he do that? The rumblings of anger inside made her cry even more and when she lifted her eyes to look at the clock it was 2.45.

She knew there would be no sleep for her tonight. She might as well make a cup of tea. As she stood she gazed around the room and noticed the wardrobe door and the bedside cabinet door were both open.

After examining the wardrobe she realised Cole had taken a white shirt and his navy-blue jacket: they appeared to be the only clothes missing. She had never really looked in Cole's bedside cabinet but she did now. She could not tell if things were gone; all she found were books and papers. Carrying them through to his study, she flicked on the light and there on his desk sat an open box. She placed the books and papers beside it. The lid was off and it was lined in silk. Whatever had been in here he had taken. But a single bullet was lying at the bottom of the box, half hidden in the silk. She had not even known he possessed a weapon. This box always sat on his desk and he had told her it had his father's private papers in it. It was quite beautiful, made of walnut with a pattern of mother-of-pearl inlaid on the lid, but now she noticed that on the inside of the lid, which of course she had never seen before, were the initials LB in gold leaf. She took a deep breath. 'Cole, what does this all mean?'

She shivered.

Some hours later as the dawn stole over Apple Gate Farm and the blades of grass in the paddocks bent under the glistenings of overnight dew, Shelly sat at the kitchen table staring in disbelief at the items in front of her. She had found them in Cole's service trunk up in the loft. Opening the trunk had taken her half an hour during which time, on and off, she could not stop herself from crying. She had used three knives and bent them all, until finally she resorted to a small axe she fetched from the wood crate in the back room. The noise had been horrendous but she had not cared. After all, the nearest people were Jim and Moston, the farm hands, who lived down by the creek half a mile away.

She was amazed at what lay in front of her: a flick knife which had *Fait dans Lyons* on the end; four lengths of a type of elastic rope; an RAF uniform; a skull cap; a tiny object that she thought must be a camera but that was hard to believe for it was the smallest one she had ever seen – minute; a celluloid fountain pen with the same LB in gilt on it and a French identity card belonging to a man called Antoine Balfour.

The last items were the most startling. There was a silver ring with a death's head on it which, inside, was engraved with the same mystifying letters LB, as were on the interior of the walnut box and on the pen. She was not sure, but she thought this could have been a Nazi SS ring. Though she soon became sure, for two of the remaining objects were medals. The first was a blue Maltese cross attached to a silver and black ribbon and upon it in gold were the words *Pour le Mérite* and a crown with an F below it. At first Shelly assumed this was French but as she studied it she saw the pattern between the arms of the cross were gold eagles reminiscent of the German eagle. The second medal left no doubt: she opened a leather case with the shape of a cross pattée printed on the outside and inside sat an Iron Cross with a swastika in the centre and 1939 on the front and 1813 on the back. With it was a folded neck ribbon in black, red and white and an ivory-coloured document more than a foot long. It was obviously the certificate which accompanied the Iron Cross. It had been given to a major in the SS called Lucien Bayer and a tremor ran through Shelly as she read Heinrich Himmler's signature at the bottom of the page along with the *Reichsführer SS*-embossed stamp.

Himmler was the monster responsible for the extermination of millions of people in the death camps! The ongoing Nuremberg Nazi War Crimes' Trials were informing the world of exactly what unthinkable horrors had been perpetrated by Germany during the war. Shelly shuddered; just to see Himmler's signature was a shock. What was Cole doing with all this?

She was mystified and frightened as she sat staring at the eccentric collection in front of her. So . . . the LB inside the lid of the box stood for Lucien Bayer, an SS officer.

But the final items were to Shelly the most interesting and worrisome of all; they had devastated her.

They were two sepia photographs inside a worn grey envelope: the first image was of a palatial villa with a row of trees running to a marble staircase at the entrance. It was taken from a distance and had the words: *Uncle Glenro's villa* on the back. The second was a picture of one of the most beautiful and striking women Shelly had ever seen other than on film at the pictures. Her figure in a clinging silk evening gown appeared to be flawless as she leant against a stone pillar, her long dark hair nestling on her shoulders. A murky view of water could be seen behind her and her eyes glowed wide and fiery. It was not a snap but looked professional and a photographer's studio stamp was on the corner of the back: Printemps & Co, 63 Avenue de la Costa, Monte Carlo. But it was not that which disturbed her: written in a round, flowing hand were the words *Laetitia de Witt at Uncle Glenro's villa, on the lake: 1938*. And underneath it, penned in the same hand, presumably at another time, for it was in a different-coloured ink, glared the statement:

My Darling ~~Lucien~~, Cole,
We'll live together here after the war.

What in God's name did that mean? The name *Lucien,* the same as the SS officer, was crossed out and *Cole* written in its place?

A tear – in the long procession of tears of this night – slid down the side of Shelly's nose.

Chapter Five

The morning sunlight greeted the kitchen to find Shelly bathed, dressed and sitting again at the table. She had cleared a space in the kitchen dresser and placed the items from the trunk there, though the photograph, identity card, the certificate and the ring she had put carefully in her brocade travelling bag.

A lukewarm pot of tea sat in front of her and she rested her chin in her hands and eyed the note Cole had left. He said he was coming back and he asked her to wait for him. But how long would he be gone? When would he return? And, most importantly, where had he gone?

Clattering began in the yard outside and she knew it would be Moston and Jim making ready for the day's work. She stood and, picking up six bananas and two apples from the fruit dish on the dresser, walked out on to the landing and called to them, 'Jim? Moston?'

They lifted their heads from where they were washing milk buckets at a trough. Moston waved and Jim's greeting rang across the yard, ''Mornin', Mrs Wareing.'

'I have to go into town today. My husband's already gone. So I just want you to look after the place until I return.'

'We'll do that,' Jim answered as she came down the steps and walked over to hand him the bananas and apples.

'Give these to Sweet Face and Victoria along with their pellets.' She had named her pet pigs and both of them were fruit lovers. 'I'm not sure what time I'll be home.'

As she turned away Moston asked, 'How did the boss get into town?'

Shelly thought it useless to lie so she replied as she walked back to the house, 'On his bicycle.'

A quizzical look passed between the two farm hands, but both being laconic countrymen, neither commented.

She walked slowly back to the steps and as she did she noticed something on the ground. She picked it up: it was a tiny notebook with a cardboard cover obviously dropped by last night's visitors. The first page had on it the sentence: *Perhaps see Andy again* with the word *Holland* beneath it and a question mark. The second page began with *Ipswich, Queensland* written at the top and underneath a list of Australian villages and towns south-west of Sydney from Campbelltown to Goulburn and directly south from Helensburgh to Woolloongong. There were eighteen and they all had lines through them except for *Bowral*, which had a tick beside it. So that's how Tudor had found them hidden away here at Apple Gate Farm; he had been to Ipswich – probably even seen her mother and learnt enough to comb this part of the countryside. She slipped it in her pocket and climbed the stairs.

By 0930, when clouds had appeared from over the hills and rain began to fall, Shelly had learnt that three men, who said they were *travelling around Australia*, stayed the previous night at the Grand Hotel on the corner in Bong Bong Street, Bowral. She had been informed by the housekeeper at the Grand that they came to town driving a Ford truck which carried bicycles in the back and that they spent yesterday away from the hotel. The woman told her they had left money for the stay on their beds and that they were not in their rooms this morning. Shelly thanked the housekeeper and made her way to the station, where the plump station mistress, who was wedged into the ticket office, revealed that the only people who had caught the 07.40 to Sydney were 'the usuals' and that no strangers had bought a ticket on any train which had departed since.

Shelly smiled her thanks and asked, 'I thought my husband might have caught one of the Sydney trains this morning?'

'No, haven't seen him today. He went up yesterday, didn't he?'

Shelly nodded and hurried away.

She drove back to the farm in a downpour and sat for a long time on the front verandah gazing at the avenue of trees and watching the geese and ducks wandering across the yard back and forth to the tiny pond in the first paddock, in the still gently falling rain.

She could sit here and wait as Cole had asked her to do. The one thing she was now certain about was that the strangers had come to do Cole harm, real harm . . . probably to kill him. Why?

A sick feeling ran through her. How did she know they had not caught up with him last night and already killed him?

She must decide what to do. And as she sat staring at the big birds in the rain, she made up her mind: she would wait a week and if she had heard nothing from Cole by then she would go home to Queensland to see her mother.

✳   ✳   ✳

Eight days later Shelly and her mother stood on the iron-lace-clad front verandah of the old colonial house overshadowed by tall cedar trees in the isolated area of One Mile outside the town of Ipswich.

As her mother spoke, Shelly stared beyond her parent to the dark shape of Tam the cat stretching himself in a beam of the dependable Queensland sunshine.

'Of course I'm trying to understand, Shelly, I'm your mother, for heaven's sake.' Mavis Longford turned and put down her teacup on the small outdoor table. 'You didn't fool me, I realised you were in love with Cole from the minute you met him at the cricket match in the North Ipswich Reserve.'

Shelly remained silent.

'Oh yes, he's a looker, I'll agree with that and in that air-force uniform he was a knock-out and he's got a silver tongue with it. But . . . to marry him no more than two weeks after he returned from the war and to up and leave home without telling even me where you were going!' She let out an exasperated sigh. 'How do you think I felt?' She sniffed and looked down at her hands.

'Mother, please. Cole just wanted to be with me alone for a year or two . . . away from everyone. After all he'd been through, I understood; pity you didn't. And I did write to you a few weeks after we left.'

Mavis blinked in frustration and her tone became pained. 'Oh yes, you wrote – after I was nearly a physical wreck wondering where you were and even then you didn't inform me properly, did you? *South of Sydney on a farm*, you said. God, that could have been anywhere!'

'Mum, he asked me not to tell you even that.'

Mavis continued to look wounded. 'Ah yes, and so now you

know how it feels. He's done to you exactly what you did to me.' Her eyes filled with tears.

'Mummy, please. It's not the same at all.'

'Darling, you trusted him and he's gone.' Abruptly her eyes widened. 'Oh dear, perhaps he's got another woman.' She dabbed her eyelids with a pink handkerchief from her apron pocket. 'Yes, that'll be it. Oh, you poor love.' Mavis wrapped her daughter in her arms. 'Why, oh why, didn't you marry Captain Tommy Madison?'

Shelly closed her eyes over her parent's shoulder. Tommy Madison was a decorated American flyer who had shown an interest in Shelly while he had been stationed nearby at Amberley air-force base, during the war. He had been keen on the relationship but there had never been a real romance except in Mavis Longford's eyes.

'Mum, stop it.' Shelly had not yet told her mother of the men who had come in the night. She drew out of her mother's embrace and looked steadily in her eyes. 'Mummy?'

Mavis released her and leant back on the railing.

Shelly took a very deep breath. 'I know it was hard for you to accept that I slipped away with Cole straight after we were married and I'm sorry. And I know sometimes you get dramatic.'

Her mother's eyes widened. 'Shelly Longford, whatever do you mean?'

'Please, Mummy, listen. But I love you very much and I also know you're strong. So I probably should tell you something else . . . actually, a lot more.'

Mavis Longford adjusted her spectacles and, in doing so, studied her youngest child.

Shelly's father had been in World War One and survived death in the Somme Valley in northern France and Ypres in Belgium fighting the Germans. He had come home wounded and an invalid;

but with his wife's help he had run a newsagency in Ipswich for ten years until finally his war wounds had killed him. Mavis had continued the business on her own, and alone brought up Shelly and her brother Russell. Yes, she knew in her heart that sometimes she was histrionic about things, but she had suffered and worked hard and it had toughened her. Though when her daughter had married Cole in a civil ceremony and simply told her she was leaving without any explanation of where she was going, it had certainly hurt her.

She had received only three letters in almost a year. They told her that her daughter was well and happy and that she was enjoying life on a farm 'south of Sydney'; the postmarks had been SYDNEY GPO, then today, out of the blue, Shelly had come home. And now this!

Mavis picked up Shelly's hand in hers and spoke deliberately. 'Then whatever this *lot more* is, you had better tell me and we'll see what we can do about it.'

'Well, sit down then, Mummy.'

Ten minutes later Mavis leant back in her chair. She had not spoken while her daughter told her the tale. She was surprised by it, but not shocked. The war had turned the world upside down; the Japs had raped South East Asia and almost invaded Australia, she was not a schoolgirl. She nodded to herself in recollection as she replied, 'Darling, this will interest you: a man came here about a month ago asking about you . . . perhaps thirty or so, pleasant, polite. He put on a good show. Said he had come out here from England as a teenager with his family and had been at the Teachers' College in Brisbane with you before the war. That they were having a reunion and wanted to contact all the class. I had no reason to disbelieve him and I mentioned you were living on a farm south of Sydney and that unfortunately I had no address for you. I even mentioned that if he found you I'd like your address . . . thought no more of it until now.

'You see, I went into Ipswich that same afternoon and was in Whitehouses' Café buying some cakes when I caught sight of the same man sitting in the back at a table. He was with a male companion who was *such* a good-looking man with fair hair and a limp arm hanging at his side. From what you've just told me, that man was Tudor Harrington.'

Shelly nodded. 'Yes, trying to trace Cole through you.'

Mavis pursed her mouth as she was reminded of other things. 'Now, darling, didn't Cole speak fluent French?'

'Yes, he was always good at languages. His mother taught him.'

'Of course. I tend to forget she was born in France. Now, you said you thought the identification card you found was for a Frenchman.'

'Yes, I'd say it is.' Shelly drew it from her purse and showed her mother.

Mavis examined it. 'Cole was a POW, wasn't he?'

'Yes.'

'Where?'

'Oh, Mum, I don't know, somewhere in Germany: he won't talk about it, any of it.'

'And didn't he have a complete command of German too?'

Shelly hesitated. She had left out of her tale the SS ring, the pistol box and the Iron Cross.

'Well, didn't he?'

'Yes . . . the lady he called his "grandma" taught him.' A weird feeling rose in Shelly's chest. 'He always says languages are easy. I suppose they are if you have that sort of brain. He'd not long come back from over six years in England and Europe when I met him.' A fine line lodged between her eyes as she sighed. 'Oh, Mum, what am I going to do?'

'I think you should go to the police.'

Shelly had a bad feeling about that advice. 'No, Mummy, not yet. With your help I'll try to work out what to do, but I have a very strong urge to go back to Apple Gate soon. Will you come with me?'

Mavis nodded. 'Yes, darling, I'm sure your brother Russell will mind the shop for me.'

'But first I think I should visit Cole's mother in Warwick.'

'Oh, darling, do you think it's wise?'

'Well, I feel obliged and she might know something.'

Mavis squinted and made a doubtful sound. 'I don't think so. I must say she's been a dear, commiserating by letter with me on a regular basis.' She gave a loud sigh. 'We were both so affected by the way you two went off like that, but I know if she'd seen these men she would have written and told me. I mentioned my visitor in a letter to her that same week he came and I've had two from her since. The latest one is on the dresser in the kitchen. If you go to her with all this you'll worry her terribly again. She's just getting over it all. Her sisters have been wonderful in helping her.' She patted her daughter's hand. 'I truly believe the most comforting thing you could do is write her a long letter sometime.'

'But, Mummy, don't you think she has a right to know her son has disappeared?'

'Darling, only take my advice if you think it's right, but in this instance I believe you'll upset her dreadfully and have nothing to gain.'

Her daughter sighed and slowly nodded her head.

✳ ✳ ✳

Shelly and Mavis arrived at Apple Gate Farm half an hour before the boy bicycled in with the telegram.

> *In Perth. Going Europe or England. Please don't worry. You mean so much to me. I'll return.*

> *Cole*

Chapter Six

27 December 1947

The English West Country wind was at his back as Cole strode through the straggling trees on the edge of Rainbow Woods to head down the slope towards the town of Bath in county Somerset. His footprints were the only dents in the snow which had easily survived the fleeting sun of noonday; ice hid in the roots of the trees and the smell of coming rain hung in the air. He paused as he came to the last tree: above him in the afternoon haze a solitary bird sailed beneath pallid clouds.

Recalling the last time he had walked down here, he shuddered. The war had raged: it was 1943 and prior to his third espionage operation in Nazi-held Europe. His scarf had fluttered in a rising wind, his boots had left tender impressions in the spring grass dotted with daffodils and the sky above had been clear blue.

That April afternoon was seared upon his memory for Andy McClure had hinted at what was to become Cole's most dangerous operation: his boldest, most improbable mission in enemy-held territory. That day he had visited the man he was now about to call upon: Andy McClure, one of the instructors who had given him his paramilitary training in Arisaig, on the western coast of Scotland; wielding Vickers guns and Schmeissers and Bren guns in the wild and bleak grandeur of Inverness-shire. Andy, who had prepared him twice previously for missions in France as an operative for SOE, Special Operations Executive: the force of secret agents created by the Prime Minister, Mr Churchill, to harass the enemy in German-occupied territory, at great personal risk to themselves. Cole's mouth hardened and he shook his head at the recollections before striding on down to the grey stone cottage nestling on a ridge in a scattered row of similar dwellings as if a giant hand had dealt them out like cards.

Andy lived here these days, whereas, in those yesterdays of war, it had been his occasional hideaway.

The dead remains of summer hollyhocks lined the short pebble path to the front door and when Andy McClure opened it Cole felt the Scot was not surprised to see him, though his next words gave lie to that.

'I never thought I'd see *you* again.' His heavy Scottish brogue had not altered.

'Can I come in?'

Andy gestured behind him to the sitting room and Cole bent his head to enter. Nothing had altered since Cole's visit that summer afternoon years ago except for the small Christmas tree standing beside the two tabby cats lying on the hearth. One lifted her head lazily, noting his arrival.

The Scot sniffed and used his handkerchief. 'Did you have a nice Christmas?'

'No, did you?'

Andy gestured to the cats. 'Aye, the girls and I had a fine old time. We like our own company.'

Cole remained in his overcoat and went immediately past the crackling fire in the grate to the window and looked out, speaking without turning round. 'Look, Andy, I reckon Tudor's been here, so you know what I've come about.'

'Tudor?' The Scot watched his visitor's stiff back. 'I haven't seen him for six or seven months.'

'So you're alone?'

Andy nodded at that. 'No one here but me and my girls.' He knelt and stroked the nearest cat. 'It's cold enough for a tipple. Will you join me in a whisky?'

'No, too early.' Cole spoke over his shoulder, remaining at the window peering through the lace curtains to the street as his host rose, poured two measures in a glass and stood silently waiting.

It was another minute before Cole turned. 'I was living quietly in Australia until I had a visitor a couple of months ago. In fact, a number of visitors. They came with the intention of killing me. Tudor led them.'

The Scot swallowed a mouthful of his drink before replying. 'Obviously they didn't succeed.'

'Come on, Andy, you and I could talk honestly once. Let's cut out the hedging. You say you haven't seen Tudor . . . or Mako? Or Felix?'

'Aye, that's right. I haven't in recent times.' The wiry man shrugged and sat on the arm of the shabby floral sofa eyeing his visitor. His eyes had always been bloodshot; they still were. 'I suppose it was last July or August Tudor came to see me. He was pretty sick there after the war . . . in and out of hospitals for a year or more, his arm and all, and then rest homes. But he was over that when he came here; though his arm would never work properly again – bit of movement in his fingers – but it just hung at his side. He wanted

41

to know if I had an address for you, if I knew where you were living. He seemed to be pretty sure you'd gone to Australia after your stint with the RAF in the Orient before the end of the Pacific War and your demobbing in '46. Asked me about Brisbane – and Ipswich, the town out there, not the one here.'

Cole pursed his lips in thought and turned to the window again and Andy's eyes narrowed, watching him; remembering how all SOE agents were unusual coves, had to be to do the bloody job. Even though SOE tried to recruit people who appeared quite normal, Andy knew from experience that even if they began that way, most altered; some became self-important and aloof, others postured, some faked cheerfulness, while others were, in fact, cheerful. All were self-assured, even those who were otherwise quiet and thoughtful. Yet Cole Wareing had differed from all of them: older, more complicated, somehow imperious, impossible to read.

Their only true common characteristic was courage; beyond a normal person's understanding, so why the hell wouldn't they have their idiosyncrasies?

Andy's gaze followed Cole as he broke from the window and wandered around the room, almost prowling, moving into the hall and out to the front door, halting and returning, walking with just the faintest suggestion of a limp. In his final secret agent role he had become so used to limping for so long that unconsciously it came back now and then.

It was from that particular time 'in the field', as it was known in SOE parlance, that Cole Wareing came back with certain proof that the Nazis had a real and systematic plan worked out to exterminate all European Jews. He had been one of the first with evidence of the *final solution*, as Hitler and his lieutenants

42

called it, and at the time it had shocked the British High Command to the core.

On his first two operations in France, Cole had refused to take the L pill with him – the death pill which killed the instant it was swallowed – but he had carried it on his ultimate mission. Andy remembered that night in mid-June 1943 as the four agents who were to work with Cole departed together for Groningen Province in Holland. Cole was there to see them off, he would follow in two weeks after they had made preparations for his arrival. Andy pictured them all now, it was imprinted on his mind.

There was no moon that night, a canopy of light clouds ensured the east coast of England was bathed in ebony. Cole stood with the four operatives who had done their final check to see nothing had been overlooked in their packing and organisa-tion and they now drank tea in the drawing room of the big old house, hidden from the road by elms and not far from Norwich Castle. In the front hall, also drinking tea and eating a scone, waited Flight Lieutenant Lewis Hodges of No. 161 Special Duties Squadron, ready to fly the agents into Holland in his Hudson and soon to be promoted to command his squadron.

Cole and Tudor stood side by side. Rarely had Andy seen a more fascinating pair: real names Squadron Leader Tudor Harrington and Wing Commander Cole Wareing. Tudor, working under the cover name Dirk Hartog, nonchalantly smoked a cigarette. He was an American pilot who had come over to England in 1940 and volunteered for the RAF. Both were immensely attractive men, even another man could see that, almost vying with each other in magnetism: one dark, one fair, both chatting as if they were off to a pleasant evening at a country pub. They had been recruited together and both had been on previous missions into France: multilingual, Tudor had been requested this time because he spoke fluent Dutch and German.

All SOE agents were given cover names to use as their own abroad, their true identities were kept secret. The operatives also took their own codes and code names plus a personal poem to identify themselves when they radioed into SOE.

The third of the group sat nearby on a windowsill and went under the cover name of Mako Vanderbilt, born Jack Coeman, a Welshman with Dutch father; an explosives' expert and one of the most sinister-looking men possible: face all angles, sunken cheeks, burning dark eyes, feline movements. He was carrying the pencil bombs which they were to use in the coming operation.

With him was a twenty-seven-year-old, cover name Felix Lansing: a knife thrower extraordinaire; his real name was Hammersmith and he had been, remarkably enough, born in Hammersmith of a Dutch mother and an English father. He could hit a moving target at great distances, but within fifteen yards his knives became as deadly as a gun. With wayward black curls and wiry diminutive stature he was a tough Londoner who could drill all day and not tire. The last member of the band, cover name Leopold de Vries, was the wireless operator. Just twenty-two, with Irish mother and Dutch father, Leopold moved nervously from one foot to the other, reciting to himself his personal poem. His real name was David Holt and he was on his first mission. He would be shot dead by the Germans within three weeks.

But tonight, along with the others, he listened to Hans Buckhout, the Dutch officer who had put the operation together, who had believed in it so vehemently and who was turning Cole Wareing into a colonel in the Nazi SS.

Tudor was on his third mission and Felix his second. It was dangerous for an agent to go 'into the field' multiple times; a number of them had been arrested on their third operations, including Peter Churchill, one of their best, the previous April.

Finally Hans offered the L pills to them; he proffered the phials in the palm of his hand. This was something that was usually done earlier in the night so it had surprised Andy McClure.

Leopold swiftly took his phial, followed by Mako and Felix, who closed their fists over the tiny object before Tudor stepped forward, picking his up as he would have done a cigarette, between his index and middle finger and nonchalantly slipping it into his trouser pocket.

Andy watched Cole's reaction to all this, knowing the man had refused the L pill twice previously, but it was impossible to judge what he was thinking as he spoke light-heartedly to the four departing men.

'Well, toodooloo, lads, I'll be seeing you in Holland in a couple of weeks.' He shook hands with them each in turn as they took up their belongings and moved towards the door after Hans.

Once they were out of sight Cole turned to Andy. A deep frown lodged between his eyes and he blinked. 'I'll take the L pill too, when I go into Holland this time.' He spun on his heel and left the room.

Chapter Seven

Andy was eyeing Cole as he finally came to rest back at the window, yet his body remained taut as if he still expected an intruder any moment. 'I thought I could go back to Australia and live my life. But no, Tudor has other ideas. Blast the man; to think I even went looking for clues to where he might be once Holland was liberated.'

'That's right, you were over there with an airborne unit, weren't you?'

'I had permission to go into Apeldoorn and the Doetinchem area as soon as the Canadians were in there. I had Canadian Intelligence as well as our boys searching everywhere for the bugger once our forces were in Germany.' He shook his head. 'Though why I bothered . . .'

The visitor gave a supercilious grunt and the Scot sniffed and sipped his drink before he declared, 'So, Cole, you turn up here now athinkin' I might have seen Tudor of late, eh? But I haven't. So for old times' sake and to fill in a dull afternoon, why don't you tell me what happened to bring you here?'

Andy pointed to the chair near the hearth and Cole moved to it. 'All right, Andy.' In tentative fashion, he sat on the arm where he still had a view out the window. He recounted the night Tudor and the others had come to Apple Gate Farm and what had subsequently occurred. The Scot poured himself another whisky during the tale and Cole finished with the words, 'So I caught a steamer and came to England, because I realised I finally had to find out what the hell it was that triggered off Tudor's need to kill me. I thought you or Buckhout might know something.'

'Hans Buckhout? Ah, Hans lives in Paris now. He knows everybody from De Gaulle down, of course, so he might be worth a visit sometime. Lives at sixteen rue d'Anjou near the Elysée Palace.'

Cole repeated the address as Andy leant forward enthusiastically. 'So your escape route out of the farm was pretty darn sophisticated, eh? Tricked them good and proper, eh? Now, laddie, that makes me think you were expecting him –' his bloodshot eyes locked with Cole's – 'just as a guilty man would be.'

The visitor made an exasperated sound. 'Of course I was expecting him. The last time I heard from Tudor he said he'd get me wherever I went.' He gave a sneering laugh. 'I didn't take that threat lightly.'

'Understandably.' The Scot shrugged his bony shoulders again. 'And when was that?'

Cole's impatience sounded in his voice. 'When was what?'

'The last time you were ahearin' from him?'

'In England, after the war. Before I was sent to Burma. I didn't see him, I got a message from him.' Now he threw his hands in the air in a frustrated gesture. 'But first . . . Come on, Andy, spit it out, what did he tell you about me?'

The Scot studied his visitor through half-closed lids. He did not speak for some time and when finally he did, he spoke slowly and thoughtfully. 'He said you worked for the Nazis. That you changed sides. That your last operation corrupted you and you and Laetitia de Witt were in cahoots with the German secret police and informed on him and his men. That because of you and Laetitia de Witt, they were taken by the Gestapo.'

'Hell, Andy! I guessed all that.' A disdainful expression rose in Cole's eyes. 'Tell me, why hasn't Tudor taken this to the authorities, if he's so damn certain of it?'

Andy nodded in agreement as if that particular dart went to the centre of the board. Silence followed until the Scot broke it. 'I reckon he believes it would be his word against yours . . . after all, you're a hero in the old SOE ranks and he's probably heard you've given an affidavit against Erich Naumann in the current trial in Nuremberg of those Nazis who ran the mobile killing squads. By the way, did you give one against Rauter for his trial at the Hague too?'

A callous, hard edge made Cole's voice grate in his throat. 'I certainly bloody did; I wrote them before I left for Burma – and one against Seyss-Inquart as well. I hope they all burn in hell for eternity.' He took a long, noisy breath and shook his head. 'And for heaven's sake, Andy, if I'd joined their ranks, don't you think Rauter and Naumann would have already implicated me?'

The Scot gave a sceptical grin. 'It's not what I think, laddie, it's what Tudor thinks. Despite the fact that he's aware the British authorities regard you as a hero.'

'You're enjoying this, you old bugger. It's not you he's after. That'd wipe the smile off your face.'

The clock on the mantel began to chime and Cole stood up hurriedly. 'Jesus, I must be aging, I'm getting edgy.' He began ranging around the intimate room again like a caged big cat, half talking to himself. 'How could Tudor think I worked for those degenerates? How in Hades could the man believe it? How could any of them believe it?'

'Listen, matey, you and Tudor were skilled, so skilled you were probably the best operatives I ever dealt with, but that also made you the best liars I ever knew. So who to believe, eh?'

'Damn it, Andy, you of all people should be aware that nothing and nobody could have made me into a murdering Hitler robot.'

Andy sniffed loudly, it could have been in agreement or it simply could have been a sniff. He cleared his throat. 'Tudor had an idea that playing the role insidiously ate away at your soul and finally encompassed . . . now how did he say it? encompassed . . . *your whole persona*, that's it – until you believed what you pretended.'

Cole shook his head murmuring, 'Damn fool', as he began to roam around again and a long silence endured while the ticking of the mantelpiece clock magnified in the room. He paced into the hall, along to the front door and back once more to end up, as usual, at the window, while Andy sipped his drink.

Finally, the younger man turned and took a paper from his pocket. 'Here, this is the message I mentioned before, I've kept it in my wallet since I left England. It was handed to me by Tonia at SOE headquarters, the very morning of the day I flew out to Burma to take over the RAF Special Operations Wing. She said it was hand-delivered to her at her flat in Bayswater the previous night. This was how I knew Tudor was alive and coming after me. It's definitely his handwriting.'

Andy read:

I'll get you, Cole. You're dead, it's just a matter of time, Nazi scum! You fooled a lot of people but I'll get you wherever you go. I know you turned

because of Laetitia de Witt. We know she's gone but you'll join her. There
will be nowhere on earth you can hide. I'm coming.
T. H.

As Andy raised his eyes from the paper Cole pointed to it. 'That's why I was expecting him, even as far away as Australia.'

Andy McClure wagged the note in the air. 'That's right, I remember he and Mako didn't return from Sweden until the day prior to your departure for Burma. They came into Dover on a merchant ship . . . had spent all that time hiding out in Sweden until the war was over. I saw him that afternoon and he and Mako asked a lot of questions about you.' He shook the paper in the air. 'He moved fast to get this to you.'

'Yes . . .'

'He hated Laetitia de Witt.'

The visitor's eyes changed as the edges of his mouth drew down in memory. 'I know.' He shook his head and turned again to the window. With his right hand he moved the lace curtain to peer out before he faced back to his host. 'Since I got that note I've always realised he thought I was a double agent along with Laetitia.' He paused. 'God, I still don't know what to believe about her myself; and of course Tudor thought she was a Nazi. It sure as hell looked like it from certain standpoints . . . but me in with her? I've never guessed why he included me. He must have told you; come on, Andy, why?' Cole's eyes were cold again, the expression that Andy remembered so well: the confident, imperious, self-sufficient look that had been his trademark. He stared straight at the older man as he took the note from Andy's hand and pocketed it.

The Scot cocked his head on one side. 'He told me that when he was in the German holding prison outside Doetinchem he learnt without a shadow of a doubt that Laetitia de Witt had worked hand in glove with you to trap them. He said he saw you and Miss de Witt together at the prison. And from that day he has lived only to seek revenge.'

Chapter Eight

Cole's eyes flicked back and forth in disbelief and he stood stock-still.

Andy contemplated him carefully as the moments passed and he noted the deliberate way Cole brought his apparent astonishment under control until finally he spoke in a normal tone. 'This can't be. Why would he say he saw us at the prison? I was never there. I'm not even sure I know where it was.'

Andy's gaze did not leave Cole's face. It certainly appeared that this statement had shocked the former agent; that his reaction was genuine. *If you actually weren't astounded by that information, lad, then you're still bloody outstanding. Just as outstanding as you ever were.*

Andy nodded. 'Well, that's what he said. He's convinced you two sold them down the river.'

The visitor began to pace around the room again while his host asked, 'The holding prison outside Doetinchem? That's where he was taken after they caught them all on the banks of the Oude Ijssel, wasn't it?'

'Yep. This makes no sense at all. Why would he say that? What the hell was he raving about?' Cole was back at the window and he brushed the curtain aside to stare at the pane of glass in front of him. He could see his image in it and he spoke as if to his reflection. 'He learnt without a shadow of a doubt that I had worked with Letta to trap him? What in Hades does that mean? Why do I think Von Bremen had a part in this? It was a big favour to the world when I wiped that bastard off the face of the earth.' He leant forward to rest his head a moment on the iciness of the glass. 'What *does* it matter now – any of it?' Andy saw Cole's shoulders drop as if the weight of memory were too heavy. 'But oh no, Tudor won't let it lie.'

The Scot continued to watch his visitor closely while the younger man straightened up and turned and Andy noticed a tell-tale tightening of Cole's jaw as the muscles contracted. His reaction appeared truly authentic; he certainly seemed to be continuing to have trouble accepting this piece of information and Andy felt somehow gratified that he had seen the cracks in the ex secret agent's façade. Everybody working with Andy and Hans Buckhout in 1943 had guessed that Cole Wareing was in love with Laetitia de Witt when he had told them he was bringing her out of Holland with him.

Andy finished his drink and cleared his throat. 'I know you're aware Tudor and Mako escaped from the lorry taking them to Amersfoort camp and that, in due course, they got across to Sweden.'

Cole grunted. 'Yes, where they remained for the duration of the war.'

'Uh huh.'

Cole was talking to himself again. 'Saw me with Letta in the holding prison? Found out Letta had worked with me to trap them? All that bull dust . . .'

Andy shrugged. 'Ah, laddie, so it might be, but Tudor believes it and in war the most absurd things happen, eh?'

Cole now spoke dismissively. 'God, man, we all know that.

53

Absurdity after absurdity: I lived a lie in the middle of a den of high-ranking murdering Nazis for month after month . . . killed you a few of them too.' He waved his hands in the air for emphasis. 'Jesus, Andy, have you ever lived every night and every day expecting to be arrested? No, of course you haven't, we were the bunnies who went into that. Well, it's no flaming picnic. You get to thinking all manner of mad things. Holland was a mess, the Resistance was infiltrated by German collaborators, double agents, the lot; and our people were caught all the time.' Cole gave a short sarcastic laugh. 'Holland was full of bloody *V-manner* everywhere. I was a bloody *thaumaturge* to survive!'

Andy grunted, 'Whatever that is, eh, lad?'

'A bloody magician is what that is.'

'Mmm, and survive you did.' It did not escape Andy's notice that Cole used *V-manner* – the German colloquial form of *Vertrauensmanner*, meaning 'those who could be trusted'.

Andy sighed. 'Ah yes, in 1943 the Germans were certainly playing *the game against England*, eh? *Englandspiel*, as the German counterpart to us at SOE called it at the time.'

'You don't have to tell me.' Cole was revealing his anger now and his voice began to rise. 'Andy, what did we expect from Holland? The bloody Kaiser lived there under their protection after the Great War; his grandson died fighting for Hitler's bloody Wehrmacht in 1940. The decent good men in Holland didn't have a lot of chances, their country was riddled with collaborators . . . and in Tudor's eyes I'm supposed to be one?' He let out a groan of frustration. 'I sent Hans and you all sorts of secret information: Peenemünde, where to bomb, intelligence on airfields, factories, troop movements . . . I wasn't a double agent. You, of all people, know for certain I wasn't.'

'All you say is so, and none of us knew in '42 and '43 that the entire Resistance movement in Holland was penetrated by the enemy, even though some of us, Hans Buckhout in particular, suspected it.' Andy sighed. 'That was the reason Hans worked autonomously with you and Tudor and the others.'

Cole prowled the room again, paused and abruptly asked, 'You do believe me, don't you?'

Andy blinked and nodded. 'Aye, lad, I do. I always have.'

'Thanks.' He gave a small smile. 'Well, look, I thought you might have had a recent visit from Tudor but as you haven't and you've enlightened me about what he claims, there's not much point in my remaining here.'

Andy raised his hand to stay his visitor. He did have one more piece of information for him and he knew he must reveal it no matter what the consequences. He pointed to the chair near the hearth again. 'Listen, laddie, sit again a minute, eh? You're starting to make me nervous the way you've continued to roam around this blasted cottage like a tiger on heat. Tudor hasn't been near me recently, and if he does come again, I'll tell him what I'm about to tell you.'

'I don't want to sit, old man, just tell me whatever it is.'

'All right . . . About two months ago an old pal of mine from SOE came to visit. Taylor, do you remember him?'

'No.'

'Ah well, he'd worked in SOE's camouflage section for years and was close to our leader, Gubbins. Well, while we sat here gabbing – he was in the very chair you're standing near now – he got to talking about all sorts of people and how Prime Minister Attlee had closed SOE down last year with only forty-eight hours' notice. Bloody foolish move, of course; it was a perfect worldwide communications' network with people in it who were Britain's friends; but I reckon as Winston Churchill had opened it, he was all for closing it – "a sheep in sheep's clothing", as Churchill called Attlee, eh?'

He chuckled at this, a deep throaty amused sound and his bloodshot eyes gleamed with mirth. 'But I digress . . . well, Taylor was one of the few who went over to MI6 last year after the closure of SOE. Well, here we were atalkin' about some of you agents in the field – and your name came up. He was full of praise for you and your stint in Nazi uniform, said you should get a George Cross, which, by the way, appears to be happening, but—'

'Really?' Cole knew nothing about this. The George Cross was the highest non-battlefield award bestowed in the British Empire. Cole grinned at this news. 'I reckon I should get two of the buggers.'

'Aye, laddie, so do I, but this is the part you should know . . . Taylor then told me that there was evidence, hard evidence, that Miss de Witt didn't die as we'd all believed, that she is still alive . . .'

Cole's grin died on his mouth.

Chapter Nine

For a moment Cole blinked violently and took a small involuntary step backwards as if he had been prodded in the chest. He locked eyes with Andy and his voice dropped to almost a whisper. 'Letta? You mean Letta's still alive?'

'I do.'

Andy could see the man with him tried to control himself but the shock had affected him so greatly that his jaw clenched again and this time a tiny muscle twitched in the skin below the scar on his cheekbone. 'What are you talking about? I know she's dead.'

'Apparently not, laddie. MI6 now have proof that it's certain she spent the last part of the war in northern Holland and then at the cessation of hostilities passed through the French zone in Allied-occupied Germany with some sort of pass from a Canadian general. It's believed she went from there through the American zone, before disappearing completely, until now, when she fleetingly turns up in Alexandria in Egypt. They have reopened the file on her and are dealing with the Americans and Canadians on it.'

'No.'

Andy stood from the sofa as Cole hung his head in contemplation, his face was a shade paler than before. The confident, supercilious

Cole Wareing was completely gone. Rents had appeared in the cold clandestine cloak the ex-agent wore. 'This cannot be. I told you all when I got back here. I saw her dead. I felt her pulse . . . there was none. You all knew that. What in God's name is this trickery?'

Andy took hold of his companion's arm. 'Listen, lad, I know it's hard for you to believe, but Taylor showed me a fairly recent photograph. He thought it was taken about a month before his visit here. It was Laetitia de Witt, it seems to be indisputable.'

'God in heaven, Andy! It was you who told me to forget her.' He shot his arm in a cutting movement away from his body and stepped out of Andy's grasp. 'SOE closed her file.' His voice dropped and he stared at his hands. 'I saw her. I know what I saw . . .' He turned away and held his head in his hands. He relived the moment: she lay on the floor, her head in a pool of blood – blood on her face and hair; her blue dress, the one that had been his favourite, stained with red blotches. The white collar scarlet with blood; her body lifeless . . .

A note of sympathy sounded in the Scot's gravel-like voice. 'I remember. And as far as I'm aware, that's what Tudor still believes as well; that she's dead. We informed him of that on his return from Sweden. Well, we all believed it until Taylor's evidence came to light.'

A dog began barking outside and abruptly Cole spun back to the window to look out as Andy continued, 'Shortly after it was taken, the photograph fell into the hands of a man called Notts from the MI6 North African Branch. This Notts was acquainted with Laetitia de Witt's father in the thirties, had met Laetitia and had worked with Hans Buckhout for a short period during your months in the Netherlands. He knew your file intimately and the ones on Tudor, Mako, Felix and Laetitia de Witt. Notts was astounded when he saw the picture for he was sure he recognised her. Taylor said Notts reported that he spoke to her a day later as she left a small hotel and there was no denying it was Laetitia de Witt although she was calling herself Martine Thalberg.'

Cole flinched as if he had been stung by a bee, but he remained at the window.

Andy had not missed this reaction. 'So the name means something to you, lad?'

'You might say, Andy, you might say.'

Complete silence fell and neither of the occupiers of the little cottage spoke. Two minutes passed during which time Andy's eyes flicked around the room: from his visitor to the cats by the hearth and to the half-bottle of whisky, until finally Cole nodded to himself and turned abruptly. His expression was once again unreadable. 'All right, Andy . . .' The afternoon was beginning to close in and shadows lingered about the room, making Cole's dark-blue eyes black and icy. The sharp, experienced mind of the secret agent was again at work and his feelings were now outwardly under control. 'So you saw a photograph of her, supposedly taken when? Three months ago?'

'Aye.'

Cole's eyes closed briefly. 'Where is it?'

Andy crossed to a small desk and opened a book lying there. He removed a picture and handed it to his visitor.

Cole studied it and he felt his pulse quicken. It was only a snap but it had been enlarged significantly and was clear enough. It was obvious that it was at some sort of a restaurant or nightclub for two people danced and she was seated at a table to the side of them, with a glass in her hand, looking away to the side of the camera and wearing that same alluring smile on her mouth; the one he knew so intimately. Her eyes oozed charm even in black and white. Her hair nestled on her shoulders but it was styled differently, parted on the left and swathed over her forehead to cover her right temple. Half of her companion was visible: a man in a dark suit. She appeared thinner and older than when he had last seen her four years prior, but undeniably it looked like Laetitia de Witt.

Andy scrutinised his companion and if he had not been with Cole in the previous five minutes he would have believed him completely at ease and in control as he murmured, 'It could be . . . her.'

'Taylor and Notts are certain. The information given to me was that every night she accompanied an elderly man to a club and watched him play roulette in the casino on the premises. That by day she went south in a jeep to the outskirts of the city to the same place near the Villa Antoniadis.'

'Can I keep this?'

'Aye, laddie. I was sort of aholdin' it for you. I had a strong feeling you'd turn up sometime, unless, of course, Tudor had realised his desire to put you in the next world, eh?'

Cole slid the black and white photograph into his pocket and put out his hand. Andy shook it. 'I suppose you need to find her, eh?'

'Uh huh . . . I suppose I do.'

'Any ideas where to go?'

Cole shrugged and his host did not press the matter as they walked to the door and he opened it, patting his visitor on the back as he exited. 'Come back and see me sometime. I'd like to hear the outcome to all this . . . you know how it is, once SOE is in your blood you desire to tie up the ends if you possibly can, eh?'

'Sure, Andy.' Cole clicked his heels and his head bowed automatically in accurate Nazi fashion. 'Bugger,' he said with a shake of his head, 'now why the hell did I do that?'

Andy pursed his lips and winked a bloodshot eye. 'Ah, laddie, it's still living down in ye somewhere, eh? All our training, still intrinsic.'

Cole did not comment, he simply gave an air-force salute and walked down the short path as the Scot raised his hand in farewell and closed the door.

At the cottage gate Cole hesitated, his fingers on the latch. He stared at the back of his hand.

She removed her pale fingers from his and ran her nail — a perfect ellipse shining in the light of the candle — across the skin on the back of his hand. 'Your hand is so brown compared to mine.' She turned her head and kissed his cheek. They rose and he wrapped the cape around her shoulders and they moved to the door. Outside the breeze dallied round them and her hair rippled gently on her shoulders as she walked, her heels making distinct clicks on the stone of the footpath. He could smell the faint sweet essence of her perfume, exotic like herself, wafting around him.

Abruptly Cole stiffened and removed his hand from the gate in the chill of the closing afternoon.

Martine Thalberg? Yes she would use Thalberg, that made sense. The name had meant nothing to Andy and it would mean nothing to Tudor and the others . . . but it meant a lot to him. So she had been in Alexandria three months ago. Yes, he might have to go to Egypt, but he would try one other place first. The other place he knew she might be.

Letta alive? How could it be true? It seemed absurd, bizarre.

But if she were still alive, he had to find her, find out the answers that only she knew, even though he was married to Shelly. Thank heaven his darling Shelly was in Australia, safe and away from all this at Apple Gate Farm.

Chapter Ten

Shelly stood a short distance from the dock and the cargo ship SS *Royal Orb*, which had brought her here, watching two youths playing ancient violins. The cries of seagulls drifted in on the breeze from the Mediterranean Sea as the moods of the grey chill December day settled in over the port of Toulon. She had recognised the melody of the Christmas carol, even though the playing had been hardly expert, but just hearing 'Silent Night' this far from home had brightened her soul a little, and because of the lifting of her spirits she walked over and dropped two sous into the hat on the ground in front of the players.

The swarthy-faced younger of the two smiled a thank-you at her, showing broken teeth – sad in one so young, he appeared no more than fifteen. She supposed dental care had not been at the forefront of general needs in the previous six years here in France.

The city of Toulon had altered little from how it was during the war. British and American naval ships were in the harbour and so too were the remains of the French fleet scuttled by their own hands in November 1942 when Hitler, in his usual fashion, betrayed them, broke his word and attacked the city, even though it was part of the Vichy-controlled area of France which was collaborating with him.

A British military transit camp was currently within the environs of the city though not many servicemen were in the streets as they were forbidden to fraternise with the locals because of their Vichy association. The streets were full of bedraggled people selling all manner of wares from military blankets to scissors and at times their enthusiasm for a sale caused them to intimidate. Shelly had been accosted earlier in the day and her schoolgirl French was good enough to say – *'Je suis désolée, mais je n'ai pas d'argent pour acheter quelque chose. Pardon: I have no money to buy anything, excuse me.'* And to hurry on by.

Restoration of the harbour was underway but mountains of rubble still decorated the foreshore and the town looked grey and dismal under the eternal watch from the dominating hills and Mount Faron looming over the city, beyond.

She smiled now at the boy as he asked, *'Aimé "Douce Nuit"?'*

'Yes, I liked it. *Oui, merci. Je l'ai aimé.'*

'Un autre?'

She shook her head. *'Non, merci.'*

The young man pointed to her hair. It was revealed beneath her warm beret and curled above the collar of her overcoat. *'Jolis cheveux,'* he commented and she gave him another smile.

'Thank you.' She believed she was not beautiful, but she was often complimented on her golden fair hair . . . but what Shelly did not realise was that, with her slender figure, wide green eyes, high cheekbones and candid smile, she exuded a charm far in excess of what she believed possible.

She walked on. She had boarded the merchant ship SS *Royal*

Orb in Sydney six weeks ago. It had been a miracle the captain could take her aboard, for the ship had space for only twelve passengers and one berth had come free just when Shelly inquired about a passage to Europe. Her mother had said she wanted to accompany her and had cried there on the dock in Darling Harbour in Sydney as her daughter had sailed away, but in her heart Shelly felt Mavis Longford did not wish to leave her brother Russell and his young family. In any case, Shelly had decided it was better that she travelled alone.

Her decision to follow Cole had been made in haste and the two farm hands had readily agreed to run the farm in her absence. Her bank manager had been co-operative and she felt comfortable that Apple Gate was in capable hands.

She sighed as she gazed around at the rubble lying in heaps and the three small black cats wailing as they made their way through the fragments of broken stone. Thinking of her well-taken-care-of-animals back at Apple Gate Farm made Shelly feel sorry for them. No doubt they were homeless; poor 'displaced' cats like so many millions of displaced persons. Europe was still full of camps for those with nowhere to go; often with no relatives and some even with no name. Toulon was typical of most cities: in the brief period since war had ended there had been little time to tidy and rebuild the ubiquitous destruction.

The breeze was gentle though its tenor icy, as it roved through the tunnels of open spaces. She shivered, turning up the collar of her overcoat to hide her ears peeking from under her felt beret, and pulling the coat more firmly around her.

Crossing a square she passed the ruins of the Saint-Louis church where children played, their laughter rising in contrast to the colourless melancholy of the environment around them. She paused a moment to watch them and her hands slipped around her middle to clutch her body. A sorrowful expression turned the edges of her mouth downwards as a powerful feeling rose stinging in her throat. For some moments the emotion overwhelmed her until she swallowed and opened her mouth to breathe the cold air deeply into her lungs. How badly she was missing Cole. She had miscarried last June when she was just over two months pregnant. The doctors had told her it would be unlikely for her ever to conceive again. She had come to accept that because she knew there was no alternative and people had to endure all sorts of things in this life.

When she had lost the baby, Cole had taken her in his arms and stroked her hair and smiled tenderly, his tone of voice warm and sympathetic. 'Shell, you're a wonderful girl and you would have been a splendid mother, but I'd be lying to you if I said I'm sorry. I know I don't speak very often about the war, but I saw too much misery, watched men die and saw many innocent men and women . . . innocent children, even babies – suffer horribly – beyond what you could imagine.' He took up her limp hand from her lap and held it. 'I know that, now – post Hitler and Tojo – it's supposed to be a new world where humans will be kind and tolerate one another but, my dear, I'm a cynic about that and it'll surprise me if they don't just go on with all their old hatreds and indoctrinations just as strongly ingrained in them as ever. The history of this third planet from the sun proves that. I can't truly say I want to bring children here.'

He had looked into her eyes and she saw, deep in his, the intense belief in what he was saying. 'So if you had carried this child, then I would have accepted the fact of its being here; I would have attempted to be a decent parent; but as you haven't, let's believe that it's gone to another world, a finer one where goodness prevails.

65

Let's be calm and content just with each other. I want peace and harmony – and just you – very badly.'

Shelly had leant forward and kissed the sides of his eyes and the scar near his mouth and watched his vehement expression soften. 'Since I first told you, Cole, I thought you were lukewarm about it, and now I know why. I'm glad you've expressed all this to me and released that now. I'm hurting but I understand what you say. Tell me, darling, was what you did . . . that bad?'

He gave her one of his wan half-smiles and his eyes glazed to where he seemed to look somewhere beyond her at something she would never see. He remarked very softly, *'What I did?* No, Shell, I have no regrets of any kind about what I did. It was what Hitler and his stinking rabble did. It was what I saw . . . and what I could *do* . . . nothing about . . .'

He said no more, he simply held her close and kissed the top of her head and called her darling. She felt so sad for him and hoped one day he would explain more to her so that she could truly understand his deepest feelings. But she also knew that time had not yet arrived. She was aware of her own strengths and she knew she could wait.

He whispered, 'I need you, darling Shell', into her hair and that had been enough for her to rally; that he needed her was more important than their *might-have-been* baby. She loved him and would support him always. It was easy then, back at Apple Gate, for he had been with her and they were united, but now she was alone ten thousand miles from home without him. Here, on a fanciful whim that she could find out things for him and somehow help him. She had spent a deal of their savings getting here and momentarily she felt ridiculous and lonely. But the next minute she pulled herself together and mentally scolded herself. She was here and nowhere else. She had come to find that woman in the postcard and she would darn-well do her utmost to do so.

Suddenly she became aware of a ball rolling to her feet and a boy of eight or nine chasing it. He ran to her and grabbed it, looking up and smiling, showing a missing front tooth. She responded in kind and ruffled his hair and he picked up the ball and ran back to his playmates.

'Right, Shelly,' she said aloud, 'get on with it', and urged herself forward to enter the rue Nationale where she looked to the mountains beyond and thought that perhaps from up there on a sunny summer's day with the blue Mediterranean Sea in the background, distance might lend some charm to the town.

She traversed Place Victor Hugo and entered a small street, the left-hand side being still garnished with the remains of destroyed buildings. Four boys played soccer in an open space which had been cleared of broken stone and fragments as if rebuilding were about to begin.

She hurried to No. 13. It was an unprepossessing façade of dark stone and the door was open. As she stepped through the opening a loud voice hailed her, '*Madame Wareing, n'est-ce pas?*'

'Yes, *oui*, I am Mrs Wareing.'

A stout body followed the voice as Monsieur Gavare appeared from the darkness beyond into the pool of light made by a single electric bulb hanging on a cord from the ceiling. The bland illumination reflected in the dark eyes of the stocky, swarthy man of middle years as he eyed his visitor. He attempted to welcome her. 'Ah . . . you *ici. Bon.*' He looked cold and kept his hands in the deep pockets of his jacket as he spoke. A cigarette had burnt down to perhaps an inch in length and it balanced on his lower lip in the corner of the wide, amiable smile he used to greet Shelly. He looked her up and down and nodded to himself, 'Good, yes.' He seemed to be fond of this phrase and it was repeated over the coming days many times. He rambled on, 'Cost travel. *Est-ce que ma femme* tell *vous* cost travel?'

Shelly replied. 'Oh yes, *oui*, when I was here yesterday, er . . . *hier*, your wife — told me, *combien* . . . I have the money. *J'ai les fonds pour vous payer sur moi.*' She handed across an envelope from her purse and he gave her a wide grin and, after repeating 'Good, yes', looked back into the darkness and called loudly: '*Yvonne, la dame est ici.*'

A moment later his wife appeared, a fine-boned, tiny woman who coughed as she came forward to greet the newcomer. Shelly had come here the previous afternoon on the recommendation of the ship's mate and met Madame Gavare and explained her needs. 'Good day, it is nice to see you again.' Yvonne Gavare spoke competent, understandable English, having been educated at the Sorbonne. It was evident that she was a class above her husband, though the bond between them revealed itself to Shelly as time passed.

'Ah, *ma chérie*,' Gavare began and he spoke so quickly to his wife that Shelly lost track of the ensuing conversation.

Yvonne Gavare patted his arm as she coughed again and turned to Shelly. 'My husband and his partner will take you in our good solid sailing boat to Monaco. It will be less expensive to go that way rather than any other . . . petrol is still hard to get in any quantity and the trains are unreliable. Are you a good sailor?'

'I believe so. On the long voyage here I was not ill even though we hit rough seas at times.'

'*Bon*. Because the wind is right for sailing today: there will be a small swell in the sea so it will not be, er . . . perfectly tranquil, but Pierre could sail you to the Porquerolles Island this afternoon. We have fishermen friends there, so we'll have a bed for the night and we'll be under way. Can you start in a few hours?'

Shelly hesitated only momentarily. 'Yes, I can start today.'

'Then it is settled. We hope to sail on to the little port of St Tropez tomorrow. The Allies landed there during the war, so much was destroyed, but they are rebuilding it.'

She met Shelly's eyes as she cleared her throat and Shelly frowned. 'You said *we*, are you coming with us?'

'Of course. Pierre's English is hopeless and his partner Gerard is not much better. You will need me with you to translate.'

Shelly had liked this woman immediately on meeting her and now she warmed to her even more. 'How kind of you.'

'And if the seas are not rough, we will sail on to the fishing village of Villefranche the next day and possibly even on to Cap d'Ail right next to Monaco; but we make no promises. Pierre has a cousin who lives above the beach at Cap d'Ail near the principality so that will help with a place to stay.' Yvonne's eyes were big, almost too big for her fine-pinched face; they were a limpid brown and gentle, reminding Shelly of the cows at Apple Gate. 'I see you travel alone, my dear. That in itself is brave. We have many alien people around; not all of them with good intentions.'

Shelly shrugged. 'I had no one to come with me. My mother said she wanted to accompany me but I think the truth is she did not wish to leave my brother.'

Yvonne nodded. 'Ah, I understand — mothers and their sons, my mother was like that.' She gave another cough. 'She cried for a week when my brother went to war . . . the Great War, not this one. He was shot in the Battle of the Marne.'

'Oh, I'm sorry.'

'No need to be, he was lucky. He simply lost his leg . . . but he came home, when so many did not. We regarded it as a blessing that he was wounded.'

Shelly did not know what to say to this so she asked a question, 'Am I right in thinking the distance to Monaco is about one hundred miles . . . er . . . one hundred and sixty kilometres?'

'As you say in English . . . *as the crow flies* . . . yes, but it is a little further by sea.'

Pierre Gavare broke in at that point and rattled on to his wife, gesticulating and grinning at her in the insipid yellow light.

Yvonne turned back to the visitor. 'Can you be ready by, say, one o'clock today? On the dock near your ship?'

'Yes, I'll be there. I shall speak with the ship's mate as soon as I get back. He has been very helpful.'

'Now how many bags do you have?'

'Two and this.' Shelly held up her black leather handbag in front of her.

'I think perhaps you had better only bring one valise.'

This startled her listener, but Yvonne patted her arm. 'Don't worry, Pierre's cousin Danton will be at the dock with us. He will take your spare case and look after it, so only bring the items you need most with you. Now, my husband shall see you back to your ship.'

Shelly felt she was being organised by the frail French woman with the big heart, but she did not mind. 'Thank you.' She was in a part of the world she did not know and since leaving Australia she had seen sights on her way to Europe, in the Orient and Asia Minor, which had revealed to her what she had always suspected, that she had been brought up in a very cosseted society. When she saw the squalor of Singapore, Bombay, Aden and the like, she had almost wished she had not been so cavalier as to rush after her husband with her only clues two postcard photographs and a few Nazi trappings.

However, for all that there was a strong streak of her mother's temperament in Shelly, she was a realist and would face up to whatever she had started in motion. In Australia she had decided to come to Europe and go to Monaco and see if she could find out about the woman in the photograph. She had an overwhelming feeling and at times a sorrowful one, that if she learnt about the woman, she would find out a lot more about Cole.

She now had confidence in Yvonne Gavare and she could thank the mate of the *Royal Orb* for that. On the long voyage here, the captain and his second in command had taken her under their wing and looked after her. The mate, Lawrence Banks from Port Pirie, an ex-petty officer in the Royal Australia Navy during the war, who was in his first peace-time position as mate of the ship, had been particularly kind to her. It was through the captain and his knowledge of the town that the mate had gone out and found Pierre Gavare for her.

Yvonne patted her visitor's shoulder in farewell and Shelly and Pierre hurried back through the small square that was Place Victor Hugo. The cold seeped through their clothing and Pierre's hands did not leave his pockets while he and Shelly hurried down the streets leading to the docks until the looming shape of the ship straining at its ropes appeared beside them on the wharf. There he removed his right hand from his pocket, doffed his cap, said, '*Jusqu'à une heure*', and hurried away.

'Yes, until one o'clock,' she repeated in English.

Shelly was greeted by a sailor in a greatcoat standing watch at the gangplank. 'You're back, Mrs Wareing; did you like Toulon?'

Shelly answered with a platitude, and hurried aboard.

Chapter Eleven

The gunmetal waters of the harbour lapped against the small sailing vessel hanging off the wharf in front of the bow of the SS *Royal Orb*. Partial sunshine seeped through breaks in the cloud and the breeze had become a wind which danced across the harbour to lift Shelly's overcoat skirt and flutter her scarf as Larry Banks, the ship's mate, followed her down the gangplank carrying her luggage.

She waved at Pierre Gavare standing waiting with two men near one of the ship's lines tied to a large bollard. As Shelly approached, they stepped over the rope and Larry handed across the bags. Pierre took the brocade travelling bag and a tall man, Pierre's cousin, reached out for the second case as Gerard, his partner, began to untie the shore lines and Yvonne, wrapped in a warm overcoat and bonnet, called out, 'Climb aboard.'

Feeling somewhat heady from the strong, crisp smell of ozone in the air, Shelly turned to Larry.

On the voyage she had often dined with the mate and they had become genuine friends. He was aware that she was seeking information about her husband but knew none of the details and had respectfully not asked. Shelly had realised in the last few weeks that Larry felt a little more than friendship towards her and now, as they stood together to say farewell, the thought crossed her mind that she could abandon this search and stay with him on the ship and travel to England.

When, for the first time, she had seen the photograph of Laetitia de Witt that night at Apple Gate, she had sensed in her very bones that the woman was a key to all the mystery surrounding her husband. It had been a bombshell to her already disturbed world to read the words on the back of the picture and she had repeated to herself, *But he came back from the war and married me, not her*.

That thought had comforted her, but as the days and weeks had passed on her voyage to the South of France, her moods had swung to and fro. Sometimes she believed that Cole certainly loved her and wanted her for herself and then that thought would fade into the conviction that for some reason he could not marry Laetitia de Witt whom he truly loved and so he had married her for companionship alone. She thought how he rarely used the word *love* to her and in the past it had not troubled her, for he always spoke tenderly to her and called her *darling* and told her how happy he was with her; and he treated her with love, even if he did not use the word. That had been all she needed for she knew he was not a man who openly revealed his feelings. But now she was questioning everything.

One part of her mind told her, as it always did, to *buck up* and not cloud her head with indecision, but only ten minutes ago, before she had disembarked from the *Royal Orb*, she had sunk to her lowest point. She had taken out the photograph of Laetitia de Witt and studied it and compared it with herself in the mirror. While she was content with her own slender, firm figure and supposed she could be called attractive with her fair hair, clear skin and large green eyes, the woman in the picture was breathtakingly beautiful. There in her cabin, Shelly had felt her eyes cloud with tears and it had been only her sheer willpower that had forced herself to be sensible and to wash her face and put on lipstick just prior to Larry Banks's knock on the door.

And as the mate said, 'Mrs Wareing, I shall miss you', and she hesitated, that powerful voice somewhere inside her told her not to falter now and she answered, 'Goodbye, Mr Banks, thank you for coming here to see me off. You've been awfully good to me and I do so appreciate everything.'

He withdrew a piece of paper from his pocket. 'I have written two addresses here for you. One is my home, the other is of a friend of mine in London where I shall visit. I have a month's leave there before the ship sails on to Savannah, Georgia.' He handed her the paper. 'I hope I don't sound presumptuous, but if ever you need a friend, please remember me.'

A swell of kind feeling for him ran through her. 'Thank you, again. You've been most kind.' She took the paper and held out her gloved hand to him before he gave a half salute and turned and walked away.

Within two minutes Shelly was aboard and they were waving goodbye. Before long the sailing boat was making progress from the roadstead of the Petit Rade – via the opening in the breakwater which ran across the harbour – into the Grande Rade and out into the undulations of the Mediterranean Sea.

As Pierre and Gerard sailed the sturdy wooden thirty-footer southwards and Shelly looked back to see the silhouette of the *Royal Orb* disappearing in the distance, she sank down beside Yvonne in the keel and the two women wrapped themselves in blankets.

The wind filled the patched sails and the boat rode the swell until Porquerolles Island came into view and Shelly looked up to the sky where clouds were herded together by wind.

Was it fancy or truth that allowed her to see a human profile she recognised in the large cloud that now separated itself from the others as she watched?

For the seconds that she believed she witnessed Cole Wareing's profile riding in the sky that day, any despondence Shelly still carried waned and a powerful feeling of determination overcame her. The icy air which moved across her face roused her spirits and an energy filled her with the certainty that, after all, taking this voyage to Monaco was right, no matter what would be found there.

And so with wisps of sea spray in Shelly's hair, the little group sailed on to the rickety wharf in Porquerolles Island and the shouts of welcome from the fishermen and their families. The notion that somehow she had been given a sign when she thought she saw the outline of Cole's face in the cloud in the sky stayed with Shelly and she continued to become even more positive.

And when they landed, the buoyed-up feeling remained to such an extent that even the pungent marine aromas which hung in the fishermen's cottages were not unpleasant to her. She smiled at the merry faces of the children and as the shadows lengthened, she actually looked forward to the next day and the continuing voyage to the tiny port of Saint Tropez: a village since medieval times . . . another step on her way to Avenue de la Costa in Monte Carlo.

Chapter Twelve

The same hour: Bath, England

Cole knew he was being followed a few minutes after he left Andy's gate. He had passed the string of cottages and crossed a green to enter a more crowded part of the town when he realised he had a tail. He speeded up and turned a corner, walked diagonally across the road and entered a park where the wind chased him as he darted by a row of elms and accelerated. He ran on a hundred yards to the rubble of a bomb site and crossed another road, but did not lose his follower. He hastened on down a side street, ducked into a whitewashed corner pub and stood looking out.

The stale smell of smoking yesterdays hit him as he saw the man hurrying down the road: Mako!

Cole's body tensed.

He spun round and took in the scene: a few empty wooden tables and chairs on a frayed rug; three workmen in overalls at the bar and a woman and a man playing darts in an alcove beyond the counter. 'What'll ya have, matey?' called the bartender, but Cole did not reply, merely lifted his hand in negation of the question.

Crossing the room he eased himself through a green-beaded

curtain into a corridor at the side of the bar and ahead of him saw 'Gents' written on a door and 'Ladies' on the one beside it. Beyond was another door which probably led out to the back of the pub. He hurried to it and turned the handle: locked!

Swiftly returning to the 'Ladies' door, he tried it and it opened: no window! He had better luck in the 'Gents': above the urinal was a window which opened when he pushed it. Two seconds later he was standing on the porcelain and thrusting the frosted window which opened out to a lane. He carried the smatchet knife and the Walther P38 in the pockets of his overcoat but he hoped he would not have to use them. He did not want to kill Mako. Once in the lane there was a chance of getting away.

He pulled himself up and had one leg in and one leg out of the window, when the door burst open and the deft hands of Mako grabbed at his dangling foot as Cole kicked out and smashed him in the jaw with the heel of his shoe.

Mako swore loudly in pain as his head flicked back, his cap fell off and he went down, but the blade of the dirk in his right hand did not miss the flesh of Cole's lower leg as he pulled it up and threw his body out the window. The knife slit his trouser leg and went deep. Blood spurted back over the lavatory as Mako fell on to the porcelain urinal but rallied immediately and regained his balance to leap up at the window and follow the disappearing figure through the opening.

Cole felt the searing pain as he stumbled to his feet on the surface of the lane and Mako dropped heavily behind him to cast out his left hand and grasp the escaping man's overcoat tail.

As he was jerked backwards Cole tumbled into the greedy arms of his pursuer who swung the dagger, still in his right hand, round towards Cole's body. But even as he toppled, Cole's instinct was to fling his forearm up to meet Mako's wrist with such force that his fist opened and the blade dropped to the ground, clanging on the stones.

They grappled and rolled over. Each man knew the other's tactics. They had been trained by the same experts in self-defence and, as Cole's fingers closed around his pursuer's neck and the manic eyes widened, the assailant forced his arm up through Cole's grasp and broke away.

'Jesus, Mako . . . you're wrong . . . about me.'

Cole was on top now and as the man beneath tried to throw him off, Cole brought his elbow thudding down into Mako's temple. The man went limp, his resistance vanished and he slipped into momentary unconsciousness. At that second a woman screamed from the mouth of the lane, 'Police, get the police!'

Cole rose instantly and looked round for the fallen knife, but could not see it. *It must be under Mako.* He had no time to waste and jumped up and ran past the screaming woman. Thank God it was Mako after him and not Felix. With his remarkable aim, Felix would have dared to throw the dirk from a distance.

He emerged into a street where a group of children played cricket in front of an upturned crate and as he darted by them a taxi appeared. It halted and a man alighted as Cole leapt over the dirt towards the vehicle and the children took up the woman's call, for they had noticed the trail of blood left behind the running man. 'Eh, 'ee's bleedin' . . . Police! Police!' And they ceased their game for the more intriguing sport of following the bleeding man.

Cole waved and yelled at the driver of the taxi, charging towards it Pied Piper-like with his string of howling children. He flung open the door and jumped in shouting, 'Nearest railway station, please.'

The driver looked round. 'What'd you do to those kids? Why are they yellin' at you?'

'Nothing, they just saw me fighting with a bloke, that's all.'

'Ah.' The driver shrugged and pulled away from the collection of shouting boys on the kerb.

'So nearest station, eh? Well, that's Bath Queen Square.'

'Right, good, that'll do.'

They had not covered a hundred yards when the driver noticed that his fare's trouser leg was dripping blood and staining his carpet. 'Eh? What the bloody 'ell do you think ya doin'? That's a new rug back there. Me brother got it on the black market.' He pulled over to the side of the road, his voice rising and his face reddening. 'Out, you.'

'Listen, matey, I'll make it worth your while. I'll pay you however much you reckon it's worth to replace.'

'Gawd! Cost me eight shillings, that did!' But he did not move on, the vehicle remained at the side of the road.

Cole glanced around across the shining black boot, where, sure enough, he saw the group of young cricketers still standing watching, but now, looming behind them, came the spectral form of Mako holding his temple.

His voice rose. 'Listen: just get going. I'll give you five pounds.'

'Five quid?' The driver's mouth contorted in disapproval. 'You're barmy; why would you give me that much? You a burglar or sommat?'

Cole groaned. Why did he have to run into the only taxi driver in Bath who refused a goodly profit? He leant forward. 'Look, we'll come to an arrangement. I'll give you whatever you think's fair.' He looked back through the rear window and now Mako had started to run towards the taxi.

Cole's heart began pumping. 'Just take me to the station. Listen, I'll pay you anything you say.'

'Gawd!' The driver cleared his throat. 'Oright, but you're a one, you are, and 'ow'd you come by the bleedin' leg anyway?'

'I'll tell you. Just move. Come on.'

And much to Cole's relief, the driver shrugged and turned back to his wheel and pulled away.

In the taxi Cole wrapped his calf in his handkerchief and pulled the ripped, stained leg of his trousers down over the bandage as best he could. The driver settled on a pound and two shillings to cover the mess in his cabin and Cole jumped out and ran into the ticket office.

The female ticket seller asked, 'Where to?'

'What's the first train out?'

'The one to Bristol via Mangotsfield. It's in now.' She nodded her head in the direction of the platform.

Cole frowned. 'When's the next train to London?'

'Isn't one. London train leaves from Bath Spa Station.'

Cole took a deep breath. His one chance was that Mako would think he had gone to Bath Spa for a London train.

'Give me a ticket to Bristol, then.'

'What class?'

'Second.'

Ticket in hand, Cole hurried down the platform under the impressive roof of vaulted glass in a single-span wrought-iron arch. But as he ran, Cole was not looking up to that refinement where the cold winter twilight presently seeped through the remaining holes in the still-damaged glass from bombing raids during the war. He chose the last carriage of the train from where he would be able to watch the entire platform and see if indeed his old associate arrived. Jumping aboard he entered the corridor. It was empty and so too was the first compartment. Once inside, he pulled down the blinds over the two windows to the corridor.

Six tense minutes ensued as he stared out to the stationmaster who finally blew his whistle and the carriage shunted forward, allowing Cole to make his way to the men's room. There he removed the linen hand towel from the rail and, using his silver and enamel penknife, cut the cloth in strips. He saved a piece in his pocket and wrapped his still-bleeding leg while the train drew out of Bath and picked up speed to rattle over the bridge across the Avon river flowing below.

Chapter Thirteen

Under the anaemic illumination in the railway carriage Cole sat, eyes wide open. The soporific click of the train wheels on the rails had no power to entice him to sleep. He was deep in thought as the iron engine drew its burden across the fields under the darkening sky.

His leg began to throb and he lifted it up next to his overcoat folded on the seat opposite. There were ten seats: plush green but threadbare – five on both sides. They would have looked smart when they were new. The seat frames could even be walnut: all typical of the compartment interiors built before the war.

He shook his head: Letta was not dead? It was bizarre. But then he had seen many a bizarrerie. He removed the snap taken in Alexandria from the inside pocket of his jacket and stared at it. The memory of what he had seen four years ago stung his mind.

But here she was in the image he held in his hand looking very much alive – older and thinner, but still lovely, holding a glass of wine, taken just three months ago: September. He returned the picture to his pocket and stared ahead. *How can it be?* He still would not have believed this even with the photograph – except that she used the name *Thalberg*. That had convinced him.

For a year with Shelly he had found a little peace, a little tranquillity. In that time at Apple Gate his wife's infectious laugh had helped him forget the ugliness; her trusting green eyes and smiling face had allowed him to live in the present with her; allowed him to veil the past.

And now? Letta was alive. The past had returned to the present.

How in God's name could she be alive? He frowned in remembrance as the event he had filed away in his head in the fog of time came back in full force again. He stood looking at her; she wore the blue dress with the white lace on the collar, her head and the collar were covered in blood; he felt her pulse . . . none. He lifted her dead body and took her to the sofa . . .

I knew her with the wind in her hair and the blue dress snuggling around her curves, with her eyes glowing and her tinkling laughter . . .

He sat upright and brought out the photograph to study it once more. It was her — no one else but Letta. *Letta, how can you be alive? And yet you are: Martine Thalberg.*

He took a deep breath and looked at the ceiling of the carriage, where his trained eye automatically noted the peeling paint in the corners as his thoughts turned to Tudor: *You believe we were both traitors, eh? You maintain you found out she was a traitor at the prison; that you saw us there. How in the hell could that be?*

He turned his gaze to the window but all he saw was his own reflection. Night had fallen.

Tudor, who had been his pal — his closest friend — now turned deadly enemy. Ah, how different it had been that summer evening in 1941 when they had met.

The breeze lifted Cole's dark hair as he sat near the open window in the mess. The squadron had just returned from bombing a target in northern France and the boys about him were relaxing in cheerful, rowdy style. En route to their objective, one of the Blenheim bombers in No. 18 Squadron had flown over St Omer airfield and dropped, by parachute, a box containing a spare right artificial leg for Douglas Bader, the renowned English fighter pilot ace, who was now a prisoner of the Germans, having been shot down over France ten days earlier.

Cole had raised his eyes from his beer and a hand had shot in his direction. The owner was a young man who could have made the grade as a 'matinee idol', he was so damn good-looking. He met Cole's eyes with a direct gaze from his own vivid blue ones. 'Howdy, Wing Commander. I'm pleased to meet you.'

'You're an American.'

Tudor grinned, revealing a row of faultless teeth. 'Sure. Flight Lieutenant Tudor Harrington at your service.'

Cole took the proffered hand. 'You're a long way from home.'

'You bet, sir. I've been flying since I was a kid. I joined up during the Dunkirk evacuation. I thought you guys could do with all the help you could get.' Tudor's easy Southern accent was comfortable on the ear.

Cole nodded. 'Yep, you're right about that.'

They had liked each other immediately. Tudor had an eye for the girls and they for him, but it was all good fun to the 'guy from North Carolina' and he never tied himself down to any of them. Cole was older than him and began to regard him as the younger brother he never had. By October they were in Egypt and five weeks later Tudor was made a squadron leader and they were back in Great Britain. Cole remembered the December day when they heard that Germany had declared war on the USA and the USA had retaliated with its own declaration of war on Germany. Tudor's handsome face had been sombre. And speaking slowly and deliberately breaking the vowel in true southern mode, he had announced, 'We . . . ell, sir, it's finally my wa . . . ar too.'

Before year's end they were both recruited into SOE.

Cole delivered a cynical grunt in recollection: to think Tudor, of all people, could turn against him.

The train slowed and chugged into Bitton Station where he

focused on a dimly lit small brick station house with two gables facing the platform. A man and two women boarded and a minute later the carriage shunted forward and began to move. He leant back, considering what he should do next. His leg was throbbing now.

The journey from Bath to Bristol was not long, even via Mangotsfield, and fifteen minutes later, after they had criss-crossed the Avon river a number of times, the train was gathering speed from its final stop before Bristol when the door abruptly slid back. Cole's eyes lifted to the newcomer, and a tingle of needle points shot up his spine as he leapt to his feet.

Chapter Fourteen

Mako!

How the hell did you get aboard?

The man stood menacingly inside the door and closed it behind him. His right hand was in his pocket and Cole was very aware what he held in it. Cole's right hand slid immediately into his own pocket.

"Evening." The menace in Mako's tone hung in the air.

Cole's own pistol and the smatchet knife were in the pocket of his overcoat lying behind Mako on the seat, so he bluffed. 'Don't make me use the pistol I've got aimed at your heart, Mako.'

The intruder's sunken eyes widened and he hesitated and, at that second, the door which Mako had just slid closed, rattled open.

'Tickets, please!' the conductor announced, edging Mako to one side.

Cole watched his old confederate sit down in the nearest seat and oddly enough he noticed that his straight dark hair had become tinted with grey. The newcomer looked to Cole who remained standing and proffered his ticket.

The inspector clipped it and rounded back to Mako. 'Ticket, please?'

'Didn't have time to buy one, got on the train in a hurry.' His Welsh accent seemed more pronounced than when Cole had known him.

The inspector eyed the big man over his spectacles. 'Ah well, now, no time to buy a ticket, eh? Ah . . . we've heard that before . . . we have to teach you a lesson, sir. Where are you headed?'

'Bristol.'

'Where did you board?'

'Bath.'

So his pursuer had been on the train since Bath; Cole could not help but admire the way Mako had managed to hop on the train without being seen.

'Right . . . so let's see what you owe.'

While the inspector calculated the amount Mako needed to pay, Cole looked down at him. 'Tell Tudor he's wrong about everything.' And he grabbed his overcoat, pushed by them both and left the compartment.

Cole raced along the corridor and out on to the carriage landing to bound across the bridge over the coupling to the next carriage. On and on he sped towards the front of the train, hastening through the hallways of second-, third- and first-class carriages until, as the train decelerated and drew into Bristol Temple Meads, he opened the door in the very first carriage and jumped on to the platform. Even though the vehicle was slowing greatly, as he landed he could not retain his balance; he fell and somersaulted over and instantly regained his feet. Startled people stepped quickly away from him protesting loudly but he kept running, ignoring the escalating pain in his wounded leg.

He knew Mako would not be far behind, it just depended on how long the inspector had detained him.

For the second time that day Cole jumped into a black cab: the lone one outside the station. 'Take me to Taunton, please.'

'Taunton?' The man turned round and eyed him.

'Yes, Taunton.'

'You a millionaire, old chap?'

'What does that mean?'

'Yikes, fella, it'll cost you a fortune and, in any case, I don't have enough petrol . . . I don't get my ration till Monday. You won't find a taxi in Bristol to take you, matey. Your best bet is to go by train. Go back inside and catch one.' He pointed with his thumb to the building Cole had just exited.

'No, can't do that. What's the nearest station where I could still catch a train to Taunton?'

The driver remained with his thumb in the air pointing backwards.

'Other than this one, for Christ's sake? Come on, man, we need to move.'

The driver sighed loudly in exasperation. 'Well, they all come through here, as I said, and the seven forty will be the next one out, but it doesn't stop at Bedminister – that's the first station on the Exeter line . . . it's the Exeter line Taunton's on, you see . . .'

'Yes, damn it, I do see, where does it stop?'

'No need to get hot under the collar. I believe the seven forty will stop at Flax Bourton, we could head there, but you'd still be best to go back inside and—'

'Look, just move, will you? Take me to Flax Bourton.'

'All right . . . keep your hair on.' The driver muttered to himself as he drove away, 'Strange coves about nowadays.'

Cole looked back towards the lit station but to his immense relief there was no sign of the menace which followed him.

He rubbed his leg gently to assuage the constant ache. *This will be another bloody scar . . . as if I don't have enough.*

The driver turned his head sideways to ask, 'Where're you going in Taunton, then, sir? If you don't mind my asking.'

Cole paused before answering. 'As you aren't taking me there, you don't need to know.'

'No need to get uppity, just making conversation. You from around here?'

'No.'

'Where are you from, then?'

'Listen, I'd like to get some sleep, if I can.'

'That's all right, no offence taken. You close your eyes.'

Cole leant back on the seat as the driver's eyes lifted to the heavens.

Chapter Fifteen

Same time: France

'I do not wish to pry but this journey to Monaco . . . will it bring you happiness?'

Shelly looked up at Yvonne Gavare from where she sat in the small stone room with the two bunks which would be their beds for the night. Her honest green eyes were linked by the frown line between them. 'Happiness? I don't know. I hope it will explain some things to me. Things I need to know and which I am at a loss to understand right now, Madame Gavare.'

'Oh, please call me Yvonne.'

'Thanks, I will, and you should call me Shelly.'

Yvonne coughed and sipped the coffee, which their host, the Porquerolles fisherman Axam Moreau, a gregarious sunburnt individual, had made for them. Pierre, Gerard and Axam were ensconced in the only other room of the hut, talking and smoking pipes. Their voices drifted through the closed wooden door to the two women.

'It must be a powerful need indeed which brings you all the way to France from Australia. I know a little of geography and it is a long, long way.'

Shelly gave a small smile. 'Yes, it sure is.'

'"*It sure is*." That's an American phrase.'

Shelly smiled. 'I learnt it from American soldiers during the war.'
'The American Forty-fifth Infantry Division landed here in 1944
. . . they used to say *Goddam* and *swell* a lot too. Before they came I
thought a swell was in the sea and something that grew larger.'

Both women laughed and Shelly turned her head to where the
glow from the fire and the candles revealed light rain pattering
outside on the single pane of glass in the room. It had begun to
rain as twilight descended.

Shelly felt that the woman with her was honest and kind, that
her heart was generous. She badly needed a confidante, and as her
gaze swung back to her companion she made up her mind.

'I am trying to find out some things about my husband. He is
somewhere here or in England. He was in Europe during the war.
We've been married just a little over twelve months; wonderful
months – at least I thought so . . .' She stopped. The potent optimism of the afternoon was slipping from her. Her face stiffened
and she fell silent.

The French woman put down her cup and came to her and
spoke soothingly. 'Please don't feel obliged to tell me anything. I
am too inquisitive, I shouldn't have questioned you. Forgive me.'

Shelly raised her head to look up at her new friend. 'Oh no,
that's not so. I've decided I want to tell you.'

'Then I want to listen.' Yvonne sat down beside her and patted
her hand.

And as Shelly looked into her companion's eyes she took up her
tale.

In the many minutes that followed, Pierre knocked on the door
more than once to inform them that supper was ready and when

they did emerge to eat with the men, Shelly felt strong again. Her new friend Yvonne had listened closely and sympathetically to her story and with a keenness of mind had supported Shelly's plan to go to Monaco to see if she could find out about the woman, Laetitia de Witt. '*Oui*, the photographer's will be a good starting place, *ma chérie*.'

The same time: back in England

Fire crackled in the grate, the bar was warm and hearty laughter lifted through the cosy atmosphere where the customers sipped ale and basked in conviviality.

The mullioned-glass front door reflected twinkling colours from the electric light as it swung open and those nearest it were sharply reminded of the icy December chill lurking just outside in the streets of Bath. Feeling the gush of wind, Felix lifted his head from the *Evening Standard* newspaper and beckoned the tall dark figure who entered the pub.

Mako saw him and after some gentle pushing and shoving he parted a lively group to join his friend and slip into the seat opposite Felix in the wooden booth.

The expression on Mako's face brought forth the comment, 'You've seen him and you've lost him.'

'You're right. When I took over the vigil there from you this afternoon, he turned up only a couple of minutes later. I waited and when he came out I followed him and cornered him in a pub lav; gashed his leg, pretty deeply too, but he climbed out the window. I caught him, though, and we fought . . . he got the better of me and actually knocked me out for a few seconds.' Mako rubbed his head as he went on, 'That was enough for him to give me the slip in a taxi. I caught up with him again on the Bristol train but the bugger's got the luck of the Irish . . . he was saved by the inspector.'

'What?'

'Well, I didn't have a ticket, did I? So while I was held up buying one the target got away.'

'Pity I missed him with the smatchet that night in Australia; I won't miss him next time.' Felix shook his head disconsolately. 'That was my favourite Fairburn-Sykes I used on him, too. I've only got two left.' He pushed a beer across to Mako. 'I bought this for you – hoping you'd show up soon.'

'Ta.' He took up the beer. 'But do you know what?'

'What?'

'As Wareing left the train compartment he looked at me and said, "Tell Tudor he's wrong about everything." He said something similar when I caught up with him earlier as well.'

Felix sat up straight and cleared his throat. 'Heck. Well, naturally he's going to say that, isn't he? Did you two stop and have a breather and a bloody conversation or something?'

''Course not . . . don't be ridiculous.' As he spoke Mako shifted his weight on the seat and moved into the corner of the booth. He felt more comfortable with his back to the wall and his severe features lightened a fraction. He cast his eyes around the smoke-filled room.

Felix shook his head and his curls danced. 'Look, naturally the man's going to profess innocence.'

Mako grunted, 'Yeah, Felix, you're probably right.'

'Strange, isn't it?'

'What?'

'The way you and I still use our SOE cover names as if they

were our real names. You still call me Felix and I call you Mako, even though I've known your real name for years.'

Mako's lips twisted in a grin. 'I like Mako. It suits me and you'll always be Felix to me.'

'But we don't call Tudor "Dirk", do we? Though Dirk was his cover name. And, for that matter, we call Wareing by his real name too. Now why is that?'

This was becoming too technical for Mako; he leant forward from his corner and pointed a spindly forefinger at his companion. 'As Publilius Syrus said in the first century BC: "Not every question deserves an answer."'

'Who the heck was Publilius Syrus?'

'Look up an encyclopaedia.' Mako threw his glass back and finished his beer in successive gulps.

Shrugging, Felix took this in his stride and tilted his head towards the door. 'We need to get going. Tudor's train's due in an hour, we'd better get to the hotel.'

Chapter Sixteen

Same day: six hours earlier

Tudor Harrington, his fair hair jutting out on his forehead from under his felt Fedora hat, walked along West Street in Farnham in Surrey beneath a burst of winter sunshine. He had been in Paris visiting the Dutchman Hans Buckhout who now lived in France, but to no avail. Tudor had skirted around the real reason for seeking out Buckhout and simply asked if he had seen any of *the old SOE gang* lately. He had not, so the visit ended rapidly.

He had sent Felix and Mako ahead of him to England on their return to Europe after the Australia expedition, to maintain surveillance on the one place he suspected that Wareing might turn up in due course: Andy McClure's cottage in Bath. And he would travel to that town of natural hot springs later today and meet up with his pals.

He mused on the past as he walked by the businesses and the colourful shop windows of Farnham to pause beside a woman, wrapped in a blanket and sitting on a low stool, with a basket of small bunches of lily of the valley upon her lap. As his shadow fell across her she lifted her head of white hair and with a warm, cheeky grin held a bunch up to him. 'Grown in me own indoor garden, dearie. You won't find 'em anywhere else this time of year – only tuppence each.'

He hesitated and she added, 'Whoever she is, dearie, she'll like them . . . especially from you.'

'Yes, all right.' And carrying the posy in his good hand he made his way along the street and stopped at number twenty-seven, a bakery shop with a window displaying bread and cakes. Two stone steps led up to the door and from where he stood it appeared as if there were a house attached to the back. Abruptly he felt uncertain. Why had he come? This was foolish and ill-thought out. His main reason for living was to terminate Wareing's life and even thinking about this place was a diversion he could not afford.

The quixotic conclusion to come here had been made on the train from Dover to London this morning. He had been reading the newspaper and glancing down the columns when he saw a headline: *Town of Farnham in Surrey Stages Reunion for Land Girls*, and a tingle of emotion ran through him.

He had looked out the window at the passing landscape of mottled green and there she was in his head, her eyes wet with tears. '*But why can't we still be friends?*'

'*Because this war is taking me away and it's better like this. I can't have any ties . . .*'

'Goddam,' he had whispered aloud to himself to the clack of the train wheels, 'she might still be in Farnham – twenty-seven West Street, Farnham, Surrey.'

The address had remained locked in his mind for years. Many times he had decided to come here and many times he had checked himself. The priority always was for him to get well and strong and to find Wareing and annihilate him.

Yet he had thought of visiting this house a thousand times: when he was lying in hospital beds after the war while they operated on his arm; when he was in the series of military rest homes and again before he had gone out to Australia; but he had always resolved not to come. Today it had suddenly been different. It seemed to him that the reference to *land girls* and *Farnham* in the newspaper was a signal of some kind and the knowledge that he had hours to spare before he needed to catch a train west to Bath had pushed him to making a snap decision.

So he had travelled to this historic town with its Georgian buildings and streets of small shops and made his way to this very place only now to stand doubtful and wavering in front of his destination.

Jane Morley had been a land girl in Suffolk during the war: one of the women's land army who replaced men in the fields and farms of Great Britain so the males could join the fighting forces. The first thing he noticed about her was her figure. He had been physically attracted to her immediately, but once he was acquainted with her he saw the beauty of her nature and he had been captivated by the warmth of her heart. He had been constantly surprised by her kindness to everyone.

She would stop and talk in the street to lonely elderly people and take a genuine interest in them. In the evenings she worked for the Red Cross and on her one day off a week she visited hospitals and the local military orphanage. He remembered how on one of their country walks she had made them both spend an hour removing a cow's head from where it had been caught between two palings. He had been ready to leave it there and let the farmer take care of it in due course, but not Jane. Somehow all this compassion had impressed him, for he admitted in his heart that he was the opposite and he was aware of how she had revealed values to him which he had never previously considered.

And now he was standing in the chill of a December day on a concrete footpath in this street looking at the address she had given him back in 1941 . . .

He glanced down at the delicate white flowers in his good hand and suddenly he completely lost his nerve. He was a broken thing; he was a blasted fool to do this.

He had discarded personal needs and wishes for years in his seething desire to eliminate Wareing. It had kept him alive in Sweden between their escape from Holland and the end of the goddam war; and after the war it had restrained him from going home to his mother in North Carolina – his great regret, for she had died without seeing him. It had taken him to Australia and it had brought him back to England and it had seen him through the operations on his arm – his crippled arm – which remained the constant reminder of his consuming desire . . .

And now he had succumbed to his emotions because he thought he saw some type of blasted message in a goddam newspaper!

'Jesus,' he whispered and even as he said it and made to turn away, the door opened in front of him and a middle-aged woman in a velvet hat and an overcoat with a green skirt peeping from the open flap, stood gazing down at him.

'Are you looking for someone?' She smiled at him. And as he did not speak she descended the two steps to the footpath.

He took a deep breath and removed his hat with the hand that held the flowers. 'I . . . er . . . Does Jane Morley live here?'

A crease formed between the woman's eyes and she looked closely at him: tall, brilliant blue eyes, fair hair, one of the best-looking men she had ever seen. 'Who are you?'

For the first time in years Cole Wareing slipped to the back of Tudor Harrington's mind as he answered, 'My name's Harrington . . .'

'Oh my heaven! You're the American, Tudor Harrington?'

He nodded. 'Uh huh.'

Her expression instantly hardened. 'So you're the one my daughter's carried a torch for all these years? You broke her heart, you know? Spoilt her for other men. She won't look at anybody even after all this time and there are a number who come calling.' She sniffed, pursed her lips and looked disapprovingly at him.

So Jane had waited for him . . . he pictured her as he last saw her, her russet hair tied at the nape of her neck to hang down her back, her eyes framed by the dark arched eyebrows, her tender smile.

'You're her mother?'

'Of course I'm her mother. And Jane's out.' She said it with satisfaction and glared down her nose at him.

Tudor stared past her at the painted window box and the sun reflecting on the shop window. There had only been two women who had ever got under his skin. One was dead and he hated her memory with a seething enmity; this woman's daughter was the other. He had become very close to Jane prior to the day he had been recruited as a secret agent. It was SOE's desire – if at all possible – for its agents to have no, or minimal, relationships, which had forced him to break things off with her and he had always regretted it. He remembered how drunk he had become the night they parted.

Of all the women he had known, and there had been many, Jane was the only one he had really admired; the only one who had stayed in his heart.

And now here he was standing with her mother who looked

askance at him; reproach in the very way she held herself: chin tucked in, taut shoulders, tense mouth.

Years ago, prior to being wounded and captured, he would have tried to charm this woman but now he simply spoke the truth: 'Mrs Morley . . . this is very hard to say and I'm not sure how to say it and I don't blame you for your attitude, not at all; I understand it; but the fact is . . . I've *carried a torch*, as you put it, for your daughter all these years as well.' He dropped his gaze to his bad arm. 'I was wounded. And . . . things have always stopped me from coming here before today. Suddenly I felt I must see . . .' His voice trailed off.

Elizabeth Morley stared at him and her bitter look softened. Her shoulders dropped as she replied, 'Oh, I see . . . it's like that? Well, listen, Mr Harrington, Jane's away for the day. But I know she'll want to see you and she'll be back this evening, so if you can return, say around six, she'll be home.'

Thudding back into his mind came Cole Wareing. He had to be in Bath this evening. Yes, he admitted he very dearly wanted to see Jane Morley, but being here was an indulgence. He had come here on a whim.

Tudor's eyes closed momentarily as he moved from one foot to the other. Abruptly he replaced his hat before he pushed the posy into the woman's hands. 'Mrs Morley. Please give these to Jane from me. Tell her . . . tell her . . . I have to do something important . . . that it might be a little while . . . but . . . I'll do my darnedest to come back here.'

He spun on his heel and strode away down West Street, his heart accelerating. He had to deal with Wareing, but he had learnt that Jane was free.

Please, God, let me somehow come back to Jane.

* * *

100

That evening on her arrival home, Jane's disappointment was patently evident: 'You mean he was here, Mum? Tudor was here? And I missed him.' Her chin quavered as she attempted to remain in control of her feelings.

Mrs Morley handed her the flowers and patted her daughter's shoulder. 'But he left these for you and said he would do his darnedest to come back – those were his very words. And darling, as much as I've been against him in the past, well, I believe him.'

Jane clutched the posy of flowers to her chest as her mother added, 'He has a bad arm, I suppose he was wounded in the war.'

'Oh no, poor Tudor.' The young woman's eyes filled with tears as she shook her head. 'But that doesn't matter to me . . . as long as he comes back.' And she looked for affirmation from her mother as she continued hopefully, 'And he wouldn't have come here today if he didn't care, Mum, would he?'

'Of course not. I'd say from the way he acted, he cares very much; it's just that he has something important to do first. Now, darling, I've had a real turnaround about him. I truly feel that he was wounded and all and couldn't write or get here before this, for some reason.' She wrapped her daughter in her arms and made a motherly comforting sound as Jane held the white flowers up to her lips.

Chapter Seventeen

Mako and Felix saw Tudor enter the dining room and so did a number of the female diners whose gazes followed his tall striking figure as he crossed the dining room of the Old Mill Hotel overlooking the Avon river and stood looking down at his allies. His eyes gleamed in the radiance of the art nouveau lamp beside him. 'I can see by looking at you that he slipped through our fingers.'

Mako groaned. 'Yes, he did, but he got a mighty bad leg out of it, I can tell you. I gave him a right awful gash in his calf.'

'So we've given him a natural limp at last.' Tudor laughed. 'Now that's very funny . . . very funny indeed.' And placing his greatcoat on the back of the vacant chair he sat down and laughed again.

Mako's mouth twisted into an amused grimace. 'Yeah, isn't it? It was a fairly deep cut, reckon I hit the bone.'

'Sounds like he's in need of stitches.'

'For certain. He turned up at Andy's just as we thought and I tailed him.'

The waiter arrived at that moment and as they ordered steak and kidney pie, Felix made conversation. 'How was the journey in from France today?'

Tudor smiled. 'Rough as hell early this morning. Pity they don't have a tunnel under the Channel.'

'Heck, imagine it.' They all found the thought of that phenomenon amusing and Tudor toyed with his knife and fork as the waiter moved away. 'You have no idea where the target went, Mako?'

'No, I wounded him when he tried to climb out of a lavatory window in a pub. Stayed with him into town and on to the train from Bath to Bristol and almost had him when a damn inspector came in and he gave me the slip. I reckon he got into a taxi at Bristol Temple Meads.'

Felix nudged Mako's arm. 'Tell him.'

Tudor frowned. 'Tell me what?'

Mako let out a sigh and leant forward confidentially, 'Well, it's like this. Just as he was leaving the train compartment, he eyed me, and said, *Tell Tudor he's wrong about everything.*'

Tudor grunted. 'Sure, of course he's going to say that.'

Felix tapped a rhythm with his fingers on the white tablecloth. 'That's what I said, boss. He's not going to say you're right, is he?'

Silence fell until Tudor broke it. 'He's guilty all right, as guilty as she was. We knew they worked together and what I heard and saw in that goddam prison I'll never forget.' His mouth twisted and he lifted the forefinger of his good hand in the air. 'You know what? We should go to Andy McClure's tonight. See what they said to one another.'

Mako grunted. 'But when you saw Andy before we went to Australia he told us all he knew.'

'Yeah but that was back in May, old pal.' Abruptly Tudor sat straight upright. It was so unexpected that the two others started in their chairs.

Now Tudor's eyes shone with the stimulation of an idea. 'I

know where that louse is. Down in Taunton. The Castle Hotel! That's where he's gone. I'll bet on it. He has a surrogate father who lives there . . . sort of permanent guest. And he's a blasted medical doctor! God, Wareing took *me* there twice.' He leapt up and the other two rose in unison to their feet. 'He's wounded . . . needs stitches . . . needs a friend. We have to get a taxi, a car, a lorry, anything. The manager here must be able to help us with something. You cancel the food, Felix, we'll meet you outside. We'll drop in on Andy right now to find out what he said to Wareing and we'll hot-foot it to Taunton.' Tudor grabbed his greatcoat with his good hand and Mako helped him on with it before they hurried to the door.

As they moved, Tudor was calculating. 'Taunton's some forty miles as the crow flies. By road it'll be more like fifty.'

'We should be there well before midnight,' Mako answered, his lips parting in a wide grin. 'Tudor, I think he's got a pistol . . . just before the inspector entered the compartment he said he had it trained on me.'

'Did you see it?'

'No. It was in his pocket.'

'Sure he might have a gun, but so have we.' Tudor tapped the pocket of his dark greatcoat. 'But first we see Andy.'

Shelly rolled on to her back in the darkness to the sound of the sea. In the bunk beside her she heard Yvonne's regular breathing; her new friend was fast asleep. Pierre and Gerard slept in the next room with Axam, who had kept them entertained with rollicking sea stories over a hearty seafood supper.

The fire which had burnt vigorously some hours previously had turned into glowing cinders and the big baskets and fishing tackle cast strange shadows in the dying light from the grate. A damp cold had descended and Shelly's nostrils twitched with the aroma of the burnt wood mixed with the lingering smell of their lobster meal.

Pulling the blanket more tightly around her she heard the patter of rain on the roof. She had always liked the sound of rain and it reminded her of when she was a little girl and they had lived in a small house in North Ipswich before they had moved out to the big house in One Mile. Her mother and father had run a news-agency nearby on the 'top road', as they had called it. Both buildings – their house and the newsagency – had corrugated iron roofs and one of her happiest memories was of her father singing a lullaby to her as she lay in her cot with the sound of rain pattering on the roof.

The memory made her sigh and as her thoughts returned to Cole and what might be happening to him, she could not stop the tears which slid from under her eyelids to dampen her pillow. She missed her husband and prayed for his safety. She was on her way to Monaco, and after that? Who knew where? Well, she would face it all as she came to it.

With a deep breath and rationalising that she knew it was the middle of the night when things always seemed at their bleakest, she wiped her eyes and turned on her side and whispered, 'Cole Wareing married me, Laetitia de Witt, not you. He *wanted* to marry me. I'll do my best to find you and to learn whatever it is I need to know.'

Chapter Eighteen

By the time Cole found Edward Shackleton his leg throbbed constantly.

Outside the Taunton railway station he had broken a small, firm branch from a tree and, using it as a stick, limped as fast as he could for over ten minutes in light rain through the empty streets until he entered the Castle Hotel through the slender pillars on the small porch at the entrance. It was Friday night and the dining room and bar were noisy with activity and chattering couples came and went through the foyer. A desk clerk in a neat black suit revealed that Dr Shackleton was in and up in his room.

'My boy, my boy, I didn't even know you were in England!' Edward Shackleton threw his arms around his visitor, a warm smile beneath the grey moustache on his ruddy oval face. But his delight at seeing Cole soon turned into concern as he saw the makeshift cane and his leg.

'Cole, sit down. Now hold tight. We need to cleanse and stitch this wound, lad. My hand's as steady as it ever was.'

The cut bled and it was difficult and painful to cleanse but finally seventeen stitches were completed. Edward Shackleton had worked in silence but as Cole lay back on his bed with his leg raised and bandaged, the doctor looked over his spectacles with a loving expression and spoke gently. 'You've lost a lot of blood and you look pretty done-in, son. I'd dearly like to know what happened to you but I think you need sleep and sustenance first. I was just about to eat my supper, cheese sandwiches and a pot of tea, but I believe you need them more.' He picked up a tray from a low table and brought it to his visitor.

Edward Shackleton had been Cole's father's closest friend. The two had joined the Australian army as young men in 1902, Edward as a medic and John Wareing as an engineer. In the Great War they had been sent to Belgium and northern France with the First Australian Imperial Force and when Major John Wareing had died of his wounds on his fortieth birthday, 2 April 1918, he was in Edward Shackleton's arms. Cole had been about to turn thirteen. For the next decade until he retired from the army at fifty-one, Edward Shackleton had been moral support to Cole's mother and a surrogate father to Cole. In the spring of 1928 he had met an English lady in Australia and at the advanced age of fifty-two had married her. He had migrated with his wife and his single sister, Myrtle, to England where his wife had inherited land in Somerset.

In 1930, when Cole's mother had gone to live with her sisters in the town of Warwick and Cole had completed his law degree, it was to Dr Edward Shackleton in England that Cole had gone. He remained with 'Shack' for seven years travelling back and forth to the continent for lengthy sojourns in France, Belgium, Holland and Germany and working with various law firms.

Shack knew Cole intimately and he was aware he did not need to pry further into what was going on, that Cole would tell him what he needed to know at the right time, and that was good enough for him.

Cole felt desperately weary and his leg ached but he recognised the calibre of the men who were after him and he was conscious of the fact that one of them had been to this hotel and met the man who tended him. 'Thanks, Shack . . . it's been a hell of a long time since breakfast. I'll have the food, but then I must get on my way.'

'No, Cole, you can't leave with this injury. You're exhausted.'

Cole shook his head and raised himself on the pillow. 'God, Shack, you know some of what I did during the war; you're one of the few who do. Well, it's all catching up with me. Harrington – you remember him? – and a couple of blokes who were agents with us in Holland, are after me. Want to kill me.'

'Why would they want to do that?'

'Tudor believes I turned double agent. Betrayed him. The security police took them, they were in the hands of the Gestapo . . .' His mouth turned down and his breathing became heavy.

Edward blinked behind his glasses in disbelief. 'You? A traitor?'

'Apparently . . . and another thing, you'll recall the last time I saw you before I went out to Burma, I told you about Laetitia de Witt?'

'Yes, the woman in Holland?'

'The same. Andy told me tonight that she didn't die.'

Shack's intake of breath was loud in the quiet room. 'What?'

'Yes, I'll tell you all about it, but right now –' he slipped off the bed and gave a grunt of pain as his foot hit the floor – 'one thing I would be grateful for, is a new pair of trousers.'

Shack was happy to oblige. 'Of course, and I'll get you some other clean clothes and a shaving razor while I'm at it.' He took a small leather case from under the bed as the younger man sat back down, holding his head as he continued talking.

'I can't stay here, Shack, I'm compromising your safety. The man who stabbed me doesn't know about you, but Tudor Harrington does. He'll soon put two and two together. I can't risk staying here, I'm vulnerable and that puts you in grave danger. I just needed to see you and to get your help.' He was beginning to mumble. 'I have to keep ahead of them now. They'll turn up here for certain . . . in the morning . . . or sooner . . . in an hour . . . can't compromise you . . .'

'Listen, lad, I've got an idea. Your Aunt Myrtle lives in a village about ten miles away – Hambridge. Tudor Harrington knows nothing about her. So we go to her. We can stay there for a day or two till your leg improves.'

The younger man shook his head. 'No, I've got to get to Europe. This can't wait.'

'Well, at least we'll go there for tonight.' Shack was already taking out clothes for himself. 'We'll get Tom, the new night porter, to give us a hand with you and we'll tell him we're going to Bridgewater. That way, if Tudor does show up, Tom will give him a false lead. What with the rationing. I've only got petrol in the motorbike and sidecar, but in oilskins and hats we should get to Myrtle's place dry enough.' He moved to the wardrobe and when he turned around, Cole's eyes were closed.

Shack smiled and spoke optimistically. 'Don't worry, lad, we'll be at Aunt Myrtle's place in no time.'

Tudor eyed Andy McClure as the night wind wailed around the thatched cottage and the cats still lay on the hearth where a fire flickered in the grate. He was not sure how he felt.

His reaction to the news that Laetitia de Witt was alive bore similarities to Cole's. He had fallen silent, unable to speak, his bad arm began to ache and he felt very odd.

While Mako and Felix protested he had contemplated all Andy had said and finally he asked, 'How in Hades did SOE get that wrong?'

Andy sniffed and sipped his eternal whisky. 'I don't know but of course, lad, you'll recall that the two parts to the authentication of her death came from the Dutch Resistance organisation De Kern who could find no trace of her and from Wareing's own statements made on his return to England after his escape from Holland. He said unequivocally that he witnessed her lying dead in her house.'

'Yeah, I know, and obviously you're convinced she's now not dead at all?'

Andy nodded. 'Aye. There's no reason to doubt it. Notts's evidence and the photograph prove it. She's calling herself Martine Thalberg and I noticed when I said that name to Cole he recognised it straight away, even though he didn't acknowledge it.'

Tudor frowned. 'So the phoney knew the name Martine Thalberg. Have we ever heard that?' He looked to Mako. 'Have you?'

'Nah, never.'

'Martine Thalberg.' Tudor slowly repeated it to himself.

'MI6 have reopened her file.' The Scot moved from where he stood warming his back on the fire, put down his glass and lifted one of his cats in his arms. 'If it's of any interest, my opinion is that you have the wrong drum on Cole. Remember, when he came back he gave us at SOE a pretty convincing brief on what had transpired in Holland. I believed him then and I still do. A deal of the intelligence he brought with him went straight to Prime Minister Churchill, for God's sake.'

Mako loudly swallowed the remains of the whisky he held. 'We know you're sympathetic to him, Andy, but remember, we weren't here to tell our side of things. We were bloody lucky to be alive and hiding in Sweden. He could say what he liked without contradiction. We've always felt once he lost her he decided not to stay in Holland. He didn't know we'd escaped . . . probably thought we were done for, the rat.'

Andy sniffed and made a scoffing sound of disagreement.

'Swe-ell. Andy, you go on believing Wareing.' Tudor shrugged and his tone of voice sank into sarcasm as his gentle southern drawl suddenly became more pronounced, breaking the vowels in his words. 'But, frankly, you weren't taken by the secret police and in the hands of the Gestapo like Mako and I were, see? You weren't being sent to a bloody camp where they were going to torture the hell out of you. Funny how that sort of thing stays with you; you tend to hold grudges, it tends to make you just a smidge . . . bitter.'

The Scot willingly conceded this point. 'Understandable, Tudor. But I told you months ago and I'll tell you again – what you hold against him doesn't make sense. He had a bullet in him, for heaven's sake.'

Tudor's mouth tightened and he grunted in disagreement. 'Yeah, yeah, we know. But we also know *what I heard and what I saw* . . .'

Andy squinted at them. 'This is peacetime, fellas. Have you forgotten that what you're trying to do carries a murder charge?'

Tudor's ice-blue eyes were indifferent. 'So?'

'It's not murder,' Mako replied. 'It's retribution.'

'Let's just say this, Andy,' Tudor added. 'You're the only one who knows what we're intending to do and you know why. Your goddam wooden heart's full of SOE secrets, you old bugger . . . so just add our intentions to the list already there – get it?'

Andy cleared his throat and said nothing; he just stared at them through his bloodshot eyes.

Felix finally revealed his point of view and his dark curls shone in the firelight as he pronounced, 'The two of them were in it together . . . what happened to break them up, we don't know; but we'll catch up with him and if she's alive, then we'll catch up with her.' He drew his hand across his throat.

The Scot nodded. 'I see you've made it your fight too, Felix, even though you weren't on that second operation into Holland.'

Felix gave a sharp laugh. 'If I hadn't caught pneumonia, Andy, I'd have been there as well – besides, I need the target practice now the war's over.' He patted his waist, where under his overcoat his knife rested in its pouch.

'Well said, matey.' Mako put down his empty glass. 'Thanks for the drink, Andy, it's bloody windy and cold outside.'

'Have another.'

Tudor held up his hand. 'No, we'd best move on. We appreciate what you've told us, but we need to get to Taunton now. We'll let ourselves out.'

As they left Andy called out, 'Remember, lads, that things aren't always what they seem.'

'How philosophical,' Tudor commented as he closed the front door. As they moved down the path he spoke to himself. 'So she didn't die? And Wareing and I both know.'

On the road to Taunton in the small cabin of the utility truck with Mako driving and Felix tucked in between them, Tudor rested his head back, closed his eyes and listened to the driving rain. Laetitia de Witt was alive! The woman he had trusted and cared about. The woman who had joined forces with Wareing and betrayed them to the Nazis. She was calling herself Martine Thalberg and his enemy recognised the name immediately . . . Andy had said so.

Mako had never heard it, yet something was triggered in Tudor's brain. What was it about *Martine Thalberg* that sort of struck a chord with Tudor as well?

There is something about that name . . . come on, Tudor, what is it? Think.

He remained with his eyes closed, half-hearing his pals beside him commenting on the rain that had begun to fall and the dark roads and the cold, but it was no use, he could not recall why he felt that the name Martine Thalberg should mean something to him too.

Chapter Nineteen

It was after midnight when the lithe figure of Felix dashed through the narrow portals at the entrance to the Castle Hotel and shook the rain from his shoulders to find Tom Field, the night porter, reading a newspaper in the now silent hotel.

'Good evening.'

The porter put down his paper and when he spoke revealed a missing front tooth. ''Evenin', sir, what can I do for you?'

'I'd like a room for the night.'

In his six weeks as night porter Tom Field had never had guests arriving at this hour and he looked over the counter top and down to Felix's legs with a sceptical glance. 'Where's your luggage?'

Felix sighed and leant on the desk. 'Oh, outside in the car with the wife. We had a flat tyre earlier in the night, I've had a devil of a time. We were meant to reach my mother's house in Exeter tonight but instead we're here and my wife won't go another yard. I'm using all my petrol ration to get her down there too. Only reason I've come to the Castle is that a good friend of mine resides here, Dr Edward Shackleton. What room does he have again?'

The war was over. The need to be tight lipped and mistrustful had passed and Tom Field was a naturally gregarious and forthright fellow. He grinned. 'Oh, 'ee lives in 212 but you've missed 'im, I'm afraid.' He pushed a pen and the hotel registry book towards Felix as he rattled on, 'I'd just come on at eight – I'm on till six in the morning, you know? – and Dr Shackleton called me up to 'elp 'im bring 'is nephew down from 'is room. They went off on 'is motor-cycle and sidecar, they did, and in a downpour, would you believe it? The nephew 'ad a sore leg so we 'elped him down the stairs. Bit odd really.'

Felix held the pen in his hand. 'Oh dear, I was so looking forward to catching up with him. Yes, his nephew, I think I know the fellow. Where did they go?'

The night porter could answer this and he inclined his head in a northerly direction. 'Bridgewater, north about ten to twelve miles, but don't ask me why. I've no idea. Dr Shackleton just said "Good night, Tom, I'll see you when I return from Bridgewater." That's just what 'ee said.'

Felix manifested a smile. 'Ah now. I haven't seen him for ages. You have no idea at all where he went in Bridgewater, do you?'

'None at all, I'm afraid.'

'Well, does he have a relative there or something?'

'Sorry, sir, I don't know that either. 'Ee's a man who keeps to 'imself so it's surprisin' 'ee told me that much. None of us 'ere at the 'otel know too much about 'im. Now you sign the register and I'll get a brolly and go out to your car and bring in your wife and the luggage.'

Felix grinned and held up his hand. 'No, don't bother, I'm wet anyway, bit more rain won't harm me. You get the room key and I'll pop out and get the wife and the bags.'

Tom was happy not to have to go out in the icy wind and the rain. 'All right, sir, if you insist.'

Felix signed the register and took up an umbrella from the stand by the door before he walked outside to the waiting Hillman light utility truck which they had paid the manager of the Old Mill Hotel extortionate rates to borrow.

Tom heard the engine start and realised that his supposed guest had driven away. He looked at the hotel register and whistled in surprise through his missing tooth. Felix had written: *King George VI.*

Felix slid into the seat beside Tudor, now in the middle, with Mako at the wheel. 'Let's get going; he's not here; they've gone to Bridgewater . . . to the north about ten or twelve miles, the porter said. Porter helped Wareing down the stairs. They went by motor-cycle and sidecar.'

Mako shoved the utility truck into first gear and drove away. 'Where in Bridgewater?'

'Dunno.'

'Wait a minute.' Tudor elbowed Mako in the ribs and the driver took his foot off the accelerator and slipped the gear-shift into neutral.

'So Shackleton *told* the porter he was going to Bridgewater?'

'Uh huh.'

'Well, then, think about it. Would you tell the goddam porter where you were going if you knew we were tailing you?'

Felix shook his tousled curls. 'Blast . . . you're right, it's a hoax.'

'Just as sure as General Lee was a Confederate, pal. They want us to go to Bridgewater. They'll have gone in the opposite direction.'

'Of course,' Felix agreed. 'The porter said Shackleton was a man who keeps to himself and that no one knows much about him.'

Mako pulled the compact truck to the side of the road. He shivered as his fist closed more tightly on the wheel and he leant forward on it staring into the misty rain revealed in the yellow beams of the headlights. 'What's the answer, Tudor?'

'I think it's time to reassess. What have we learnt today that we didn't know before?' He answered his own question. 'That Laetitia de Witt is alive. That she was in Alexandria with some old guy three months ago. Sure we can head to Egypt but three months is a long time, she could be anywhere now. But we learnt one other thing: Wareing recognised the name or something about the name she's using – Martine Thalberg – and, oddly enough, I think it sort of rings a bell with me.'

'Gosh, really?' Felix turned to look at his leader.

'Yeah, there's something . . . well, I keep thinking there is; but maybe I'm wrong because if there is, it's damn well evading me at present, that's for sure. Now it's flaming cold. So we can drive around all night long looking for Wareing in the wind and rain and getting pneumonia. We can even sit here frozen and cramped in this truck till morning and then hope to find out where Shackleton might have gone. But it's like looking for a needle in a haystack and we've learnt from the night porter that he's a man who keeps to himself, so the chances of finding where he is are slim. And bloody Wareing will possibly go to ground for a while; but he'll head for de Witt as soon as he can.'

Felix spoke up as he retied the scarf more tightly around his neck. 'Yep. Then we can give them both what they deserve. I reckon we should head back to Bath and have a hot toddy.'

'My sentiments exactly.' Tudor smiled. 'All those in favour?'

'Aye.'

'The ayes have it, let's scram.'

Mako shoved the ute into low gear and took off down the road as Tudor gave a self-assured smile. 'We'll head off to London in the morning and then go to Holland. There are a lot of people in Apeldoorn and the Zelhem area who'll remember Laetitia de Witt. All we need is a lead to her . . . and as we've said, when we find her, we'll find him.'

His two companions made rumbling noises of unity.

Tudor continued to muse as they carried on, closing his eyes now and then and leaning his head back and a minute later sitting forward with his hands on the dashboard. Half-clear memories flowed at the back of his mind like leaves in a stream after stormy weather, but nothing materialised except for a hunch that he *had* heard the name Martine Thalberg before somewhere. But where and who had said it? It had to be in that rotten year of 1943 . . . had to be in Holland surely? Now, had he read it or heard it? Was it Rada Vermeer from the Dutch Resistance who said it? Could it have been his German captors? Was it her? What in hell was it about that name?

On the road to Hambridge, the downpour had increased, the wind had blown the rain in their faces and Shack had been forced to drive slowly but when they saw the glow through the trees from the lighted front window of the thatched cottage which was their destination, their spirits rose.

Myrtle Shackleton was overjoyed to see Cole and her brother and was solicitous when she was told about the *accidentally* injured leg. She soon had the two men dry and sitting before the fire drinking hot tea and eating her ration of ham and tomatoes. 'I

118

can't give you any bread, my dears, as Clement Attlee is even rationing that now, but I do have two slices of fruit cake.'

'Never mind, Aunt Myrtle, I had some bread when I ate Shack's sandwiches earlier.'

Myrtle peered through her horn-rimmed glasses and began to question Cole on his appearance 'out of the blue', as she put it, but Shack put his finger to his lips behind the younger man's head and she dropped her inquisitive stance.

While Myrtle prepared beds for them Cole confided in Shack. 'I'll tell you the whole story in time, Shack, but I have to get to Europe as soon as I can.'

'We'll go wherever you need to go, but a good night's rest is a priority now.'

Cole was tired and fading fast when he climbed into a twin bed under a knitted patchwork quilt. As he lay down his eyes caught a petitpoint picture hanging on the wall in a gilt frame. It was of a man and a woman in eighteenth-century costume sitting on a river bank with the words of an old Somerset folk song worked in shades of blue underneath.

As I walked through the meadows to take the fresh air,
The flowers were blooming and gay;
I heard a young damsel so sweetly a-singing,
Her cheeks like the blossom in May . . .

. . . The very next morning I made her my bride,
Soon after the breaking of day.
The bells they did ring and the birds they did sing,
As I crowned her my Queen of sweet May.

How simple and uncomplicated. That was what he coveted most: a simple, uncomplicated life and for a time with his lovely Shelly he had found just that.

His thoughts turned to his wife and he pictured her at Apple Gate Farm in the yard. She stood by the pond wearing a soft, floral-printed dress, her bare lower legs golden from the sun. She wore a straw hat and in her left hand she carried a billycan full of hens' eggs she had collected; and she raised her right hand to beckon him as she smiled and called to him, 'Time for a cuppa.'

Shelly, the beautiful quality of you. You made me forget, even if only for a little time.

He took a long, slow breath and closed his eyes. Ah, to be there with Shell now; to walk with her in the fading light past the beds of flowers down to the pond as eventide enveloped them in their own little world at Apple Gate. To feel the warmth of her close within the crook of his arm.

I married you believing absolutely that Letta was dead . . . I needed you. I needed your artlessness, needed your lack of understanding of what I'd known; needed your inner strength and constancy; the simplicity of your love for me . . . yes, I wanted all that normality without complication, very badly.

But now Letta is alive.

He lived again the moments when he saw her still and lifeless, the blue and white dress blood-soaked. But now he was told all that he saw was a lie.

Martine Thalberg: of course *he* knew why she would have taken that name as her alias, he was the only one who would. He had committed to memory at her request the address of Villa Thalberg on Lake Geneva in Switzerland. He had to keep ahead of Tudor and he had to find her. *Letta, what is the truth? How can it be you were dead and are now alive? Where are you and how much of what Von Bremen told me is true? Why does Tudor say he saw us together at the prison?*

He opened his eyes and switched off the standing lamp, aware of the old, tight feeling rising in his throat, of tense anxious emotion clouding his mind.

If I live to be the oldest man in the universe I'll never forget 1943.

THE WAR

Chapter Twenty

On 3 September 1939, Great Britain and her colonies and Australia, New Zealand and France had declared war on Germany after Germany invaded Poland. On 10 September, Canada declared war on Germany.

For years Hitler's war machine had been gathering speed and threatening Europe. A prescient minority, including Winston Churchill, had warned the world about the menace of Adolf Hitler, his ambitions for the Third Reich and his indoctrination of the majority of German people with an irrational hatred for Jews.

In 1940, the Netherlands were conquered in five days, the defenceless city of Rotterdam being bombed by the German Luftwaffe and 30,000 civilians killed. Belgium, Luxembourg, Norway and Denmark fell swiftly to the Blitzkrieg in succession and Italy entered the war on Germany's side.

Most of Europe was under Germany's heel.

London, 10 April 1943: Three and a half years into the Second World War

Light fog had given way to insipid sunshine as Cole opened the door of Andy McClure's Baker Street office in one of the buildings taken over by SOE: Special Operations Executive. Formed in deadly secret in 1940 with direst insistence from Prime Minister Churchill himself, it was a unit of highly trained secret agents who, at extreme personal risk, operated as guerrilla-like saboteurs to create havoc in German-occupied countries.

The creaking of the door caused the Scot to lift his head and grin at the entrant. Sitting in a heavy serge overcoat, sipping tea, he winked a bloodshot eye at Cole as he entered. 'Ah, there you are, Wing Commander. It was good of you to visit me last Sunday in Bath and now you're about to find out more of what I intimated to you then. Pour yourself a quick cup of tea and we'll get on our way.' He pointed with his bony forefinger to the teapot wrapped in a knitted cosy.

Cole did so. 'Where are we going?'

'Over near Gloucester Place to meet Captain Ovitz of the Special Intelligence Service — MI6 — and Captain Hans Buckhout, a Dutchman. Apparently, Dutch Prime Minister Gerbrandy and the government in exile here in England have given this Buckhout fella permission to run a small autonomous department of section "N". He's the one who wants you.'

'N' stood for Netherlands. Some enemy-occupied countries had a section in SOE — 'F' section for France, 'N' section for the Netherlands and 'T' for Belgium and Luxembourg. On his two previous missions — *going into the field*, as it was known by all secret agents — Cole had worked for Maurice Buckmaster who ran 'F' Section. The most recent time under the cover name, Antoine Balfour.

Cole spoke as he slid into an unoccupied chair. 'I thought SIS and SOE didn't get on?'

'They seldom do; diverging interests, as a rule, but in this instance

Buckhout and Ovitz know each other well and co-operated. Can't imagine it'll last long though.'

As Cole sipped his tea he informed the Scot of his feelings. 'Since I've known that "N" wanted to see me I've been at a bit of a loss. I mean yes, I can get by pretty fairly speaking Dutch, but no way in the world could I pass for a Dutchman.'

Andy grinned. 'Aye, I knew you'd be athinkin' that. But it doesn't matter in this instance.'

'It doesn't? This Hans Buckhout wants me, yet I don't need to speak fluent Dutch? That's an odd one. Well, it would appear it's not French I need, so that only leaves German . . . I'm all out of languages.'

The Scot gave a chortling laugh. 'Good deduction.'

Cole frowned. 'German? That's intriguing.'

'Aye, it is. Now, if you agree to go into the field for Buckhout you won't work through any of the current channels being used in the Netherlands. As I said, Buckhout is on his own: he has an idea that much of the Resistance in Holland is infiltrated with informers. Though Seymour Bingham, who currently runs "N", appears not to agree, eh? He still continues to work through the people there on the ground as his predecessor Blunt did.

'Buckhout informed me confidentially that one of SOE's "N" section agents in the Netherlands has asked for permission to train local Dutch wireless operators and to use more wirelesses. Buckhout maintains that's a red flag – double-agent stuff – and is very suspicious about it, but no one else seems to be taking any notice of it.'

'Jesus, yes, I'd agree a hundred per cent with Buckhout on that.'

Andy stood up, 'Well, he's the one you're about to meet, so swallow your tea and we'll get going.' The Scot headed round the desk and kept talking. 'Anyway, Buckhout is a sort of maverick. Most of "N" are opposed to him, of course. They see him as a rival.

'He's impressive, running a smaller, tighter ship. He's not your usual type of manager here in the *Ministry of Ungentlemanly Warfare*, as Mr Churchill dubbed us. He holds a commission in the Dutch Army but has a dubious sort of past out in the east.'

Cole grinned. 'Dubious past? Well, a lot at SOE have; old Hayes in the forgery section spent most of the thirties in jail.' He put down his cup.

'Aye, I reckon half of them in there are ex-crims, but as forgers they're princes, eh?'

They left the office and Andy went on as they headed to the stairs: 'And you'd probably be aguessin' that there's been one heck of a to-do behind the scenes with Hans Buckhout and Maurice Buckmaster who wanted to keep you for another mission to France. Some of us have been calling it the *Battle of the Bucks*.' He chuckled at that and his Adam's apple rose and fell above his shirt collar. 'But Buckhout has won that round.'

Chapter Twenty-one

Captain Hans Buckhout turned from the window where the muted sunlight managed to elicit a gleam in the Dutchman's fair hair. He stretched out his hand as he came forward to the arrivals. 'How do you do? I think we should get straight into it.' Hans Buckhout was of average height and muscular and he spoke quickly, giving the impression that he had to rush off somewhere.

'Please do.'

He introduced Captain Lane Ovitz and after everyone had shaken hands he gestured to the chairs.

'This is not a simple operation, Wing Commander Wareing.'

'Are any of them?'

'No, but this is much more complicated than normal.'

They sat and the Dutchman perched on his desk and directed his words to Cole. 'We're going to ask you to impersonate *Standartenführer* Lucien Bayer of the *Schutzstaffel*.'

'*Impersonate* a colonel in the SS?' Cole grimaced and glanced to Andy who winked and leant back in his chair.

'*Ja.* He's originally *Waffen SS-Verfügungstruppe*; went into a special combat support group and was wounded on the eastern front. And by a trick of fate, has been recuperating in Denmark where Captain

Ovitz and the SIS have been able to help me get information on him. He has been seconded to the Civil German Authorities in Holland where he'll work with the security police: this is probably due to his wounds. He worked with the German security police in the late thirties. We have chosen him for all sorts of reasons which we'll explain in due course – one being that we have a copy of his army records and his personal details.

'Now, you are a highly skilled British agent used to clandestine operations, intensive training, planning and secrecy and adept at taking on other identities, to the extent that when awoken in the middle of the night you can immediately establish your alter ego and respond normally.'

Cole's mouth turned down wryly. 'Hang on, we're all supposed to be able to do that.'

'Indeed, Wing Commander, but you have a few other qualities that make you the perfect choice. You speak fluent German with the right accent – Bayer was born in Hamburg – and you are quite passable in Dutch and, more than that, your appearance is right . . . Bayer has dark hair and deep blue eyes and the two of you could be twins.' He pulled out a file from a cabinet at his right hand. 'Look here, we've something to show you. We've enlarged these photos of Bayer so you can see the subject more clearly.' He handed Cole a photograph of a man in uniform and jackboots standing with Heinrich Himmler, Hitler's head of the SS and the German police and, as was becoming known, a mass-murderer.

A resemblance to Cole in the size and shape and general appearance of Bayer was apparent. Buckhout proffered a second photograph of the same man's face in which he was smiling. In this picture it was clear that there was a strong resemblance to Cole but Bayer was not quite the same around the mouth, it was

130

a fraction smaller and Cole thought the Nazi's teeth looked different to his own.

Cole remained silent as he was given a third photograph showing the man in profile: from the side, the forehead, nose and chin appeared identical; it was just the area above the top lip and the mouth, again, which differed. 'Now look at this.' Buckhout gestured and Ovitz moved to a film projector on a bench and started it. The film was grainy and old, but three men were seen walking on a promenade with the sea in view.

'Look at the one on the right. That's our man.'

Bayer was younger and in mufti. Ovitz shut off the projector and both men turned to Cole. Buckhout spoke. 'I've had this idea of substituting a Nazi officer with one of our secret agents for some time and finally the conditions fit together. What do you think?'

Cole leant forward uneasily. 'Hold on. You want me to pretend I'm Bayer. What? For a day? A week? How long does this masquerade last?'

Buckhout's fast speech delivery slowed down considerably. 'Ah, we haven't yet decided on a time limit; you see, we intend to eliminate him and we want you to *become* him.'

Chapter Twenty-two

Cole leant back in his chair. His eyes narrowed and a supercilious expression rose to his face. 'Look, I'm pretty game for most things but . . .' He caught Andy's eyes. 'No wonder you didn't tell me what this was about.'

The Scot stared at the ceiling as Cole shook his head. 'This is too far-fetched, fellas. Yes, this bloke's forehead and eyes are virtually identical to mine and so is his nose and chin and his body shape and size are pretty much the same too, but the differences are obvious to me. I don't walk like him. His mouth is not quite as wide as mine and his top lip comes out a suggestion more than mine does and his teeth differ. His hair is brushed straight back – well, at least it was in the film. It's just not feasible that I can double for this bloke unless it's for five minutes on a dark night. There's no way I can *become* him.'

Ovitz and Buckhout glanced momentarily at one another and back to Cole. Buckhout waved his finger in emphasis. 'We agree with all you say, Wing Commander Wareing, but – and here's the interesting bit – this Nazi now looks different. We have two snaps which are current and your comments – while all being quite pertinent – don't apply any more. Look. This is Bayer now.' He proffered three large sepia photographs. 'Two are of the same image, one is an enlargement of the face and neck. They were taken in the grounds of a nursing home. See, here he is leaning on a cane . . .'

Cole held the pictures and examined them. The man wore a light-coloured shirt and shorts and his left leg was bandaged around the knee. His hair was not straight back but semi-parted on the right. He had a bandage around his forehead and one on his throat and in the enlargement it was clear that a scar at the edge of his mouth had the effect of widening it. He was smiling in one snapshot and the teeth were visible.

'This is Lucien Bayer today, in Denmark, recovering from his wounds. Wounds which fortunately allow us to *make* you a replica of him. The shrapnel which hit his knee has left him with a permanent limp and therefore his gait becomes unimportant – you can limp and lean on a cane. We also think we can get your hair to look like his. You are both very similar in colouring. Our belief is that because your nose and shape of face and, in particular, your eyes, are virtually indistinguishable from his – this ruse will work. We have it on impeccable authority that the mouth and teeth we can fix, *ja*?'

He glanced to Ovitz who joined in. 'We do. We have a Swiss orthodontist called Durst who is a genius with teeth. He uses some concoction of natural plant adhesive as a dental bonding material; his porcelain crowns are amazing and he has seen photographs of you and Bayer and is adamant he can make your teeth match Bayer's and, in doing so, bring your top lip out that mere suggestion which will give you pretty much his mouth.'

Hans Buckhout hurried on, 'There'll be a need for that tiny scar he now has at the corner of your lips and you'll require other obvious scars on your temple, throat and ribs and a large one on the side of your knee. If you agree, we'll cut and stitch them fast and we have an expert who believes he can age them so that eight weeks from now they will look more like five- to six-month-old scars.'

Cole made a rumbling sound in his throat. 'How bloody clever of him.'

'The other miracle for us is, as we've said, that you speak perfect German with a sort of formal, stiff upper-class Hamburg accent which we'll continue to work on. He was brought up in Hamburg, son of a doctor; so that's ideal . . . and you speak French like a native and passable Dutch; so does he. By the way, our information is that he also has a little Russian. Do you?'

Cole met the speaker's eyes. '*Niet*.'

'Very funny, Wing Commander. Well, that shouldn't matter, as you aren't going to the Russian front.'

'No; one is pretty certain the destination is Holland.'

Buckhout nodded. 'Indeed it is.'

'But what if this bloke has a shrill high voice or something? Voices can be bloody dead giveaways.'

'I knew you were no fool,' Buckhout answered. 'But we're not worried about his voice. Fact is, he was hit by shrapnel in five places: knee, ribs, temple, edge of mouth and to the side of his Adam's apple: all on his left side, so he'll have scars in all those places. We've discussed it with medical experts who believe the throat wound could have affected his voice but as we don't expect you to meet anyone other than one man who knew Bayer previously, and that was briefly and five years ago, we're not too concerned.'

Cole raised an eyebrow and the bite of cynicism sounded in his tone of voice. 'Easy for you not to be concerned. Anyway, who's the bloke he knew?'

'A man called Fritz Schmidt, he's a Nazi civil commissioner in Holland, represents the interests of the NSDAP, the National Socialist German Workers' Party, but we'll come to him in time. We expect to have photographs soon of all the men you'll deal with.' He cleared his throat and continued, 'Now Bayer has been assigned to the Netherlands to work with the German occupation's civil authorities beginning Saturday the nineteenth of June, when he will start with a meeting in the town of Groningen in Groningen Province . . . as we said previously, he's been given a soft job because of his wounds.

'This June meeting will be attended by some top Nazi civil officials plus a number of others from the Centralised State Employment Office – euphemism for the State *Slave Labour* Office, of course. They're getting together because in recent times a number of well-known Dutch National Socialists, in other words, collaborators with the Nazis, have been assassinated by certain Dutch patriots. And we intend to blow all the buggers at the meeting to kingdom come!'

Cole leant back in his chair, staring at the mid distance. 'It's April now . . . not a long time to *become* Bayer.'

Buckhout agreed. 'It isn't, but it's all we've got and if you acquiesce, we intend to immerse you in all things Bayer. We've been working with a trusted link in Denmark and the miracle is that Bayer's a colonel. We would have been delighted if he'd been a captain or a major, even; but being so high-ranking an officer is pure gold, it will get you in and out of all sorts of places.'

Cole did not speak and Ovitz added, 'That's if . . . er, indeed you go on this operation. No need to make up your mind now, but we want a decision very swiftly, can't give you more than twenty-four hours, we're afraid.'

The listener's expression transformed into one of indifference which had his companions baffled. He held silence for ten seconds or so, examining the black-out blind above the window as they waited.

Suddenly Cole stood up and, thinking he was leaving, Buckhout held out his hand. But Cole waved it away. 'If I'm going to Holland, I'll need all the time I can get. Might as well agree and start today.'

Andy rose and met his eyes. 'You don't want a day to think about it?'

'No.'

Buckhout's voice could not hide his excitement. 'Is that a formal acceptance to become Lucien Bayer?'

'Yep.'

Now Buckhout's glee bubbled over; he came forward and grabbed both Cole's hands in his own. '*Wonderbaarlijk.*' Lane Ovitz smiled widely and Andy gave a supercilious sort of a grin as if he had known the result all the time.

Ovitz held out his hand to Cole. 'Good luck, you won't see me again. I've co-operated as much as my superiors will allow me. Now you've agreed to the operation, I'll be melting away.'

Cole shook his hand. 'Good to have met you.'

'Well,' Hans Buckhout hurried on, turning to Andy McClure, 'get Dr Gordon Campbell, he's the expert and he's standing by. We'll cut and stitch the Wing Commander today.'

Two weeks later, in a farmhouse in Essex rented by the powers of SOE, Cole sat practising the signature of Lucien Bayer. Ovitz of Special Intelligence had done one last favour and supplied a Danish hospital form which carried Bayer's signature.

Cole now displayed a two-inch pink scar which ran from his temple

136

to his cheekbone and a half-inch one at the edge of his mouth, as well as others on his neck and his ribs and one on his left knee. The stitches had come out a few days prior. The dental work was in progress and opposite him sat Herr Helmut Schultz, the man who was turning him into a Nazi. Helmut Shultz had been recruited into the SS in 1932. He had risen to the rank of captain but had become increasingly disillusioned with Hitler. He had broken his leg in 1937 and while recuperating had fallen in love with an English girl in Berlin and his change of heart towards the Führer became cemented. He had been refused permission to marry and they had fled together to England eight months before Germany invaded Poland.

He had been interned briefly at the beginning of the war but the Member for Parliament in his area knew him and knew his sympathies were not with Hitler. After intensive checks, Schultz was released and had been working on and off with SOE since July 1941, a year after its deadly secret inception. He was Cole's authority on the SS.

Cole's two other pundits were a Swede who was an expert on the Russian front, and an advisor to the Dutch government in exile who had been brought up in the same Hamburg suburb where Bayer had been born. He knew a number of the German cities well, including Berlin and Dresden where Bayer had spent time. They were endeavouring to give Cole all the information he would need to submerge himself into the Bayer persona.

A knock on the door made them both lift their heads from the papers they were reading. In walked Cole's German language coach who had the very unGermanic name of Dorothy Smith, but who also had a very decidedly Hamburg accent, having lived there for twenty-six years.

'I believe it is my time now, Mr Schultz.'

Helmut looked at his watch. '*Ja*, you are right.' He shook hands with Cole. 'I shall return after lunch.'

Dorothy eased herself into the chair he had vacated as Cole opened his exercise book and glanced out the window where two pheasants ran across the lawn. Dorothy stood and deliberately closed the window and pulled the curtain. She spoke to him as if he were a schoolboy. 'Mustn't be distracted, must we? Now we need to concentrate, so we'll start where we left off yesterday. Repeat the last phrase we were saying, please.'

Cole grinned and replied, '*Die Straße hinunter und um die Ecke . . .*'

'No, *nein, es ist nicht richtig.* I want it to be perfect.'

Cole groaned. 'It's easier in English – *down the street and around the corner.*'

The woman frowned, her expression severe. 'Please say the phrase again, Wing Commander, the accent needs more concentration . . . in German, *bitte.*'

He repeated it. '*Die Straße hinunter und um die Ecke . . .*'

'*Gut.* That's much better.' She eyed him over the rim of her spectacles. 'Now let's repeat it twice more.'

Chapter Twenty-three

A May breeze murmured around the farmhouse while Cole stood at the window watching a fox make its way through the bracken beyond the lawn and near the pines which hid the front gate. He had just completed a lesson with Dorothy Smith and he awaited the arrival from London of Hans and Andy.

Fine rain was falling and the pines and oaks in his vision stood like moody guardians around the lawn and the beds of flowers. Cole liked the tenor of this view; the harmony and the stillness, the only activity coming from the fox. For a brief interlude he forgot the war and why he was here.

He contrasted this misty green realm with the stark sunshine of his native Queensland and the undulating hills and valleys often filled with dry grass and drooping pallid-leafed trees yearning for rain.

Into his mind slipped a picture of Shelly Longford, the girl he had been seeing before he left Australia. A year ago he had written her a letter telling her not to wait for him. He had decided when he became a secret agent that death could be just around the corner and it was not fair to Shelly: better not to have any sort of liaison. It had been hard for him to do, for he had regarded her as his girl and had been pretty stuck on her; but SOE preferred it that way. They saw it as a real advantage that he was from Australia and had only one close associate in Edward Shackleton in Great Britain. The fewer friends or relatives in proximity, the less need for SOE operatives to lie about what they did and where they went.

Yet Shelly's letters to him had kept coming. He never replied, even though he had almost weakened a couple of times. And now, as the tail of the fox lifted and the animal darted under the fence and into the woods, he imagined her fresh face, round green eyes, and direct smile. He pictured her hair billowing from her shoulders as she brought her favourite horse, Cromwell, over the hedge near the barn on the property where she lived in One Mile across the creek outside Ipswich. He remembered the nights with her in that last month before he left Queensland: the feel of her close within his arms, the soft silkiness of her bare skin on his, the touch of her lips and the way she whispered his name. He grunted as he took a deep breath for she was his no longer and by his own choice. Yet the one thing he hated was the thought of any other man with her.

He shook that uncomfortable notion off with the shrugging of his shoulders as a dark green Rover appeared through the trees from the lane.

Within two minutes Hans Buckhout and Andy McClure had been greeted by Dorothy Smith in the front hall and they stood beside Cole in his room. The Dutchman held forth at his usual fast pace while the Scot seated himself in the single armchair. 'Dorothy tells us your accent is perfect. It was your grandmother who taught you German, wasn't it?'

Cole shook his head and gave a brief, tender smile. 'Actually, she was no relation to me. She was a lonely elderly lady whom my mother took in, gave a home to, prior to the Great War. She treated me like her grandson. She had no relatives and I had no grandma . . . worked perfectly. Anyway, it gave me an understanding of German and the Hamburg accent you're so keen to have.' Cole winked at him.

Hans shot Cole an odd look; he had not quite latched on to Cole's humour. '*Ja*, right. Now today we want you to see photographs of the bastards whom Bayer is supposed to join forces with in Holland, though, as you know, we're hoping to kill a few of them on the nineteenth of June in the bomb blast. We have three more photographs for you.' He took them from an envelope and spread them on the table.

'These are the Nazis you will deal closely with in your guise as Bayer.' The first was of a group of men in suits and uniforms standing with Hitler. Hans pointed over Cole's shoulder towards two very tall men: the first possessing a large forehead with hair receding on both sides and milk bottle-thick glasses. 'He's the German supreme authority in the Netherlands and known as the High Commissioner; one Dr Arthur Seyss-Inquart*, balding and lame in one leg. We are all aware that in Holland, like all the occupied states of Europe, the enemy is sucking the workforce dry. The civilian administration of Holland under the Nazis is being run by this man.

'Seyss-Inquart and his staff have the task of *Nazifying* the Civil administration of Holland, which means finally getting rid of all Dutch patriots and replacing them with Nazi hacks.'

Hans pointed to the man next to Seyss-Inquart. 'This is the other individual who holds ultimate power in the Netherlands, an

---

* Arthur Seyss-Inquart: see Author's End Notes, page 529

Austrian general called Hanns Albin Rauter[*] who is a general of the Waffen-SS and the Higher SS and Police Leader and therefore head of all the SS troops and police units in the country: you could say he's Himmler's General plenipotentiary in the Netherlands. He's the man you'll be working for.'

'If Rauter survives the bomb blast,' interjected Andy McClure.

Hans grunted in accord. 'True. Yet the Wing Commander must learn as much as he can about these men.'

Cole translated, 'So he's the *Hoherer SS und Polizeiführer*. That lot are fond of the *führer* word.'

'They are,' Hans agreed.

Cole studied a huge man with balding head, weak chin and large hooked nose, standing six feet four or five, holding his cap in hand. 'Rauter and Seyss-Inquart are not two of the prettiest Aryans I've ever seen!'

'*Ja*, they're ugly, inside and out,' commented Hans with a sigh. 'Rauter's a fanatic, a militant, and a radical national socialist, typifying all we expect from the extreme SS and he reports only to Himmler and Hitler. We think Lucien Bayer is being brought in to watch and report to Rauter on two commissioner generals under Seyss-Inquart: Friedrich Wimmer, Internal Affairs, Administration and Justice – though I fear there won't be much justice for the Dutch – and Fritz Schmidt, Commissioner General without portfolio.'

Cole remembered this name. 'He's the one Bayer knows?'

'Correct. He and Bayer had a passing acquaintance years ago; we have some details of that but not a lot. Schmidt, apparently, is ambitious and intelligent but unbalanced. Acts very oddly at times without apparent reason.'

* Hanns Albin Rauter: see Author's End Notes, page 529

Cole gave a cynical laugh. 'Don't all Nazis?'

'Good point. He's thirty-nine, and we have no photograph of him, unfortunately.'

'No photo . . .' Cole groaned. 'And yet he's the one Bayer's acquainted with . . . Jesus!'

'Sorry, old man.'

'*Old man?* You've become very British recently, haven't you, Hans?'

'*Ja*, rubs off, I suppose. Now the next picture is of Wimmer.'

He was a portly oval-faced uniformed man of average height standing in front of a group of SS soldiers.

'Dr Friedrich Wimmer, born ninth of July 1897, so he's coming up to forty-six. He's a weak man – likes the good life. Apparently comes to loggerheads with the SS wing under Rauter.'

Cole leant forward, still studying the image. 'So which of these do we think will be at the meeting in June?'

'All except Seyss-Inquart. We believe Wimmer, Schmidt and Rauter will be there, and of course others.'

'So when they get blown into the next world, what's Bayer's job then?'

'We all believe that Bayer will be put in charge of a number of departments, certainly Wimmer and Schmidt's in the short term, possibly even in the long term. So that will give you, as Bayer, access to all their records.'

'Who's this bloke?' Cole touched the last photo. It was of a hardened-looking older man, perhaps in his early sixties, wearing Luftwaffe uniform.

'Now he's another of the pretty gang terrorising Holland. As you can see – a Luftwaffe general: Friedrich Christian Christiansen. He's in charge of the Wehrmacht, all three branches, in the Netherlands.'

Andy stood from the armchair and came forward to slide into a seat at the table. 'Cole, this next piece of intelligence for you is highly classified, top secret, and it comes directly from Prime Minister Churchill's office.' He paused momentarily. 'The Germans are experimenting on unmanned flying bombs — long-range rockets with the ability to fly from Europe and hit London and beyond. Five separate secret reports on these rockets have come in since the end of last year. It is a terrifying new aspect of the war and we have reason to believe Christiansen is involved somehow. Our information shows that he visits the place where they are being assembled: the tiny port of Peenemünde on the Baltic Coast of Germany. The rockets are being designed by Nazi scientists and built by slave labour, many are Poles.'

Hans leant forward over the table. 'If it is possible for you, as Bayer, to get close to Christiansen, you might be able to find out more about this for us. We are especially hoping to pinpoint factories that are manufacturing the parts or get some photographs or details of what is happening at the Peenemünde site.'

'Will Christiansen be at this nineteenth of June meeting?'

'We don't know.'

Cole held his bottom lip in thought. 'A daylight bombing like this is pretty dangerous stuff. Pity we couldn't be doing it at night.'

Hans nodded vehemently. '*Ja*, we all agree, but this is the only chance we'll get. We are working with Rada Vermeer, a man who runs his own Resistance cell. I knew him before the war and I trust him. He has a cousin, a woman, who works at the hotel. She and another will plant the bombs.'

'We'll land you in Groningen Province in Holland's north-east. It's sparsely populated. No one on the ground there will be informed of your arrival. We mean *no one*. It's better we keep your existence secret from anyone in Holland, even Rada Vermeer.'

'I agree.'

'Four of our operatives will be sent in two weeks prior to your arrival to make contact with Vermeer and to get to know the countryside and do the ground work for your arrival. They'll take in the pencil bombs and one is an explosives' expert. The bombs will be set prior to the meeting and before you turn up at the meeting place. They'll explode and then, fifteen or so minutes later, you'll arrive.'

'What's my excuse for being late?'

'You'll be mock-attacked on the way in by our people and tyres will be blown. Hence your late arrival.'

Hans Buckhout unfolded a map and tapped a spot in the north-east corner of Groningen. 'We already know that Bayer is spending the two nights prior to Saturday the nineteenth of June here and alone, at the Zwann Inn. That's where you make the switch with him on his arrival.'

'The Swan Inn, right. When do I go in?'

'On the night of Monday fourteenth, or Tuesday fifteenth of June, whichever we believe will have the best weather.'

'And when do I come out?'

'That will be up to you. There'll be two escape routes. You'll be thoroughly versed in both.'

Cole made a sarcastic noise in his throat. 'Always nice to know there's a way out.' He nodded slowly to himself, taking in what had been said as Hans stood and moved across to the window.

The Dutchman pulled aside the tasselled curtain and looked out. 'The operatives who are going over to Holland before you're due here. And if I'm not mistaken, they're all entering the farm in a van this very minute.' He headed for the door. 'Wait here.'

In the hiatus, Andy poured himself a cup of tea from the trolley and a few minutes later the door opened and Hans came back, followed by three men. They were introduced by their cover names: Mako Vanderbilt, tall and gaunt but giving the impression of physical strength and, behind him, Felix Lansing, the knife thrower extraordinaire, with Leopold de Vries, the wireless operator.

They all shook hands and greeted one another and Cole glanced back to the door. 'Well, where's the fourth?'

There was a pause and Cole experienced an odd feeling, half suspecting he might know the man about to enter.

Abruptly through the doorway breezed Tudor Harrington, oozing energy and smiling widely. 'Howdy, *Standartenführer* Bayer; for this mission you'll call me Dirk Hartog.'

'Somehow I knew it.' Cole paused and held out his hand. 'So, Dirk Hartog . . . suits you; your alter ego was a Dutch explorer who visited the western shores of my native land . . . I believe in 1616.'

'You don't say?'

'I do say.' They laughed as they shook hands and the American gave Cole's shoulder an affectionate slap. 'How are you, buddy?'

Cole and Tudor had been recruited for SOE together when they had both been in Bomber Command of the RAF: Cole a wing commander and Tudor a squadron leader.

Hans held out his arms as if to embrace them all before he spoke directly to Cole and Tudor. 'You realise that it's highly improper for two agents to know each other prior to going into the field; but in this case we have had to make an exception.'

'Yes,' Tudor answered with another broad smile, 'Hans *had* to take me, his other mark came down with something, didn't he?'

'Broken leg in a motorcycle accident,' the Dutchman informed them grimly.

'So I'm the last-minute substitute.'

'*Ja*,' Hans nodded, 'I couldn't find anyone else who spoke good enough Dutch and had pretty perfect German . . .'

Tudor turned back to Cole. 'Seems a long time since the recruiting officer for SOE took us aside that Saturday afternoon after the sortie into Germany.'

'Doesn't it? What did he say — "I'm told you two speak some European languages fluently"?'

Tudor nodded. 'You bet, and then I think he said, "We know you're valuable to the RAF, but would you be interested in doing something else for the war effort? Something very dangerous which will require more training?"'

Cole broke into a wide grin. 'And you burst out laughing and said, "Hell, man, we've just brought a wing of bombers back from a blasted daylight raid targeting factories in Germany where we were narrowly missed by a fog of flack . . . we had a near escape from freaking Messerschmitts on our tail all the way back across Holland and over the Channel, where one put holes in our tail so that we limped home and you're talking about *something very dangerous*. Are you wacky or just some sort of a comedian, pal?"'

They laughed loudly together reliving the memory, while Hans Buckhout smiled around at all of them like an indulgent parent.

Chapter Twenty-four

Thursday, 17 June 1943

In the haze of evening's fading light, an eddying mist stole in from the North Sea and swallowed the Dutch foreshore in the Eems estuary where a German light cruiser strained against the ropes holding it to the pier. The click of jackboots sounded on the dock and the voice of a *feldwebel* cracked out in the porous atmosphere: '*Heil* Hitler. *Untersturmführer* Hertz and escort are here for *Standartenführer* Bayer.'

A minute later, wearing the uniform of the SS which stung so many hearts with contempt or dread, a colonel appeared and limped down the gangplank, leaning on a polished ebony and ivory cane. He held a leather briefcase and behind him came an *oberfahnrich zur zee* – a midshipman – carrying two black suitcases.

The SS colonel raised his hand in the Nazi salute in reply to the second lieutenant. 'You are Hertz?'

'*Ja, Standartenführer* Bayer. *Hoherer SS und Polizeiführer* Rauter sends his compliments and asks if you are fully recovered from your wounds.' He addressed the colonel as '*Standartenführer*', unlike those soldiers in the Wehrmacht – the traditional German army – who used the word 'Herr' before the officer's rank. The SS did not, they addressed superior officers simply by their rank as the British Army did. Hitler had made this compulsory.

The SS *standartenführer* gave a sharp, amused grunt under his death's head cap. 'I have a few scars and aches and pains but am able to walk, so yes, I am sufficiently recovered.'

'That is excellent, sir. The Police Leader also says to tell you he looks forward to seeing you in Groningen at the meeting on Saturday.'

'*Gut.*'

'I also have a message from Commissioner General Schmidt. He welcomes you too and remembers old times, he said.' Hertz handed across an envelope. 'I believe the woman's name is inside and a note from Commissioner General Schmidt. She will stay with you.'

'*Gut.* As long as she is not a Jewish whore; I cannot stand to put my hands upon them.' He slipped the note into the pocket of his jacket.

'Oh no, sir, she is Dutch. She is not from a camp, she's *V-manner*, trusted and very lovely indeed.'

As they reached the edge of the wharf the lieutenant attempted to make conversation. 'Were you close to Commissioner General Schmidt, *standartenführer*?'

'I knew him before the war.'

'I am delighted indeed to make your acquaintance, as Commissioner General Schmidt told me you are from Hamburg: my mother was from Hamburg like you, and her sister's son was in Dresden with you in 1939.'

For a moment Bayer's cold eyes revealed a degree of interest. 'What is his name?'

'His name *was* Lockermans, he was killed a year ago. He also spoke Dutch and French like you, *standartenführer*.'

Bayer nodded. 'I do recall him, we worked together for a time; *ja*, it was Dresden, he liked to hike. So . . . he's gone?'

'*Jawohl*, he's gone.'

The senior officer began limping across the grass in the direction of the port gate and the lieutenant followed. 'What time do you want an escort back on Saturday morning, *standartenführer*?'

'How long is the journey from the inn where I am staying to Groningen?'

'Perhaps forty to forty-five minutes. The roads are old and narrow.'

'Then I shall wish to leave at oh seven hundred. And I hope the inn is quiet.'

'*Ja*, it is, *standartenführer*.'

'*Gut*, I am fond of peaceful weekends *when war permits*.' This amused him and he gave a short, barking laugh.

'The Zwann Inn sits alone not far from tiny Zandeweer and has many interesting walks nearby along the dykes and over the fields; apparently there are a few farmers' cottages and one or two very old churches not far away.'

Bayer grunted. 'Walking is not as pleasant as it used to be. More importantly, the innkeeper speaks German, I'm told.'

'*Jawohl, standartenführer*.'

'Will it be you who returns for me, Hertz?'

'It will indeed. We have a small squad of Wehrmacht soldiers in a camp half a mile away. They will be at your disposal.'

'I have no wish to be disturbed until Saturday morning. Is that understood?'

Hertz hesitated, looking uncomfortable. 'But my orders are to stay with you. It could be dangerous to leave you alone.'

Bayer stopped and turned in the wind. 'Hertz, I have been on the Russian front. I am able to take care of myself. Don't let this leg fool you. I don't want you with me. If you have orders to stay within range of me, so be it, but I do not want to see anybody . . . except my female visitor, is that understood?'

'Of course, *standartenführer*.'

Bayer shuffled on.

A sentry gave the Hitler salute as the entourage passed through the gate and halted at a large black Mercedes-Benz. The driver, a corporal, opened the rear door and Bayer climbed in as the lieutenant saw that the suitcases were placed in the boot before he slid into the front passenger seat. As the escorting soldiers climbed on to their four BMW R75 military motorcycles with permanently attached sidecars, the convoy moved.

Across the road, up a gradient overlooking the end of the small port, in the attic of a house, Leopold watched through field glasses. He tapped out a message and Hans Buckhout in England replied.

Soon Hans in London re-transmitted the message that the target was moving – to Cole, Tudor and the others. It was a cumbersome way of operating but SOE had learnt undeniably that the only safe and secure way to function was to transmit through England, therefore no secret agents were allowed to make direct radio contact with one another in the field.

In the back of the moving car, the superior officer leant forward and spoke to the driver. 'I believe it is close to half an hour from here. I'll sleep. Wake me on approach.'

Hertz turned his head. 'I shall wake you, *standartenführer*.'

Nightfall closed in as Bayer leant back on the mustard-hued leather of the seat and, making his injured leg as comfortable as possible, shortly began to snore.

Thirty minutes later, he opened his eyes. 'You did not wake me.'

Hertz spoke quickly. 'I was just about to, *standartenführer*; around this next bend we are within a kilometre of the inn.'

Bayer smiled to himself. He wondered if the girl would be fair or dark-haired, not that he cared; as long as she did what he wanted and had firm breasts he would be satisfied. Anyway, she was supposed to be beautiful from what the *untersturmführer* had said. He nodded to himself. Being a colonel back here away from the demoralising Russian front certainly had its advantages. He was pleased that he had been wounded; many of the men in the front lines prayed to be hit by a bullet just to get invalided out. Yes, he had been badly wounded and his ribs and knee ached on and off, but he was away from the hell of the fighting and keen to do his duty here in Holland.

As the motorcycle escort slowed and the black automobile came to rest, Bayer shivered. Holland was a fool of a country, flat and no hills to stop the North Sea winds; even though it was a June evening, he could feel the chill. Never mind, he was in luxury here and the girl would warm him. A surge of expectancy ran through his body as he thought of the night ahead.

'We're here, *standartenführer*.' A soft yellow glow through the windows of a small stone building promised cosiness. The lieutenant jumped out as the innkeeper appeared. They spoke briefly and Hertz gestured to one of his soldiers to open the car door.

Bayer stepped out, briefcase again in his hand, and moved inside, as swiftly as his limp would allow, followed by his driver with his suitcases.

'Close the door, the wind is cold,' he barked as he entered the front hall. 'It's June, it should be warm.'

The innkeeper followed him and in obsequious manner bowed and pointed up the wooden stairs, speaking in German. 'Best room in the house, *mein Herr*. Top of the stairs to the left. There is a small sitting room as well as the bedroom. Bathroom is convenient, in the corridor immediately opposite.'

Bayer took no notice of him, but turned to the *untersturmführer*, who glanced longingly through to the smoke-filled bar. Ignoring the obvious desire of the lieutenant, the SS superior officer spoke dismissively, 'You can leave me now, Hertz. I'll expect you on Saturday at oh seven hundred.'

Hertz responded with a '*Heil* Hitler', clicked his heels and spun round to the door, closing it as he left.

As Bayer swung on his cane past the innkeeper waiting at the bottom of the stair, he spoke dismissively, 'Bring me two glasses and cognac. What is for dinner?'

'I had much good fortune and managed to obtain a chicken, *mein Herr*, and kept it especially for you tonight. It will be roasted to perfection.'

'Are there fires in my rooms? I want a fire. How is it so cold in this damn country when it's summer? The place is starting to remind me of the Russian front.'

'Of course, *mein Herr*. It was a warm day but once evening fell the temperature dropped so I lit a fire myself. Your rooms will be quite snug now. Shall I show you up?'

'*Nein*, just bring me the brandy and my bags in a few minutes.'

Outside in the rising wind, the soldiers stood by their vehicles waiting in hopes that a beer would be their reward for the escort, but the wave from Hertz to remount quashed that thought.

Hertz heard their groans above the wind as he climbed back into the car. '*Standartenführer* Bayer has given strict instructions that he wishes to remain entirely alone until Saturday. Thank heaven we do not need to stand around in this wind to dance attendance upon him.'

Chapter Twenty-five

Lucien Bayer leant heavily on his polished cane as he entered his bedroom and a curse slipped from his lips: '*Verdammt!* The blasted innkeeper is an incompetent fool!'

The room was cold. The fire had gone out in the grate: the balcony door was open and the curtains billowed in the air. His rage rose as he limped hurriedly to the open door and reached out to the handle to slam it closed. But in the second his fingers touched the metal there was a movement outside on the balcony and his mouth opened in shock as the first knife hit his chest and the second hit an inch to the right, a moment later. Blood spurted from him and oozed from his mouth and he crumpled dead to the rug at the door.

'Get him off the rug quick-smart, don't want blood on that.' Cole, Felix and Tudor entered the doorway and leapt into action. Cole was already dressed in identical uniform, except that he was not wearing the Iron Cross which hung round the dead man's neck. Rapidly, Cole dropped the small leather suitcase he carried on to the sofa and removed the dead man's medal from his neck and tied it round his own. He went through Bayer's pockets while Felix wiped blood from the wooden floor where some had landed. Slipping the Nazi's cigarette lighter into his own pocket Cole followed that with the note Bayer had received from Hertz and a leather wallet and a handkerchief.

He found two loose keys and assumed they belonged to Bayer's luggage. Swiftly he took off the German's belt with pistol and holster attached and strapped it round himself while Tudor and Felix dragged the *standartenführer* outside. Lifting his body to dump it over the railing, Cole suddenly saw his hand. 'Wait!' A death's head ring glinted on the corpse's finger. 'God, we nearly missed that.' He slipped it off and put it on his own. It was firm but it fitted. 'Right, let it go,' and they dropped the body over the railing to the ground below where Mako pulled it into the bracken. Felix slipped over the balustrade after the body and eased himself down until he hung from the balcony before he dropped the remaining eight feet to the ground.

In the room above, Cole stood leaning on Bayer's ornate cane. Tudor nodded and spoke quietly. 'You're a little taller than him, I reckon, but otherwise, you're a double, all right. It's amazing! You'd fool me.'

Cole winked. 'That's not hard. Though looking like that bastard is no real compliment.'

His companion frowned. 'I guess if anybody in the SS here in Holland knows him they won't have seen him since before he was wounded anyway.'

Cole's mouth twisted wryly. 'Yeah, that's the fervent hope.'

A rap on the door halted the whispered conversation and Tudor sped to the chintz-covered sofa to the left of the fireplace, lifted Cole's case and crouched down in hiding.

Cole crossed to the door and opened it to reveal the innkeeper with a bottle of cognac and two small glasses on a silver tray and behind him a boy with the black suitcases.

Cole leant on Bayer's cane and pointed to a table just inside the door. The innkeeper placed the tray down as he spoke to the boy and pointed to the bed. 'Put the *standartenführer*'s luggage on the bed.'

Suddenly the innkeeper looked around. 'Oh, *mein Herr*, your fire has gone out. How on earth could that happen? I am so sorry. I shall attend to it immediately.' He took two steps towards the hearth but Cole halted him.

'*Nein!*'

The innkeeper froze and turned around.

'I'd rather unpack a few things first. Come back in twenty minutes.'

'But you asked specifically for a fire.'

'I said, come back in twenty minutes.'

'Of course, just as you wish, exactly as you wish, *mein Herr*.' The host retreated in haste to the hall, followed by the boy.

As the door closed behind the two, Tudor stood up. He whistled softly. 'That was close. Right, let's see his papers.'

Neither of the two keys Cole had found fitted the briefcase catch but they were deft at opening locks and a few seconds later they spread the papers they found out on the bed.

Cole sorted through them, tapping a number with his forefinger. 'These are for the meeting on Saturday in Groningen. Looks like some correspondence from Schmidt and Wimmer: the two I'm to watch for Rauter. *Nice* people, the SS.'

'Yeah, well, you'll fit in.'

Cole grinned. 'Ta.' He picked up another sheet of paper. 'Here it is, we were right. The meeting's oh eight hundred in the Boomgaard Hotel, just as we thought, commandeered for the purpose.' He flicked through more papers. 'Hans said they're Nazifying as much of the civil administration as they can. Here is a list of Dutch mayors they still need to replace with *reliable* men.'

'Reliable *traitors* to Holland, they mean.'

'Uh huh. Just a matter of time before the whole country is dominated by *V-manner*. Oh . . . and here are the names of the attendees.' He ran his finger down them. 'All those I expected are on this list.'

'Good, we'll get rid of a batch of the bastards.'

'Yep. Pity we can't set pencil bombs for an exact time.'

'Don't worry, they'll go off, all right; Mako will set them for oh eight twenty, and he says that means between oh eight ten to oh eight thirty.' Tudor winked. 'He swears this type is dependable to ten minutes either way.'

'Mmm, well, we have no option but to believe him.'

'Now, remember the attack on your vehicle will take place at the bridge near the village of Winsom. Early on a Saturday morning we believe that particular back road will be deserted. Mako and Felix will make sure they kill the motorcycle troops who accompany you and they'll blow a tyre on your car, so you'll be slowed up all right. We want to delay your arrival at the inn until after oh eight thirty when the bombs have gone off . . . can't have an early arrival and find you blown to kingdom come, along with the targets, old buddy.'

'My attitude exactly.' Cole slapped his friend's shoulder. 'Just make sure the buggers don't kill me when they fire at the car.' He grinned and showed his top six front teeth, all of which had been covered by veneers to give his mouth the appearance of Bayer's.

Tudor smirked. 'We'll try to avoid that. That's why I've left the strike on you to Mako and Felix to handle alone. If we brought anyone else into it, they might just accidentally kill or wound you.' He frowned as he met Cole's gaze. 'Rada's asked a few tricky questions about Monday morning but I've skirted them. He's a good man but we've managed to keep your existence a secret from him and everybody else since you got here. Now you're really *Standartenführer* Bayer, old pal!'

'Reckon so.'

'I still wish we'd been able to do the bombing at the hotel just with Rada and without bringing others into it.'

Rada Vermeer, the old friend of Hans Buckhout, had appeared to Tudor to be solid and trustworthy, and had helped the agents hide since they arrived. But Tudor and his companions had noted some strange things going on in the Dutch Resistance even in their short time here. One of Rada's men had been picked up by the Gestapo, and a house on the edge of Groningen, where Rada and Leopold had visited the first week, had been raided the following day.

Tudor frowned as he added, 'But my dilemma came when we had to get the false work passes from a forger called Frans De Groot in Veendam. I had to deal with him.'

'It's only you and Leopold who've met De Groot, isn't it?'

Tudor's blue eyes picked up the light from the lamp on the table. He blinked and his mouth turned down in thought. 'Yes. Though he's aware there are four of us. He knows zip about you, of course.'

Cole stepped closer to his friend and spoke quickly. 'By Monday night you'll be south-east down near the Zuider Zee waiting for good old Lewis Hodges and the RAF pick-up to take you out of here, you lucky damn Yankee, you.'

Tudor shook his head. 'That's an insult, buddy, I wear the grey.'

'My mistake.' Cole was trying to keep the coming parting on a light note and he managed another grin. 'Goodbye, *Dirk*, see you in the Old Dart when I get back.'

Tudor frowned. 'What's that? The Old Dart?'

'The *old country*, you ignorant southerner! England.'

Tudor took a deep breath and slapped his friend's shoulder. 'The scars suit you, make you mysterious. Good luck, *Lucien*.'

'Good luck to you too. Now *scram*, as you would say.'

They shook hands and Tudor crossed silently to the door and outside on to the balcony; he turned to wink and salute before swiftly disappearing over the balustrade into the black night.

Cole felt strange as his partner left and he closed the door and pulled the curtain. Now he was truly on his own. Turning away he caught his reflection in the mirror and he paused. He had seen himself dressed as Bayer a number of times previously but suddenly it had immense impact. He had been into the field twice before in France and taken on aliases but this was extreme. This was existing as a Nazi colonel and infiltrating Hitler's SS and not knowing for how long he must do it. He had been game for a lot of things in his life so far; he hoped like hell he was up to this. The man in the mirror looked back. It was not himself; it was a Nazi colonel. 'This is it,' he murmured aloud.

He blinked and turned away to the small leather case he had brought with him; it contained the compact wireless set for contacting London. He used one of the keys he had found in Bayer's pocket to open the larger of the black suitcases, took out some clothes – uniforms, a pair of shoes and boots, and slid the wireless in its own case down to the bottom. Beside it he placed the German-made wallet Hans had given him containing thousands of guilders and marks.

All secret agents were given large amounts of money in the local currency of the country in which they were operating for they often had to buy on the black market or bribe the locals.

Within a minute there was another rapping on the door and as

Cole crossed to it he called, 'I thought I told you to leave me for twenty minutes.' He opened the door expecting to see the landlord and instead he had to steel himself not to open his mouth in surprise. A woman of thirty or so, with dark alluring eyes and brilliant auburn hair tumbling to her green velvet-covered shoulders returned his gaze.

Her voice could have been velvet as well, '*Guten Abend, Herr Standartenführer*, I am Laetitia.'

Oh Jesus . . . this was the part they didn't tell me about. Now we know why he was coming here for two nights, to this lonely inn all by himself!

Chapter Twenty-six

Over her arm was draped a jacket and in her hand she held a large fabric bag. She tilted her head sideways and her red lips parted in a semi-smile; he noticed the tiny beauty spot at the side of her mouth. 'Aren't you going to ask me in?' She spoke good understandable German.

His expression must have altered for she asked, 'You *were* expecting me tonight, were you not?'

'*Ja*, of course, I simply thought you might be later.'

'Oh no. I told them I'd be here before eleven.'

He had not gone through the papers. He had not sorted through the suitcases. He had to prepare himself for Saturday and now this.

'Ah *ja* . . . then come in.'

His mind raced. His mammoth deception had been planned by Hans and Andy and experts at SOE. *Well, thanks, boys, if the rest of my information is as good as this, then I'm bloody done for, before I start.*

Bayer, the dead bastard, had obviously ordered a harlot to have some fun with before Saturday came around and he began working on some new ways to terrify the Dutch into a larger output for the bloody Fatherland. What the hell was he going to do with this woman? *I've got to get her out of the way so I can prepare. But Bayer ordered her . . . oh hell.*

As she passed him and the fragrance of her perfume wafted to him, Cole noticed the innkeeper lurking at the top of the stair and he had a sudden thought. 'You! Bring that dinner, get this blasted fire going and . . . where is the *Klosett und Badezimmer?*'

'Right here, as I mentioned, *mein Herr.*' He pointed to the bathroom door opposite Bayer's room.

'Then get somebody to run a hot bath for the lady immediately. *Fahrt kommen!*' Cole pointed with his thumb and the innkeeper got going just as he had been told to do.

Cole took a deep breath and re-entered the room. *At least I'll have some time to think while she takes a bath.*

She had moved to the sofa and now had the coat round her shoulders; she was shivering. 'It is pretty chilly in here.' She looked up at him meaningfully.

Remember you are Bayer. 'True. There was a fire, but the doors were left open and it went out. The innkeeper's an idiot. I have ordered a hot bath for you. It will be warmer in the sitting room next door. You sho— *will* wait in there.' He moved across to the adjoining open door and pointed. The woman stood and hastened through.

'Oh yes, this is better, it's warmer in here.'

'*Gut.*'

Another knocking at the door made him turn. 'Come in.'

It was the same boy who had brought the suitcases earlier. He pointed to the fireplace and gestured he wished to light a fire.

Cole nodded sharply. '*Ja,* go ahead.'

The woman waited in the small parlour and Cole handed her the brandy and a glass before he returned to the bedroom where he read the note he had found in Bayer's pocket. It began by

162

saying that he looked forward to seeing Bayer on Saturday and that he remembered their friendship in those good days before the war.

Cole wished he had written more about that but he had not. The message continued:

The woman you requested is called Laetitia de Witt, Dutch, but half-French, hence the French first name. They say she was Walther von Reichenau's mistress on and off till he went to the Russian front, but she denies that. I know she was very friendly with our prominent Dutch friend, old Hendrik Seyffardt, who was murdered by the Dutch who resist us in January this year . . . so don't get too close to her, it might be dangerous! This is a joke, Lucien! She is Vertrauensmanner *and a friend of mine, and will conduct business on my behalf at the Groningen University and consequently is in the vicinity. I told her you want companionship and therefore I expect she understands you wish her to sleep with you. I believe she will stay Thursday night and return Friday night. The price will be what I gave you in our last communication. She has a taste for good champagne.*

    Until Saturday,
    Heil Hitler,
    Fritz Schmidt
    Commissioner General
    NSDAP

He had to get rid of her!

Another knock on the door heralded the innkeeper, who shuffled obsequiously a foot inside the door to say the bath was ready for '*die junge Dame*' and should he set the table for dinner?

'*Ja, selbstverständlich* . . . obviously.'

Cole watched her leave. He believed he was mentally prepared to take on the life of Lucien Bayer but not to have his whore into the bargain. This was a massive complication. His hoax as Bayer was intricate and risky; if he made one mistake his life would be forfeit. From the letter he had learnt that Fritz Schmidt had been in previous communication with Bayer, another complexity, but not one he would worry about now.

Cole blew out a long noisy breath and bent to open the other suitcase.

He lifted out three books: a copy of Hanns Joshst's *Ruf des Reiches, Echo des Volkes, Call of the Reich, Echo of the People*; a copy of *Mein Kampf* and Alfred Rosenberg's *Der Mythus des 20 Jahrhunderts – The Myth of the Twentieth Century*, which had been a German propaganda best seller before the war: Cole could not help but elicit a grim smile. 'Good little Nazi,' he said to himself before he rummaged through the rest. He found striped pyjamas, shirts, underwear, socks, casual clothes and the usual toiletries a man would carry. There was a leather case with the shape of a cross pattee printed on the outside; obviously the container for Bayer's Iron Cross and a certificate signed by Himmler was lying beneath it. In a corner of the case he found another leather container with a German blue-and-gold order of merit medal inside and a box for the Walther P 38 automatic pistol which he now wore. It was walnut with mother-of-pearl on the lid and inside were three eight-round magazines lying beside a celluloid fountain pen. Both items carried the initials LB. He took the pen and slipped it in his uniform pocket.

Cole had to get rid of this woman: why would an SS officer who had ordered her suddenly decide he did not want her? *Come on, Cole, think. She won't be in the bath all night.*

There was a sound behind him and he looked up. She held the

door open, her semi-smile parting her lips again and wearing a slinky satin evening gown which exposed a great deal of her smooth, pale flesh. He could see the innkeeper poised behind her with a tray of food.

As she entered Cole limped over to her, took her roughly in his arms and kissed her hard on the lips while the innkeeper pretended not to notice as he hurried to the table in the parlour.

Chapter Twenty-seven

Cole's eyes snapped open. *I am Lucien Bayer.* The thought he had forced himself to think coincident with waking up, flashed through his mind.

He became aware of the early vapid light of morning seeping through the space between the curtains and at the same time the woman at his side murmured in her sleep.

A frown lodged between his eyes as he turned towards her. He had played the part of Bayer even to having sex with his whore. She was lying on her back, one bare arm on top of the blanket. There was enough illumination to see the planes of her face; smooth, almost flawless skin, dark eyebrows and long eyelashes, the generous bottom lip and the round chin. Hard to believe it was the face of a collaborating harlot.

He had hardly spoken to her after kissing her at the door. He had acted as he had been conditioned to believe that Bayer would act. It had been instilled into him hour after hour, day after day, week after week that Bayer was the quintessential Hitler follower: fervid believer in the Nazi doctrine that Jews were the enemy of the Aryan race and must be exterminated, along with all other *degenerates*: homosexuals, dissenters, communists – he was a fanatical disciple and completely loyal to Himmler. He saw anything that he was commanded to do as legitimate, sanctified by SS doctrine and therefore desirable. There were no contradictions in his personality: he was an inflexible believer in the rights of the Fatherland.

Bayer was a solemn and, at times, sardonic man who had been engaged to be married to a schoolteacher in Bavaria briefly in 1936: the engagement was severed at Christmas that year. He had fathered a son he had never seen with a Danish woman in 1938. He was estranged from his mother who remained living in a small village outside Hamburg. He had no brothers or sisters and his father died in 1929 of tuberculosis. He had been raised in rank three times on the eastern front and when he was wounded he had been given up for dead and left in the snow but he had managed to crawl – most of one night – back to safety. As was to be suspected, he enjoyed Wagner's music. The nuances of his personality were not known and Cole fervently hoped that he would never meet anyone who was, in fact, acquainted with them.

Once the food had been served, Cole had told the female to eat, which she did, and he had taken some food for himself into the bedroom. Finally he returned to the parlour where she sat reading a book. 'What is that?'

'Victor Hugo – poems,' she answered meeting his eyes.

He grunted as if in disapproval of the French poet and gestured to her. 'Come, I'm tired.'

He had taken her to bed and she had performed as he had expected a good slut to perform. It was a bizarre experience: acting as *Bayer*, perceiving her as *Bayer* . . . and as his hands slipped down to the small of her bare back, it was easy to detest her. For Cole

Wareing did detest her. To him she was a Dutch bitch who had allied herself to the murdering Nazi bastards of this world . . . and yet as he rolled over to face away from her, he found himself unable to simply ignore her and go to sleep, so he asked where she was born.

'In Deauville in southern France,' she answered, her tone of voice luxurious, sensual. 'My parents were visiting my uncle there in the countryside when I was born, my father was French. Have you been there?'

'I know where it is,' he cut her off.

'So you have been there, *Herr Standartenführer*?' she asked.

'I told you I know *where* it is.' Cole had been to Deauville in 1937 and he remembered the area well but he had no idea if Bayer had ever been there.

'Of course. I think you would like it. I like that part of France. I've been back a couple of times. My uncle has a home in Switzerland as well. I've been there often on holiday.'

He remained facing away from her and yet he spoke once more – to wish her good night. '*Gute Nacht.*'

'*Gute Nacht, Herr Standartenführer.*'

And now . . . she appeared to be waking, for her hand moved on the blanket. He noticed her nails were perfect pink ovals as she moved and opened her eyes.

He spoke immediately. 'I have changed my mind. I want you to leave now, this morning. I wish to be alone.'

She took a moment to weigh what he had said before the velvet voice answered. 'Of course, *Herr Standartenführer*, I have my own transport, my car is here.'

'Who bought that for you?' He sat up with his bare back to her.

She did not answer but touched his skin below his scapula. The pressure of her fingers aroused him. He hated that her touch had any appeal. He shook her off and stood. He faced away from her and reached out to take the dressing gown which lay on the back of the sofa.

'I have always had a car. My uncle bought my first one for me.'

He slipped into the dressing gown and replied as he took fresh clothing. 'You're indeed fortunate to have a vehicle and fuel, when most of your compatriots are lucky to ride bicycles.' He tried not to let sarcasm slide into the statement.

As he walked to the door she spoke again, 'Do I still receive the full amount?'

He turned so quickly to look at her that he caught the last half-second of a vanishing expression: had it been hostile? Venomous, even? A quizzical smile replaced it instantaneously, leaving him unsure. He did not answer and she spoke hastily, 'My friend Commissioner General Schmidt said you would be kind enough to grant the full hundred guilders.'

'*Ja*, of course.' He walked to the dressing table and took a hundred guilders from Bayer's wallet; returned to the bed and dropped it beside her. She put her hand out, the long ellipses for nails resting on it as she smiled up at him, a full-blown lavish smile. '*Danke*. I hope we meet again, *Herr Standartenführer*.'

He gave her a steady Cole Wareing unidentifiable look before he left the room.

When he returned after bathing and dressing she was gone.

The note she had left sat on top of one of the locked black suitcases.

Herr Standartenführer,
I believe I have offended you. That was not my desire. I hope we meet
again.
Laetitia

She had written in large open, right-slanting letters. He slipped the message into his pocket and as he did his eyes wandered over to the briefcase on the sofa. It had been moved: only slightly, perhaps merely an inch or so, but it was not in the exact position he had placed it in last night. He had set it upon the seat and noted that one end covered the red rose in the floral pattern of the material, now part of the red rose was exposed.

He crossed to it and lifted it. It was locked. When he and Tudor had picked it, they were such experts that they had not broken the workings of the lock and he had fastened it again after replacing the papers. Later he had found the right key in Bayer's wallet.

Swiftly he opened it and now he was certain. As a precaution he had placed two hairs from his head inside the first and second and fifth and sixth sheets of paper. Neither were there. He had not left the rooms until this morning to bathe and dress. It had to be the woman! No one had been in here except Laetitia de Witt and, more than that, she had to be conversant with breaking into locks to do this. This was no ordinary traitor. It appeared she had been close to a Nazi general and a high-ranking Dutch collaborator! Had she been sent by Schmidt or someone else to spy on Bayer? And if so, why?

He turned back to the suitcases and opened them. The hairs he had left in position in the suitcases were still in position. So they had not been opened, only the briefcase. He let out a breath of relief as he spontaneously touched the case which held the compact wireless set he was to use to contact Hans in England.

It was impossible for her or anyone to know he had taken Bayer's place. The answer had to be that she was actually spying on Bayer!

So what was Laetitia de Witt up to? Who the hell was the woman he had slept with?

Chapter Twenty-eight

The wind had endured overnight and it pursued low grey clouds across north-eastern Holland to follow the lone black Mercedes-Benz limousine – minus the military motorbike outriders – into Groningen town. Inside, Cole sat dressed in grey SS uniform with Bayer's Iron Cross at his throat and tall black boots on his feet. Beside him on the seat to his right lay the cap with attached death's head and German eagle and to the left Bayer's briefcase. Outwardly he swaggered with self-importance, inwardly he was tense.

Hertz had greeted him with a formal Nazi salute, '*Heil Hitler! Gut* to see you again, *Standartenführer* Bayer.'

Oh, oh so we've already met. Cole was well aware of the small *gruppe* of troops camped by the canal. He and Tudor and the others had seen them on Thursday night as they approached the inn to lie in wait for Bayer. They had also heard the arrival of Bayer's car and the innkeeper's greeting as they waited in the dark on the balcony of the hotel. But they had not seen who delivered him.

'*Guten Morgen, untersturmführer.* I do not wish conversation this morning, I have much to think about.'

'*Jawohl,* of course.'

Hence the ride had been silent until the attack by Mako and Felix as they approached the bridge near Winsom.

The first sweep of bullets hit the two leading motorcycle soldiers who dropped off their machines as a front tyre exploded and the car swerved off the road across the flat pasture of grass and into a low thicket of leafy trees. The escort troops following were hit in the second hail of bullets. Hertz and Cole leapt from the vehicle as the back windscreen shattered and they crouched behind the engine of the car. As they took stock of the scene they saw the two perpetrators fleeing on a motorbike of their own towards the windmills in the distance near the villages of Winsum and Obergum. The second lieutenant fired after them; Cole took a little longer to remove his pistol from his holder and to fire, making sure it went wide. Hertz was ashen but soon regained his colour when he realised that the attack had come from two men only, who now fled.

The driver was slumped over his wheel and they quickly ascertained he was alive but had been hit in the shoulder. The escorting soldiers were all dead.

No one had come by so Cole and the lieutenant had changed the tyre themselves. They had to use the intricate hand pump to inflate the spare tyre so it was a time-consuming exercise and thus they approached the Boomgaard Hotel later than estimated at 0846.

The hotel sat on a canal which emptied into a small lake to the north-east of the town and as they advanced along the narrow road they could see across the flat fields to where hundreds of soldiers massed and two armoured tanks blocked the road.

Hertz, who was now behind the wheel with the wounded driver beside him, turned his head and spoke. '*Standartenführer* Bayer, it appears there is something happening in the vicinity of the hotel.'

'*Ja*, I can see that.'

They drew up behind a group of workers on bicycles who were halted by soldiers blocking the road. Hertz jumped out and yelled and the workers soon separated so that the Mercedes-Benz could drive up to the soldiers.

The second lieutenant spoke through the open window. 'What has happened here? I am carrying *Standartenführer* Bayer for a meeting at the Boomgaard Hotel. We were attacked on the road . . . our escorts were shot and our driver is wounded. What is this pandemonium about?'

The sergeant saluted. 'We only know that a plot to blow up the hotel has been uncovered. We are told the culprits are being rounded up.'

Cole's pulse quickened. 'Get me to the hotel immediately.' *Jesus, the bombs didn't go off. There I was believing an explosion had taken place and that was the reason for the troops and the commotion . . . and it's the opposite.*

Hertz managed to push the bonnet of the car through the milling troops to within forty yards of the front of the hotel.

Cole leant forward on to the back of the driver's seat. 'Wait for me.' He stopped himself from asking to get the driver to a medic.

'*Jawohl, standartenführer.*' The second lieutenant jumped out and opened the rear door for Cole to vacate the limousine and limp on his cane past soldiers of the Wehrmacht up the steps to an SS officer who was barking orders.

As soon as he saw Cole he came to attention, looked with interest at Cole's Iron Cross and down to the ivory and ebony patterned cane before clicking his heels and giving the Hitler salute. Cole returned it with a desultory copy.

'What is going on here?'

The SS captain was happy to explain.

'*Standartenführer*, pencil detonators in an explosive charge were found just as an important meeting was about to begin in a wing of the hotel.' He pointed. 'It was a plot, but we believe the perpetrators are being rounded up as we speak.'

'Rounded up? Where?'

'I don't know. There is a lot of confusion at the moment. I believe the *polizei* have names. *Polizeiführer* Rauter himself is here.'

Oh God, Tudor, I hope you aren't anywhere near here. Cole took a deep breath. 'Where is he?'

'I believe he and the commissioners have commandeered the small post office along the canal, *standartenführer*.' He pointed. 'They left here in case there were other bombs which had not been found. Though we now believe there were no more.'

Cole tried to hold down the sick feeling which was rising through him. 'Where was the bomb found?'

'In the tea urn.'

Yep, that's where it was meant to be, all right.

Cole could hear Tudor's words in his head. '*I still wish we'd been able to do the bombing at the hotel just with Rada without bringing the others into it.*'

'I shall find someone to drive you down to the post office, *standartenführer*.'

'*Nein*.' Cole shook his head. He needed time to weigh all this in his mind. 'I must walk . . . it is good for my leg. Oh, and make sure no one removes my car until I come back. I'm making you responsible.' He turned away as the *hauptsturmführer* 'heiled' Hitler. He sure needed to get used to that!

Passing groups of soldiers he limped down the side of the canal towards the post office while he attempted to bring his muddled thoughts together. He must find somewhere secure enough to radio London. This operation had gone amuck and he urgently needed to speak to Hans. Besides, somehow he must get to the lonely cottage on the small lake south-west of Groningen town where he and Tudor and the other operatives were to meet if anything went wrong.

Tudor had found the abandoned cottage ten days prior when he had been reconnoitring the district and had shown it to Cole on his arrival. They rode there on bicycles and noted that it could be approached on foot as well, even though two of the fields closest to the cottage were partially waterlogged and therefore unused, but they could be circumvented. Half of the dwelling had fallen into ruin but it was an ideal hideout for a brief period and they decided to use it as a gathering point for any or all of them, if the operation went wrong.

All this coursed through Cole's mind as he made his way to the small brick post office standing alone near a tiny park. Outside the building near beds of bright red tulips stood two sentries. They came to attention as he strode up to the stone and cement steps and mounted them. At the door stood a sergeant. On the wall behind him were two posters: one showing a drawing of Hitler's head with the caption *Be True To The Führer*, the other revealed two young men stripped to the waist arm in arm, one holding a shovel. The message on this was: *Reichsarbeitsdienst – we build body and soul* . . . suggesting that Dutchmen should volunteer for the *Reichsarbeitsdienst* – the Nazi labour service.

Cole's gaze returned to the German soldier. 'I am here to see *Polizeiführer* Rauter.'

The sergeant stood aside and Cole took a slow, deep breath and entered. He recognised Rauter and Wimmer immediately. They stood just to the left of the door with a third man, all drinking out of mugs. Perhaps fifteen to twenty others, most in uniform, two or three in civilian suits, milled in the room. Cole clicked his heels with precision, the way Helmut Schultz had taught him, and the heads of Rauter's pack turned towards him. Rauter put down his mug on a windowsill and moving away from the others walked over to Cole; in the flesh he was massive; his height must have been six feet five and with his wide shoulders it was his bulk which made his overall size threatening. He must have appeared a terrifying figure to prisoners.

Cole stepped up close to him. *I am Lucien Bayer. I am Lucien Bayer.* He met the SS general's studied gaze with a candid expression. 'Heil Hitler, *Obergruppenführer, Polizeiführer* Rauter, I am Lucien Bayer.'

Chapter Twenty-nine

An hour later Cole was still in the post office. Rauter had abandoned the meeting and rescheduled it for a week hence in Apeldoorn about sixty-five miles south where many of the civil administrative offices were and where Rauter was to spend some time over the coming months. A few of the men around him had been noticeably disturbed by the planting of the bombs but the overall reaction of those gathered was anger at the 'insolence' of the Resistance. The Nazis called the Resistance fighters *criminals*, which Cole, of course, found absurd, but he had been thoroughly schooled and so he used the word even though it did not roll readily off his tongue.

It had been explained to him that Fritz Schmidt, the commissioner whom Bayer knew, had become ill with some sort of fever and so had not attended the meeting. Cole was relieved. He would prefer to meet Schmidt without an audience. He would have to thank him for the woman and wanted to do it as swiftly and as fast as possible.

Rauter dominated the assembly in every way and introduced the newcomer with his arm around Cole's shoulder.

I have to get rid of this surreal feeling and accept all this. I must accept that this is normal: I am Lucien Bayer.

Subsequently, as some of those gathered began to leave, Rauter was brought news by a courier and he came over to Cole, his massive face still pink with anger. 'Commissioner General Fischboeck has just heard that we have already made an arrest.'

Cole felt a chill through his veins. He forced himself to sound matter of fact. 'Who have they arrested?'

'The woman who planted the bombs.'

Rada Vermeer's cousin who worked at the hotel. Cole nodded. 'Do we know about anyone else?'

He gave an optimistic growl. 'We soon will and then the security police will be out rounding them up. You'll be welcome to see them interrogated, if you wish to remain that long. We'll make reprisals for the attack on you as well; don't you worry. We cannot allow these animals to think they can attack SS officers. I had to use the reprisal method here to put down the general strike about six or seven weeks ago.'

Cole knew all about it. General Friedrich Christiansen, the head of the Wehrmacht in Holland, who at this moment was leaving the building with his aide, had issued a proclamation that all Dutch Army veterans were to report for reinternment in Germany which had resulted in strikes across Holland and many former Dutch soldiers going into hiding. Rauter had executed about eighty Dutch patriots and randomly shot another sixty before the Dutch workers went back to their jobs.

'You see, they only understand force,' Rauter proclaimed.

All Cole could *execute* was a nod.

Rauter called over his second in charge, Wilhelm Harster, the Commander of the *Sicherheitsdienst* – the SD, the Nazi security service – a short and stout man who looked like a midget beside the giant Rauter. They made ready to leave, but before they departed Rauter

179

suggested they all eat at the same table for dinner and Cole had thought it judicious to readily agree.

As the members of the SS and the German civil staff peeled off, Friedrich Wimmer, who ran Dutch Internal Affairs, walked over to him. His grey tunic pulled tightly across his expanding middle and in his fleshy face his eyes almost disappeared. 'We return to Castle Trentaneborg near Noordlaren. I believe you have a staff car but no driver after that shocking business on your way here.'

'*Ja*, that's right.'

'Who brought you in? Was it Hertz or Hoffmeyer?'

Cole, who had no idea, hastily answered. 'I have requested a new driver. One is being supplied to me . . .'

The door slammed behind them and they both turned to the noise.

'Ah, only the wind,' Wimmer remarked. 'We're getting edgy, thinking there are bombs everywhere.'

Cole hurried on. 'I shall remain here a little longer . . . I am interested to see what happens.'

Beads of perspiration were forming on Wimmer's forehead even though it was a cool day. He wiped his face with his handkerchief as he commiserated. '*Ja*, as you were nearly killed I understand your curiosity. But don't worry, they'll get what's coming to them. Personally, I'd rather return to the castle for lunch and a nice bottle of French wine.'

The invaders had commandeered a castle nearby and ousted the owners a year ago. Rauter and the commissioners and their staffs had stayed there since the previous Thursday; it was a beautiful moated structure built in the Middle Ages along with its sister castle, Fraeylemaborg, in Slochteren.

Wimmer stepped closer and his voice dropped as if speaking to a brother-soul. 'We have an excellent mobile brothel at the castle; some are quite artistic – you and I could go down there together tonight. I hear you've been with a girl already,' he giggled. 'You didn't waste any time.'

Cole thought he had better get a reputation for being a *loner* as fast as possible. 'Commissioner, respectfully, I don't like to discuss my women . . . with anyone.' He inclined his head and stepped away. 'And as for the offer to join you tonight, *nein, danke.*' He clicked his heels. 'I shall make my own way to the castle later.'

Wimmer's face revealed confusion: it was clear he did not know how to take the *standartenführer*. 'As you wish.' He cleared his throat, heiled Hitler, turned and left the building.

Finally Cole was the only one remaining and the post office staff began returning. He limped back along the road and after sixty yards a motorbike with an empty sidecar stopped beside him.

'Do you wish a lift, *Herr Standartenführer?*'

He nodded. 'Back to the Boomgaard Hotel.'

Getting out to the cottage – where he prayed Tudor and the others would show up – was imperative now, and besides, having to limp extended distances was difficult. When the Wehrmacht soldier deposited him at the Mercedes-Benz he found that the key was in the ignition. *Good.*

He looked around for the second lieutenant who had brought him into Groningen, but was delighted that he could not see him. As he opened the door of the Mercedes-Benz he glanced beyond the small garden of the hotel and caught sight of the SS captain he had spoken to earlier.

He beckoned him over and the *hauptsturmführer* spoke as he approached, smiling behind his spectacles. 'We have good news.

The security police have more information about the planting of the bombs and are out making arrests, we understand.'

Cole kept the sick feeling from rising. He spoke nonchalantly. 'Where will they take them . . . after they make the arrests?'

'If they don't shoot them, then the town jail briefly, for inter-rogation. After that, I don't know.'

'If you see the second lieutenant who brought me here, tell him I've taken this vehicle.'

'But your leg . . .'

'I am quite capable of driving.'

'Of course, *standartenführer*, if you say so. But you were attacked this morning, it's imperative that you have an escort.'

'We cannot let such incidences frighten us, *hauptsturmführer*.'

He turned sharply away and climbed into the car as the surprised captain lifted his arm. '*Heil* Hitler.'

Cole raised his cane and mumbled the same incantation before placing his briefcase beside him on the front seat and closing the door.

It was nearing noon when he arrived at the small whitewashed inn about a quarter of a mile away from where the cottage sat. He had decided it was better to leave the car parked near a building than alone on a road. He drove the big black Mercedes-Benz into the open space beside the public house and as he stepped out he noticed a young woman at the window.

He gestured to her and tentatively she opened the window a little wider. Her eyes were round with fear. 'We are closed . . . for the duration of the war.'

He answered her in Dutch. 'I do not wish to come in. I am here for exercise in fresh air for my bad leg.'

She looked past him down the road the way he had come. 'Where are your soldiers?'

'I don't have any.'

Her expression altered to surprise. 'Oh . . .'

'Don't you see officers here alone?'

'Never.'

'I might leave my vehicle here for some time.'

She nodded.

Now he could read confusion along with the dread in her face. 'There is nothing to fear,' he added and, leaning on his cane, limped away.

She stared at him until he was lost beyond a clump of trees. He left the road and doubled back across a field, through more trees and out on to the lane that ran down by his destination. The inn was hidden from view.

The sun came out from behind the clouds and glinted on the broken windows of the cottage as Cole rounded the trees which hid it from the lane. He traversed a garden which had gone to seed and limped across the arched courtyard, his boots and stick resounding on the stone. He gently pushed the broken wooden door open and it squealed on its single hinge as he passed inside where the musty smell of mould hung in the stillness. He called softly, 'Anybody here?'

Chapter Thirty

No answer came except the whistling call of the wind. He gazed around at the walls discoloured with damp, the peeling ceiling and the lone wooden table in the middle of the stone flagging. A rag doll, the only other object in the room, lay on the floor in the dust — faded and without arms, it had been abandoned with the house.

Striding through the tiny cottage it was obvious there was no one in it so he returned outside and peered across the fields. All still, no movement except for the constant waves of wind in the tall verdant grass and the reeds at the edge of the lake. Two swans sailed by the mass of beech trees in the near distance as the sun disappeared behind a cloud. With a noisy exhalation he went back inside. He was unsure how long he could wait. The officer he had left at the Boomgaard Hotel would be wondering where he was and even Rauter and his cohorts would eventually be curious about why he had not joined them at the castle. Thank goodness he had told Wimmer he might remain to see who had been arrested. That would help.

He decided to wait an hour.

He sat looking out the side window towards the courtyard,

wondering what had really happened and why the bombing had failed. He hoped with all his heart that Tudor and the others had not been taken, otherwise it was one hell of a sorry start.

If, in the months to come, he lost contact with Hans and England, he knew he had two separate escape routes out, one via an RN torpedo boat from Dutch shores and the other a land route through Belgium, France and Spain. He shook his head and stood up and paced about. His deception had just begun: he had to stop thinking of escaping! *But if Tudor and the others have been caught and one of them talks, I'm in for it . . .*

He kept glancing at his watch.

He paced up the small staircase to what had been the bedrooms and back down the steps to his window. *Where the hell are you, Tudor?*

He was back at his window when he checked his watch and noted forty-six minutes had passed. His head flicked up as he caught a movement through the beeches beyond. Rising, he hurried around to the door which sat half-open and watched through the crack, his Walther pistol in hand. Three men emerged and a sound of relief escaped through Cole's lips as they widened into a smile and he pushed the door open for Tudor, Felix and Mako to enter. 'Thank heaven it's you, Dirk!' He spoke in English as they entered.

Slipping his pistol back into the holster he held out his hand. 'God, it's good to see you.'

Tudor was pale and Mako's hand shook as he wiped his brow with the back of it. Felix stood silently, head down.

Tudor spoke first. 'It's sure swell to see you too, buddy, but it's been a bad morning. I'll fill you in with all the details, but Leopold's been shot.'

'What?'

'Yes, poor kid. I was in Groningen at the viewing spot across

185

the canal waiting beside my bicycle at oh eight hundred when all hell broke loose at the hotel – people yelling, Fritz running everywhere – I knew immediately that we'd been sprung and the bombs had been found so I got the hell out of there. I went straight to the farmhouse to warn Leopold, and ran into Mako and Felix returning from attacking you. We met on the side road south of the farm. So we began separating the one big pile of stones there into two as a warning for Rada not to go into the farm but to scram, when suddenly we spied a convoy of goddam trucks belting along the main road to the east. We couldn't do a damn thing to warn Leopold. We could see the farm buildings clearly across the fields and they entered the yard and rolled right up to the main house. As dozens of Germans leapt out and surrounded the place Leopold ran from the side door. He didn't have a ghost of a chance. He was firing at them but they cut him down as he headed for the sheds. We reckon he has to be dead.'

Cole shook his head. 'Bugger.'

'Yep.'

Mako sighed loudly. 'If we'd been a few minutes earlier and the Krauts a few minutes later, it would have been us as well in the flamin' farmhouse.'

'Trouble is,' Tudor went on, 'the lorry we were meant to get away in was standing in the yard so that was the end of our transport. We got out of there the back way, Mako and Felix on the motorbike and I was pedalling like hell. Then as we entered the lane leading to the fields to come here, we saw a woman waving to us from a parked car. Lo and behold we knew her; met her yesterday with Rada. She's on our side but works as a double agent of sorts. The Germans trust her: risky way to live but she does it . . . has her own car and access to plenty of petrol; amazing, really. She lives in Amsterdam but was up here doing things for Rada. She and Rada go back a long way.

'Anyway, yesterday Rada told us that if something went wrong today and we didn't have the lorry she would help us. She has bridge passes and everything. She had an agreement with Rada to wait there for him on the back road and we came along instead.' He took a deep breath and wiped his eyes with the back of his hand. 'All the woman knows is Rada was in Groningen town at oh eight hundred this morning. She doesn't know what's happened to him and nor do we.' He shook his head as he went on, 'I hid the bicycle and came in her car, the boys travelled on the motorbike.'

'Yeah, she came here with us.' Mako grunted affirmatively.

'What?' Cole's brow furrowed and his eyes narrowed with scepticism.

'That's right,' Felix confirmed. 'She's outside in the trees. Has left her car hidden in a thicket back near the road.' He pointed over his shoulder.

Cole looked around with concern. 'You really believe this woman is trustworthy?'

Tudor was adamant. 'Rada swore by her, said he knew her mother well and – even though this has been a debacle – Rada's a patriot, I'm sure of it. Hans Buckhout trusted him completely.'

Cole could not deny that.

'Yep,' agreed Mako with a surly nod of his head, 'she told us she heard this morning that the operation went wrong and as Dirk said, the skirt came to meet Rada, but found us instead.'

Cole let out a long noisy breath. 'Bloody hell, it gets worse. I know for sure one woman was caught at the hotel, but I don't know about anybody else. I just don't like any of this and now there's a strange female in it.'

Tudor held his chin in thought and cleared his throat. 'Lucien, we have to trust this dame, we have no option. As I said, Rada introduced her as one of his most trusted confidantes. He said she was like a daughter, really. She keeps low because she hoodwinks the Germans and deals with the underground by way of Rada alone, as far as we know; but I get the strong feeling she *will* get us to the RAF pick-up point tonight. She says she can do it . . .' He paused as Mako added his piece.

'Yeah, Lucien. We have to believe she's ridgy didge. What do you think, Felix?'

He was in accord. 'I think Rada's as straight as a die and he vouched for her. Said she worked with him on and off whenever she could.'

'That might be,' grunted Cole, 'but somebody informed.'

Felix was adamant. 'Look, we'd swear it wasn't her.'

'All right, then.' Cole accepted this with a shrug of his shoulders. 'So, Dirk, where the devil is this blasted paragon?'

Tudor lifted his thumb over his shoulder. 'Come on, we'll get her and we'd all better go back to speaking Dutch.'

'*Ja, natuurlijk.*'

Followed by his companions Tudor strode out through the doorway where he halted and waved and forty yards away a female form separated itself from the greenery and bracken.

Cole's eyes met a flowing blue dress and his face stiffened in astonishment as the shape became one he recognised. Walking with a gentle sway of her hips and looking as seductively alluring as the last time he saw her, Laetitia de Witt came towards them.

Chapter Thirty-one

The woman in blue stopped dead as she recognised Cole. She was so astounded she could only speak one word. 'You?'

Cole duplicated the word and the expression. 'You?'

The heads of Tudor, Mako and Felix whipped back and forth. 'You know each other?'

There was complete silence before Cole answered, 'We met at the Zwann Inn.'

No one spoke until the woman asked, 'Are you . . . all on the same side?'

Tudor glanced at Cole and when no one answered, Laetitia de Witt managed to say, 'I'm having trouble accepting that it is you I am seeing here, *Standartenführer Bayer.*'

In the thick atmosphere of bewilderment, Cole responded slowly, 'Indeed, I feel the same way.'

'Well, this is a blasted turn up of events . . .' Tudor was shaking his head as the sound of a woodpecker's staccato refrain began on a tree nearby as if he, too, were commenting on the phenomenon.

Laetitia de Witt's delicate gaze lifted to Cole's. 'But how can this be? You're a German colonel in the SS.'

His mind was racing. He was astounded. He was here on the

189

utmost top secret operation. No one in Europe other than the men with him were intended to know who he was or what he was doing here. But that was all too late. Bad thoughts about this whole operation now flashed through his brain: the bombing had gone wrong and this woman, of all people, had turned up. His astute mind calculated the situation and he responded curtly, 'You can see I am. I am *Standartenführer* Bayer. But these men are . . . my associates.'

It was evident she remained in shock; amazement still abided in her eyes as she glanced around at them all.

When no one spoke she looked again at Cole. 'I am close to Rada Vermeer and I will help your friends; they are in dire need. They must get to an RAF pick-up point tonight and I believe I can take them there.'

Cole held up his hand to silence her. 'I think we should continue this inside.'

Tudor turned and urged them into the disused cottage. 'Sure. Let's go inside.'

Their footwear clicked loudly on the stones as they crossed the courtyard and on entering Laetitia turned to face them and spoke immediately. 'I am having difficulty accepting this, but obviously I realise that you, *standartenführer*, are working for the British too.'

He hesitated momentarily before he acknowledged her statement. 'I am.'

'Listen, Laetitia,' Tudor began, 'we're all baffled by this and we cannot tell you what part the *standartenführer* plays. Best you just accept what you see.'

'All right.' She nodded. 'Then I want you to know this, *standartenführer*: that Rada Vermeer is like a parent to me. He knew my mother. They were close. He is in the Resistance and has managed to avoid the German labour draft because he is over fifty. We have worked together against the aggressors and he has been vigilant in keeping my identity secret.'

She paused and sighed. 'He has always treated me like a daughter. I knew of what he organised at the Boomgaard Hotel, though none of the people working with Rada saw me. We met alone always: it is best that way. And when I became aware this morning that things had gone wrong, I had a previous plan to meet Rada, but instead,' she looked to Tudor, Felix and Mako, 'I found you three and when Rada never appeared, you told me you had to get here, to this place.' Her voice was still that honeyed sound from Thursday night.

Cole's eyes narrowed. 'Hold on, you didn't come here to help Rada Vermeer. National Socialist Commissioner Schmidt wrote me a letter of welcome. I received it the night I arrived; it mentioned you. He said you were in Groningen doing business for him at the university.'

She answered vehemently. 'Of course, for that was right.' She glanced down and blinked and he noticed how long her eyelashes were. 'I know a number of our *German masters*. They believe I'm one of them. It is how I get all sorts of things, including my papers and passes. I did come here on an assignment for Fritz Schmidt *but* at the same time I met with Rada.'

'God, that's dangerous,' commented Mako and she turned to him.

'*Ja*, it is, but I choose to do it. Holland is being raped by them.'

'Hold on,' Tudor interjected. 'How was it that this German commissioner wrote to the *standartenführer* about you? And how on earth did you meet each other?' Tudor looked from Cole to Laetitia.

Her expressive eyes turned to Cole and it was he who answered. For some reason he could never explain to himself, he decided on the spot not to mention that they had slept together or his previous assumption that she was a Nazi whore and collaborator. He simply lied and said Fritz Schmidt had formally presented her to him in the letter of welcome. 'I required a companion to dine with me and Fräulein de Witt was the lady who arrived . . . with an introduction from Commissioner Schmidt.'

Tudor rounded on Cole. 'Could I have a word with you alone?'

They went together to the next room where he faced his friend with a grimace. 'Lucien, I see you're letting her remain with the assumption that you're an SS officer.'

'I must. Why would I tell her I'm an imposter? As far as she's concerned, I'm a Nazi who's gone over to the British. Why disabuse her of that? We don't even know if she's trustworthy yet.'

'We have no option but to believe in her, Lucien.'

'Correct, Dirk, I'm afraid we don't; but it's best to leave her with as little real knowledge as possible.'

'She knows plenty already.' He thought a few moments before he went on, 'Bloody amazing that you've already met her. Listen, do you want to come out with us? Your mission's altered. If she gets us to the pick-up tonight that's one thing, we're up and away from here; but if you stay in Holland, you remain with the fact that she knows you're working for the Allies.

'Look, Lucien, I actually trust her. She found us, brought us to you and was definitely in Rada's confidence. But the whole thing has gone awry and I can understand if you abandon all this to escape with us. Hans would sure understand.'

Cole's mouth twisted as he examined what his friend had said. He had come here to be Lucien Bayer. He could not leave after one day; that was not possible for him. The thing he hated was what Tudor had just recognised: that once Tudor and the others were back in England this woman would be the single person in the whole of Europe who knew he worked for the British. 'You're prepared to continue putting your lives in her hands, then, Dirk?'

Tudor blinked. 'Hell, Lucien, I have to be prepared, just as you have to be, if you stay.'

'You've just said it, mate. Go or stay, I have to . . . you have to . . . we all have to trust her. I can't leave. I'm Lucien Bayer.'

'That's it, then.'

'Yeah, reckon it is.' Suddenly Cole looked at his watch. 'Jesus, I need to go.' He spun round and re-entered the room where the others waited and as he did so, his boot caught the rag doll lying on the floor. He nudged it closer to the wall as he brought his eyes round to the beautiful, anxious face of the human doll in the room. 'We are all at risk', he stated. 'All in the gravest possible danger.' He locked eyes with her. 'You have my associates' lives in your hands and, it would appear, mine too.'

'*Ja.*' She said it very softly. 'But they are safe and so are you.'

He hoped like hell that was the case and as they all fell silent Tudor turned to Laetitia. 'We have no option but to trust you and believe in you. You came with us to this place with the prospect of great danger to yourself and now you say you can get us away from here and to our rendezvous point for oh two hundred in the morning.'

'*Ja,* I believe I can do that. In reality the co-ordinates you mentioned are not that far away but we'll have to wait until dark, of course.'

Tudor nodded in agreement and moved to Cole and held out his hand. 'For the second time, goodbye and good luck.' Cole was strangely aware of the firmness of their grip upon one another as their palms met.

'Take it easy,' he said as he released Tudor's fingers and shook hands with the others and limped towards the door.

He was halted by Laetitia de Witt's silken voice calling quietly, 'Standartenführer Bayer?'

He turned.

'I believe you stay out at the castle?'

'Ja, for three or four nights.'

'Then I shall come and tell you news of your friends.'

He met her eyes again. 'Is that wise?'

'Oh ja, it is.'

He had no idea what to say to that so he said nothing and simply turned and limped to the door where he raised his cane in a sort of salute over his shoulder and departed.

Chapter Thirty-two

Three days later: Tuesday, 22 June

The breeze lifted Laetitia de Witt's hair as she sat behind the wheel in the small dark-blue Rosengart and slowed down as she reached the sentry box. Leaning out of the open window of the car she eyed the German soldier. 'I am here to see *Standartenführer* Bayer.'

'Does he expect you?'

'Not perhaps right now, but I believe he will wish to see me when he knows I'm here.'

'What is your name?'

'Laetitia de Witt.'

'How is it you have petrol for this motorcar?'

For reply she handed him all her papers which he read and handed back with a nod. She watched him enter the makeshift sentry box and ring the telephone bell to the castle. When he returned he gave the Hitler salute. 'Wait in the courtyard.'

As she drove across the moat her eyes lifted to the keystoned arch of the drawbridge lit by a burst of the summer evening sunlight and as she entered the castle she was greeted by an array of red and yellow roses in tall barrels decorating the yard. Beyond their tranquil beauty and to the side of a line of Kübelwagens painted with large swastikas on their bonnets, drilled a unit of German soldiers. As she pulled up into a spot designated by a corporal, the eyes of many of the men in uniform followed the car.

'I am here to see *Standartenführer* Bayer,' she repeated, resting her bare arm on the door as the soldier smiled appreciatively at the expanse of smooth skin which showed above the light summer frock she wore.

Cole saw her the second he stepped out of the doorway on the far side of the courtyard. He had a troubled feeling inside as he limped across leaning heavily on the ivory and ebony cane. It was hard for him to believe she was a Dutch patriot: he had truly accepted her as a Dutch traitor and a whore on the night she had slept with him. Yet here she was, as good as her word, no doubt to give him the news she had promised to Tudor and the boys.

He was trying to remain dispassionate about her as he drew closer but he could not help recalling her response to his lovemaking in the Zwann Inn: erotic, sensual; the way her body had moulded to his – he had tried to act the way he believed Bayer would act, and yet he knew he had ended up making love to her the way Cole Wareing would have done. He paused when he was some ten yards from her car. As the days had passed since Saturday, part of him had hoped she would not come here and the other part had wished she would. He had found himself thinking of Shelly too. And that had resulted only in a vague anger and an uncomfortable, sensitive feeling for he did not want to be reminded of Shelly Longford and her loving ways and tempting charms at the same time as he thought of this woman: there was no comparison. He was in German-held Holland a million light years from Queensland and he had released Shell, she was no longer his. He would be lucky to get out of this bizarre existence alive and any attachment he might have felt to her had nothing to do with this.

He remained still while his visitor opened the car door and slipped her bare smooth legs lithely down to where her shoes met the ground. Rising she moved round to rest against the bonnet and wait for him.

He could see the effect she was having on the German soldiers. He had hated her on Thursday night; and he admitted he still found it distasteful that she chose to sleep with the enemy: for good reason, if you listened to her, no doubt.

A warm smile greeted him as he approached her and when he came to a halt a few feet away he presented a calm, disinterested exterior.

She could not read the expression on his face so she gave him another glowing smile and speaking in a low voice, said, '*Guten Tag, Standartenführer Bayer*.'

He replied in German, 'Good afternoon to you', and clicked his heels and with his head indicated a small private square of lawn through a gateway in a stone wall. 'Come this way.' Turning from her he led her through the opening where additional barrels full of lavender softened the stark stone walls of the castle. He continued to converse in German. 'What have you to tell me?'

She glanced at a sentry, away in the distance. 'Your friends – are still here.'

He scowled. 'What?'

'There was heavy mist that night . . . the wind dropped away and the mist rolled in. I did not get them to the pick-up point till close to the appointed hour. I thought it would be simple but it wasn't. It was not an easy journey – there is a curfew from midnight to four and, in any case, no aircraft came in.'

'Oh hell. Here I was thinking they were in England. Where are they?'

'Safely hidden in a house on the coast.'

'Where?'

'Not far from Harlingen. It took nearly two days to get them there. We could only move at night. Though Holland is riddled with informers the place they are in is safe, it belongs to a man I trust completely.'

'I hope so. I know there are plenty of *Vertrauensmanner* here.'

She nodded to that. 'Yes, it's why Rada always protects me. I have not met the people he deals with – I am at arm's length from them, but I help Rada in my own way.'

He knew he had to tell her that he had learnt of Rada Vermeer's death. The man had been caught and shot as he tried to leave Groningen town after the failed bombing, but Cole did not want to tell her here in this exposed place.

She stood studying him. Laetitia de Witt had thought a lot about this German SS officer in the last couple of days; just as she had thought about his handsome fair-headed friend whom she had in hiding. These two men were so different from any men she had ever known; so far out of the ordinary that she was fascinated by them.

The expression in Cole's eyes was hard. 'Why should I believe that my associates are safe?'

She blinked in shock. 'What?'

'They might not be where you say they are.'

She sighed. 'Please listen to me, *Standartenführer* Bayer, I understand your reluctance to deal with me, but I am your friend. You must begin to trust me as your three friends have done. I am helping them. Things will be complicated but I believe I can get them out of this country. If I am not to be trusted why have I not told the German authorities about you? Answer me that.'

That arrow hit home and he went quiet, considering the situation and looking down at his cane as he tapped it on the grass near his boot. When he lifted his eyes to hers he grunted affirmatively. '*Ja*, all right. I accept what you say.' Perhaps he needed to concede that Laetitia de Witt appeared to be a very brave woman. For a moment he wondered whether to tell her he had been unable to contact London by wireless, that there was something wrong with his set, but he quickly resolved not to mention it. 'Are you sure the British agents are safe?'

'I believe they can hide there an extended time.'

That relieved him.

'I know the names they are using, Dirk, Mako and Felix.'

He nodded. 'Please inform Dirk and the others that I've been asking questions and have confirmed that our wireless operator was shot to death at the farm.'

'Oh, I'm so sorry.' Her mouth trembled with emotion and she clutched her hands together in an agitated way, moving her fingers up and down. He was pleased he had not told her Rada Vermeer was dead, seeing her reaction to the death of Leopold. He needed to be somewhere alone with her to tell her about her friend.

At that moment a voice behind them said, 'Laetitia, what are you doing here?'

She started noticeably but Cole turned slowly and steadily to see the face of Fritz Schmidt. This was the man who knew Bayer and who had written him the letter of welcome the night Bayer had arrived in Germany. He was thin and quite good-looking with a fair Aryan aspect. He was the only non-Austrian in the top German civil officials in Holland and had been born in Westphalia. Cole had been warned

199

by Hans that he was thought by some to be unbalanced and as he stood looking at them now, there was a penetrating, unnatural look in his handsome eyes. Schmidt had collared Cole on the first night at the castle and talked about *their days in Bingen and Berlin.* Cole thought he had acquitted himself capably but had tried to avoid him as much as he could since.

Schmidt mechanically clicked his heels together and came forward. 'How nice to see you two together, considering I introduced you. To find you here having a tête-à-tête like this, so cosy, the meeting last Thursday must have been very successful? But didn't I hear that you only spent one night together?'

Cole made a quick decision and took a deliberate step nearer the woman. 'Whatever you heard, commissioner, it was successful. In fact, we are just now going for a short drive.'

Schmidt answered with a frown. 'I thought you had the reorganising of the Groningen Province mayors to handle with Wimmer now?'

'No, I've been with him all afternoon, we are finished for today.'

Schmidt blinked and abruptly smiled. 'Ah . . .'

Taking Laetitia's arm, Cole guided her past the German and as he did so, Schmidt's hand shot out and latched on to Laetitia's forearm to halt her. 'Come and see me again soon,' he said.

She met his eyes as she slipped out of his grasp with a pleasing smile. 'Of course I will, Fritz; but I have business with the *standartenführer* today.'

Schmidt surprised them by bursting into a barking laugh. 'Ah, I see it is more serious than I thought . . . and so soon.'

As Cole urged her on by the flower barrels, Schmidt called, 'Don't forget we are up early, *Standartenführer* Bayer. Tomorrow we go to Assen then on to Apeldoorn.'

Cole's clipped tones rang back along the path. 'I won't forget.' They walked back to the car and Cole opened the door. 'Get in, we'll drive out of the castle . . . we'll go somewhere we can talk.'

She deftly crank-started the Rosengart's engine as Schmidt moved to the gateway in the wall and stood watching. They drove across the drawbridge where the sentry brought his arm up in the pretentious Hitler salute and lifted the drawbridge without hesitation.

Once they were along the road four hundred yards Cole pointed to a lane ahead where he could see woods and a canal. 'Turn down there.'

She brought the car to a halt under some beech trees facing the canal and switched off the engine. They were both silent and the sharp call of evening birds sounded nearby as Cole faced her. 'I don't think you are aware that Rada was arrested along with his cousin?'

'Oh no!' Her eyes widened in shock. 'God, so that's why he was not at our usual appointed place this morning. I only returned from the coast at eleven a.m., you see.' Tears welled in her eyes and ran down her cheek and she lifted her hand and wiped them away.

'Rada's cousin was taken when she tried to get out of the hotel and Rada when he attempted to leave the town.'

She closed her eyes. 'Do you know where they're holding him?'

'I'm sorry, but he's dead.'

Her eyes snapped open and her mouth trembled and he felt a strong desire to hold her in his arms and soothe her, but he quashed that and instead handed her his handkerchief.

She wept into it, murmuring, 'No no no.'

'I'm afraid they shot him; from what I understand, his cousin, the poor girl who was caught planting the bombs, gave them his name and he was taken leaving town. He ran. Perhaps he preferred to die that way, than to be a prisoner. It's obvious that some bastard was collaborating. Didn't they have to use a man from Veendam for the forged papers?'

She sighed. '*Ja.*'

'Well, somebody talked.'

'I don't understand why Rada was in town . . . he was supposed to leave before eight. Why was he still there?'

'I've no idea.'

'I can't believe it was the forger, we've used him before,' she sobbed.

'And apparently one other woman and a man were taken. Unlucky devils might be better off dead.' He paused a few seconds before adding, 'So that's the head count.'

She brought her sad eyes up to his and continued to cry softly.

Chapter Thirty-three

As time passed she dabbed her eyes but did not speak. She appeared unnerved and kept looking out the window.

He touched her on the arm and she brought her gaze round as he asked, 'Have you made any contact with anyone here since you came back this morning?'

'No, when Rada was not on his usual seat in the park, I came straight to tell you what had happened.'

'God knows how many others will now be arrested. Relatives, friends of the Dutch who were shot and taken.'

She winced but made no comment.

'Was Rada married?'

'No.' She sighed. 'He had friends, acquaintances . . . and he was always fond of my mother: very fond. I've known him a long time. I cannot believe he is gone. He was so strong and brave . . . and . . .' She broke down again and wiped her tears with his handkerchief. She seemed very vulnerable and evidently had loved Rada Vermeer.

When she quietened she turned to face him. 'I'm sorry about the wireless operator. Dirk said he was very young. How old was he?'

'About twenty-one or -two, I think. I was told he took out two Germans before they got him.'

She shook her head and her chin fell on her chest in thought.

'*Politzeiführer* Rauter is going to kill five civilians tomorrow in Groningen.'

Her dark eyes still glinting with tears, lifted to him, 'Do you mean in reprisal?'

'Yes, and also because of an attack on me when I entered the town. Four Germans – motorcycle soldiers, were killed.'

'I did not know.'

'Why should you?'

A thoughtful expression crossed her face. 'If Rada had anything to do with it I think I would have known. I wonder who it was who attacked you.'

'I've no idea.'

She turned away to gaze out the window again, her hands holding her body around her waist. '*Ja*, Rauter is cold and cruel and heartless.' She sighed. 'They all are – they're fanatical.'

He stared at the back of her head, the thick auburn hair cascading around her shoulders; her arms firm and smooth and her skin a gentle pale honey colour, as the sun – low to the horizon – radiated through the opening in the trees to fall on her chest and on her bare arms. He tried hard to ignore the feeling he had as she faced to the wheel and leant her head back so that the skin on her throat gleamed too.

A racking sigh broke from her. 'Rada was perhaps my best friend and now the Nazis have killed him.' She said it as one might read the last sentence of a book, in a final definitive way.

A moment later she inclined her head towards him and met his eyes with an enigmatic look on her face as she said very softly but distinctly, 'I have been thinking a great deal about you. Thinking and wondering. How is it that an SS officer works for the British? When did they recruit you?'

She sat up straight again and he replied, 'I think the less you know about that the better for you.'

'Perhaps. But you don't need to protect me. I'm up to my neck in this by hiding Dirk, Mako and Felix.'

'*Ja*, I realise that. You and your friends are courageous people.'

'And you are courageous too; very different and very courageous.' Her gaze dropped to his body and back up to his face and she lifted her forefinger to the side of her mouth in deliberation. 'I've been contemplating you ever since you left that disused cottage; contemplating the weirdest thing I've ever seen or heard of in my life: that an SS officer is working hand in hand with three British operatives. Yet there's a part of my brain that tells me it's impossible.'

'Give your brain a rest, Laetitia de Witt. You've had enough to contemplate for one day. Let's get back to my friends. What are you planning for them?'

'The man who is hiding them might be able to get a vessel. His son runs a boatyard. But it will be some time before we can organise it. Everything has to be clandestine and it will cost money.'

'How much money?'

'I'm not sure. I will tell you when I know. Things need to be bought.'

'I suppose so.'

She sighed and looked intently at him. 'I'm very lucky. Fritz Schmidt has been very useful. I have petrol and along with my identity card I have passes to go through various cities and on some forbidden roads.'

'So I understand.' He was wondering what she had to do for Fritz Schmidt to receive these benefits, when, as if she read his mind, she informed him, 'He is very strange: all he asks of me is to dine with him, hold his hand and occasionally massage his head.'

'Massage his head?'

'*Ja*. Odd, isn't it? Has he always been strange?'

'Why do you ask?'

'Well, you've known him for a long time. He told me so.'

Cole nodded. 'I'd say he has always been strange, but he's never asked me to massage his head.'

She gave a small smile at that and he liked to see it. He sat back a little from her and appraised her. 'How is it you know men like Schmidt and Rauter and are accepted by them?'

Laetitia hesitated before leaning further towards him, her eyes wearing an innocent and meaningful expression. 'I'll answer that with a little story.' She touched the mole at the side of her mouth with a delicate movement of her long fingers as she went on, 'I was in France, when Poland was invaded and I remained. My father was French, a colonel in the Great War – he was at Verdun with Philippe Pétain who was a general then. *Mon père* became a general himself later. His family had always run shoe factories in France, Belgium and here: I was the only heir. My father and my Dutch mother separated when I was very tiny and my mother brought me home to Holland to live but I spent holidays in France with my father and my uncle and I was with Papa the night he died a few months into the war.

'Through Papa I knew most men of importance in France. I was acquainted with Pierre Laval – he's disgusting –' she threw this comment as an aside and went straight on speaking – 'and a number of politicians who went with Marshal Pétain to co-operate with Hitler in the puppet Vichy French government.'

206

Cole made a sound of disgust. 'Ah, Pétain, the man who said in 1940 when Germany overran France that *in three weeks England will have her neck wrung like a chicken*.'

'Yes, the very same.' She lifted her hands and gestured, palms open in frank fashion, 'You see, that's how I met certain high-ranking Germans — through the shameful Vichy French.' Giving him a direct gaze, she continued, 'I am not proud of *mon père*; he knew many people I regard as traitors — collaborators with Hitler: Pétain and Laval being two. I suppose, if he'd been alive, *mon père* would have co-operated with the Germans as well — out of fear and knowing what nearly happened in the Great War when France was practically on her knees and the flower of French youth died fighting.'

To this Cole raised his eyebrow and commented sardonically, 'The flower of many countries' youth died fighting.'

'True, I agree, but some people are weak and afraid.' She looked out across the canal and tapped the steering wheel with her fingernails.

'Even generals?'

'Yes, even generals.'

Laetitia had gone so far she decided to finish her tale. 'I remained in Paris and saw Holland, Belgium and France invaded by the Germans in May the following year. And when so swiftly in June, France fell, I came back here, just in time for my mother to die. Strange how my parents died within a year of each other.' She paused and gave him an odd look. 'I actually came back here with an important Dutch collaborator whom I'd met when he visited Paris.' She ended with a matter-of-fact tone. 'So I have remained.'

'You *came back* with a Dutch collaborator . . . you mean you were his mistress?'

She gave a wan smile. 'No, just because I stayed a night with you, *standartenführer*, does not mean I sleep with every man I meet. He was a friend of Marshal Pétain and accompanied me back here in the train, that's all. It is easier if the Germans trust you.'

'I suppose it is.' He had no idea what to make of this beautiful unusual creature in the car with him. He attempted to consider all these revelations. It was easier when he was not held by those dark, beguiling eyes. He did not look round as he asked, 'How is it your name is de Witt, if your father was French?'

'De Witt was my mother's name. I always use it here, though . . .' she paused a few seconds and he turned to her. 'I used to be Laetitia Leroye in France, for that was my father's name, *Standartenführer* Bayer.' She pronounced his name in an assertive fashion and met his eyes.

'Perhaps you should call me Lucien.'

She moved on the seat with a feline action, almost stretching herself. 'I suppose I should, Lucien.'

The sound of aeroplanes in the distance reached them – the continuous whine of a fleet. The noise grew louder and came closer, until Cole looked out the window into the gathering twilight hoping they were the RAF on their way to bomb Germany. Gazing up a little longer he could not see anything, so sat back in his seat.

'British aircraft on their way to bomb your home country,' she said, looking intently at him.

'Let's just call it the country where I was born.'

She touched the base of her throat with her index finger and locked eyes with him. '*Ja*, I understand. It's clear you are certainly disillusioned with it.' She paused and produced the hint of a smile. 'When shall I see you again?'

Chapter Thirty-four

Cole stared at her. 'Let me think about that. It's time we went back to the castle. Where did you put the crank?'

'Under your seat, but I can do it.'

He did not reply but bent down and reached it and, leaving the car, started the engine. It roared into life and he came back and slid in, closing the door.

The sun had dipped towards the horizon and shadows melded on the road ahead as they travelled in silence until the Rosengart neared the castle and Laetitia spoke. 'You've had many questions for me, now I have one for you, if you will please answer?'

'What?'

'I heard Fritz Schmidt say you go back to Apeldoorn; is that where you will work?'

'*Ja*, in the civil offices there and also in the Hague.'

'I have a small house not far from Apeldoorn which I visit, though I've been living in Amsterdam. I have another property too, a farmhouse over near the German border; it was commandeered by a German regiment for a time but it's empty now.'

'How is it you have country houses? What do you exist on?

Sounds like you've got a stash of money somewhere. I would have thought the Germans would be very interested in that?'

Laetitia gave him another serious look. 'The houses belonged to my mother's family and *ja*, I have my inheritance from the shoe factories my father owned; part of that is safely in Switzerland with my uncle, but so far our Nazi masters have left most of my money alone, thank heaven.'

She brought an elegant finger up in the air towards him. 'Listen to me please, I have a suggestion. If I were seen as important to you by the German authorities . . . if it appeared you had taken me for your woman, your girlfriend, mistress, we could see each other. I know the sort of man you are; working alone is what you prefer, but won't you want to know when your friends leave? If I can see you I can tell you what's happening. You might wish to send a message back with them. I can be a help to you on a lot of things.'

When he did not comment she continued, 'With Rada gone, I will not come back here and as none of the people working with him knew me, there is no concern about a link between me and the aborted sabotage at the Boomgaard Hotel. If you will only trust me as Dirk and the others trust me . . . it could be a most successful liaison. We have already sown the seed with Schmidt back at the castle.'

She was right about that last point. Yet he could not help but be dubious about an obvious liaison with her; all his training went against it. He tried to critically appraise what she was saying: yes, he wanted to know when Tudor, Felix and Mako escaped. He was certain to want to send a coded message to Hans, especially if his wireless continued not to work. It baffled her that an SS officer would be a British spy but she accepted it, of course, so, even being able to keep a close eye on her might be a good thing. He wavered back and forth . . . perhaps what she suggested might work. He could smell the sweet fragrance of her, the car was filled with it; it somehow annoyed him that he found it pleasing and he pointed through the windscreen as they neared the sentry box. 'Let me out where I got in.'

The soldier strode forward and waved them through.

Inside the courtyard she braked and left the engine running as Cole turned to her and stared silently at her. When he still did not answer her proposal she sighed. 'Tomorrow I will see your friends and the next day I'll drive back to my house in the country outside Apeldoorn; it's on the edge of the Veluwe.'

He knew what that was – the Hoge Veluwe, a huge national park of many square miles containing forest-rich ridges where deer and wild boar roamed. There were grasslands and sand hills and the occasional farm plus areas of vacant land criss-crossed by tracks and certain dirt roads. Much of it remained today as it had been for centuries.

'*Standartenführer* Bayer. Please, when will I see you again?'

He heard himself answer her before he considered any more about it. 'On Friday, if I'm back in Apeldoorn.'

She smiled and, bending her head towards him, she said softly, '*Wunderbar*, there is a café still open near Raadhuisplein Square. It has a vine-covered trellis. The flowers are in bloom.'

'All right; if I'm not there by eleven hundred I'm not coming.'

She slipped her hand into her purse and took out a piece of paper and drew upon it. He watched her in the gathering darkness of twilight. She handed it to him. 'This is a map of how to get to my house if you ever need it . . . it sits alone.'

He took the paper and met and held her gaze fleetingly in the gloom. 'Be careful. And I'm sorry about Rada.'

'*Danke,* that is kind of you.'

As he limped away he thought what an enigma she was, though amazingly brave in her own unique fashion. Perhaps, allying himself with her would not be a mistake. Perhaps having a friend here in this maelstrom could be for the best after all. One thing he finally admitted to himself; he believed he could trust her; and he wanted badly to do so.

Behind him she watched him leaning on his black and white cane and limping away past the barrels of summer flowers. He did not look back.

Chapter Thirty-five

Laetitia de Witt drove away from Castle Trentaneborg with Cole's handkerchief on her lap. To think there was an SS colonel who was a British spy! She knew this would continue to amaze her.

She had stayed the night with him last Thursday to spy on him and see what she could find out for Rada: what an irony. The thought of Rada made her eyes fill again with tears. How she would miss him. He had not approved of some things she had done and he had spoken scathingly to her at times but he had always treated her with love. He had never been happy that she pretended friendship with certain of their Nazi masters, and he had continued to warn her more than once how dangerous that was.

Dear Rada, he had always been careful to cover her tracks with him and had dealt with her in a completely covert fashion. She did not know who else he worked with and he had always met her alone. In reality it had been for Rada that she had agreed to go to the Zwann Inn and she had reported to him the following day on what she had read when she opened Bayer's briefcase.

Rada would have been astounded if he had lived to find out that the four British operatives who came in to help him bomb the Boomgaard were in liaison with the very SS officer she had spied upon that night.

She remembered the last day she had met Rada in the Groningen park and talked about the Zwann Inn. He had worn a straw hat tilted in a jaunty style and his light eyes had held her in a serious gaze as she told him, 'Commissioner Schmidt has a friend arriving by boat from recuperation in Denmark after having been wounded on the Russian front. He is a colonel in the SS and Schmidt wondered if I would go to join him at the Zwann Inn on Thursday.'

'Join him? What does that mean?'

'Dine with him – companionship . . .'

Rada's wrinkled brow had puckered even more. 'Why would you do that?'

'Rada, Rada, the more we know the better. Schmidt told me he is here to go to the very meeting you are intending to bomb. He'll have papers – all sorts of papers – and I can open most locks.'

The Dutchman had shaken his head. 'No.'

'I do dangerous things. You do dangerous things.'

'But going to meet with him that way? He could take it for granted that you will stay.'

'Then I'll stay.'

'Oh, Laetitia, Holland does not expect you to do that for her. I forbid you to do this.'

She shrugged and patted his arm. 'Don't worry about me. I am not exactly virtuous. I'm like my mother.'

'Don't say that!' A flush of anger rose to his face. 'I don't want to hear it. Never sully your mother's memory, it's not worthy of you. Why do you say these things?'

Laetitia sighed. Rada had loved her mother, she had realised that, but it had not been mutual, though Laetitia had seen her mother's series of lovers. 'All right, Rada, I understand how you feel, but I'm going to the Zwann Inn anyway.'

And she had. And Rada was gone . . . the nearest thing she had to a father was gone. Her ample mouth tightened and her hand clenched on the wheel with emotion.

So now she had met *Standartenführer* Lucien Bayer, the most extraordinary German of all, with the ensuing consequences. A shiver ran through her as she remembered his kiss and the feel of his body and her hand left the wheel to drop briefly to her lap to touch his handkerchief.

When she had met the British agents with Rada the day prior to the failed bombing it was well-nigh unbelievable that the very next day her *standartenführer* would turn out to be their associate. She knew Dirk and his friends had never mentioned to Rada that they were working with a German double agent.

She was still recovering from the entire circumstance and she continued to analyse it as she drove along.

As her mind turned to Dirk she gave a sigh. He was the most physically beautiful man she had ever met. She dearly wanted to help the three of them escape anyway, especially since Rada had been killed; but she admitted that the thought of seeing Dirk again did not dampen her enthusiasm.

Yet the strange thing was that *Standartenführer* Bayer fascinated her too. Against her better feelings he had appealed to her the minute she had seen him at the door of the room in the inn, although she had not wanted to feel that way. The scars on his face and neck did not detract from his looks at all and with his dark blue eyes weighing her sceptically, she thought he had a most dashing adventurous appearance.

215

Ja, these two men were the two most attractive men she had seen for a long time, perhaps ever . . . She slowed as a torch waved in the darkness ahead and she pulled up beside a checkpoint.

'Papers.'

She handed them through the open window with a wide smile as the soldier shone the beam upon her face. 'Didn't you come through here earlier?'

'*Ja*, I went to the Castle Trentaneborg to visit my friends.'

'Of course.' He nodded in recollection. He knew that the SS were in residence there. He handed her back her papers. 'I hope you enjoyed your visit.'

'I did.'

He heiled Hitler and opened the barrier.

At the same time

Tudor leant on the still of the open window in the stone cottage by the canal in north-west Groningen. He listened to the harsh, chirping, almost jarring call of a nightjar and wondered momentarily where it might be as he breathed in the fresh breeze frolicking across the level lands from the North Sea.

He had been feeling restless and he found it soothing to abide here in the darkness while Mako tinkered and talked endlessly to Felix who did push-ups and calisthenic exercises on the floor in the living area.

The disappointment of missing the RAF pick-up to take them out of here was still raw and not knowing how long they would now have to remain in hiding was something which Tudor found difficult to accept. The woman, Laetitia, had repeatedly told them she would be able to organise it but that it would *take time*. They were completely in her hands.

That rankled with Tudor. He liked to be in charge and found it hard to accept a woman as the voice of authority in his life. This was not a true condescension in him as it was in many males of the era, it was more his belief that matters relating to fighting wars and taking part in covert missions were more suited to men. Had he made the RAF pick-up and been transported out of here, he would have been forever grateful to Laetitia de Witt and thought of her as briefly taking over the role which Rada was meant to play; but now that he had no one to turn to except her and must rely on her every decision as the only recourse for escape, he was almost bewildered.

She was sensually beautiful and that threatened him more, for she represented that which he would like to protect, an object of desire. He knew the others did not feel this way. While they thought her attractive, they also admired her for what she was doing to resist the Germans and they appeared comfortable with the situation of being in her hands.

He pictured this woman who was his only current link with freedom. She sure was something: something he wanted to conquer, to have and to hold. She had left this morning to go to Cole and inform him that he and the others were still here. She had said she would return in less than a week.

As the nightjar exclaimed again, the memory of last night when she had come to him, lingered in his mind. He had been here in this very spot, leaning on the sill and peering out at a three-quarter moon which gave a feeble illumination to the landscape of trees and flat fields beyond.

'I've brought you a cup of tea,' her liquid gold voice had sounded behind him and they had talked a long time. She told him she realised that he could divulge nothing of his life to her. 'Being who you are I know you can't tell me anything of yourself but I would like you to know a little about me. It might help you to be more comfortable with me.' He thought she had looked knowingly at him in the moody haze of night, as if she could read his mind. She began by telling him of her childhood in a farmhouse somewhere to the south near a little village outside Doetinchem, a town on the Ijssel river. She talked of her mother's numerous Shetland sheepdogs and how her mother's friends came and stayed for weekend house parties. She mentioned Rada's lifelong fascination for her mother and his devotion to her. After a time she mentioned people who came to stay with her mother. He did not know of most of them but apparently they were famous in Europe: an architect called Jacobus Oud and a German tennis player named Hans *somebody* and a couple of film stars, one who was known in Germany as 'the Little Dutch Cheese'.

'Quite a hostess then, your mother, eh?'

And Laetitia had answered, 'Oh yes, she craved reflected glory.'

She had moved nearer to him, close enough for him to smell the sweet scent she wore. Briefly he mused on where she would locate fragrances in occupied Holland with people having difficulty finding food. She had gone on talking about her family: 'My mother's half-brother was quite an entertainer too. Ran in the family . . . he has a home, Villa Thalberg, on Lake Geneva where I holidayed often. Theo van Doesburg and his wife came to stay there for a week with us when I was about seventeen; they brought Mondrian with them, you know, the painter. He taught me a lot . . . we painted every day on the foreshores of the lake. It's beautiful there at Villa Thalberg, my uncle calls it paradise . . . I like it in summer; in winter, not so much.'

Tudor put out his hand and touched her shoulder. 'So you paint?'

'*Ja.*' Her tone of voice altered, it became more intimate. 'Perhaps sometime I might do a portrait of you – if you would like me to . . .'

The moon had gone behind a cloud as he pulled her into his arms in the darkness and kissed her: the feel of her mouth warm and exciting and the taut firmness of her body arousing him. She had not resisted and had returned the embrace, but when his hands slipped down her back and took hold of her buttocks to allow him to press himself into her, she had pushed him away making a negative sound in her throat. Yet the sound was not truly reproachful, it was one which made future promises to him.

He could see her eyes in the night as she informed him, 'I have to leave in the morning but I'll be back next week.'

'How long will you stay here?'

'Long enough.'

So now he waited for her return: impatiently.

Tudor knew he was what Cole called 'a ladies' man'; he admitted that. Women did flock around him and he had known a lot of them in his time. He smiled in the darkness recalling how Cole used to eye him in that way he had of sizing up a man and say, 'You know what, Tudor? In that RAF uniform you're a real matinee idol.'

Sure Tudor was aware he was good-looking, but so was Cole, in a distinctive way that perhaps, strangely enough, he would have preferred to look like: dark-haired with lean features and that sardonic air Cole could muster – even the scars now enhanced his appeal somehow – rather than fair with regular features and urbane appearance, as he saw himself.

Tudor had all sorts of girls who were wild about him. Yet there was one girl Tudor could not forget: Jane Morley, his land girl in Suffolk. Just imagining her made him long to hold the softness of her once more in his arms and he exhaled noisily, shaking his head and dreaming of yesterday. She was originally from Surrey and he had met her only a couple of months prior to joining SOE. He had seen a lot of her; but when he and Cole decided for certain that they would enrol in SOE, he told her he was being transferred away and it would be no use to go on with the association. Jane's big round eyes had brimmed with tears and she had shaken her head and said, 'But I'll wait for you.'

Tudor had negated that.

'But why can't we still be friends?'

He had almost faltered at that moment and agreed, but then he thought about what he had consented to do. 'Because this war is taking me away and it's better like this. I can't have any ties. I'm off somewhere dangerous; you'd better forget me.'

And he had gone back to the mess at Wattisham Airbase and proceeded to get drunk. He recalled the night. It was late one Saturday and he had sat holding a beer opposite Wing Commander Cole Wareing at whom he pointed his free index finger. Tudor had himself been raised in rank to Wing Commander only two weeks prior, but because he was leaving the RAF to join SOE, ostensibly both he and Cole were being transferred to overseas commands.

'Well, Cole, I broke off seeing Jane earlier tonight.'

Cole nodded. 'Is that why you've had a few too many?'

'Yep. Really stuck on that girl, have never felt this way before. She's just . . . beautiful.' He hiccuped. 'Goddam war, ruins so much in everybody's life.' He lifted bleary eyes to his friend. 'But now we're changing course, you and me, that is . . . they've told us it's better not to have liaisons of any kind, eh?'

'That's right.'

'Besides, I have to remember there are plenty more fish in the sea.' He hiccuped again and raised his forefinger. 'That's always been my philosophy, you know. Best not change it now.'

Cole had laughed at that. 'You're incorrigible, Tudor, my friend, you really are.' He finished his beer and stared into the distance. 'I've said virtually the same to a girl or two myself; one in particular, out in Australia. Wrote to her recently and told her she might not hear from me for a long while . . . suggested she shouldn't wait for me . . . not fair to ask a girl to wait when you can be killed any old time.'

Tudor had never heard Cole talk about women before and he blinked and refocused his eyes upon his friend as he asked, 'Are you in love with her?'

Cole paused a long time and made a steeple of his fingers, eyeing it thoughtfully before he responded, 'Look, *Wing Commander*, love is something I'm not certain about, but one thing I definitely know, thinking of her has the effect of tying me in knots and it would be heaven to hold her close right now.'

'That sure sounds like you're well on the way there, sir.'

'Mmm, well, you are too, by what you say about Jane, and the state you're currently in.'

They had both made themselves laugh at that and Cole had leant forward and added, 'But you've done right tonight, Tudor; with the work we're going to do, it's desirable not to have romantic entanglements of any kind.'

Bringing himself back to the present Tudor nodded in the gentle night air of Groningen province. Yeah, Cole was right about that, but he would always remember Jane Morley: always. Even his philandering heart had believed it might have stayed true to her . . .

The grating declaration of the nightjar interrupted the stillness again as he remonstrated with himself – he had to remember there were plenty more fish in the sea. And Laetitia de Witt was one of them and a beautiful, voluptuous one at that. Yeah, she was one swell-looking dame and he sure looked forward to her return.

Odd how both he and Cole were reliant on Laetitia de Witt; he needed her to make his escape and Cole had to trust her to remain silent.

He took a deep inhalation of the quickening breeze. This was no joy-ride he was on, but then this was his choice – to join SOE and take these risks and there was no one he could blame for being here in enemy-held Holland but himself. At least he had the hope to cling to that Laetitia would come through and get him out of here; it was his good buddy, poor old Cole, who was in for the long haul.

Chapter Thirty-six

Cole stood looking over the head of Rauter's second in charge, the stocky five-foot-four-inch high SS *Gruppenführer* Dr Wilhelm Harster; beyond them stood a few of Harster's staff, and in the rear, Fritz Schmidt tapped his toes impatiently in the dirt of the railway station inside the barbed-wire enclosure of Kamp Westerbork.

Cole had accompanied Rauter and his staff from Groningen to the town of Assen where Rauter's ugly police work had continued. He was bringing in harsher measures in the district to increase farmers' quotas for feeding the German army. Even the highest civil German authority in Holland was on hand – High Commissioner Arthur Seyss-Inquart. The tall Seyss-Inquart had surveyed Cole through his thick milk-bottle glasses which magnified his eyes in a weird alien-style look. The civil head of German-occupied Holland appeared to warm to Cole; perhaps because he, too, walked with a distinct limp. He had smiled meaningfully as the SS *Politzeiführer* Hanns Albin Rauter explained who Lucien Bayer was.

Seyss-Inquart and Rauter stood side by side as Seyss-Inquart

223

shook Cole's hand. '*Gut* to have you here with us, *standartenführer*. Holland has benefits not found on the Russian front.'

Cole had forced a smile, he was getting good at smiling at people he detested; but there were no smiles on this dank morning while they waited within the confines of the Jewish transit camp near the small village of Westerbork. The summer temperatures of the previous day had disappeared, even the sky was grieving, lowering with bleak, menacing grey clouds above, and despair, like a tangible thing, hovered on the rising wind.

Early this morning in the town of Assen, Rauter had explained to Cole that a 'batch of Jews', as he called them, were to be sent off to Germany including one who had incited some sort of uprising: a Dr Frank Cohen. The authorities were to witness his embarkation on the train for the German death camp of Auschwitz. The Germans had used the Westerbork camp inmates themselves, to extend the railway line the six miles from the village of Hooghalen to the north-east – right into the penal yard; for the convenience of loading the trains more easily and away from the view of ordinary Dutch citizens. This way the unfortunates were taken directly to the gas ovens of Auschwitz.

In all, over 103,000 Jewish men, women and children were to be sent from Westerbork to extermination in Germany. When *Politzeiführer* Rauter had suggested Cole accompany Harster and Schmidt to witness the deportation, he had spoken in a matter-of-fact tone. 'I can't go, so my commander of the security police, *Gruppenführer* Harster will be there. I think you should accompany him, Lucien.'

Cole had calmed himself and mildly protested. 'Ah, I have much to do tomorrow morning to get my papers in order for you for your meetings in the town hall, *polizeiführer*; I'm afraid I cannot go along.'

Rauter liked Bayer, but he little liked disagreement with his directives; he shook his head. 'Lucien, work on the papers this evening; as a conscientious SS officer, I wish you to attend. We'll meet afterwards and go down to the town hall together.'

Hence Cole stood now, smelling a foul odour – human smells mixed with something like the strong stench of mildew – emanating from the camp around him. It stung Cole's nostrils as he turned to see a group of people appear from the side of distant huts to be herded to the waiting train, the snorting blasts of steam echoing like ominous trumpets on the morning air.

'Exactly how many are there?' Schmidt asked, holding a handkerchief to his nose; and one of Harster's officers replied, 'A hundred and sixty-one adults, twenty-four children.'

Those who were weak stumbled as the soldiers, a number leading Alsatian dogs, drove them across to the train. Perhaps half carried possessions in their arms, six or so carried small children and one, a baby.

On his earlier operations into France and now in his brief stay so far in Holland, Cole had heard of these slave camps, and of the extermination camps in Germany and Poland. It was hard to believe that such places existed, and very few people in Great Britain or the rest of the world had any conception of what was happening here right in front of him.

Cole steeled himself as the elderly, the middle-aged, the young and the children all alike, all with the yellow star of David with the word *Jood* marked on their clothes, moved towards him. Those who protested were clouted with rifle butts and one man who touched a guard as he bent to pick up his fallen bundle was battered across the side of his head. There was a crunch as he fell to the ground bleeding but those nearest him managed to help him to his feet.

As they came closer and the first few began to pass by, Cole did not make eye contact with any of them. The guards began to push and harass them into what had been three cattle transport carriages; there were no windows, only one sliding door.

'Which one is Cohen?' sounded Harster's voice.

One of his staff pointed out a man of medium height with glasses, though he walked tall, his expression defiant as the guards urged him along. He looked stronger than the rest, many of whom appeared frail; he had only been caught a week previously. It was as he was some thirty yards from Cole's group that Cohen moved like lightning – he tripped the nearest guard with his left leg and brought his arm down in a rabbit-killer punch on the man's neck as he stumbled. The next second Cohen had torn the rifle from his hands and, as he managed to get a shot off at Cole's party, two of the nearest guards fired at him in unison and a third fired a moment later. The prisoners screamed and fell away from Cohen as a young girl was hit by a stray bullet and Cohen's rifle went off loudly as he pitched forwards into the dirt: he was dead before he hit the ground.

In the disarray, loud wails lifted from the Jews as the other guards leapt into action, indiscriminately butting the prisoners with their rifles as they forced them towards the carriages. Harster began screaming, livid with rage that a *Jew* had dared to rise against them. The veins in his neck bulged and his face turned scarlet. His arms flayed the air. 'Get them in!' he screamed. 'Get them in.'

Cole braced himself, showing no emotion. *Well done, Cohen, well done. At least you tried and died like the hero you obviously were.*

The wounded Jewish girl was dragged up and thrown in through an open carriage door. Cole looked away. Within another minute, they were all herded – like the animals which had ridden in these transports before them – into the daunting dark interiors and the doors slammed closed on their pale, appalled faces.

In the last second as the door in front of him slid to a close, Cole forced himself to lift his gaze. There, looking out at him, was a little boy held in the arms of his weeping mother. He was about six years old, his face aged and grey with terror as his mouth twisted in shock and his eyes widened in disbelief. The door clanged shut and the little face was gone, replaced by screams and yells rending the morning air as they battered on the inside of the door.

Cole had fought in dogfights and seen aircraft plunge to the earth in flames; he had flown bombers and dropped explosives on enemy targets; that was war – enemy to enemy; this was obscene, base and mindless against defenceless human beings.

He knew that in his nightmares for all eternity he would see that small boy's face and hear the cries and the hammering on the interior of the carriage. *The child should be playing in a field; laughing and carefree.* Swallowing hard to keep down the bile which had risen in his throat, he turned away as the steam train jerked forward, taking its human cargo inexorably onwards to all forms of unspeakable horrors.

Beside him the runtish figure of Wilhelm Harster spun away in annoyance, his gross face scowling. He spoke in a clipped, dismissive manner, his voice rasping like a saw scraping on metal. 'Let's go. This is over.'

What indoctrinated lunatic world are you from?

'They are enemies of the Reich,' Harster repeated like a mantra, as they strode back across the dirt to the two waiting Mercedes-Benzes. 'They are enemies of the Reich.'

'*Jawohl,*' confirmed Schmidt.

No! Cole yelled in his head. *They are helpless men and women and children you are murdering, you evil bastards.* He hoped like hell he had not turned pale.

As they reached their car, Harster paused. 'You are very quiet, *standartenführer*.' His tone was confidential now, as if he were speaking to a friend. 'No wonder; it was a shock to all of us that such a thing could happen. It was luck that the bullet went wide.'

Cole strained to sound conversational; he was unsure if he succeeded. 'I've had a headache ever since I rose this morning, for some reason.'

'This would give anyone a headache.' Harster made a clucking sound of irritation.

As they climbed into the car, Cole was the only one who glanced back, to see three guards carrying Cohen's corpse away.

They were soon through the gate and on the ride back into Assen; the *gruppenführer*, in sympathetic tone, listed to him various remedies for headache.

They arrived at the town hall by 0930 as the sky at last began to weep. Harster looked at his watch, speaking with frustration as if he were dealing with another chore. 'It's raining and I must go to see the execution of two criminals who have been caught in subversive activity.'

Cole mentally shook his head again at the way the Germans always used the word 'criminals' for brave men and women of the Resistance.

His headache became the excuse he did not eat lunch that day and by 1600 they were travelling south towards the town of Apeldoorn. Just before they left Assen they heard the drone of aircraft in the sky and all looked up towards the sound. The cloud was thick above them but Cole thought he recognised the hum of a squadron of Lancaster Bombers on high heading towards Germany.

228

It was the single benign moment in his day as Rauter and Harster, assuming the same as Cole had, looked up and swore at them.

The fleet of limousines carrying the Nazi leaders made slow progress; it was over seventy miles to their destination and it rained on and off throughout the journey. They halted numerous times at checkpoints and twice for refreshment and Rauter's temper got worse with each half-hour. Cole spent much of the journey with his head back and his eyes closed, trying to forget what he had seen in the camp that was simply a gateway to death and, instead, imagining the eyes of Laetitia de Witt.

Schmidt, who sat in front next to the driver, intermittently attempted conversation with him about their previous association, but Cole answered briefly and pleaded his headache as reason to forgo talking. Nevertheless, Schmidt insisted and by the time they were settling in after their second stop, Rauter, who sat beside Cole in the back, tapped him on the shoulder. 'Commissioner Schmidt, *Standartenführer* Bayer and I would like to get some sleep, we're all off to Paris on Saturday and we'll have no rest there, so let's get some now.'

Schmidt answered in restrained tones. 'I was only trying to make the journey go faster, *polizeiführer*.'

'Well, don't.'

Schmidt was obviously irked and he spun to the front and did not speak again until they reached their journey's end. This suited Cole and he leant back in the corner of his seat and tried to sleep.

He knew of the impending trip into France to meetings and to a military base, and he had records to get ready for Rauter.

It was after 2200 hours when they reached the magnificent Het Loo Palace which had been the Dutch Queen Wilhelmina's favourite residence prior to fleeing from the Nazis to England and safety.

The German high command and their staffs had seized it and resided in it when in the district. Rauter went straight to bed. Cole was delighted; he had dined every night with him at the police leader's insistence. The massive Nazi liked to talk about the war with Russia and every time Rauter brought up the subject, Cole mentally thanked his Swedish expert who had instilled into him minute details of the SS divisions on the Russian front.

Cole used the excuse of his headache again to follow suit with the *polizeiführer* and retire to his room, and finally, as the long evening faded, he lay in bed and thought of Cohen and his thwarted attempt to take a Nazi along with him. For the first time in many years he looked into the night and offered up what resembled a prayer. He spoke not to a Christian God, he had ceased to believe in one, but he hoped he had the attention of what might be an ultimate universal power.

If you're listening, make them all suffer never-ending pain . . . as they have made the innocent suffer . . . and give Cohen a nice life on a decent faraway planet.

Chapter Thirty-seven

Friday morning: Apeldoorn, Holland

Laetitia and Cole sat at a bench-like wooden table near the front window of the café. She wore a pale summer dress and a pearl necklace. Her hair was pulled back and he could not help but notice how the morning light sat lovingly on her face and neck. He had resolved, at the last moment, to meet her when he had left the *polizeiführer*'s presence ten minutes previously. So, departing the town branch of the SS offices, he had walked the short distance to the café to find her waiting.

He had decided that he would agree to a fake close liaison with her for he needed to know when Tudor and the others left the country and he wanted to use them as couriers if he had any information to send Hans Buckhout. He had convinced himself this was all for the best and now, as he sipped his ersatz coffee, he spoke quietly. 'I need somewhere to look closely at my wireless set.'

'Why?'

'I have only had the opportunity to try to use it once and there is something amiss.'

She glanced down to the table and back up to him, lifting one finger in a graceful movement to rest near the tiny dark spot at the side of her mouth. 'You can come to my house and look at it there, away from the eyes of your SS companions.'

He had thought of this, of course. 'Perhaps. Though I won't try to contact London from your home. I am better off somewhere in the wilds of the Veluwe where I can feed out my antenna away from roads and the possibility of passing people.'

She smiled. '*Ja*, of course. I don't have a wireless. Any kind of radio is forbidden now. That rule has been vigorously enforced since there was a strike here in April and May; it went right throughout Holland.' She made a melancholy sound.

'Yes, I know all about it; it started when Christiansen issued the announcement that all Dutch former soldiers must report for re-internment in Germany.'

'That's right.' A frown appeared between her dark, appealing eyes. 'After the strike was put down, Rauter ordered the confiscation of civilian radios and instigated stiffer and stiffer penalties for those found harbouring any sort of wireless. Nowadays, people are terrified to keep one, though of course there are those who dare and who listen to the BBC and live in great danger for doing so.'

'Do you know Rauter?'

She met his gaze. 'I have met him a few times with Fritz.' She made a grimace of distaste. 'He's big and ugly.'

'I agree.'

'He asked me out once, but I politely refused. I will do a lot of things,' she met his look with a self-conscious gaze from under her eyelashes, 'but I refuse to do them with Rauter, he's horrible.'

He realised he did not want to think about *the things she did* and he abruptly pushed his chair back from the table. 'I shall pay. I must get back now.'

As he stood she asked softly, 'When will you come to my house?'

He hesitated for just a moment, looking down at her, before she stood and he answered, 'We leave by train tomorrow evening for France. I have found out this morning that General Christiansen is coming along and we go on to Germany. I think I'll be away a week but it could be more.'

Together they exited the café, passing under a large poster on the stone wall near the door. It depicted an effete youth in a suit smoking a cigarette and, in front of him, a physically powerful, virile-looking man in the uniform of the Netherlands Legion – an army of Dutchmen who were German collaborators. The caption read: *Who is the true Dutchman?* proposing that true Dutchmen united with the Germans. Posters like this were all over the occupied cities of Europe. Some were defaced, but this one was new and, so far, pristine.

Cole had not mentioned to Laetitia about what he had witnessed at Westerbork prison transit camp forty-eight hours ago but it had made him quiet and introspective. He did not wish to speak of it and be reminded. She had noticed his mood shortly after he sat down and inquired about it, but he had deflected the query by saying he had much to think about, which, of course, she accepted.

Outside the café they walked side by side beneath the vine-covered trellis where the blossoms hung in profusion and a sweet, cloying fragrance trailed in the air. Avoiding a host of workers on bicycles they continued on towards the Raadhuisplein – the town hall square – while behind, on the cross-street, they could feel the vibration of German tanks trundling along.

The sun had gone behind a cloud but in a burst of summer warmth, it appeared to endow them with shadows as they halted near the stone bust of King Willem the First on its pillar, draped in a Nazi flag. At the other end of the compact square, perhaps a hundred yards away, huge swastika banners hung from the front of the red brick town hall. As they paused, two German staff cars swung round the corner and parked in front of the building as uniformed officers of the occupying forces clambered out and hurried up the stone steps past the sentries. The square was empty except for sentries outside the town hall and an old man who sat on a doorstep thirty yards away. The sun felt good on Cole's back as he stood close to Laetitia and briefly touched her arm. 'When will you see the men you have in hiding again?'

'I am not certain, perhaps while you are in France.'

'If you see them, tell them I might have some intelligence for them to take back to England when they go. I'd like them to be couriers for me.'

She smiled up at him. '*Ach ja, gute Idee.* My compatriot organising the escape has a plan he thinks is possible to put in place. These things take time, so it will be perhaps two to three weeks.'

'You are sure of this man? After what happened in Groningen?'

'He had nothing to do with Groningen; although I met him first through Rada. His son has an extra vessel hidden away from his boatyard. It is stolen but it has a motor and will get your friends back to England. I'm guessing the cost will be around one thousand guilders. Dirk tells me he has that much.'

Cole took a deep breath. Tudor was completely in her hands and the hands of some mysterious *compatriot* of hers. A thousand guilders – well, it would be cheap if they got back safely. He stared down at her as he asked, 'And how much of that do you get?'

A flash of affront sparked in her eyes. 'Why do you insult me? None of it. We have to pay for the boat and for the fuel.'

'But you said the boat was stolen.'

She nodded. '*Ja*, but the risk, it is the risk which is costly.'

'All right.' He could do nothing but agree; they were all in danger all the time so it was understandable some of them demanded payment. 'Tell my . . . associates that I think of them and am envious that they'll soon be on the way to freedom.'

She was thinking of the one called Dirk: his electric-blue eyes under his light hair and the way his body moved, lithe and muscular, imbued with life and virility. When he laughed she had laughed, it was somehow contagious and his personality was big and bold like himself. She answered in an undertone, '*Ja*, I will.'

Cole's hand tightened on her arm. He urged her forward and they began to walk across to the town hall. As they moved he slipped his hand from her arm to the middle of her back, speaking again in a low voice. 'If I don't come to you next Friday, I'm not back. I think we need to set up a regular visit together if we're to . . . keep up this pretence.'

'*Ja*, of course, I agree.' She leant in towards him, looking up at him. 'When we are alone, I can help you to perfect your Dutch and you can help me to perfect my German.'

'*Vielleicht* . . . perhaps. Your German is already *gut*.'

They reached the town hall where the German sentry who had watched them heiled Hitler as they paused in front of the steps.

Cole's voice remained low. 'Rauter says we'll be working here in the offices in Apeldoorn for the next month. After that I think we go to the Hague.'

'I shall hope to see you Friday, then . . . what time?'

'Perhaps by three in the afternoon.' He leant in towards her and took her hand. She clung to it as he looked down into her eyes and she smiled gently before he limped away up the stone steps.

As he moved inside the first person he saw was Fritz Schmidt. 'Ah, *standartenführer* . . .' he came over, 'there you are. How about coming with me to lunch? The Dutch cook here makes such a good *hasenpfeffer*.'

This was German rabbit stew. Cole had been avoiding conversation with Schmidt, he hoped the man did not realise it.

'Ah, rabbit stew, I like that.'

Schmidt nodded. 'I know, I remember, that's why I'm telling you.'

God, Cole, be careful, you didn't know that. You could have said you didn't like it. 'Fritz, it would be my pleasure to join you but I can't, I feel obliged to work at understanding my position here and what's needed from me before we leave tomorrow evening for Paris.'

Schmidt gave him a sceptical look. 'Oh, do you? Yet I see you had time to meet our mutual friend, Miss de Witt.'

Cole ignored the look and grinned. '*Ja*, true. So that makes it even more important for me to do some work today.'

Schmidt was not to be put off. 'Perhaps, then, we will get together on the overnight train?' His tone became oddly urgent which only succeeded in confusing Cole. 'Surely you'll find some time for me on our way to Paris? After all, we haven't talked since you arrived.' He was obviously disappointed.

Cole nodded and answered in friendly fashion. '*Ja*, of course, I'll look forward to it.'

As he limped on down the corridor he was aware of Schmidt's gaze on his back. 'Enjoy the stew,' he threw over his shoulder.

236

Chapter Thirty-eight

The next day: 26 June 1943

The train trundled on through Belgium towards France as the stars glinted like diamond specks in ebony and the moon rode smears of drifting cloud in the silky sky. It was the first fair night since Cole had been in Europe.

He moved through the last carriage past the boxes of munitions, slid the door open and stepped out on to the small platform at the back. It was narrow – perhaps only a few feet deep but enough for him to stand holding the iron rail and take in large gulps of air. After having been all day in the company of Rauter and Harster and their staff plus Schmidt, Christiansen and Hans Fischboeck – their Nazi Commissioner General for Finance and Economy – he needed to get away from them, to be alone. He had to clear his mind after hours of being involved with the decisions that were being made on how to instil terror into the populace and rape the Dutch workforce and the economy, all for the betterment of the Fatherland. He must become used to it, he had no options, but it was a strain, even for a man like Cole, whose self-belief was virtually unassailable. He was convinced that as time passed he would become immune to it.

Fortunately, already he had established certain peculiarities of character with his associates: one being his proclivity for privacy, which those around him were already accepting. And when the conversation turned to the Jews he went into a sort of 'other state' where he did not listen to the offensive indoctrination and simply nodded to himself as if in agreement. It seemed to be working.

The sights he had seen at the camp in Westerbork would not leave him and now as he stood here he relived in his mind Cohen's attempt to fight back. *On the one hand it was pathetic, Cohen . . . and yet at the same time you were majestic . . . in that grotesque arena for those moments you frightened the hell out of them.*

He grunted to himself as he listened to the rhythm of the wheels clacking on the metal lines and, as time passed, the gentle swinging of the carriage through the darkness had a calming effect on him. He stood watching the night for perhaps ten more minutes while the train slowed down to pass through a station and then gained in momentum for the overnight, eight-hour journey. As he stood breathing in the night air his mind turned to thoughts of *her*: Laetitia de Witt.

He was still unsure of what to make of her. He had rarely seen such a woman, all gentle curves and winsome smiles and dark enigmatic looks from under long eyelashes. He recalled the tiny dusky beauty spot just to the side of her mouth – her sensuous mouth with the perfectly formed teeth. He shook his head in the night, cleared his throat and in conjunction cleared his mind of Laetitia de Witt and took another deep breath.

Rauter had told him that he had been brought along to watch Commissioner Fritz Schmidt. The *polizeiführer* had already given Cole some vague clues as to what he wished to accomplish. There was a political rivalry going on in Holland between the Schutz

Staffel, the SS, and the NSDAP – the National Socialist German Workers' Party, run by Schmidt; and Rauter wanted evidence of some kind against the commissioner. Though what the devil that was, Cole was unsure. It was clear to Cole that Rauter, as the head of the SS in Holland, had little or no time for Schmidt or his superior, Martin Bormann, at Hitler's headquarters.

The Austrian general's heavy face had worn a scowl when he referred to Schmidt. 'I do not like the way he does things. He does not represent *our* interests – that is, the interests of the SS; he is greedy and thinks only of power for himself and his civil authority. He has seen a lot of High Commissioner Seyss-Inquart lately and I think it would be better for us if some time in the future we could replace Schmidt with someone more pliable. So, Lucien, see what you can learn. See if he will speak about his relations with Seyss-Inquart.'

It was not a duty which Cole cherished as he had been avoiding Schmidt all he could, but this evening aboard the train he had noticed the man was drinking heavily and he had decided that over dinner he should face up to sitting with him and would ask him a barrage of questions and hope that Schmidt did not ask too many in return.

He took another deep breath of air. He must soon return inside to the first carriage where the fitted tables would be laid for the meal and he would seek out his dinner companion.

He looked up into the night sky. *It's a good night to bomb Germany. I hope my old squadron is doing just that.*

He recalled the excitement of flying and coming back to the mess and the camaraderie with other flyers; but there was no doubt that this secret and sham life of masquerade, with its double edge of constant danger, suited him. The risk and the ever-present menace sent adrenalin pumping through his veins. He thrived on fooling the Germans; it had become a perilous stimulating game to him with immense and terrifying consequences. His original incentive to become a secret agent was to see Britain and her allies win the war, to defeat these iniquitous ideologues who were mercilessly jackbooting their way through Europe.

And after the Cohen incident, how dearly he wanted to see them annihilated. But something had happened to him along the way. This was his third operation and the feeling of triumph at hood-winking the enemy, of successfully completing what was nigh impossible, had intensified. He tried to analyse himself here in the pleasant night air as it sped by him and he tilted his head to look up at the galaxy and contemplate the iniquity which was Hitler's rule of Europe.

The train was accelerating. The carriage gave a sudden sharp swing and he braced himself against the railing as he heard a scraping noise and looked around. A man issued from the carriage behind him and on to the small platform. It was Schmidt.

'I thought this was where you might be.' He took out a cigarette and offered one to Cole.

Cole shook his head in the darkness. '*Nein, vielen danke*. Shouldn't we go back in to dine?'

Schmidt shook his head. 'We've plenty of time.' His words ran together and the seedy smell of alcohol wafted in the air as he lit a cigarette in his cupped hand and turned to Cole. 'Why are you avoiding me?'

'I'm not.'

'It seems to me that you are, especially as we used to be so close.'
Oh hell . . . more I don't know.

'Lucien?' The man stepped a pace closer and now the strong

240

fumes of liquor were directed straight at Cole. 'I have been looking forward to being with you again.'

Cole could see the Westphalian's eyes glinting in the moonlight. 'Have you forgotten the days we spent in the spring of '37? At Bingen canoeing on the Rhine? That was something, eh? Who was that fellow we met? The one who smoked the pipe?'

Cole's voice was calm, controlled. He gave a short shrug of his shoulders. 'Those days are gone, Fritz. Never to return. We should simply remember them with affection and leave it at that. That was years ago. I am different now, you are different.'

'No, I am *not* different . . . but *ja*, you are. You've altered. We used to talk for hours.' His words ran together. 'Perhaps it's your wounds that have changed you.' He gave a high-pitched wheeze. 'The Russian front – was it there you altered?'

Cole gave a sarcastic snigger. 'Almost having my brains blown out might have done it.'

The train was picking up speed now and it swayed as the German stumbled sideways before steadying himself and in the ambient light from the moon and stars he looked up to the top of Cole's head. 'You are very different! Why, you're even taller than I recall . . . *ja*, you are.'

'What? Don't be silly, no one grows at my age.'

'That's what I thought.' Schmidt continued holding the railing and staggering a little as he took small steps back and forth, stabilising himself. His words were really slurring now. 'Lucien – how – did you receive your wounds? Tell me about it.'

'Shrapnel and a bullet, that's how.'

'See . . . you never elaborate these days – and once you were so voluble. You're almost withdrawn and certainly quiet. I did not expect – to see you again, but when I found out you were coming here I looked forward to it . . . but you've spent every night with Rauter.' He staggered again. 'Rauter does not like me.' Puffing out more smoke, his voice became strained, nervous. 'No, the *polizeiführer* and the SS do not like me . . .' He returned to his original subject as his words ran together. 'I know it was six years ago, but you and I were close – you can't deny that. Why do you seem to forget? To be changed?' He put his near hand out and covered Cole's with his own.

Oh, bugger.

Into Cole's mind flashed Hans Buckhout's words: '*Schmidt, apparently, is ambitious and intelligent but unbalanced. Acts very oddly at times without apparent reason.*'

Cole removed his hand and took a sidestep away from his companion of the night before he turned square on to him presenting an equable, relaxed exterior. 'Fritz, we'll stay friends but we have our mission here in Holland. We must remember always that we are here to enforce the rule of the Third Reich. I am very conscious of that.'

'What?' The German's voice rose and his tone became quarrelsome. 'Do you think I'm not conscious of it? Why do you say that to me? I work hard every day for the Führer . . . I have the stinking Jews to contend with, always trouble . . .' He broke off and hit the railing with his fist. 'Damn them all. I have given many speeches – and – I asked them politely to register properly for deportation to the Fatherland, but no! They don't. They make trouble, always trouble. The Führer specifies that Jews must be removed . . . removed!'

He leant forward and the odour of his breath carried again to his companion as he rambled on. 'We have all the civil records; the Dutch state has excellent details on all Dutch nationals.

When we took over, it was easy to assess who was Jewish. But they create trouble, they do not . . . do as requested; they disappear, they try to hide. We must rid the earth of them – they are vermin.' His words were badly slurring now and he hit the railing again with his fist. 'Filthy, vile Jews . . . why don't they come quietly to the assembly points?' Continuing his slurring, stammering diatribe, he flicked his cigarette out into the night in disgust. 'Like yesterday, when that Jewish scum dared to – dared to . . .'

Cole's voice burst from him like a gunshot. 'Who dared to what? To not go quietly to extermination? Tell me, why should they *come quietly*? When you bastards are trapping them, maiming them, torturing them and starving them first – before you murder them. Would you come quietly, you stinking bastard?' Even as he was saying it, he knew he should stop. Change his words, alter the meaning, make a joke even, but he did not. He completed his statement clearly and explicitly. 'You're the filthy vermin who should be wiped from the face of the earth, not the Jews.'

Schmidt spun drunkenly round to him in horror and amazement, his voice rising in high-pitched rage, a gleam of perspiration on his forehead. '*Gott im himmel!* Who are you?'

The train was travelling fast now and the wind was picking up and at that moment the carriage lurched and the Westphalian toppled towards Cole. Cole moved back to balance himself and his cane slipped to the floor as Schmidt's arms went round him and his hot alcoholic breath covered the side of Cole's cheek.

Cole elbowed him firmly away but the German's fingers were on his revolver.

'You're not Lucien Bayer!' He tried in his drunken state to take the pistol from its holder on his belt but Cole stepped in immediately and punched him hard in the solar plexus, following up with an open-hand chop to the jaw.

Schmidt grunted in pain as he doubled up and stumbled backwards just as the carriage swung savagely again. His hands flailed the air to grab the railing, but they clutched nothing. Bent over, he staggered, called out, overbalanced and dropped out of sight.

The black shape of Fritz Schmidt slid straight through an opening in the railing and disappeared head first into the night to be lost down an embankment. All Cole heard was a strangled screeching sound issuing from the darkness.

Jesus.

He stood there clutching the railing and looking down into the inky darkness as he took large draughts of air into his lungs to steady his pulse. A minute later he picked up his cane and limped inside. He passed through the munitions van and along a corridor to the lavatory without meeting anybody. Inside the cubicle he took long, deep breaths again and washed his face.

Hopefully the bastard is dead. He'll be pretty badly damaged, in any event. If he lives, I'll decide what to do. I'll take that prospect as it comes.

But one thing played loudly in his head. He knew he could never afford to lose control again. He had been Bayer a mere week, and he had allowed himself to openly reveal his contempt to Schmidt. Was he losing his touch? He had virtually only just arrived – there were bloody endless months of this ahead. *Peace, Cole, calm . . . peace.* The minutes passed and, when he felt settled, he exited the lavatory and continued on to the first carriage where Rauter saw him appear and beckoned with his big hand over the heads of his grey-garbed companions. 'Here, *standartenführer*, we are just having a glass of French Bordeaux, *sehr gut!*'

'I will eat with Commissioner General Schmidt tonight,' Cole said meaningfully as he joined the group and the huge man winked at him.

'*Ja*, of course, you should.' As the *politzeiführer* grinned he appeared like a massive bear pulling back its gums. 'Schmidt was telling me earlier in the day – a mite jealously, I thought –' this sentiment amused Rauter and he grinned again – 'that you have become a friend of Miss de Witt quite quickly.'

'Ah, *ja, obergruppenführer*, that's true.'

'*Gut*, she is well liked; a trusted one of ours and what a beauty, eh? Many of us have been interested in her but to no avail, so, *viel Glück*.'

Time passed and Cole sat alone until Rauter called out, 'Come and join me. Schmidt took a lot of gin earlier, perhaps he is resting somewhere.'

Dinner was four courses cooked by a French chef and no one thought of Schmidt again until 2300 when questions were asked about his whereabouts, but nobody had any idea where he was.

Large amounts of alcohol and wine had been consumed and Rauter leant over to Cole and whispered in his ear, 'I want to talk to you again tomorrow about Schmidt . . . and Wimmer. We'll go through a plan with Heklestein, one of my men – he's come up with it. It will give you access to their records.'

The rats spying on the rats . . . how convenient for me. 'Very good, General, what time?'

They had moved on to champagne, and Rauter emptied his glass. 'Nine hundred hours.'

'Certainly.'

At 0800 the following morning after some hold-ups on the line, they were in Paris and the talk at breakfast was all of the disappearance of Schmidt. Fischboeck turned in his seat to gaze at Cole across the carriage. 'At one point Fritz went searching for you, *standartenführer*. Did he find you?'

Cole looked him straight in the eye. 'No; I was to have dinner with him, but, of course, he never turned up.'

At 0900 Cole met Rauter and Heklestein and at 1000 they departed the train and travelled to a Waffen SS military base.

At 1500 hours they returned to the city. At 1530 hours Rauter, Harster and their staff and Cole, along with Christiansen, Fischboeck and two Paris-based SS generals and a host of lesser lights, sat under a tall mural-covered ceiling decorated with eighteenth-century fretwork in German headquarters at the Hotel Meurice. A knock on the door ushered in an aide who marched to the *polizeiführer*, clicked his heels, heiled Hitler, and handed over a piece of paper. The big man read it and looked around the faces of the men at the long walnut table. 'Commissioner General Schmidt* has been found. He appears to have fallen off the train. He is dead.'

The way Rauter glanced around those gathered and added the words, 'He was very drunk; I am not at all surprised,' Cole was aware with relief that Rauter would make sure there would be little or no investigation into the matter.

---

* Commissioner General Schmidt's death: see Author's End Notes, page 530

Chapter Thirty-nine

Friday, 9 July

Laetitia de Witt glanced through her wide front window and saw the black staff car enter her gate and drive up past the oak trees to her house, a compact construction adorned with gabled windows in the roof and a blue front door. She stood painting at an easel in her lounge room where the light flowed through the wide front window to fall upon her work. It was a pastime she had been devoted to since girlhood, and before the war, a small gallery in Paris had sold a number of her works. She put down her brush as her pulse quickened and the motorcycle soldiers ahead of the big vehicle came to halt at her front steps.

'So he has come,' she said to herself as she hurried to her front door to open it to his uniformed, imposing figure. She gestured for him to enter. 'I had believed you were not coming.'

Cole took off his cap and hung it on the hall stand as she beckoned him through to her sitting room.

He halted in surprise, gesturing to the canvas. 'You paint?'

'I have as long as I can remember. Though it's impossible to find oils so I'm reduced to using house paint and I severely lack colours.'

He made no more comment as he limped to the window and stood watching the staff car and the soldier escort leaving. They would return in an hour, he could afford no more time today; he had to be at the Police Academy back in Apeldoorn where Dutch police were 're-educated' with Nazi ideology.

But he would not think of that yet: ahead of him was the grassed open yard dotted with wild white narcissuses and on the right two sheds stood framed by beech trees. A broken-down fence in the distance formed the edge of the property where beyond lay a stream. Two black-and-white ducks waddled across his vision past the sheds and over towards the fence. The view appeared so normal and yet he was in German-occupied Holland, where nothing was normal.

He turned his head to her. She wore an apron dotted with paint stains to protect her grey dress. Her shining hair nestled on her shoulders, a flush of pink coloured her cheeks and her brown eyes welcomed him. Even in a dirty apron and dull-coloured attire she outshone most women he had ever seen. She was removing the apron to exhibit a neckline which dared to plunge just far enough to reveal the beginning of the smooth mounds of her breasts as she said, 'I have managed to find a few ounces of tea, would you like a cup?'

'*Ja*, I would.'

'When did you come back to Apeldoorn?'

'Last evening.' Rauter and Christiansen's party had returned via train from Germany the previous day. Cole did not mention that he had accompanied Christiansen to a series of airfields where he took note of the geographical position of all of them and photographed and recorded in detail the camouflaged huts and hangars. He would pass all this on to Hans Buckhout in due course.

Cole had been in the presence of various Nazi generals and leaders of the Luftwaffe, including Gunther Rall the Luftwaffe fighter Ace born in the Black Forest: in the short time they spoke over a beer in a Luftwaffe mess, he seemed to Cole a reasonable sort of man simply fighting for his country. Not so with Field Marshal Erhard Milch who entertained Christiansen's party to a lavish dinner. He had been a prime mover in founding the Luftwaffe and presented himself as a fanatical follower of Hitler, even though rumours abounded that Milch was half Jewish and his mother had been made to sign a document saying his Jewish father was not Milch's real parent. Cole noted that Hermann Goering, the original Luftwaffe leader, had recently fallen from grace with Hitler, so he was not present at any of the dinners or meetings.

'Make yourself at home.' Laetitia motioned with her hand and Cole walked back out into the hall and familiarised himself with the rest of the house.

He was in the storage room near the front door where three bare canvases rested against the wall when she called him and he came to the kitchen. They sat opposite each other at her table of washed wood where he told her that Fritz Schmidt had died the previous Saturday.

'Fell off the train on the way to Paris?' Her smooth brow puckered in amazement.

'Ja.'

'But how could that happen?'

'I have no idea.'

'Damn! He was a bastard for certain, and I'm glad he's gone; it somehow makes up for Rada, but he was my main supplier of perquisites.'

'I'm sure I can be of service to you on some of those matters.'

249

She stared at him for a few seconds realising the truth in this. 'Yes, *danke*, of course, I suppose you can. I know Rauter really disliked Schmidt . . . wouldn't be surprised if he had him pushed off the train. Schmidt told me all the SS here were against him and against Wimmer too.'

'Did he now?'

'*Ja*, there is some sort of power struggle between the civil administration and the SS. I thought you'd know.'

'I do, but I didn't know you did.'

She said nothing but the corners of her mouth turned up in a half-smile as she sipped her tea.

Suddenly he asked her something that bothered him. 'How did it come about that Schmidt supplied you to me that night at the inn?'

There was an edge to his voice and Laetitia answered defensively, 'He didn't supply me. I chose to come to your hotel.' She glanced at him in that manner she had of turning her head and looking up from under her eyelashes. 'You might not approve of me and I understand if you don't, but when Schmidt told me you were arriving I saw it as an opportunity. He said he knew you of old, you were his friend and that you were looking for a woman for company.' She looked steadily at him. 'I have skills and can find out things.'

'Mmm.' He was reminded of the way she had opened Bayer's suitcase at the Zwann Inn. 'Then perhaps the question should have been, how often did Schmidt supply you to others?'

Now she bristled openly as she put down her cup, clinking it in the saucer. 'It was the first time.'

He did not know whether to believe her or not. 'Then why did you spy on me?'

She sighed as she answered, 'It was for Rada. When Schmidt said that you were one of the SS going to the Boomgaard Hotel I knew you would be carrying papers of importance. As you are very aware, Rada hoped to blow you all apart and so . . .' She stopped talking and blinked as her index finger lifted. 'That's it, I see it now.' A knowing expression crossed her face. 'You were attacked on the road going into Groningen. It was by your friends, wasn't it? The British agents deliberately waylaid you to delay you so you would be late at the hotel and arrive after the bombing was over. Ah, *standartenführer*, *ja*, I'm right, aren't I?'

'I have no idea what you're talking about.'

She gave a soft laugh. 'It doesn't matter. I understand.'

'So you came to my room and you opened my briefcase the following morning when I was showering.'

An expression of astonishment rose in her face. 'How on earth did you know I opened your case?'

'As we're on the same side I'll tell you.'

When he explained about the hairs he had left between the pages, her eyes widened in wonder. 'Ah . . .' she made a throaty sound of appreciation, 'how clever.'

He wanted to ask her why she thought it acceptable to sleep with a Nazi just to gain access to his papers. He wanted to know why she allowed herself to be used in that manner and what real justification she could have. He admitted he hated the fact that she had so easily slept with him and all the while he gazed upon her smooth skin and watched the graceful way she moved and how her hair framed her face and her sultry eyes met his. He did not want to remember the feel of her body against his own.

A sigh escaped her lips again. '*Ja*, of course I came to your room, but I was not sure what I would do . . . whether I would stay or not.'

251

He gave a supercilious grunt. 'Oh really? Schmidt said you knew I expected you to sleep with me.'

Her dark eyes locked with his. 'Did he now? Well, that's what he thought, isn't it?'

He leant back in his chair, appraising her, the cup to his lips. 'And the fact is that you did stay.'

She paused and looked away for such a long time that he decided she was not going to comment yet, finally, she did. 'Mmm, I stayed.'

'Laetitia, it's not my business how you conduct yourself. But now that we are allied and I spend time like this here alone with you, I'm bound to ask you questions. I need to understand you a little.'

'Of course, and I would like to learn about you.'

He was not sure that was such a good idea and he stood. 'Can I see some of your paintings?'

She nodded and rose to follow him.

They returned to the front room where she kept a number of works stacked against the wall. He looked through them silently and took one of a woman in a forest scene and stood it on a credenza leaning against the wall. 'I'm not an aficionado, but I'd say your work is pretty good: interesting brush strokes.' They reminded him of the Australian artist Grace Cossington Smith. He kept that thought to himself for Laetitia de Witt was obviously intelligent and would certainly wonder how he knew the work of an Australian. She had assumed from the first moment she met him that he was German and he was not going to disabuse her of that belief.

Her smile grew wide. '*Danke* for the compliment. I'm having to be very careful with my canvases. In fact, I'm painting over certain pictures I don't like, to save the few spares I have.'

'I knew a Scot who did that, though it was because he was too poor to buy blank canvases.'

'What was his name?'

'I forget. It was before the war in Hamburg.' It had actually been an artist called Fairweather, a strange solitary man he had met once in Sandgate back home in Queensland in early 1939. He pointed to the painting he had placed against the wall. 'I think the want of colours makes this better; gives it a certain distinction. The woman is a more powerful figure painted in tones of brown than she would be if you had her in vivid colours. The muted quality brings a sort of compassion to her and enhances the entire picture.'

She walked over to stand beside him, her arms crossed in front of her and her hands holding her waist. 'You are different from the others, you know?'

He turned his head to her. 'What others?'

'The other Nazi officers and officials I know . . . you are somehow not quite like them.' A frown lodged between her perfectly arched eyebrows.

Tiny stings of alarm registered in Cole's spine and he scowled at her. 'What the devil does that mean?'

'Well, the way you speak of my painting; you use the word *compassion*. I just can't imagine Rauter or Schmidt or Harster or Seyss-Inquart talking this way . . . any of them. It's just that you surprise me.' She shook her head. 'Perhaps that's why you are the enigma you are . . . an SS officer who is an agent for the British.'

She was too damn close, he could smell the pleasing fragrance of her and he turned on his heel and limped away to the window. 'Don't be foolish,' he growled.

'I'm not being. That's probably the reason you are different. Being near you like this I see something in you which is not in them.'

'*Ja*, I've been wounded in the head, they haven't.'

She came up behind him; too close again. '*Standartenführer*, I am complimenting you.'

'Well, don't.'

She was looking at his profile: his straight nose and his firm jaw. She could see the scar on his temple and the one near his lips and another near his Adam's apple. She knew there was no use in asking him how he got them. He would not tell her. They were obviously wounds and they gave him such a gallant appearance.

Recalling the first night of meeting him she thought of how much he had aroused her and she had hated herself for feeling that way about him: a Nazi *standartenführer*. But now she knew he was brave beyond understanding and must have become completely disillusioned with Hitler, Himmler and the rest of them. Yes, he was unlike the other Germans and he fascinated her.

But then, so too did his fellow undercover agent, the calmly spoken golden-headed Dirk, who held her in his riveting gaze and whose hearty laughter brought reminiscences of happy days. The minute Rada had introduced Dirk to her, she had found herself drawn to him; wanting to be close to him and to help him.

As Laetitia de Witt stared at the man beside her she admitted that an immediate magnetism had occurred with these two men and it disconcerted her to acknowledge that she desired them both.

Cole was conscious of her body close to his, too conscious of it, and he moved away again and picked up his cane which rested near his chair. 'My escort will be back soon.'

Her soothing voice followed him. 'I think I see them coming in the gate.'

She walked with him into the hall by the staircase to the front door and before she put out her hand to open it, she turned back to him in the semi-darkness of the vestibule. 'You know, I think I shall not return to Amsterdam at all, but shall remain here indefinitely.' She paused and lifted her hand to his arm. 'Will I see you before next Friday? It seems too long to wait till then.'

She had put into words what he, too, was thinking. 'If I can come prior to Friday, I shall.'

She smiled at that and he asked, 'Is there anything firm about the others returning to England yet?'

'My contacts are trying hard to get everything planned. Nothing is simple and everything is a serious risk. But you know that. I hope to have some news next week.'

He stepped back from her and her hand slipped from his arm. As he limped down the steps, he pictured Shelly Longford with her vivacious green eyes and candid smile born of sunshine and open spaces, but he shook his head. She might as well be on another planet.

Chapter Forty

Friday, 16 July 1943

Shelly Longford dropped her hand from Captain Tom Madison's shoulder as the swing music of 'Tuxedo Junction' – made popular around the world by Glenn Miller's band – came to an end. Leaving the dance floor at the Ipswich Golf Club which sat not far from her home across the One Mile Creek on the western side of the town, they made their way back to their table and sat down.

Every Friday night a dance was held by the club members to raise money for the war effort and a number of American airmen from the Amberley air-force base nearby attended. Captain Madison was with the 431st Fighter Squadron of the 475th Fighter Group United States Army Air Corps – USAAC – and had been stationed in the small mining town of Charters Towers in North Queensland until two weeks previously, when they had been transferred with their P-38 Lightning aircraft to Amberley for maintenance. Since early 1942, numerous American squadrons had used the airfields of Australia and, in particular, Queensland, as their interim bases before moving north to fight the Japanese, and those here now, like Tom Madison's squadron, were to be the last of the American air

256

force units to utilise Amberley. Soon they would all have departed to forward airfields in the continuing war.

As the couple passed a porcelain jardinière full of gerberas – one of the few blooms that still grew in the Queensland winter – and sat down at their table, Tom looked admiringly at her. 'You look lovely tonight.'

'Thank you.'

Shelly's long hair was styled and worn up in curls. She was above average height and the emerald-coloured dress with the pale green collar sat enticingly around her slender figure and enhanced her eyes.

'You have such beautiful eyes.'

She smiled. 'Thank you again.'

'Now, what about a drink?'

'Yes, I'll have something, perhaps a gin and tonic. That is, if they have any gin. If they don't, just something soft like a lemonade will do.'

Captain Madison stood to go to the bar. He was an attractive man in his early thirties with straight black hair and a neat moustache. He had met Shelly and her mother at a fete the very day after his arrival here and he had shown an interest in Shelly immediately. Her mother had been impressed by him and it was partly because of her insistence that Shelly had been out with him twice before and now again, tonight.

As he moved to the bar her eyes followed him. He certainly cut a handsome figure in his uniform and she saw the heads of more than one woman in the room turn towards him. She sighed and looked down at her hands. She could not help it, her mind was on the man she loved, but he was far away in England in an RAF squadron, though she had no idea where he was now. The last time she had heard from him he had been stationed in Suffolk, but that had been the beginning of the previous year. Oh, she knew he was still alive, well, he had been a few months ago – for she remained in periodic contact with his mother who lived in the town of Warwick about sixty miles away.

It would be sensible to forget Cole but she could not. Her prayers were full of him: to keep him safe; to bring him back to her; imploring that he did not fall in love with some other girl. She became annoyed with herself at times for what she saw as weakness: the way she still carried a torch for him, but it did not extinguish her hopes and almost every day she recalled the last night she had spent with Cole.

It had been three years ago when it was confirmed he was being sent overseas. She thought of the way he had kissed her and caressed her and held her close. Surely when it had meant so very much to her it had meant something to him too? He had loved her with passion that night and a slight tremor ran through her as she recalled the touch of his lips upon her bare skin and she gave an involuntary tremor.

'You're cold?' Tommy put a gin and tonic in front of her and sat down.

Shelly shook her head. 'No, Tommy, not cold, it was just a shiver.'

'Someone walking over your grave?'

'Yes, that's what they say. Not very nice, is it?'

'No, not very.' He looked beyond her and raised his hand. 'Hey, there's my pal, Greg and his girl, I'll ask them over. Do you mind?'

'Of course not.' In fact, she was relieved to have other company.

Three hours later she and Tom were in his lightweight Dodge military truck pulling up under the cedar trees outside her home. Tom leapt around the vehicle to open her door and they walked over the grass, past the flowerless bougainvillea vine, and up the wide wooden steps to the front verandah in the light of a starry Queensland sky.

'Thanks for bringing me home, Tommy.'

'Say, ma'am, it was no trouble at all. Sorry I couldn't get a staff car. The big brass has them.' He lifted her hand and kissed it and as she removed her fingers, he stepped very close. 'I had a swell evening, Shelly. It wasn't so bad going out with me again, was it?'

'Oh, Tom, of course not. It was very nice.'

His tone of voice altered. '*Very nice* is really not the sort of approval I was looking for, Shelly.' He put his arm around her waist and she slipped out of his grasp.

'Oh, Tom, I'm sorry. Really I am.'

He released a noisy breath. 'I know. It's that flyer guy, isn't it? The one you mentioned on our first date?'

'Yes.'

He stepped nearer again and took her chin gently and looked into her eyes in the gloom. 'No hope for me, eh?'

'There's no sense in lying to you, Tom.'

He grinned wryly. 'Guess not, though it would have been swell for a while.'

'I'm not a good liar, Tom. I enjoy your company but if you want more than that, then . . .'

His hand slipped to her shoulders. 'Yeah. You're as honest as the day is long and as lovely as any girl I've ever known. I won't be here for much longer, Shelly . . . we'll be going into combat any time soon, and I would have liked to think that you felt like I do; that you'd write to me.' He took a deep breath. 'But I guess there's no hope of that, huh?'

259

She did not answer and he leant down and kissed her very gently on the mouth. When he lifted his head he gave a sigh. 'I don't want to beat a dead horse, Shelly, but if you ever change your mind any time you know what squadron I'm with.'

She nodded. 'Yes, I do. Thanks, Tom.'

He touched her cheek for a moment, spun on his heel and leapt down the four steps in one bound.

Shelly stood leaning against the verandah railing as the sound of the engine disappeared and she looked up at the countless stars. All was silent, there was no noise out here and the night air was cold. She wondered where Cole was and if he, too, looked at the stars and ever thought of her.

She could see him in her mind's eye playing cricket on the Ipswich Reserve ground near the Bremer river; all dressed in white with his Reserve Grade cap on his head as he stepped forward and drove the red ball to the fence for four runs. She heard his voice in her head and pictured his walk and the way he moved. She felt the touch of his lips on her mouth and on the skin of her throat. She leant her cheek against the wooden post of the verandah and her eyes brimmed with tears.

Suddenly she stood up straight and decided she had to do something, though she did not know what. His last letter had made it clear that he carried no expectation of her waiting for him. And here she was acting like some naïve wide-eyed teenager.

Abruptly she spoke aloud. 'Damn, why do I feel like this? Why can't I fall for someone else? Why can't I even enjoy another man's company? What the hell is wrong with me?'

The squeak of the oak front door opening behind her startled her and she turned to see the pale gleam of her mother's dressing gown in the darkness. Mavis Longford came towards her daughter exclaiming, 'Darling, who are you talking to? I heard a vehicle leave several minutes ago.'

'Oh, heck, Mum, nobody. I'm talking to myself.'

Mavis shivered. 'Good heavens, why?'

'Don't ask me.'

'All right, dear. Did you have a nice time with Tommy?'

Shelly sighed. 'I told him I couldn't see him any more . . . well, no, that's not right. Really he told me.'

Mavis could not contain her disappointment. 'Oh dear, that's terrible. Shelly, Shelly, he was such a good catch.' She made a long, sad sound in her throat. 'If you're not careful, you'll be an old maid. I hate to think it, it worries me night and day. You know it does. You're getting on.'

'Getting on? Mummy, stop it. You'll only make me angry. It's cold out here. Let's go in.' She brushed by her mother and entered the open doorway.

Behind her Mavis Longford sighed and shook her head and a moment later followed, murmuring loudly enough for her child to hear, 'Why, oh why, can't you see that a bird in the hand is worth two in the bush?'

Chapter Forty-one

The following day, in the brisk winter morning as streaks of cirrus cloud drifted high in the sky, Shelly, wrapped in a thick cardigan and pleated skirt with a maroon beret perched over her fair curls, caught the 0821 train from Ipswich Station. Passing through the tiny settlements of Rosewood, Gatton and Helidon, the steam engine travelled at a sluggish pace across the wide-open winter landscape of olive green. She arrived at Toowoomba Station just in time to catch the only train scheduled that day on to the town of Warwick.

As the station mistress explained, 'We're lucky to have the one train going to Warwick today. Two engines and umpteen carriages have been commandeered in the last fortnight to go to Brisbane for troop movements.' She made a clucking noise and shook her head. 'Blame it on the Japs, love; this war's got us all in a muddle and don't you miss the sixteen-thirty back here from Warwick or you'll be stuck there. It's the last one coming through here tonight.'

A few minutes after 1400, Shelly arrived at the sandstone railway station in Lyons Street, Warwick and was soon walking swiftly through the broad thoroughfares of the southern Queensland settlement lying on the Condamine river, just twenty miles from the New South Wales border.

On reaching the numerous shade trees of Leslie Park, named after a family of early pioneers, she halted by an old gun carriage to watch ten women in military uniform marching in three rows of three led by one carrying a baton. They all played drums except the leader and, towering over their display, was the thirty-five-foot-high war memorial surmounted by a Celtic cross and built in memory of the fallen from the Great War. Shelly could not help but wonder how many names would go on it after this terrible world conflict was over.

The women, with their drums slung on straps over their shoulders, gave a neat, precise exhibition as the leader waved her baton and the nine others stepped out past the obelisk. They were from a women's auxiliary army unit of some kind and practising for a war-related march, but it was for Shelly alone to appreciate and as they strode by she could not help applauding them. Moving on she crossed the park to come out in Albert Street and pass along to her destination, the two-storeyed wooden house with fashionable iron-lace railings on its verandahs.

As she paused at the white gate for a few moments, standing in the over-bright Queensland sunshine, she experienced that anxious feeling which people described as *butterflies in the stomach*. She had been here once before. Two weeks prior to Cole's departure from Australia he had come home on leave and accompanied her to this house to meet his mother. That was when Mrs Wareing had told her it was the first time her son had brought a young woman home, so *he must be serious*, she had said.

Shelly recalled that now as she pushed open the gate and walked up the narrow path leading to the spacious verandah. Hesitating at the steps she turned to the sound of a voice.

'Hello, there.' Cole's mother, wearing a wide-brimmed sun hat, a knitted jacket and an apron, appeared around the corner of the house carrying a trowel in one hand and a bunch of weeds in the other.

'Oh, Mrs Wareing . . . hello . . . it's me.' She waved. 'Shelly Longford.'

Janelle Wareing studied the visitor a moment through her spectacles before she responded. 'Ah, Shelly, *bienvenue*, what are you doing here?' The gentle French accent was still discernible even though this woman, who had been born in France, had lived in Australia since the age of fifteen.

Shelly took a deep breath. 'Well, Mrs Wareing, I'd like to speak with you for a little while, if it's possible.'

The older lady nodded. 'Well, now, just a minute. I'll get rid of this paraphernalia I'm carrying and we'll go inside and have a nice cup of tea. It's getting chilly out here anyway, even in the sun. Just wait here and I'll pop back around the side of the house and let George know I'm not coming back. He's waiting there on the lawn for me. He's my pet lizard, you know.'

Shelly did not know and gave a hesitant smile.

Mrs Wareing went on enthusiastically, 'The dear only comes out when I'm gardening and suns himself, you see. Won't show himself for anybody else. All about trust, I suppose. He might already have slipped away just hearing your voice.'

Shelly watched the woman's floral frock disappear around the corner and shortly she heard, 'Now, George, *mon petit*, our time's been cut short today because I have a visitor, so I'll see you tomorrow.'

Shelly waited, thinking what a quaint thing it was, a lizard as a pet . . . and talking to him as if he understood. Well, people did it with dogs and cats, so why not with lizards?

The older lady soon returned minus the trowel and the weeds and Shelly followed her into the house where a maroon velvet lounge, covered with knitting and small boxes containing all manner of goods, was the first thing Shelly saw.

'Just getting some bits ready for the Red Cross to send to our boys overseas fighting those hideous Japs.'

Shelly nodded. 'Yes, it reminds me of our place, we do the same thing.'

The woman disappeared to wash her hands and remove her apron and when she reappeared she gestured through to the kitchen. '*Voilà*, now, my dear, come on, we'll go in and I'll put the kettle on the stove and we'll talk. My sisters are out at an auction to raise money for the war effort so we're alone.'

Shelly remembered the big kitchen with the wood stove, tall glass windows and yellow and white flower-printed curtains. The homely surroundings helped to calm her nerves as she watched her hostess putting the kettle on to boil. It was obvious that Cole's mother was not as bright and happy as she had been the previous time they had met. But now, of course, the war seemed unending and everybody was a lot grimmer. As the hostess placed cups, sugar and a milk jug on the table she met Shelly's eyes. 'I'm assuming you want to talk about my son?'

Shelly nodded. 'Yes, I do. I'm in a real quandary and I've come here to talk to you about it. I hope you don't mind?'

Cole's mother gave a sympathetic smile. 'Not at all, my dear. I'm impressed you've come all this way to do so. Go ahead.'

'Well . . . I went out with a fellow last night; he really likes me . . . but I keep thinking of your son, you see. It's always the same for me when a man shows me any interest. But eighteen months have passed since I last heard from Cole. He sent me a letter and in it he wrote that it wasn't fair to expect me to wait for him. Anything can happen in war, we all know that. Well, the fact is, I have been — waiting, that is — in spite of the letter. Though I've heard nothing from him since. You see, I've sort of held on to a dream.' She lifted her hands, palms upwards, in a gesture of hopelessness. 'Oh, I don't really know what you can do about it, Mrs Wareing. I suppose I'm here just so that you can tell me he's alive and well and I'll go on my way and pull myself together and get on with my teaching and my life.' She looked down at her hands. 'Perhaps I really should decide once and for all to forget him.'

Cole's mother paused. 'Eighteen months since you've heard from him? Well, Shelly, in all that time, I've only had a few letters from him myself. The last one I received is months ago. Hang on.' She turned to the kitchen dresser and picked up an envelope and took out the papers and read silently for a few seconds. 'Now listen to this: "I'm off again overseas soon and, as you know, I can't say where. So don't expect to hear from me for quite a while, Mum; just look after yourself and keep up the gardening."'

She heaved a sigh as she put the letter back on the shelf and picked up a tin from the dresser and took out a small fruit cake as the kettle began to whistle. 'Goodness knows where he is or what he's doing. Probably his squadron was transferred.' She shrugged as she walked to the stove. '"They also serve who only stand and wait" . . . I can't make up your mind for you, dear, that's up to you; all I can say is, you're the sort of girl I'd like Cole to be serious about . . . and when he brought you here, well, I suspected that he was. But yes, war does alter things, and we all have to face facts.' She gave her visitor a sympathetic smile and added, 'Now, Shelly, I'll make the tea and we can talk some more.'

*　*　*

An hour later Shelly and Janelle Wareing stood at the red cedar front door and the older lady took her visitor's hand. 'Shelly, dear, I've come to the realisation in the last hour that one thing you and I have in common is our love for Cole. Where the heart is concerned we must all simply follow our instincts and it's mighty hard in wartime. That horrible Hitler continues to control Europe and our forces appear to be holding back the Japs in the Pacific but none of us knows what will happen or how long this frightening world war will last.'

She sighed again and a faraway look clouded her eyes behind her spectacles. 'The two men I have loved most have both gone to war: my husband and my son. I saw *mon cher*, Cole's father, go to the last war and I lost him in Montdidier – strangely enough, a little French town in Picardie not far from where I and my sisters were born. I pray every night to Our Lord that I do not lose my son as I lost his father.' She shook her head and a wan smile turned up the corners of her mouth. 'And now, Shelly, I shall persist in praying that he comes back to me . . . and to you. And remember, you and I can always be friends . . . no matter what happens.'

Shelly was moved by the older woman's words and as Janelle Wareing let go of her hand the young woman held back the tears which had begun to form in her eyes. 'Thank you, Mrs Wareing, what a truly kind and caring thing to say. Just talking to you has done me all sorts of good. Yes, I do love your son, and if he lives, God willing, he will come back and we shall take up where we left off . . . or . . . we won't. It's just that simple to me now. I've made up my mind. I will wait and see. I know he released me in that letter he wrote, but . . .' she met the older lady's eyes, 'the truth is, as yet, I have not released him.'

'Bravo, *ma chérie*.'

She walked across the verandah and her hostess called, '*Au revoir*. Please write to me now and then and come and visit me again, when you can . . . if the trains are running.'

Shelly turned and met the eyes of the mother of the man she loved. 'Thank you, I will.'

She walked away with a firmer step than the one which had brought her to this house. Life was what it was. The world was in turmoil and Germany, Japan and their confederates were the enemies of freedom, equity, tolerance and compassion. She was already a volunteer with the Red Cross and with the Country Women's Association and various church guilds who were all doing what they could for the war effort, but she would turn her heart and her thoughts to helping the drive to beat their enemies even more. And along the way she would pray that Cole Wareing would survive. She would love him always; but if he returned and did not want her, life would go on and so would she. Many people lived their whole lives with unrequited love and made decent jobs of it. *Buck up, Shelly, 'do your bit', as the war posters often say, and stay true to yourself.*

Chapter Forty-two

The next day: Sunday, 18 July 1943

A buzz of chatter lifted from the dozens of Australian and American military men who milled about on the grass taking refreshment and talking to the female volunteers at the outdoor canteen on the corner of Ipswich Hospital on Warwick Road. Coffee, tea, scones, biscuits and sandwiches were served free by the Red Cross in the shadow of the hospital to members of the army and air force every Sunday morning after church services. It was a brilliantly sunny morning and a cold westerly breeze made the hot drinks welcome.

Shelly had not arrived home from Warwick until late last night but she had been up early and pedalled her bicycle down the long One Mile Hill to cross the creek and ride into Ipswich to help the volunteers who manned the small tented café. Petrol was rationed and she usually used her bike unless her vehicle, a dark green Ford Model A compact utility truck, was needed.

She smiled as she handed across a cup filled with tea to a young army sergeant. He was about twenty-two with wide shoulders and a cheeky grin and spoke confidently. 'Just visiting my mate who lives here; I'm stationed at Redbank Army Camp, don't know many people but I'd really like to know you. You're sure easy on the eye. Who are you?'

'I'm Shelly Longford and I'm old enough to be your big sister.'

He laughed. 'That's quite all right by me if it's all right by you.'

She gave him an amused look. 'No, it's not all right by me, sergeant. Drink your coffee and find a teenager.'

He grinned. 'Now you've broken my heart.'

'Mmm, I can see that. Here, wipe up the blood.' She handed him a tea towel and he laughed and gave up.

Later when the women had cleaned up and the military men had departed, Shelly put on her overcoat and climbed on her bicycle and rode round to the front of the hospital and down the slope past the police station in East Street. Over the cross street by the Wintergarden picture theatre she glided to Limestone Street where she usually turned for home and, as she did so, she was hailed. 'Shelly, stop! I'd like to talk to you.'

James Charles Minnis*, the mayor, lifted his hat and his sunburnt face broke into a smile. He ran a chemist shop in the main street, was a good responsible community leader and had been a friend of Shelly's father. 'You're just the person I want to see.'

She liked the mayor and pulled her bike to a halt near him, beside a public air-raid shelter.

He doffed his hat. 'I was going to pop out and visit you this week but running into you like this is fortuitous.'

'Oh?'

'I'll get to the point. We of the council are looking for somebody to help Alderman Chambers run the Ipswich and West Moreton War Widows' and Wives of Prisoners' of War Fund. We decided

---

* James Charles Minnis: see Author's End Notes, page 530

we needed a female . . . better to relate to the widows in a feminine and understanding way. Part of the plan is to arrange social events where these women can meet and encourage one another and we need a woman with her own transport, you see. You do have a car, don't you?'

'A ute.'

'Yes, indeed. Well, your name came up as the ideal candidate.'

Shelly was a little taken aback. 'I see . . . is this a job on weekends?'

'No, it will be full time. We won't be able to pay a fortune, but you'll get extra petrol rations. You see, Shelly, you also have the added advantage of understanding children.'

'Yes, Mr Minnis, and I feel responsible to those whom I currently teach.'

He nodded. 'Of course you do, but a new teacher will be found. It's the sort of woman you are, Shelly. You inspire confidence and you already do a lot of volunteer work for the war effort, but this will be more comprehensive, something you can be in charge of yourself. I suppose what we're asking of you is to immerse yourself in civic duty in these times of trouble.' And making a concerned clicking sound with his tongue he finished with, 'What do you think? Is it something you might do? Don't want to rush you, but we need to get started.'

She did not answer and he added, 'We can find you an office in the town hall somewhere . . .?' He waited.

She paused before she answered. 'I'll need to know a lot more.'

'Of course, but if you agree in principle, I can deal with the powers that be at the Department of Public Instruction so that we can get a replacement teacher for you swiftly.'

'Thank you, Mr Mayor, I'll seriously consider it.'

He rested his gaze on her as he took her hand. 'Shelly, let me say something. Who are you? Who is Shelly Longford? I've known you since you were small and I believe you are the sort of person who is absolutely right for this.' He gave her a fatherly nod, replaced his hat and walked away.

Just yesterday when she had left Mrs Wareing, Shelly had decided to turn her heart and thoughts to expand the help she gave to the drive to beat the Japs – and now, out of the blue, the mayor was offering her this: a way to do it. She watched his back and he had not gone twenty paces when Shelly halted him. 'Mr Minnis, yes, I'll do it.'

She rode on feeling excited and honoured and began murmuring to herself in wonder. Twice today, in very different circumstances, she had been asked who she was. Once by a cheeky soldier and once by a responsible leader of the community.

Now as she pedalled along she considered what the real answer to this was. Who was she? She was a woman of thirty who had been to Sydney and Melbourne on holiday, with no experience of the greater world outside other than what she had read and seen in films and cinema newsreels. Her mother and her mother's friends already regarded her as an 'old maid', which, while exasperating and irritating, was an attitude representative of that particular generation who believed that women should be engaged by twenty, married by twenty-two or -three and mothers by twenty-five. Shelly found that whole anthropological viewpoint, which put enormous social pressure on young women, absurd.

Yes, her close friends were indeed all married and she had passed through the various stages of growing up in the free western democracy of Australia in what was regarded as the normal way:

obligatory boyfriend when in her teen years and more serious dating in her twenties, but there had been no one she wished to spend the rest of her life beside. That was so, until she met Cole Wareing. He had been living and working in England and Europe for years and enchanted her from the first. Older, already in his thirties when she met him, he was entirely unlike the parochial men of her acquaintance.

When she first went out with him she knew he saw other women but to her knowledge she had been the only female he had dated in that last year prior to being sent overseas with the RAAF in 1940. And when he knew he was going to North Africa he had held her close to his heart and said, 'Darling Shelly, I don't know what lies ahead, but wear this for me.' He had given her a little gold heart on a chain which she had worn constantly around her neck until yesterday. Last night she removed it. She no longer needed to wear the chain night and day like some silly symbol. She would put it on only when she felt it was right.

She was living in a country which had been seriously threatened by a Japanese invasion. The lives of all Australians had altered: boys she had known in her school days were dead and there were young women, whose weddings she had attended, who were widows or whose husbands were prisoners of the Japs: the very women the mayor now wanted her to aid in a real and constructive way.

Since December 1941 when the Japanese had entered the war on Hitler's side, they had, in lightning succession, mercilessly overrun the islands of the South Pacific. By early 1942, they were in New Guinea, the final island before landing on the mainland of Australia. In the heat and endless jungle of that country a small outnumbered force of Australian soldiers had miraculously beaten back the enemy on the ridges of the mountainous Kokoda Trail. This success plus the victories at the Battle of the Coral Sea in May 1942, followed a month later by the Battle of Midway Island, had stalled the momentum of Japanese aggression and people had begun to dare to believe in an ultimate victory. Yet the war still raged and every Australian remained aware that their enemy in the South Pacific was brutal and a fanatical and determined fighter, who had no conception of being beaten.

That was why she had said yes to the mayor. Her decision of yesterday to do even more had been tested and vindicated today by her acceptance. Now she would be able to be of service to those women whose men had paid the ultimate price or who were suffering at the hands of the Japs.

Shelly was patently aware she was blessed to be free and to be in Australia where the enemy were not in control. All the more reason why everybody here needed to stretch themselves and do even more to win this blasted war.

The westerly wind was now charging down Limestone Street as she passed the technical college on her left, followed by the Methodist church on her right. And, as she pushed up the hill with her hair billowing and the skirt of her coat flapping, she spoke aloud, 'Cole, I'm getting on with it. And wherever you are and whatever you're doing, stay safe and I pray you think of me now and then.'

Chapter Forty-three

Monday, 19 July

Cole saw Laetitia as soon as she entered the café. She glanced around and, noticing him, gave a brief wave and walked towards him, her hips undulating gently under the soft rayon of her dress. She smiled as she reached his table and as he looked up a minute dimple he had not noticed before revealed itself in her left cheek.

Cole gestured to a seat. 'You look hot.' Her face was pink and a bright rose sheen glowed on her cheeks, highlighting her bone structure.

'I've been hurrying; I thought I was going to be late.'

'You are,' he tapped his watch, 'six minutes actually.'

'*Ach, der lieber!*' She gave a mock expression of disgust. 'Forgive me.'

There were two German soldiers at a distant table, otherwise the room was empty. He grinned at her as she sat down and he leant forward from his cup of ersatz coffee, speaking in an undertone. 'I heard that the Fokker aeroplane factory was bombed successfully in Amsterdam yesterday afternoon.'

Her eyes widened with interest. 'Really?'

'Apparently. Spitfires cleared a path through the enemy fighters and the only opposition they ran into on the raid was anti-aircraft fire.'

She met his eyes as he concluded, 'I need you to tell my friends that the damage is extensive and it would appear that there were bomb hits right across the target. I will let London know if I get the opportunity, but they should tell the authorities of the success of the raid when they get back.'

She paused before she said, 'But they can't leave quite yet.'

'Why?'

'Things are taking more time than we thought.'

'By God, you've been saying that for weeks.'

'Lucien, they have the boat but they're having trouble with the motor and we've moved your friends to the place where the boat is.'

'Where's that?'

She used her hands for emphasis as she spoke, her long elliptical nails cutting through the air. 'Near Delft. They went by train. The forged papers were outstanding; they were perfect. You see, we have to choose the right night; and near the shore, in some places, there are batteries every few hundred yards. They will need to swim out to the boat and I know Felix is a little worried about that.'

Cole nodded. 'Well, Dirk and Mako are both very strong swimmers. I believe Dirk trained for an Olympic swimming team.'

'*Ja*, so they told me. I suppose they can help Felix if he needs it, when the night comes round.'

'Then when will it be?'

'They are setting it up for about ten days' time.'

Cole frowned. 'That long?'

'That's *not* long,' she protested. 'Especially when so many arrangements have to be made.'

He held his chin in his hand. 'I'll feel a whole lot better once they're gone.'

She sighed. 'I know things happen slowly, but we must all be patient. Dirk is very restless.'

'Understandably. They must all feel like caged lions.' He leant forward towards her. 'I'm off to Germany again; for perhaps five or six days, this time; we fly. Rauter's sending me to accompany Christiansen.'

The Luftwaffe general was going to be inspecting airfields again and also visiting a series of manufacturing plants, some of them top secret, but Cole mentioned none of that.

'Where will you go?' she asked.

'It's better you don't know.'

'Of course.'

'Then don't ask me such questions.' He paused and their eyes met. 'To change the subject, you're quite beautiful, you know.'

'Do you really think so?'

'Yes. Though I shouldn't tell you.'

'Why?'

'You know why. Anyway, I've said it now. I can't take it back.'

She looked down at her hands which had come to rest on the table and a moment later up to him again. He was studying her, his gaze resting on the beauty spot just to the side of her lip as the edges of her mouth puckered with amusement and she whispered in a honeyed tone, *'Danke.'*

Cole, carrying a small suitcase in one hand and a folder of papers in the other, walked out of the office which used to be Fritz Schmidt's. Along the corridor towards him stomped Wimmer.

'Ah, there you are!' Cole manufactured a smile for the

Commissioner-General for Internal Affairs and Justice. 'Glad I've run into you. I was about to bring these round: the reports on the local film industry.' He handed across the folder to Wimmer. 'I've listed all the operational theatres in the country and how many seats must now be kept free for our official supervisors and censors. We've added two per theatre to the original number. We shall distribute the new rules to all theatre management. Obviously the penalties for not complying will remain.'

'Have you included that no one must be allowed to leave the theatre while a newsreel is showing?' The newsreels were made to *educate* the Dutch in the ideology of National Socialism and to *promote* general co-operation on all levels with the Reich.

'Of course, commissioner. I believe that was always a rule.'

'*Gut.*' Wimmer tucked the folder under his ample arm. 'The Department of Propaganda and the Arts have been requesting this. Now we can keep them quiet.' He gave Cole an agreeable nod and turned away.

'Ah, commissioner?'

'*Ja, standartenführer?*' Wimmer turned back.

'Have we heard of a replacement for Commissioner Schmidt yet?'

'Not to my knowledge . . . but the High Commissioner wants to move on it soon, I believe. We might lose you back to Police Leader Rauter completely then.'

Cole thought this was a veiled way of saying he hoped so. Suddenly Cole realised he needed to become a little more friendly with Wimmer in case what he said were true. If Cole were permanently transferred to work on police and SS matters it would be convenient to be friendly with someone here to enable him to get back into this building with ease. He also wanted to be sure how much more time he had to copy the civil records which were kept in a locked office. Certainly he now had a key and could go in and out at will, and though he was above suspicion, actually photographing them and duplicating them without catching attention was taking longer than he thought.

'Ah . . . yes, that is true.' Cole paused and then grinned. 'Would you like to dine with me tonight?'

Wimmer's surprise showed on his face. It was an unexpected offer. The *standartenführer* was not gregarious, except with General Rauter – they seemed very friendly. Other than the police leader, Bayer appeared either to be with Laetitia de Witt or alone. 'Why . . . I don't know.'

Cole rattled on, 'I have found a charming rustic inn still operating out past the Het Loo Palace . . . serves excellent game. Don't know where the hell they get it, but I'm not asking.' He gave Wimmer another winning smile.

The commissioner's liking for the sensuous overrode all else. He beamed at the thought of excellent game and his eyes in his fleshy face twinkled. '*Ja*, certainly, I'd like that.' He clicked heels and bowed from the neck.

Cole duplicated the action. '*Gut.*'

As Cole walked away he smiled. He would learn things he needed to know tonight. Rauter had given Cole the task of finding out what Wimmer's real relationship was with certain Dutch civil officials. This was a chance to find out. By the time Wimmer had wined and supped with him, Cole hoped the older man would believe that he had found an ally.

By 2200 hours Cole had learnt much and Wimmer had enjoyed much.

It was when Wimmer's ample stomach was stretched with copious amounts of duckling and red wine that he gave a slightly intoxicated smile to his companion and wagged his forefinger. 'Oh, one thing I'd like to tell you, *standartenführer*.'

Cole lifted an eyebrow. 'What is that?'

'The woman you see . . . Fräulein de Witt.' Momentarily his small eyes grew larger with enthusiasm. 'She is a good choice. I approve.'

Cole's eyes met the commissioner's and just for a mere half-second the Austrian was uncertain of what he read in them but abruptly Cole broke into laughter. 'Oh *gut*, I'm pleased you approve.'

'*Ja*, she is *Vertrauensmanner* and in our confidence and she is also Dutch, so she is of an old Germanic nation and therefore, as you know, almost one of us.'

Yes, Cole did know! In Hitler and Himmler's crackpot hierarchy of racial superiority, the Dutch, Danes and Norwegians were regarded as 'super *untermensch*' and a good crop of Waffen-SS troops came from them. Mentally Cole shook his head. The poor Netherlands: the brave Dutch patriots who resisted the Nazis had to contend with more than their share of collaborators.

Wimmer licked his fingers as he added, 'I'm not sure, but I think also she has some true German blood on her mother's side.'

Cole hoped he kept the sarcasm from his voice as he responded, 'Ah, yes, well of course, that makes *all* the difference.' Cole felt a quick surge of pride in Laetitia, for she was amongst the bravest patriots of them all: one who appeared to collaborate and, in fact, did not.

'So, *ja*, I approve of your liaison with her.' The plump Austrian grunted positively as he attacked another duck leg with gusto. 'Yet you only dally with her, I assume?' he spoke with his mouth full.

Cole hesitated and was a tad slow to answer. '*Jawohl*, I only dally with her.'

'I thought so. She was a good friend of poor Fritz Schmidt. I don't know how friendly, but they spent time together. A man needs companionship.'

'Is that why you frequent the brothels?'

Wimmer's head came up sharply in affront but it met Cole's wide grin. 'Only joking, commissioner, a man needs company. I understand that; that's why we're enjoying ourselves here together tonight, eh? Let's have another glass of wine.'

Wimmer's annoyance dissipated as his hand went out for his glass.

Chapter Forty-four

30 July: Laetitia's house outside Apeldoorn

In the large front room with the curtains pulled back from the wide window and the sound of the grandfather clock chiming in the hall, Laetitia put down her paintbrush and smiled over her shoulder at Cole, who stood near the window watching. She wore her usual paint-stained apron over a blue dress with white lace on the collar and bows on her sleeves. The dress appealed to him and as she turned he deliberately stopped himself from gazing admiringly at her.

Instead he pointed to the painting. 'I like the movement in the children playing near the canal edge.'

'*Danke*. As you know, now that I've decided to forgo Amsterdam and stay here more permanently – here in the wide, flat fields of the country all alone, I badly need to occupy my time.' She laughed again and to his ears the sound tinkled like a bell. 'I once lived for a time in the village of Mittenwald in Germany . . .' she hesitated, looked away and, making a sudden annoyed sound, dipped her brush in the open tin of turpentine on the covered table. 'Oh, I don't have much of this left either. Everything is so difficult in wartime.'

'You were saying?'

'What was I saying?'

'About living in Germany.'

'Oh, nothing, really . . . my mother was there . . . taking singing lessons, can you believe it? She was enamoured of a . . . er . . . music teacher – had met him in Switzerland, I think. The attraction fizzled out, but I painted pictures while I was there.' She threw him an enchanting smile. 'It's the same here, you see, I'm alone . . . so I paint.'

'When was that?'

She answered quickly, 'Oh, a long time ago', and crossed to Cole in the strong light from the generous window. The gleam of the summer sun flooding into the room sat on her hair creating a burnished glow as if she wore a halo and her hair had been dipped in gold. He submerged the feeling which strived to engulf him as the radiant head tilted. 'Now, what am I to pass on to your friends to take back to England?'

Cole had worried at first that Laetitia was 'all talk' and that matters might just drag on, or worse, that the agents would be captured; but no, even though it had taken time, she remained as good as her word and she had organised their departure at last.

'Just this.' He took an envelope out of his pocket. It had a coded message in it which told Hans of the secret German research site on the Baltic Coast. This was the port where the Germans were building the unmanned rockets, the V-I flying bombs, that Hans had hoped Cole might find out about.

He had been with Christiansen when they visited Peenemünde to see hundreds of Poles working in the soul-destroying slave-labour camp building the bombs. He momentarily closed his eyes and shook his head as he said, 'This is of vital importance.'

'I understand.'

In the coded message to Hans he had given details of exactly where the RAF should bomb for the most effect. He had also included a description of where three U-boats lay camouflaged in Rotterdam Harbour currently being serviced. It would be an easy raid for the RAF to blow them to smithereens.

Laetitia held out her hand for the envelope. 'I'll carry it in my petticoat. I'm sure I won't be thoroughly searched. Stopped, yes, but searched no.' She gave a quick smile, 'Oh, they might look in the trunk but my identity card, passes and papers are all in order. That was one of the last things Fritz Schmidt did for me before he fell off that train you were all on.' Making a thoughtful sound in her throat she met his eyes. 'Though I still think Rauter had him pushed. What do you think? You were there.'

Cole grunted. 'I told you at the time, I have no idea, I was at dinner.' He handed her the small envelope. 'Let's hope this sets back the carpet-chewing madman's nasty little schemes by months.'

'Ja.' She tilted her head to the side again. 'What do you mean *carpet-chewing madman*?'

'Hitler – Rauter told me. It's well known within the higher order of the SS that when he gets furious, which happens a lot, he has fits and falls to the floor to bite the rug.'

She shook her head in disgust. 'Good God! But it doesn't surprise me. I have always known he's a beast. I knew a girl who met him. She said he had very little education and he was emotionally warped and that the aspects of his nature were all ugly: envy, resentment, hatred of those who were smarter, and a need to dominate. And . . .' she gave a light chuckle and put her hand to her mouth, 'she said he had bad breath too. That didn't surprise me either. She loathed him and that was fifteen years ago. Hitler

raves a lot of the time. The newsreels at the cinema are full of it
. . . and the fools think that impresses us?' She made a dismissive
sound and, holding up the envelope, she added, 'I'm sure your
associates will be very happy to take this back after the disaster
of the Groningen bombings.'

He brought his gaze to hers. 'They will and, anyway, how is
Dirk?'

'Why?'

'He's been fretting, hasn't he? That's what you've said more than
once.'

She paused before answering. 'Well, I suppose he has, he's been
frustrated to be in hiding so long. Mako doesn't seem to mind; he
tinkers with bits and pieces all day, and Felix sleeps or does push-
ups and exercises, but I don't know how well you know your friend.
He's edgy. I've done all I can to help him.'

'Have you? Like what?' He felt an odd twinge of something:
something that truly irked him.

Again she did not answer straight away. 'You know what. I've
visited him . . . well, *them*, when I can. I took games and books
– things for them to do. They say the newspapers are all propaganda
so they didn't bother with them.'

He was annoyed with himself for asking the next question. 'How
friendly have you actually been with Dirk?'

An odd expression crossed her face. That bothered Cole and he
felt irritated when she answered, 'What does that mean?'

'You know exactly what it means. You've been hiding these men
for weeks. You visit them whenever you can. While Mako is one
of the weirdest-looking men I've ever seen, and Felix is young but
pretty average, Dirk is one of the most attractive of men: all brilliant blue eyes and glittering Renaissance looks. Any woman would

285

fall for him. Besides which he . . .' He paused before adding, 'He's probably a flirt.' *Jesus, Cole, you're slipping.* He was on the verge of saying – 'He had a girl at every airfield in Britain.'

Laetitia de Witt eyed Cole closely. So *Standartenführer* Lucien Bayer was jealous.

She came over to him and rested her hip on the back of the sofa, perhaps eight inches away from him. 'You know, I *think* I prefer the dark handsome kind. They, too, have *brilliant blue eyes*, as you call them.' She stood on her toes and, resting her hand on his shoulder, looked into his eyes.

He pulled away, not quickly, but decidedly, and removed her hand. 'We need to keep this association uncomplicated. Now don't lose that envelope or I'll skin you alive. I'll see you next Friday afternoon if not before.'

'Don't concern yourself, I'll be here waiting –' she flashed her eyes at him – 'and I'll keep my skin!'

Giving an amused grunt he walked to the door where he hesitated and turned back, speaking deliberately. 'Wish them well for me.'

She was serious now. 'I will. They'll be gone just after midnight tomorrow.'

As he limped away she asked, 'How did they recruit you?'

He turned back again and raised an eyebrow.

'I'm just mystified and intrigued by the fact that an SS officer would go over to the British? I think about it all the time.'

'It's something I can't tell you; you know that and you know you should not ask.'

'I suppose I do.' She pursed her lips.

'Now good luck to you and those British agents.' For a man leaning on a cane, he left hurriedly and the *feldwebel* driver of the Mercedes-Benz and the three German soldiers of the motorbike escort all stood to attention as they saw him make his way down the steps. They had brought the *standartenführer* here a number of times now and it was generally believed that Laetitia de Witt and *Standartenführer* Bayer were having an affair.

Laetitia watched the car draw away down the drive and a pensive look crossed her face as she closed the door and leant on it feeling the hardness of the wood on her back as she tapped it with her long fingernails. Dirk and Lucien had fascinated her from the start and destiny, untrustworthy and equivocal, had thrown her together with them at the same time: she knew now that Lucien Bayer wanted her.

Perhaps she should not have been to bed with Dirk; but there was a war on and Laetitia de Witt did not consider the morality of her conduct. She was a child of 'spur-of-the-moment action', always had been. Tonight would be her final visit to Dirk before he left for England tomorrow.

She would miss him, his vitality and the power of him, his deep-throated laugh and the way he teased her. He had started off calling her 'Let' but recently he had begun calling her 'Angel'. She liked that. With his two companions he was authoritative and forceful, they turned to him constantly for leadership. He did not take well to waiting all these weeks to get away from Holland and on a number of occasions she had been forced to convince him to remain and not attempt an escape alone without help. She knew that sleeping with him was one of the reasons he had acquiesced.

She sighed there in the gloom of her front hall and justified her conduct with the excuse that they could all be caught any time and that one's code of behaviour in war was incompatible with one's code of behaviour in peace. That any pleasures found along the way in wartime were legitimate.

She tossed away any guilt which might have lurked in her mind with a physical toss of her head as she ceased drumming on the door with her fingers to hurry down the corridor into the kitchen.

The drive in the Rosengart would be slow for there were numerous checkpoints and even though she had a tin of petrol in her trunk and all the correct papers and a letter from Seyss-Inquart's office which Schmidt had supplied and which was worth more than diamonds, it would still take her many hours. But it was worth it just to be alone with Dirk one more time before he left her life for ever on the motorboat which would deliver him over the one hundred-odd miles of sombre grey water to the coast of freedom in England.

By the time she entered the kitchen a tune from her girlhood trilled from her lips while she wrapped some biscuits and an apple for the journey.

Chapter Forty-five

Cole leant back in the corner of the black German staff car watching the leaves of the forest trees flick by his eye line like reams of verdant green lace. He was elated by what he had heard from General Christiansen this morning. The German general had stormed about his office and thrown an ashtray at the wall in his fury. The two previous nights had seen successful raids by the Royal Air Force on the port of Peenemünde in Germany which was the Nazi testing site for the unmanned rocket bombs Hitler planned to use on London. Cole could hardly hold back his smile as Christiansen had ranted on and on about the RAF.

No doubt when Tudor, Mako and Felix had arrived safely on the Norfolk coast in their small boat, the envelope from Laetitia with the coded detailed information had gone via Hans straight to Bomber Command.

Nine minutes later Cole was in Laetitia's house and his eyes shone with his news. 'I can't give you any details, Laetitia, but the coded messages you delivered to Dirk have been used to great

289

success and I thank you for the part you played.' He took up her hands and swung her around joyfully in the front hall.

'Oh, I'm so pleased for you,' she cried as her skirt danced in the air and they came to rest, laughing merrily. Impulsively he hugged her to him and she felt so good in his arms that he rested his face in her hair before he let her go.

As they parted, their eyes locked and she abruptly said, 'I want to show you my latest painting.' And, beckoning him, she went on, 'Come, I've started it – without the subject – so I had to draw from memory, but I do hope he'll sit for me when he can, from now on.'

She gently urged him into the parlour where Cole halted and stood staring at his own image beginning to appear on her canvas. His mirth died as he pointed to it and spoke angrily, 'I would prefer you painted me in mufti.'

'Oh, not in uniform? But this is how I see you . . . all the time.'

'Hell, woman, that means nothing. I hate this uniform, every time I put it on I feel sick. For God's sake, you of all people must understand that? These clothes are anathema to me.'

'Oh, how stupid of me. Of course, I understand . . . what would you like me to paint you wearing?'

'Anything but a stinking Nazi uniform.'

The awkward atmosphere hung in the air before she broke it with the words, 'Then I shall paint you in pyjamas.'

His indignation dissipated and he broke into a wry smile. 'Don't tease me. If you must paint me, just make me look like an ordinary man.' He reached out and touched her arm. 'I don't want to be left for posterity in a bloody SS uniform.'

'Of course you wouldn't. I'm very foolish not to have realised it. Forgive me. I'll repaint it.' She understood his feelings and his reaction. Certainly he must hate the uniform. He worked for the British. It had been thoughtless of her not to realise that. What a mistake to begin to paint him in it. 'But all the same, do you think it's like you? Do you think it's going to be good?'

He paused. 'Yes, I think it will be very like me . . . indeed . . . very.'

'Then I am pleased after all.'

Once Cole had gone Laetitia closed her blue front door and walked down the steps to cross the yard and stroll over the pebbled path and out the gate in her broken fence by the stream. Ambling along the bank she found the same flat rock in the arbour under the trees where she used to play in childhood. Lately she had come here to sit awhile on it, resting her shoes in the long grass and listening to the sound of the bees in the wild flowers near at hand; or watching swallows sweep along the stream to land in the branches hanging above the flowing water where they hopped to and fro in restless summer activity.

Dirk was back safely in England across the sea and he had carried the critical messages home with him. She was happy about that. She would never see him again yet she would always remember him. Her time with him had been a brief, exciting interlude. There had been a powerful attraction between them which they both needed to satisfy, but she did not love Dirk; in fact, she realised that until now, she had never loved anyone. Oh, she had thought so once or twice and her mouth drew down in doleful memory as she blinked and shook her head and raised her eyes to the branches of the trees.

Lately she was beginning to recognise that her feelings for Lucien were unlike any she had ever experienced. Lucien was filling her thoughts more and more each day. She accepted that she was alone

291

here and often simply waiting for his visits and this could be influencing her; but it was not only that. She was dreaming about him at night: a phenomenon which had never occurred with any male before. Previously she had rarely dreamt in her life and now dreams of Lucien were commonplace.

She also had the suspicion that he was even more complicated than he appeared.

As she sat musing she pictured him: he was an SS officer who had decided Hitler was an evil monster and that the Germans were wrong in waging this war. Pity there were not thousands like him. Since the *Night of the Long Knives* nine years ago when Hitler had murdered many of the German leaders who stood against him, any Germans who disagreed with him were terrified to speak and so the Nazis had taken charge. Perhaps it was back then in 1934 that Lucien had defected, but if so, why did he stay in Germany and remain in the SS? He could have escaped to Britain. Instead he lived this life of audacious duplicity passing information to England to help defeat those to whom he had once belonged in spirit.

Or perhaps he had never sympathised with the Nazis. Perhaps he had been working for the British for many long years and joined the Nazi party simply to infiltrate and work his way up through the ranks. It was highly improbable, yet it was possible . . .

Oh yes, *Standartenführer* Lucien Bayer was a puzzle which was beginning to consume Laetitia de Witt.

The following Friday, Laetitia walked with Cole through the broken-down fence at the side of her property and along the stream to reveal to him her secret place. He smiled at the childlike pleasure she took in showing it and as she pointed to her flat stone she said, 'I often sit here and think – mostly about you.'

'You're wasting your time doing that, Letta. You should be painting. You're very good.' He smiled as he leant against the bole of a gnarled cedar tree. He had begun calling her Letta the previous week. 'For Laetitia is such a mouthful.'

She sat silently looking at him, holding her body around her waist as she sometimes did, until she leant forward and placed her elbows on her knees. 'You know, I was sitting here yesterday thinking about you and how you speak comparatively good Dutch – but your English must be perfect.'

Cole met her eyes. 'Why? Because I send coded messages to England in English?'

'*Ja*, that's why. Where did you learn it?'

'Don't pry.' He scowled at her. 'You know I won't tell you.'

'But how can it harm? I'm interested. You continue to amaze me. What can it matter if you tell me where you learnt your English?' She stood and tilted her head and rested her index finger at the side of her mouth near the tiny dusky spot as her eyes narrowed, studying him. She looked fresh and vital in a dress of yellow-and-white spotted cotton which was belted at the waist and dropped in a flare to just below her knees.

'Lucien, there's just so much we can say about my painting, about the weather, music and nature, I want to know more about you. You know so much about me. Tell me of when you were a little boy, I don't even know in what German city you were born.'

He stood from the tree and took hold of her shoulders. 'Letta, dear Letta, the less you know about me the better; I've said it to you over and over again.'

She raised her hand to his cheek, sliding the tips of her fingers to meet the bottom of the scar which ran from his temple. 'All right, Lucien. I'll keep trying to understand and accept what you say.' The caress of her fingers stirred up all sorts of feelings in·him; the memory of their first night together and the urgency and excitement of their lovemaking. 'Please will you help me with my English? I speak it but not very well.'

He removed her hand from his face: not sharply or quickly but slowly and gently. 'Yes, all right. But not today. Come on, Letta, it's time we returned to the house.' And as they walked along he added, 'I'm glad I have you to come and see. You are the one bright spot I have in each bleak week.' He tried to make his words sound dispassionate but by their very content they did not.

Chapter Forty-six

In heavy rain they leapt out of the little blue Rosengart and ran across the gravel over the lawn and up the steps to Laetitia's front door. She fumbled with the key while Cole shouted, 'Hurry, Letta!'

Finally she opened the latch and they stumbled soaking wet into the neat front vestibule of her house.

He slammed the door and they stood laughing and dripping water on the porcelain tiles of the entry. His hair shone and small rivulets of rain ran down his temples. The firm material of his uniform was damp and water gleamed on the backs of his hands.

Her hair glistened, her blue dress with the white lace collar clung to her body delineating the round shape of her breasts above her small waist and sticking to her hips and legs to reveal their contour. She fell forward into his arms still laughing.

He held her tightly and she pressed herself to him. They were happy, liberated from all thoughts of war and angst for these moments of simple joy: soaking wet and exuberant, they hugged. A few moments later she pulled her head slightly away and looked up at him, while at the same time sliding her hands around his back to hold him.

'Lucien . . .' She said it with a silken sound.

Her mouth lifted towards his and he felt his resolve melting away as a moment later he was cradling her within his arms as if never to release her. She tasted like the fresh wind from the North Sea and smelt of a fragrant balmy scent. His hands slid down her wet back to crush her to him as he felt her taut body moulding into his own and the mellow perfume of her enveloping him. He had been resisting her and now, in a few moments, he had lost his struggle.

Some time later the clock in her hallway chimed the hour as she murmured love words to him — suggestive, arousing. He sank once more into the warmth of her, his lips drowning her words and his body again hard with the need of her.

When he rolled away from her the thought which filled his head was how inevitable this had been. Had he ever believed it would not happen again? He supposed he always knew it was merely a matter of time. He was staring at a crack in the ceiling panel as he whispered, 'Letta?'

'Yes.'

'Are we being foolish? Too foolish?'

She gave a small echoing laugh in her throat. 'Of course we are . . . but there's a war on. You and I are in the front line. We deserve our moments of tenderness. Who knows what will happen to us tomorrow? I believe I have wanted you from the first moment I saw you.'

'Have you really?' He hesitated. 'You mean at the door of the room in the Zwann Inn?'

'Yes.' She rolled over to him and rested her lips on his.

He did not admit to himself that this answer disturbed him; he did not acknowledge the misgivings which rose in his head: that she allowed herself to find him attractive while believing he was a Nazi.

He refused to think about ethical judgements. All he permitted was his own rationalisation of what Letta had said: no one could plan for the future when there might not be one. Life was here, this minute, not tomorrow or next week – or when the war ended – but now. He had wanted to possess her again, needed to, and had. In his deep desire he dismissed the uncomfortable hazy notion that she had probably slept with others of the enemy as easily as she had with him that first night.

She was unique: she was brave, she was beautiful . . . gloriously different to other women he had known. That was all he needed to think about and he exulted in the reality that this adorable, courageous creature was in his arms.

Chapter Forty-seven

They lay on a blanket in the long grass looking up at the sky, Cole's left arm under Laetitia and around her shoulders. He stretched out his right hand, picked a long blade of grass and chewed the pale end.

Above them the elegant forms of two swans sailed by, their brilliant white wings undulating in seeming effortlessness. As the man and woman turned their faces to each other the shadows of the birds slipped like wraiths across their bodies.

It was always solace for Cole to be in her arms after being day-in-day-out with Rauter and the others. He kissed the tip of her nose and she laughed, tenderly. 'If you only knew how much this means to me, to be with you like this,' he whispered.

She sat up and looked around before she bent down over him to kiss him. He felt the seductive heat of her breasts inside her garment as they pressed his arm. She raised her face from his and sighed. 'It means a lot to me too, my treasure.'

'Oh, a *treasure*, am I? Well, thank you. Am I diamonds or pearls? I know you like both.'

It was as if they were alone in the world: it had been a fair day, the sun shone and the temperature had risen. Cole had arrived at

Laetitia's house with a few hours free so they had decided on a walk in the woods. Even now as the afternoon began to wane and the sun was just about to give up and head behind a cloud it was still warm.

She laughed, a magical sound to his ears and he pulled her down to him and they kissed again. She toyed with the buttons on his uniform and began to undo them. He watched as she continued to open his shirt. When she bent her head and rested her lips on his skin he began to undo her blouse.

'What if someone comes?' she asked, but it was not a serious question.

'Out here? *Verdammen sie*,' he replied.

'Yes, damn them,' she repeated as she lay across him and his hands slipped down behind her to pull her skirt high to her waist.

Later, she smiled up at him above her and held his face between her hands and studied him from under her curving eyelashes. 'Lucien, what's going to happen to us?'

He did not answer. He breathed heavily, a tiny row of perspiration droplets dampening his temples as he continued to look over her head into the grass while the seconds ticked away and he frowned. Suddenly she lifted her head and nuzzled his chin and whispered, 'Lucien, forget it, I should not have said that.'

He dragged his eyes from the grass and looked down at her. Very slowly he answered, '*Ja*, you should. I don't know. But I'm certain of one thing. I would like to keep you . . . for ever.'

She said nothing for a few seconds before she pulled him down into her arms, holding him close and pressing her flesh to his. 'Lucien, perhaps when this war is over . . .'

A shiver rippled through him, his eyes clouded and he rose to a sitting position covering her nakedness with her blouse. He was still breathing deeply as he drew his hands back through his hair in a slow, measured action. He hated that she called him Lucien, he detested the name, but what could he do? Could he tell her he was not a German who had become disillusioned by Hitler, but an Australian, a British agent living a subterfuge? Could he ever tell her?

He heard himself say, 'Letta, let's not talk of it now. The day's fading, night will soon draw in, we must go.'

'Yes, I suppose we must.' Her forefinger trailed down the scar on his side and she bent her head and kissed it just as he moved out of her reach and put on his shirt and began to do up the buttons.

He hurried her while she dressed and gained her feet. She moved languidly as if still attached by invisible ties to the spot in the grass near the canal. A few small insects hovered around and Letta flicked her fingers at them as she put out her hand to Cole. He was slow to take it and a furrow remained on his brow as he picked up the blanket in his other hand and they made their way through the wild flowers and the tall lush grass to the track which ultimately led back to the stream near Letta's house.

As they walked with the blanket trailing from his grasp, a breeze began and Cole glanced across a pond with bitterns wandering in the reeds, to the fields beyond, where a group of German soldiers drilled near three windmills. Their menace was impotent at this distance and they simply looked like wind-up toys for the amusement of small children.

Yet the Germans were not impotent, they were a constant life-threatening danger and he must never forget it and always remain vigilant. Yes, he trusted the woman at his side; yes, he would like to tell her everything and have no secrets – but that was the fabric of his dreams.

'Are you going over to the Hague this week?' she asked.

'*Ja*, and I'm not sure how long I'll be gone, but you'll be on my mind.'

'And you on mine.'

'And I'll be back.' He squeezed her hand and kissed her temple as his gaze rose to the heavens. *It will stay clear, I think – a good night for my old squadron to bomb Germany.*

By the time they reached the blue front door of Letta's house the gentle glow of eventide seeped across the low flatlands.

Chapter Forty-eight

21 September: The Hague

In the chill stone records office of the Security Police Command, Cole moved the paper into the light from the external window and took a photograph with his minute Minox camera. This was the list of Dutch clergy who had been brought in for questioning in recent weeks. Replacing it carefully in the file to his right, he moved to the next cabinet and took out another sheet showing German military batteries along the Dutch coast. At this very moment he could hear the boom of long-range guns firing in the distance along the shores of the North Sea; possibly at a British ship or an aircraft. He hoped like hell they missed.

At that moment he heard a key click in the lock. He immediately slipped the camera into his pocket, grabbed the page, closed the drawer and spun round to another cabinet as the handle turned and the door opened wide.

With page in hand and eyes down and with as casual an action as he could muster, he opened the drawer in front of him and slipped the piece of paper in, hoping with all his might that his demeanour was normal.

'*Standartenführer!*'

Cole lifted his head and manufactured a smile at the newcomer as he closed the drawer before turning nonchalantly to reach for the cane he had left leaning behind him.

He limped around the wooden cabinets to Rauter who filled the doorway, his massive form hiding another man. 'Do you always lock the door when you're in here?' The *polizeiführer*'s booming voice ricocheted in the small space.

Cole nodded. 'I do, we can't be too careful.'

'I suppose that's true but we are in our own headquarters, Lucien. I wondered where you were.' He moved aside to expose the man behind him. 'Meet my new second in command.' He urged forward a figure in grey SS service uniform as he went on, '*Brigadeführer* Erich Naumann*, meet one of our heroes from the Russian front and now a big help to me here, *Standartenführer* Lucien Bayer.'

The eyes of a zealot, intense, greeted Cole. Beneath the fixed gaze and above a slightly bulbous chin, a tight mouth drew back in a smile. 'Lucien Bayer. Bayer . . . Have I met you before?'

Uh oh. Cole cleared his throat, gaining a moment to think. 'Yes, perhaps, indeed. Since I was wounded I have difficulty with my memory sometimes . . . forgive me . . .' Cole's brain was racing. 'Where would we have met, do you think?'

Naumann frowned. 'Lucien Bayer. It's the name I recall. You don't really *look* familiar.'

Rauter's copious paw slapped Cole's shoulder. '*Ja,* before he was wounded he looked different to this – didn't you, Lucien? No scars, eh?'

Cole achieved a natural sort of grin and agreed, '*Jawohl.*'

---

* Erich Naumann: see Author's End Notes, page 530

Naumann was examining Cole; looking him up and down. 'Your eyes . . . *ja*. I'm sure I've met you. Never forget people's eyes.' Suddenly he recollected. 'Lucien Bayer . . . now I know . . . it was Hitler's birthday!' He gave Cole a much-needed clue. 'That's it. Before the war.'

Cole took a chance. He recalled the Nazi fuss of 20 April 1939, Hitler's fiftieth birthday, when cinema newsreels around the globe showed the massive German military build-up with their thousands of troops goose-stepping through Berlin accompanied by hundreds of tanks and armoured vehicles, rolling along in the collective show of might. Standing up in an eight-seater open vehicle with five of his staff officers seated around him, Hitler had been driven through the tens of thousands of cheering and '*Sieg Heiling*' German National Socialist indoctrinated. Enormous swastika banners and German eagles decorated the streets.

This has to be the birthday he means! 'Berlin? 1939?'

The zealot laughed. 'Absolutely. That's it. Now, was it at Caspar's Tavern? Or was it at the party in the house of that tall willowy artist's model afterwards? See, I knew I'd met you.'

Cole thought it would be safer to have met in a tavern . . . less likely that something particular would come up, so he grinned. 'I don't recall the party but I believe I was at the tavern. As I said, forgive any lapses in my memory. But it was a fine night, a wonderful celebration for our Führer. Didn't we all have a splendid time?'

'*Jawohl!* Indeed we did. Ernst Von Bremen, one of my senior staff, will be pleased to see you again; he was with us that day too.'

Oh wonderful, two of them who remember Bayer, how cosy.

Naumann became so enthusiastic about the memory that he heiled Hitler and Rauter and Cole joined his incantation in unison before Rauter took over the conversation as Cole mentally breathed a sigh of relief.

'You will both be accompanying me into Amsterdam on Saturday. We have police work there. Dozens of new directives must go out to the populace. Do you have the lists, Lucien?' Cole had become a favourite of Rauter, which had played into his hands and been very useful in getting him in and out of this very records' office. These days he did not have the easy access to Schmidt's records because his replacement had arrived: Cole thought of him as *another noxious little Nazi*. His name was Wilhelm Ritterbusch and Cole was currently trying to cosy up to him as he did to Wimmer.

Cole answered with a smile. '*Ja*, of course, *politzeiführer*, I'll bring them to your office this afternoon.'

Now the police chief turned to Naumann. 'The Amsterdam visit will be a good start for you, *brigadeführer*, to see how we do things here.' He waved his hand around the room. 'Anyway, as you know, this is the records' office. We need a larger one, don't we, Lucien?'

'Undoubtedly. But we make do.'

As Cole moved away on his cane Naumann called to his back, 'We must talk again, *standartenführer*.'

Cole was not looking forward to that.

Later, when Rauter had left the building, Cole went back to the records and found the page containing the plans of the German coastal batteries on the Dutch shore, photographed it and replaced it in the correct position.

The following evening as he left the SS hotel where he lodged behind the Palace of Peace, he halted on the stone steps. Naumann and a companion were crossing the road towards him. It was too late for him to turn back and Naumann beckoned him. Cole mentally prepared himself and limped across to them, his boots ringing on the ancient stones beneath his feet.

The man with Naumann wore the SS uniform of a *standartenführer* too. Cole realised that this had to be Von Bremen.

He smiled as Cole approached. His voice was thick with a cold and he coughed with a barking sound. 'I doubt I would have recognised you with your stick, *Standartenführer* Bayer. But now I see you up close I realise it is, in fact, you. I'm sorry you were wounded.'

A little of Von Bremen's dark hair showed beneath his cap. He appeared athletic beneath his uniform and he was probably in his late thirties. As they stood together Cole looked into blue eyes and realised they were both a similar height and size. They dwarfed Erich Naumann standing beside them. '*Danke*. But I'm all right now. *Gut* to see you, *Standartenführer* Von Bremen.'

'Did you manage to get to your *Heimatstadt* of Hamburg before coming here? I used to live there, remember?'

Oh bugger. '*Ja*, of course I do.' Cole produced an expression of regret. 'I'm afraid I did not get to my hometown. I came here straight from recuperation in Denmark.' And now he frowned in thought. 'I know we were together on the day of the Führer's fiftieth birthday, but where have I seen you since?'

'It was before you went to the eastern front. I think we'd both been to a conference at the Party's Regional Headquarters in Hamburg and afterwards we went to that bicycle club by the town hall.'

Now this Cole knew about. Lucien Bayer had been a keen bicyclist before the war and Cole was aware that he had membership of two cycling clubs: one in Hamburg and one in Berlin.

Cole gave a smile in return. '*Ja*, of course, *Der Schnelle Rad Klub* near the town hall, as you say.'

Von Bremen frowned. '*Nein*, that wasn't what it was called.'

Cole tensed. 'Ah . . . of course not, that's the club in Berlin. I'm apt to mix things up since I was wounded. Now what is the one in Hamburg called?' He was trying his utmost to recall it when Von Bremen gave a grunt. 'Wasn't it the *Unten Hugel Klub*?'

'That's it, the Downhill Club.' Cole beamed at him and clicked his heels with gusto, bowing from the neck. 'Though it is certainly good to see you again, I must excuse myself, for I have an appointment with Commissioner Wimmer who is here for a few days.'

'*Ja*, of course. We'll be seeing plenty of each other,' Naumann answered.

Cole nodded politely. *I assuredly hope not.*

Von Bremen clicked his heels as well and coughed again. 'Pity you're not free, we're going out to the Villa at Clingendael, or, I should say, the *Fortress Clingendael*, as High Commissioner Seyss-Inquart likes to call it. You could have joined us.'

As was the usual, German High Command had seized most of the stately buildings in the occupied countries and the supreme Nazi civil authority, Arthur Seyss-Inquart, lived with his family out in a commandeered villa, in the beautiful area of Clingendael.

'Unfortunately I cannot.' Cole dipped his head again in a precise movement, turned and walked away. *Thank God I return to Apeldoorn next week.*

He limped away into the city down towards De Appelyard, one of the most frequented restaurants of those which were still allowed to operate. In the fading light as night burgeoned, he passed the famous Ridderzaal, the Knight's Hall, in the centre of the city where Seyss-Inquart had informed the Dutch people in 1940 that the Germans *had been forced* to invade Holland to avoid the British and others using it as a base.

He turned down by a synagogue which was unrecognisable from the pristine red brick building it had been a few years prior. The holy building had simply been desecrated over time by the German invaders.

There was an eight o'clock curfew at present: the curfew altered with the mood of the Nazis and the streets were jet-black after dark. All windows were covered with black-out paper.

He crossed the street and entered De Appelyard. Inside, it was lit with electric light and as Wimmer saw him enter he raised the glass in his right hand to attract Cole's attention while his left rested on the pristine white tablecloth.

Cole continued to force himself to eat with Wimmer every now and then for it allowed Cole to gently interrogate the Austrian. Tonight, as the evening advanced, he asked about Von Bremen.

'Do you know much about him, *mein Freund*?' Calling Wimmer *my friend* made his words almost stick in his throat, but it was necessary to articulate them.

The plump Austrian picked up his glass and drank. '*Ah, nein*, only that he is from Hamburg originally and was an art historian. He has been with Naumann in Poland for some years now. One of my staff said he mentioned he badly wanted to visit a woman living in Amsterdam and he was looking forward to seeing her again when he could get there. I'll tell you something else,' Wimmer added quietly and leant forward, his small piggy eyes bright with the knowledge of the secret he was about to divulge. 'This is hush-hush and confidential, Lucien. Because I'm in charge of judicial matters it has been leaked to me. Naumann and Von Bremen are going to help us with cars and false identification for a new group that is being put together.'

'What group?'

'A secret assassinations group who will kill Dutchmen whom we know to be anti-German.'

Oh lovely . . . I need to find out more about this to let Hans know. Have another drink, Wimmer, so I can loosen your tongue.

'Shall we have another bottle?'

Wimmer's face broke into a smile. '*Ja*, good idea.'

Cole kept his eyes on Wimmer draining his red wine with relish as he lifted his own glass and drank a copious amount. He closed his eyes as he swallowed; he certainly was keeping nauseating company these days.

Chapter Forty-nine

Autumn Equinox: Still in the Hague

Beneath three massive German eagles and a host of swastika banners, Cole sat at *Polizeiführer* Rauter's long wooden table, which was draped with a white tablecloth and covered with drinks and food. The pillared ballroom was filled with Rauter's staff and SS-related appointees, State Secret Police and government officials, all at similar tables.

Rauter had begun the gathering by casting his heavy gaze around the room and reading a message of 'inspiration' from Hitler to his disciples which was met with the stamping of feet and a long, loud ovation.

Cole mentally shook his head: he would never get used to this – how could any rational human being ever get used to living the depraved reality of being a member of the extreme SS? *Criminals all and here I am in the middle of you.*

In the hours which followed, the food and wine flowed and Cole imbibed carefully. The official to Cole's right became more and more inebriated and began 'heiling Hitler' with each sip of his wine. He ran the Schalkhaar Police School – where young Dutch volunteers were trained to be police using SS methods. To patriotic Dutch citizens the name Schalkhaar was detested and fast turning into a synonym for inhumanity and brutality.

As the gathering became more raucous and a group in the corner began to sing a wild Bavarian song, Cole waited for the first moment he felt he could exit. He was staring at his hands. *What if they win this war . . . what if they actually win?*

'*Standartenführer?*' The voice jarred in his ear.

Cole flinched and turned to the over-bright gaze of SS *Standartenführer* Ernst Von Bremen, his mouth pulled wide in a crooked grin as he loomed over Cole's shoulder.

'Do you play skat?'

Cole blinked. '*Ja*, of course.' He had been taught the three-handed national card game of Germany in his weeks of indoctrination by Helmut Schultz and they had played many times with another of his coaches, the Russian front expert.

Von Bremen touched Cole's shoulder. '*Gut*. Do come along. *Obersturmbannführer* Stryker will play with you and me. We've got a few games going in a room along the corridor. And we've got women turning up soon.'

Cole cleared his throat as he stood and gestured to the far side of the table. 'I notice the *polizeiführer* appears to be making ready to depart. I feel I should leave with him.'

Indeed, at that moment, Rauter's bulk was rising from his chair at the table's end. 'I have much to do for him tomorrow,' added Cole.

'But that's tomorrow and this is now.' At that moment Rauter looked around and Von Bremen caught his eye and asked, 'With your permission, general, I would like *Standartenführer* Bayer to join us for some hands of skat; of course, if you have any objection . . . ?'

Rauter beamed at Cole. 'Of course not. *Gehen Sie voraus, mein Junge!*' Go ahead, my boy.

Cole gritted his teeth and at the same time bowed his head slightly and clicked his heels quite ostentatiously. 'Lead on, *standartenführer*.'

'We play for ten pfennig a point,' declared Von Bremen as they sat down. Cole looked at the ten cards which were dealt to him. German cards were adorned with acorns, leaves and bells instead of clubs, spades and diamonds, only the hearts were the same. He had been dealt a fair hand and made a bid.

Forty minutes later Von Bremen was tipsy and losing. Cole had been clever enough not to win, but a pile of money sat in front of *Obersturmbannführer* Stryker.

Von Bremen's glazed eyes turned to Cole. 'The Führer's birthday. That night in Berlin . . . weren't you with Kessler?'

Cole paused for a heartbeat. 'Was I?'

'*Ja*, you were, where did he go after that? Wasn't it Munich?'

'It might have been.'

'*Might have been*? I thought you two were good friends. I saw him in Poland, he hasn't changed, still smoking that pipe. Now what was his sister called?'

Stryker saved Cole from answering. 'It's your turn, *Standartenführer* Von Bremen.'

A lock of Von Bremen's dark hair hung over his forehead and he brushed it back with an irritated action. He was becoming exasperated. He eyed Stryker with annoyance. 'You've been winning since we started. This isn't fair.'

Women had appeared and they perched on knees and whispered in ears around the room. Light feminine giggles now intermingled with male laughter. Cole thought of Laetitia and wished he were with her. He looked at his cards as Von Bremen – who was tired of losing – put his down with a thud. 'I'm sick of this.' He caught a girl by the arm as she walked by. 'Come here.'

Cole, too, placed his cards on the table, but *Obersturmbannführer* Stryker, who was a rank lower than both Cole and Von Bremen, looked angry. 'But we haven't finished the game.' His bald head shone in the lamplight and his eyes blinked behind his spectacles. 'You're stopping because I'm winning.'

Von Bremen became dismissive. 'I am finished. I want to talk to the *standartenführer*.' The woman was balancing on his knee as he locked eyes with Cole. 'Come on, don't be coy. You know very well what Stryker's sister's name was. You were bedding her at the time, weren't you?' He held the girl in his right arm as he picked up his glass with his left and drank.

Cole met the Aryan's glassy stare. 'That's the past, *standartenführer*. Much water has gone under the bridge since then.'

'*Ja*, but what was her name?'

Damn, why do you keep asking this? 'I make it a rule to forget the names of women with whom I no longer associate.'

This brought a hail of laughter from Von Bremen and as Stryker hit the table and said, 'Let's play another hand', Cole rose.

'With your permission.' He glanced from one to the other. 'I would like to get some sleep. I have pressing meetings in the morning.'

But Von Bremen was insistent. 'Stay a little longer. Let's talk about the night we had the drink before you left for the Russian front. Wasn't Otto Becker with us?'

Cole sidestepped this. '*Ja*, I believe he could have been. But I must bid you *gute Nacht*.'

Von Bremen put up his hand to stay his companion. 'Tell me again – which part of Hamburg were you born in?'

Cole held the back of the chair as he stood, looking down. 'Blankenese.'

This made an impression. The glazed blue eyes widened. 'Ah, *ja* . . . your parents were wealthy, then?'

Cole grinned. 'We were the poorest people in a rich suburb.'

The German laughed raucously and hugged the girl in his arms.

Cole glanced down at Stryker who was counting his money. 'I have enjoyed the game. *Heil Hitler.*' He saluted with a straight arm and as Von Bremen continued laughing Cole clicked his heels and spun round and departed, leaning heavily on his cane.

Ernst Von Bremen studied Cole's departing back and he frowned in thought as he waved his free hand in the air and Cole disappeared into the corridor, but he was soon distracted by the woman on his knee and he gave his attention to her.

Chapter Fifty

2 October 1943

Cole followed the stiff back of General Friedrich Christiansen past the huge metal machines. The noise in the cold corridor between them was loud and many of the workers, all Dutch collaborators, wore grey overalls and earmuffs of the same dull colour. There was no way of communicating without shouting and it was not until they left the bunker-like machinery room and its burning metal smell and passed by the huge generators, through a soundproof door to the small anteroom, that they could communicate.

Christiansen was accompanied by Cole and two of his Wehrmacht aides, Major Freud and Captain Klose. Freud spoke glowingly, 'It's marvellous, isn't it? The components are shipped by barge straight from here across the border to the Fatherland.'

Klose agreed, '*Ja*, it is wonderful. A brilliant feat of German engineering.' He turned to the general. 'Could we view more of the factory, General Christiansen? Like the dock where the barges enter the building?'

'Oh, and the packing area,' Cole added. 'That will be of interest to see. And I'd like to inspect the canal which has been dug from the river across here to the building, with the general's approval.'

'Good ideas,' the leader agreed.

They spent another hour on the site before Christiansen tired. 'And now we head back to Doetinchem for lunch.'

The party left the factory, passing the sentries at the barbed-wire gate in the fence which ran round the building and where their six-soldier escort waited. Cole paused to take a last look back at the top-secret installation. The factory was in dense woodland some three hundred and fifty yards from the Oude Ijssel river south-east of the town of Doetinchem and about eight miles from the German border in Gelderland. The building could not be seen from the river and a trench-like canal had been dug from the Oude Ijssel to the southern side of the factory. The loading dock was actually under the factory roof, inside.

Cole was secretly elated – for this was a factory manufacturing components for the V-Is, the unmanned rockets which Hitler was continuing to build at Peenemünde, though much was now done in underground bunkers, since the RAF raids. His intention, which was to come to fruition, was to use them against the civilian men, women and children of London.

The Allies would never expect this factory to be here in Holland: no doubt that was the reason for its existence.

Calculating how he could blow the place apart, Cole felt sure that if explosives were laid on one of the barges and it sailed into the factory, the whole building would explode, even most of the underground rooms. He determined to come back as soon as possible and do more exploration around the area.

'Are you coming, *standartenführer*?' Klose's voice rang in the chill air. Cole turned to him '*Ja*, of course, just admiring the place.'

As they walked side by side, Klose informed his listener, 'It's confidential, of course, but our Führer is calling the unmanned rocket, *vergeltungswaffe*.'

Cole translated in his head. *Retaliation weapon.* 'Ja, so I understand from the general.'

Light rain drifted down to adorn the shoulders of their great-coats with tiny glinting crystals as they followed Christiansen and Freud through the forest to the point where they had left their vehicles and walked in to the factory.

Cole was in a separate staff car to the general and his two officers so he had his driver take a slightly different route. 'Stop a minute.' He got out briefly and examined that section of the river. He was a few minutes late joining the party for lunch but laughed it off. 'I did a little sightseeing. I like this part of the country, perhaps it is because our border is so close, reminds me of home.'

This brought an indulgent smile from Christiansen.

They ate in a café on the Oude Ijssel which was a branch of the Rhine river and flowed across the border into Germany. The place was dark inside and smelt of cheese, a little of which sat out on a rack near the bar. Christiansen pulled on his long nose and pointed through the café window to a lengthy grey-stone, three-storeyed building in the distance. An amused expression rose in his hardened face. 'See that building surrounded by lawn, Lucien?'

Cole turned in his chair to look.

'You can have access to that particular place any time you like.'

Cole frowned. 'Can I?'

The German's heavy greying eyebrows, which peaked in the middle, lifted and his sharp-lined features eased into a facetious grin. 'Yes, and perhaps you should.'

Cole frowned but said nothing as the Luftwaffe general gestured with the knife he held towards the building and Cole could not help but think how his mother would have slapped the German's hand and said, '*Mauvaises manières! Don't point with your knife.*'

'You can go there today, Lucien, and you can help *Reichsführer* Himmler and our father the Führer, you must know that? All SS officers and Wehrmacht officers know.'

Cole had no idea what Christiansen was talking about but he got the strong sense that he damn well should know, so he merely gave a sharp nod of the head and said, 'Of course.'

'Then, as we're here, why don't you go? This one is exclusive to the SS, as I said.'

Cole had a drowning feeling, but Klose unwittingly came to his rescue as he swallowed a mouthful of bread and gave a much-needed clue. 'I hear the women in this one are quite beautiful. So what could be hard about having a night's fun and producing a baby for *Reichsführer* Himmler?'

Freud laughed and suddenly Cole realised what they were talking about. He had heard of these places but had never seen one. Venues where SS officers, and sometimes Wehrmacht officers, cohabitated with Aryan women for one or two nights and nine months later the woman returned to have the baby. All to build *the master race* for Hitler and his deputy Himmler.

So this building is bloody Reichsführer *Himmler's Doetinchem baby factory?*

Cole took a sip of the wine in front of him and, eyeing the general, gave him a supercilious look and a shake of his head. 'Not today, General, some other time. I need my strength for my work.'

Christiansen chuckled at this. 'But you have a girl, I hear.' He stabbed a piece of meat with the knife. 'A very beautiful woman, from what I'm told.'

Cole met the general's eyes. 'People will always talk, I suppose.'

'It's true, then, eh? I believe I remember her. I was told she was a one-time friend of an old acquaintance of mine, the Field Marshal, Walther von Reichenau.' He shook his head. 'Shame about the way Reichenau died in that aircraft crash as they brought him away from the Russian front; though they say he was near death anyway after the heart attack a few days prior.' He groaned in reflection. 'And he was five years younger than me, too. Anyway, if she was a friend of his, she's a good friend of ours. So you've chosen well.'

Cole knew about Letta's so-called friendship with Reichenau. She had met him through the Vichy leader Pétain when the German general had led the 6th Army and invaded Belgium and France. She had met Reichenau only once but had used his name with the Nazis here in Holland to keep up the pretence of being like-minded. He kept the sarcasm he felt out of his voice as he answered: 'Commissioner Wimmer approves of my choice as well.'

Christiansen nodded. 'Ah, does he? *Ja*, that is *gut*.' He pointed out the window again with his knife as he lifted his glass of beer in his other hand. 'A toast to the women of the Third Reich!'

As Klose and Freud followed suit Cole took a deep breath and raised his glass. They had just finished drinking when a courier marched into the room.

'General Christiansen?' He heiled Hitler and handed over a message.

Christiansen read it and his face clouded with fury. His right hand opened and closed in agitation as he growled, 'This is terrible. The whole yard full of petrol tanks and Wehrmacht lorries blew up at Zwolle Railway Station last night, an hour before midnight.'

They all looked at one another in amazement. 'What?'

Christiansen's mouth twisted and he made a rasping sound of

319

rage in his throat. 'Just hours after we all passed through the very same yard.'

Klose swore loudly and his fist came down on the table, his tone indignant as he asserted, 'This is too much. Do we have any idea who might be responsible, General?'

'*Nein*, but we will . . . we will.' He gazed down at the message. 'It says here six guards were badly injured. *Standartenführer* Von Bremen is in charge of the investigation.'

'This is awful,' commented Cole.

Freud shook his head disconsolately. 'Good heavens, there were dozens of tanks and lorries there.'

Rising abruptly from the table, his lunch ruined, Christiansen spoke as he pushed back his chair. 'Come, we should head back to Hilversum.'

They departed the small café, all talking to one another, yet Cole was celebrating and smiling inwardly. He knew exactly how the explosions had occurred.

He had carried with him two 'pocket incendiaries'. They were relatively compact, the size of small diaries, and burnt fiercely for a full minute. In the side of each incendiary shell was a rod which hid a slot. The timer was activated by sliding a coin along this aperture.

Their party had been at the station for over an hour and it had not been difficult for a *standartenführer* to separate himself from the others, walk through the yard and place the two combustible items inside a pair of lorries, under the seats.

SOE manufactured five different types of pocket incendiaries which were set to burn at varying times: after thirty minutes, two hours, six hours, twelve hours and twenty-four hours. His had been set for six hours.

It had been around 1815 when he placed them in the vehicles so, according to the inventor, they should have blown just after midnight, yet the message had said an hour before midnight: they were not quite as reliable as Dr Dudley Maurice Newitt, Director of Scientific Research for SOE, had claimed; but they had done their job and for that Cole was grateful.

As they headed to the cars, he strode along at Christiansen's side, commiserating.

Chapter Fifty-one

Mid-October

Light rain dusted the pane of the large window in Letta's parlour as purple clouds billowed in from the west and a small silver streak of lightning etched a crazy path down to the trees. Letta was painting when the Mercedes-Benz rolled through the gate to her front steps. She watched Lucien Bayer's body unfolding from the back seat and felt her pulse quicken. Unconsciously she put down her brush and hugged herself, arms crossed, until she heard his rap on the front door.

Cole exited the staff car and paused a moment, watching the gathering storm. He had been contemplating a great deal on his way here today. He had been into the wastes of the Veluwe and, having finally mended his broken wireless set, transmitted information to Hans Buckhout on the factory he had visited which was building the components for Hitler's V-I rocket. He had conceived a plan to blow up the place. Because the rocket components were boxed inside the factory and shipped straight on barges down the river and across the German border, he believed he could hijack the last barge of the day coming back in, set bombs on it, and blow the factory apart. Hans had agreed with the idea and was working on operatives to send in to do it, for Cole knew it was impossible for him to be directly involved. Yet they needed to be met once they landed and they required a safe house to stay in and that was when he had recalled that Letta owned a farmhouse in that part of Gelderland.

Cole did not want to work with anybody in the Netherlands Resistance movement and hence he and Hans both accepted that they needed Letta's help. As he mounted the steps two by two to her small front balcony he was highly conscious that he must bring her into his confidence for the first time.

The blue door opened and she smiled as she drew him into her hall. 'I've missed you so.'

He took off his cap and damp uniform jacket and folded her in his arms. She was wearing the blue dress with the white collar and the bows on the sleeves. 'I really like you in this,' he said as they embraced.

'I know you do, that's why I wear it.'

'I've missed you too,' he whispered into her hair. 'You smell so good . . . sweet, like the jasmine vine my . . .' he stopped talking and his mouth sought hers to hold her in an extended kiss.

As they separated, she gave her tinkling laugh. 'What were you going to say? "Like the jasmine vine my" – what?'

He brought his eyes to hers. She could see the uncertainty in them, as if he argued within himself. *I'm going to tell her about the factory so . . . so why not about this?*

He continued to hesitate before he answered, '. . . like the jasmine vine my mother grew at home.'

'Your mother? Lucien, your mother grew jasmine? It's the first thing you've ever told me about your family.'

323

'Mmm, well, I do have a mother.'

'Of course, and . . .' She hesitated and added, 'I'm sure she's lovely.'

As they walked through to the kitchen she took his arm and in his mind's eye he saw his mother in her broad-brimmed straw hat with the colourful band, standing hosing the garden with her pet lizard resting in the sun on the lawn near her. It had been amazing to him how that lizard revealed itself only to her. If anyone came from the house to the garden to see his mother it would run off into the ferns to its hiding place. It trusted her and only her. He wanted to tell Letta this, too, but he would save it for another time . . . perhaps. Today it was enough just to say something insignificant and yet personal, before he told her of the coming SOE operation.

'Tell me more about your family,' Letta requested softly at his side.

'Perhaps, some other time.'

Letta had expected this. But at last, after months of knowing him, he had finally said one tiny private thing. It was a victory.

Cole's mind turned to the urgent matter. 'Listen, Letta, I've something very important to tell you. You know I trust you?'

'Lucien, of course I do.'

'I need to tell you this because – I need your help.'

'Whatever it is, I'll help you. Tell me.'

He took her by the shoulders and gazed at her. 'I have always believed the best thing for you was to know nothing about me, except what is obvious. It is deliberate that I have not brought you into my confidence about my work or myself, but now I must.'

'My dear, dear Lucien, I understand. Go on.'

'I've discovered a top-secret factory making items significant to the Nazi war effort and I want to blow it to kingdom come.'

'My heaven, where is it?'

'A couple of miles outside Doetinchem. The engineers who designed it were brought in from Germany and poor bloody Polish slave labour was used to build it, but now it's manned by Dutch collaborators who work the machines. It's surrounded by barbed-wire fences and heavily guarded, but I'm confident there's a way to explode it.'

'How did you discover it?'

'I went there with Christiansen. Rauter lent me to him again. I've been in Wehrmacht Headquarters in Hilversum for over three weeks. Keeps me away from the Hague and that blasted Von Bremen, which is a blessing.'

He let go of her and took out a map from his pocket and spread it on the table and at the same time Letta turned away quickly and walked to the kitchen sink where she stood looking out the window.

She remained with her back to him while he went on in a jubilant voice, 'We went to visit this factory, it's hidden in a wood. This is a real coup for me, Letta. It couldn't be better. It sits well back from the Oude Ijssel river, camouflaged completely from above and some of it is underground; you'd never find it flying over. As I said, what is manufactured there is top secret and gets boxed inside the factory and shipped on barges straight down the river and across the border into Germany.'

He leant over the map spread out on the table. 'Darling, isn't your farmhouse over that way?'

Letta picked up the kettle and began to fill it.

'Letta, are you listening to me? Isn't your other house over that way?'

'What way?' She walked to the hob with the kettle and bent to light the fire for the stove.

'Darling, you're not listening to me. Stop!'

She stood upright.

'Why are you fiddling with the damn kettle when I have this critical thing to discuss?'

Taking a breath, she turned to him, a tiny frown puckering the smooth skin between her brows. 'I'm so sorry, Lucien, I know it's important, please go on.'

'Didn't you say you had a house, a sort of farm, over there, near the German border? Didn't you say that?'

She appeared to gather herself together. '*Ja*, it's on the edge of a wood north-east of Zelhem.'

'But that's near Doetinchem, isn't it?'

'*Ja*, perhaps five or six miles. It's closed up and the fields are fallow. A German unit commandeered it for some months last year, but they've gone and there aren't many troops around there now, it's so close to Germany.'

'And no one lives there?'

'Well, actually, Piet does. Piet Lombard. He's been caretaker there my whole life. He's old but fit; was a trusted friend of Rada's and he was always loyal to my mother. So, he's still there. The Germans have not taken him for the labour draft simply because of his age.'

'Is he trustworthy? I mean completely trustworthy?'

'Definitely. I think he would do anything for me . . . I've known him since I was a child. He's no Nazi sympathiser; he was the one who helped Rada and me to hide four Jewish children a year ago.'

'*Gut*, and you mentioned it's isolated?'

'It is, very.'

He was smiling. 'Then perhaps we can use it. Where is it?'

She pointed to the map. 'About here.'

326

He leant over and touched the map with his forefinger, speaking slowly, 'That's pretty good.' He looked up and smiled. 'North of Doetinchem and not too far from Zelhem there's a completely vacant area of some miles beyond the moorland and heath, where an RAF aircraft could drop the operatives. It's an area of open grassland, uncultivated, solid, away from the stretches of peat bog and completely away from habitation. I was over there not that long ago. I can get the co-ordinates.' He tapped the map, 'It's only a few miles across this way to your place. That's ideal.' He was full of enthusiasm and he looked intently at her. 'Can we use your farm for their safe house?'

She nodded. 'I'll have to tell Piet. How long would it be needed?'

'About a week if it goes right.' His eyes narrowed in thought as thunder rolled outside and the rain began on the window pane. 'Letta,' he took up her hands. 'We must accomplish this before the winter weather comes so it has to be soon. We need to have someone meet the agents when they land.'

She tapped her chin in thought. 'Well, it's impossible for you to be involved so I'll do it.'

'I'm sorry I have to bring you into it at all, but I have no choice.'

Her eyes softened and clouded with love for him as she answered gently, 'We all must take risks. It's the only way to defeat Hitler and his evil.'

He did not answer but took her hand and brought it to his lips and kissed it.

They both fell silent and he returned to the map, sitting down and studying it while she stood watching him.

It was Letta who spoke first. 'So tell me the plan.'

Lifting his gaze to her he smiled. 'Right, the last barge of the day comes in from Germany at twenty-three hundred and remains at the factory overnight for early morning loading. They have dug a canal from the river right inside the factory where the barges sail in and are packed so nothing is seen from outside.

'Almost a mile from the factory there's an area where the vessels have to keep to the side of the Oude Ijssel and sail under overhanging trees for about eighty yards. All the loaded ones have six guards; the empty ones coming in from Germany have only a driver and one guard. The last one comes in to sit overnight.

'So you see, we can drop down on the final one, take over, set an explosive charge and light the fuse to blow after it reaches the factory. It'll explode inside and . . . kaboom!' He hit the table with his fist.

He was now talking fast. 'The boys who come in will need to be strong swimmers because they'll have to leave the barge before it blows and swim downriver.' He let out a noisy breath of excitement and suddenly noticed the crease of worry sitting between Letta's inky eyes. 'Darling, there's nothing to worry about, this will work.'

She replied in a low, tense voice. 'We met in danger and we live in danger. Oh God, how I wish it were all over . . . all the fear and the worry.'

He rose and moved to her. 'Darling Letta. It will be, one day it will be.'

A crack of thunder sounded right above the house and she flinched. He moved round the table and hugged her as the lightning flared outside. 'It's only a storm.'

'Yes . . . only a storm, like the one we exist in constantly.' She rested her head on his shoulder for a few moments and then drew away with another sigh and shivered as she said, 'I will speak to Piet as soon as I can. Thank God I have passes to get there. Petrol is practically impossible to obtain and I'll have to have a reason to go down there.'

'I can supply a reason and the petrol.' He smiled encouragingly at her. 'I'll think of something you must do over there for me. I'll radio the co-ordinates to Hans in England as soon as I can to get RAF approval for the drop.' Cole slipped his arms around her and kissed her hair. 'And then we'll be set.'

They stood unmoving for some moments until she turned and purposefully took his arm, pulling him towards the stove, her voice lightening to a brighter note. 'Now, the kettle's nearly boiling; how about a cup of tea? I have a little left.'

She crossed to the dresser for cups – asking over her shoulder, 'You said earlier that you were pleased to be away from somebody called Von Bremen . . . who is he?'

Chapter Fifty-two

Cole's face stiffened. 'He's the new second in command to Rauter's deputy, who's another jolly little mass-murderer called Naumann.'

'You know . . . this man, Von Bremen?'

Cole paused and looked through the window at the rain. 'Ah, *ja*. He spent some years in Hamburg. I knew him before the war.'

'What's his rank, then? This Von Bremen?'

'Same as me, a *standartenführer*. The bastard's been with Naumann on the eastern front killing Jews and Communists and other unlucky devils.'

'Oh my God! Really?' Her hand went to her mouth.

'*Ja*, really. Makes me sick.'

Letta paused and she turned her head to continue speaking as she busied herself with the cups and spoons. 'Is he a young man?'

'Late-thirties I suppose, around my age. He's a meticulous dresser, always immaculate – unlike Wimmer, who looks like he slept in his blasted uniform.'

'I see. Where is he from? Originally, I mean.'

'From? Stuttgart, I believe. Why? Why all these questions about him?'

'Nothing . . . it's just that you are obviously uneasy about the man.'

'Uneasy? No, why would I be?'

'I have no idea. You said you were happy to avoid him and to be with Christiansen.'

'Did I?'

'You know you did.'

He suddenly walked away out into the hall and she followed him.

'Lucien, are you all right?'

It was dark where he halted between the kitchen and the parlour door and he stood leaning, one hand on the wall.

'Lucien, what is it?'

He turned slowly round to her and took the three steps back to where she stood.

How desperately he hated that she called him Lucien. He badly wanted to tell her he was not Lucien Bayer, not a *standartenführer*, but an Australian, a squadron leader in the RAF who worked for the British secret service; that all these months she believed he was an SS officer who had defected to the British when all along he was pretending to be Bayer: living every day with men he despised. He wanted to tell her that Von Bremen knew the real Bayer and that was why he was a threat. That Hans Buckhout had suggested he come out of the Netherlands before Christmas; that he take the first escape route by torpedo boat soon before the water got too cold to swim out to it. And if men were sent in to blow the factory he should get out prior or around the same time. Every day that dawned he wanted to be honest with her and tell her these things.

But instead he simply folded her in his arms and kissed her hair and said, 'Letta, Letta.'

She leant her head on his shoulder and thought of the other men who had been in her life and, for the first time ever, true remorse overwhelmed her. She could not claim to have held her virtue highly, and she had used her looks to her own advantage. She had done foolish things and was sorry for them; but surely it was not too late? She had changed and this man had changed her.

'Lucien, I'm frightened.' She spoke into his chest. 'I love you.'

He turned her face up to his and kissed her a long time and when he drew away he said in the same quiet tone, 'Please don't be frightened . . . and I love you, Letta.'

'I think of you all the time . . .' She paused and did not go on as tears filled her eyes.

'Darling Letta, now why the tears?'

'I don't know . . . We can never be normal. It's all so grim and awful. You live in danger all the time. I'm horribly scared for you.'

He made a grinding sound in his throat. 'For me? Listen, I'm touched by your concern—'

'Touched by my concern?' she broke in, her voice grating in sharp contrast to her normal mellow tone. A faraway look rose in her eyes as her face fell into sombre lines. She repeated, 'Touched by my concern? That sounds so stiff and formal.'

'Letta, my lovely Letta.' He kissed her forehead.

Turning her head down so as not to look at him, she controlled her voice. 'I have this odd, ridiculous dream that you and I . . . will live happily ever after once this disgusting war is over. I know people are dying and dreams are shattered every minute of the day . . . but that's my hope, the one I cling to . . . the one that keeps me sane.' She slipped from his embrace and walked back to the kitchen.

This time he followed her and stood close behind her.

'I know I'm a fool, but you've altered me. I feel there's a purpose . . . instead of just hating the invaders and doing what I could to help Rada when he was alive and not caring much for how I did it; but now, I'm scared. Scared I might lose you and the things I want. It all matters now and I want all sorts of things: I want a future . . . with you.' Her voice broke and she sobbed the words. 'But then . . . why should my dream be the one that survives . . . when so many others won't?'

Her body sagged and he slid his arms around her waist and turned her to him, pulling her close and whispering in her ear, 'Why shouldn't it be your dream that survives? My beautiful Letta . . . why shouldn't it be?' He tenderly kissed the tear marks on her cheek and held her tightly, encasing her body with his own.

She looked up at him with a hopeful expression in her eyes and, pulling her even more tightly to him, he smoothed her hair with tender strokes.

And as he did so, she asked very softly, 'Did you ever love anyone else?'

Chapter Fifty-three

He was looking down at the woman with him, where just moments before he had seen tears and a fragility, a complete defencelessness.

Cole stared at her and thought of the women he had known but the one who overpowered them in his head was Shelly Longford. It was mostly the same picture he saw: the unaffected Queenslander with the green eyes riding Cromwell across the fields of paspalum grass on the other side of the world. He recalled taking her to his cricket matches in the North Ipswich Reserve Ground and to the soccer matches in the suburb of Bundamba on Saturday afternoons, laughing with her on the dance floor at the Trades' Hall, and going to 'the pictures' with her in the Winter Garden Theatre on East Street.

He remembered the exciting sensuous tenderness he had felt for her when she was in his arms and the amazing knack she had of making him feel content with himself.

He had written to Shelly when he joined SOE almost two years ago: he had not communicated since, though each time he went back to England her letters waited for him. He had ended his final message to her with the words: *You might not hear from me for a long, long time. I can't tell you why. But please don't worry about me. Perhaps it's better if you forget about me; in war anything can happen and it is not fair of me to expect you to wait.*

He had signed it simply: *Cole.*

Letta's eyes were on his and her head was gently inclined to the side as she waited to have her question answered. Her body moved, touching his and the magnetism of the woman he held now was overwhelming.

Hell, Shell, you might as well be on another planet. You're cosseted in the normalcy of southern Queensland. Where, even though there's a war on and the bloody Japs are near, you still have no idea of all this endless diseased disorder that is Europe under the Nazis. You can never understand any of this. It would be asking the night to understand the day. But Letta understands, understands it all, every bit of it.

It's changed me for ever, Shell, and you? You, my dear and lovely Shell, will have remained the same. QED.

Cole continued to stare at Letta as he brought his hand up and touched her mouth with his index finger, gently caressing her lips and stroking the dark spot at the side of her mouth, and now he replied, 'Letta, the love I have for you overpowers any other I have ever felt.'

Her expression changed. For a moment he thought he saw into the depths of the woman who was Laetitia de Witt, the vulnerability and unguarded sensitivity.

'Can we ever be together?'

He folded her again within his arms and kissed her hair. 'I'm working on that. There are things I must tell you: wonderful things about our future together. Not now, not today; but some time soon.'

'I know that, Lucien, in my heart I know that. And I can wait.'

And, tilting her head, he smiled down at her and kissed her on the mouth.

When they broke apart, he glanced to the window where the storm had passed and the shape of an automobile was entering the now darkening yard. 'My keepers are here.' The car and the motorbike escort had arrived to take him back to Apeldoorn. 'I tried to commandeer a staff car on my own this afternoon; sometimes I manage, but today, no.'

Letta looked round to the window and back to him. 'You know, I've been thinking you take a risk in a car by yourself. There are occasionally attacks by the Resistance on lone Germans.'

Cole regarded her sceptically. 'My lovely Letta, *occasional* is the word. People are too damn frightened to kill Germans. Rauter's lot have them terrified. Harster was bad enough as Rauter's second in charge, but now he's gone and Naumann's here, he's introducing a higher level of police terror than ever before. And Naumann's got his bloody vigilant aide, Von Bremen, making sure of that with an organised gang called Aktion Silbertanne who are carrying out more reprisal murders on the Dutch for acts against the German occupation.'

Letta trembled and he felt the quiver ripple through her as she translated, 'Action Silver Fir.'

'*Ja.*' He caught her to him. 'Darling, please don't fear for me; it's you I worry about.'

'Why?'

'I've been doing my own thinking. People, ordinary Dutch people, will regard you as a collaborator and the mistress of a Nazi.'

She answered thoughtfully, 'I suppose so.'

Cole took her wrists and held her at arm's length. 'You were saying earlier, that you're scared for me. The danger is not for me, it's in your countrymen's believing you're a traitor.'

Now she shrugged in a nonchalant way. 'Oh, I shouldn't worry about that. Truly, I'm not worried about assassination.' She stepped out of his embrace. 'Lucien?'

'Yes?'

'If anything ever happens and we're separated . . .'

'Why are you saying this?'

She took his arms in her hands holding him tightly. 'Things go wrong in wartime.'

Cole looked into her eyes and held her shoulders. 'Now let's stop this. You're getting far too anxious.'

She shook her head and moved out of his grasp. 'But you never can tell. I just want us to have another plan.'

'Like what?'

'Oh, I don't know: meeting somewhere . . . even when the war's over . . . like Switzerland. My Uncle Glenro, my mother's half-brother, has a villa there on Lake Geneva. He adores me and I used to go there for holidays before the war.' She walked to the kitchen dresser and opened a drawer, still speaking as she rifled through the contents. Suddenly she gave an exclamation of satisfaction. 'Ah, here they are!' She spun round towards him and handed him two postcard photographs. The first was obviously taken by a professional photographer; of her on a patio with water in the background. She looked a few years younger but just as beautiful.

Dressed in a clinging evening gown she leant against a stone pillar, her long hair nestling on her shoulders. She turned it over in his hands and on the back she had written *Laetitia de Witt at Uncle Glenro's villa, on the lake: 1938*. The second sepia photograph was of the villa itself, grand, imposing, with a row of linden trees to the right of the entrance.

Cole stood holding them in his hands and shaking his head.

'Listen, I told you, I'm working on a way for us to remain together.'

'Please humour me, just keep them; and this . . .' She turned to the drawer again and took out a piece of cardboard and a fountain pen and wrote something before she handed it to Cole. 'This is the address of Uncle Glenro's villa, my mother's half-brother; it simply bears his name. It's called Villa Thalberg. Please . . . commit it to memory and destroy this.'

He made a long-suffering sound and held her chin as he looked earnestly at her. 'Letta, Letta, yes, I'll humour you and do as you ask; I want to keep the likeness of you anyway but this is all silly talk.' He kissed her again and when she moved from his arms she said softly, 'Give me back the photograph of myself please.'

He did and she put it on the table and wrote on the back beneath the words already there:

My Darling Lucien,
We'll live together here after the war.

He took the postcard from her, read the inscription, closed his eyes momentarily and kissed her swiftly on the forehead. And still holding the cardboard, he slid the two photographs in his pocket and strode to the front door.

She heard the door close and, moving a few paces, she stood looking out the window to where she could see the escort waiting. When the car started and drove away she thought of those men who had been close to her; one by one. She shivered and drew her hand across her eyes. What a hopeless, superficial life she had led until the war; and even in war she had been foolish. She was reminded of the fascinating Dirk and shook her head in newfound regret.

Her fingers trembled as she lifted them to touch the window for there was fear, great fear in her heart. She was terrified to lose what she felt for Lucien.

Turning her head she gazed across the gentle gradient in front of the sheds where wild daffodils dotted the grass in summer, but now all was bare in the face of the coming winter. A shuddering sigh escaped her lips as she leant her forehead upon her hand on the glass and closed her eyes.

Chapter Fifty-four

The following day: late afternoon.

Letta was painting Lucien, stroking colour on his imitation sleeve on the canvas, her long fingers moving the brush in neat, precise strokes. The wind outside made the shutters creak but it was not cold enough to waste the precious coal which had come by the grace of Lucien for use in the depths of winter.

His eyes stared at her; she had captured the inscrutable look he often wore, yet the determination of his character was evident and at the same time her skill had revealed a trace of the arrogance which lived in his expression; not that she believed him truly arrogant like many of his race were, it was simply a look she thought he affected.

The scars on his face and neck above his collar brought a sense of mystery to the image and a tremor ran though her for she felt it was her finest work.

Stepping back to distance herself from it, she continued to eye her creation wondering, as all artists do, whether to add more paint here and there and she moved in to daub a minute adjustment on the small scar above his shirt collar, to the left of his Adam's apple.

As the brush touched the canvas Letta looked up into the eyes of the painting. What this man was doing was hardly credible: if they ever caught him he would be tortured to death. She put down her brush on the easel, wiping that thought from her mind.

She whispered, 'I love you' to the replica in front of her and lifted her right hand to stroke the side of his face on the canvas. 'What a miracle it would be if we could be together always . . .' she continued speaking softly, 'you are so different from Rauter and the others; you care about the Jews and sometimes it's hard for me to believe you ever were a committed Nazi. But you must have been, to become a colonel. What changed you and when?'

What was it he had said when she had asked if they could really be together? '*I'm working on that. There are things I must tell you: wonderful things about our future together. Not now, not today; but some time soon.*' Ja, that was what he had said.

She picked up her brushes and cleaned them and when they lay drying she crossed to the generous front window, so indicative of Dutch homes, to gaze out to the stream beyond the damaged fence. It had rained earlier and tiny rivulets had stained the glass in front of her eyes. Over the water and through the trees she could see her only neighbour, a now deserted house. The family who had lived there had been raided by the feared German 'green police' – so called because of the colour of their uniforms – who had found a hidden radio in their attic. Officially they were known as the Order Police and their assignment was to arrest, deport and execute *the enemies of Nazi Germany*.

The parents and the two children had been taken away. They had been listening to British radio broadcasts and this was '*verboten*'. On the BBC there was a special programme in Dutch called *Radio Orange – Radio Oranje* – a fifteen-minute broadcast. It was designed to give hope to the conquered Netherlands and often eminent figures such as Prime Minister Winston Churchill spoke words of encouragement to them. So, too, did Holland's own Queen Wilhelmina, who had been evacuated to safety in England on HMS *Hereward* on 13 May 1940, three days after the German invasion. She was loved by her people and her broadcasts brought some optimism to Dutch patriots. Letta had kept a radio early in the war but when Rada's had broken eighteen months ago, she had given it to him.

She felt lonely. It was unusual for Letta, for she did not mind her own company and she decided to walk along the stream to her special arbour. She put on a raincoat and boots and left the house.

As she walked over the sodden ground, into her mind came a picture of her mother and father. She could remember them together only once; when she was very small, perhaps three: *they each had hold of one of her hands and she walked between them through a darkened street on the way to a party. The family trio turned a corner and the lights of the hall where they were going gleamed invitingly ahead in the night. She was excited to be out after dark for it rarely happened* . . . and the feeling of security she experienced as a tiny tot walking between her mother and father momentarily flooded back through her.

Her mouth tightened in memory. Her parents had separated when she was four. Apparently her Dutch mother and half-French father had been ill-suited from the start.

She looked along the canal, remembering her mother: beautiful and merry and light-hearted, always out and about in society, her long, dark hair curling to her shoulders and her penchant for wearing cheerful bright-coloured bangles on her arms. When Hitler's jackbooted disciples had invaded her country her bad heart worsened and it had been Rada who had been at her mother's bedside with

Letta when she died. From that moment Letta and Rada had become truly close.

She shook her head as she walked, for now Rada had been taken from her by the enemy. How ardently she hated them. Yes, she would do whatever she could to blow up this factory Lucien had found.

Her father had been the opposite to her mother, serious and often grim, though she had loved him and visited him whenever she could. She suspected his attitudes had been formed in the harsh regime of military life. His mother had been Dutch and his father French and he had ended up a general but had been a major – a commandant – at Verdun in the Great War, yet never spoke of it.

She trembled though she was not cold.

As four geese with black faces waddled along the bank towards her she thought again of her mother and a tear slipped down her cheek. Her mother had always had a man at her side. 'Perhaps that's why I've done such foolish things, Muma,' she said to herself, 'watching your example. But I don't blame you, no, I don't. And now for the first time in my life I'm really in love.'

The thought of Lucien made her feel a little happier and as the wind was rising, she did not go as far as her secret bower but turned and walked back, lifting her eyes to the dull sheet of grey which was the sky. The geese stood as if in wait for her. In the old days she fed them here. 'I'm sorry I have no food for you any more,' she murmured as she passed and they entered the stream behind her.

She wondered what life would be like when the war was over; would it be possible that she and Lucien actually could be together permanently? Would they ever live in Uncle Glenro's villa as she had written in a moment of hope on her picture? Always her life had been complicated, and now? There was the added complexity of loving Lucien.

She had gained the path leading to the gate in the broken fence when she found herself thinking of the night she had seen Dirk and the others off on their escape to England. She shook her head as she remembered the time she had spent with the leader and the words she had said to him when she kissed him goodbye. How guilty she felt about all that now.

Halting by a trellis which stood inside her yard she bit her lip in contemplation. She pictured Dirk: the physical beauty of the man; she heard his mellow tone in her mind and his infectious laugh. Perhaps she could have cared deeply for him, if not for Lucien. But she would never see him again so it did not matter. She nodded her head to herself. Yes, it had all been folly with Dirk and she regretted it now but that was before she fell truly in love . . . so much was before she fell in love. If only she could change all that, wipe away the past as she would paint over a mistake in one of her oils. If only life could be like that.

Taking a deep breath she plunged her hands into her pockets and crossed the yard towards her house. Passing the sheds her head swivelled as she heard an engine and looked down to her gate on the road where an automobile swung in and halted. It was black and enormous; larger than the Mercedes-Benz which Cole often used and it was a different shape. Letta did not recognise it for the Maybach staff car that it was but she knew it was a Nazi vehicle. Suddenly she shivered for there was something ominous and almost sentient about the machine as the round headlamps appeared to her like huge eyes staring at her and looming over her front gate.

She watched the proceedings with a deep crease forming between her eyes. A driver jumped out and opened the gate for a man to enter and come towards her between the oak trees.

A few seconds later Laetitia's face stiffened and her pulse quickened as she recognised him. She had not seen him for years but would always remember the imperious saunter which passed for his walk.

Calming herself, she inhaled deep breaths of cool air as she watched him take off his cap and stride towards her. Nearing her he lifted his arm in greeting. 'Laetitia, *mein Liebling*, how good to see you.'

'I wondered if you would come here.' She managed to keep her voice steady.

'Of course you did. And see, here I am. You're more lovely than you were . . . nine? ten? years ago. Suddenly I realise how I've missed you.' He looked around and his hair lifted in the air as he pointed. 'Shall we go in out of the wind?'

'Why can't we talk here? What do you want?'

'I'm uncertain, but I'll let you know. Now, I said *shall we go in out of the wind?*' His tone became harsh and intimidating.

She did not reply but led him up to the blue door; she knew her hand was shaking as she opened it. Once inside he followed her through to the parlour where he stood for a long time in front of the portrait. She felt sick and wished she had not left it on the easel.

He brought his heavy-lidded eyes round to hers. 'You paint him with . . . with such . . . precision and care. I might add, it's a work of painstaking attention to every detail. I'd forgotten what a talent you have. Where's the one you did of me? I'd like to compare them.'

'Must you do this?'

'*Ja*, I must.' His eyes narrowed and his voice hardened. 'I was in the Hague and went to Amsterdam but you were not there, so I guessed this was where I'd find you. I have only just arrived in Apeldoorn to learn you are having this affair.' He flicked his fingers at the portrait. 'I'm not happy about it and don't understand it, so we'd better talk. Now offer me a drink and we'll chat about the past . . . and the future.'

'Why does it matter to you what I do?'

'Ah, I have decided it does. You have matured so perfectly, you know; into a true beauty. And you've had a big change of heart, I understand. Saw the light, did you?'

Her mind was leaping from thought to thought. What was the best way to react to him? To cajole him? To be aggressive? To be submissive? He was as strange as ever. She tried to sound nonchalant. 'What does that mean?'

'Now, now, Laetitia. Years ago you were so distressed about what I wanted to do.' He snapped his fingers. 'So distraught. Now, I find out you are *V-manner*, which intrigues me so very much.' His blue eyes narrowed, contemplating her. 'For one who hated the NSDAP and our leader the Führer as vehemently as you did, something is very, very odd about the fact that you are now a trusted friend of my associates here: a good friend of the dead Commissioner Schmidt, I'm told . . . and you have taken Bayer as a lover. He's an old colleague of mine.'

He smiled at her and she felt ill to the pit of her stomach. *Lucien an old colleague of yours . . . oh no, that cannot be.*

'By the way, for the life of me, I cannot understand what has attracted you to Lucien Bayer. He was always lugubrious. Too serious, even dull: not your type at all. And since I've seen Bayer

346

again – you know it's odd, the man is just intrinsically different, somehow, and I'm sure it's nothing to do with the fact that he's been wounded.' He gave a sharp laugh and pointed his long index finger at her. 'And you can understand why I am confused, Laetitia, my lovely one, when after the passing years I am told you are one of us . . . after all.'

The visitor departed as twilight sank and shadows deepened across the yard and a fine rain began to fall. He turned to look back as he paused on her front balcony beside her terracotta plant pots. 'I shall let your little flirtation go on for the time being.'

Is it best for him to think it means nothing? Oh God, what should I say? 'Surely it does not matter to you what I do?'

'Ah, *ja*, you've been telling me that. But I think I've decided it does.' A twisted smile stretched his mouth. 'I'll be back to see you, Laetitia, when I'm ready.' And giving a short, callous laugh he shot up his right hand to take hold of her chin between his thumb and forefinger.

She jerked her face from his grasp, uttering. 'Don't do that . . . please.'

'Now now, *Liebling* . . . you'll have to be more friendly.'

She gave him as real a smile as she could muster. 'I was not trying to be *un*friendly. You must remember that I'm still a little surprised to see you.'

He seemed to believe this, for he nodded with an equable expression on his face before he spun on his heel and strode to the steps while Laetitia remained at her open door holding the handle and watching his dark shape descend to the bottom where he turned and lifted his hand in the crepuscular light of the evening. 'Until I see you again, my dear.'

She forced herself to lift her hand in reply and stood still, watching through the falling rain until he gained his vehicle and she heard it pull away, when her head dropped to her chest and she held her hands to her temples.

Chapter Fifty-five

Deep in rolling sandhills and wood-covered ridges of the Veluwe region on the edge of a small forest reeking of mould, Cole knelt on the ground in front of his crackling radio set, his codes marked on a silk handkerchief open beside him. As he finished writing down the coded message from England, the wireless went silent. He took off his headphones and deciphered the first line fairly briskly. *Weather permitting target 9 Nov.*

So he had the date. They would come in on the seventh and they would explode the factory two nights later. The rest of the message he would unravel back in his bedroom. An order from London was now in place that no wireless telegraphy transmission was to last longer than five minutes to or from agents in the field, for some had been caught at their transmitting sets because they stayed on air too long.

All SOE agents made contact with Britain through an official receiver site. The main site was Grendon Hall in Underwood, Station 53A, and another had recently been established: Poundon House, Station 53B, in Buckinghamshire. It was because Cole's mission was so sensitive, above top secret and being guided by Hans Buckhout himself that Cole made direct contact with Hans or his two assistants at Hans's headquarters, the country farmhouse in Essex. This was where Cole had been trained and where Hans had been allowed to set up a small independent receiver site.

Cole's was the latest version of wireless set and was camouflaged inside a small leather suitcase but he had to feed out over seventy feet of aerial so he needed to be in remote spots like this one, late in the day, when he could be sure people were not abroad. He removed the crystal from the radio set and neatly reeled in the long wire antenna to fit it back into the compartment in the lid before he snapped closed his case and folded up his handkerchief.

He found it relatively simple to charge his batteries off mains power in his rooms but he had to find remote positions to call London. Nazi direction-finding vans roamed the city streets and were quick to pick up wireless signals.

But there were very few German direction-finding vehicles in the countryside and that's why Cole came out into the wild Veluwe region to the west and south-west of Apeldoorn to transmit, where there were heathlands, sand dunes and densely wooded areas. Occasional bike tracks and certain dirt roads ran over it, and there were tiny villages and isolated farms but the majority of its thirty-odd square miles was uninhabited.

Cole sniffed the damp air as he stood and brushed the tiny pieces of bracken from the knees of his trousers before he lifted his cane and put it under his arm to stride along through the wood, the leaves and pine needles crunching beneath his boots. He leapt over a mud pool and abruptly a wild boar ran across his path from a cluster of heather. He stopped and watched it disappear before continuing for some minutes, until he came out of the trees and crossed a hundred yards of heather-covered land to another small forest. He skirted the trees and traversed a thick grassy patch to a wide ditch where he leapt over roots, around bracken and through moss until he came out of it near a thick stand of elms, where a snake slithered away from his boots. Passing round the edge of the trees he descended a gentle sandy slope to another small forest.

It was dusk when he approached the road and he began to lean on his cane and limp again as he exited the wood to the dirt thoroughfare and halted as he saw *Brigadeführer* Erich Naumann. He stood near Cole's car, an empty Volkswagen schwimmwagen. *Oh Jesus, what the hell's he doing out here?* In his grey uniform and with his narrow head he had the aspect of a large, threatening bird perched by the car's bonnet.

Cole took a deep breath, waved a greeting which resembled a Hitler salute and limped forward. That was when he made out Ernst Von Bremen some thirty yards beyond Naumann in the falling gloom, waiting near a cluster of young oaks and, beyond him, four German soldiers stood at ease by their motorcycles and sidecars. In the distance was a staff car with a driver near the engine.

Cole took this all in at a glance and spoke first. '*Brigadeführer*, what brings you out into the countryside so late in the day? Are you like me? A lover of nature?' He moved across to the schwimmwagen and leant his cane on the bonnet as he casually dropped his suitcase down on the seat and turned back to smile widely at Naumann.

Naumann's thin lips parted in a reciprocal smile. '*Standartenführer*, we had no idea this vehicle was yours. When we saw it here we stopped to investigate, thinking it was abandoned.'

At that moment Von Bremen walked up. '*Ja*, we thought we should examine it, all on its own out here.'

Cole spoke to Naumann. '*Danke* for halting to check. We cannot be too careful. I occasionally come here for the solace the open countryside brings me; this country is so flat – the towns are so

351

busy, that I hanker for the mixture of woods and open land as a diversion. Yet it is all so unlike the Fatherland.'

'*Ja*, I understand.' Naumann shook his head in disapproval. 'But an officer of the Reich alone is a target for these Dutch vermin, especially here in the waste of the Veluwe.'

Cole nodded. 'Perhaps you are right, *brigadeführer*.'

'Of course I am right.'

Von Bremen's eyes wore a disdainful expression as he informed the Nazi general, '*Standartenführer* Bayer is reckless at other times, too; he visits his mistress alone as well.'

Cole locked eyes with Von Bremen. 'You have found out a lot about my habits in a short time, *Standartenführer* Von Bremen.'

'Ah, Lucien, let's use our first names, as we once did.'

Cole bowed from the neck. 'As you would like.'

Naumann's mouth drew down in dissatisfaction. 'Do you visit your mistress alone?'

Cole cleared his throat. 'At times.'

'That is foolish too and I want no more of it. You will take one of my escort back with you to Apeldoorn now.' He called forward one of the soldiers as Cole nodded again sharply from the neck answering, '*Ja*, of course, *brigadeführer*.'

Von Bremen gestured into the distance. 'Is there something of interest to see here?'

Cole was quick to answer, 'It depends if you are fascinated by nature. Are you?'

'No, I can't say that I am, but we gather you are.'

'*Ja*, that's true. There's a small spring back there – cool, clear water.' He gestured behind him. 'Today I was amazed to see a single black-tailed godwit remaining. This is the beginning of winter; it should be in Africa.'

'A godwit? That's a bird, isn't it?' Naumann asked.

Cole's manner became one of enthusiasm, raising his voice for effect. '*Jawohl*, it's a wading bird, *brigadeführer*, of the *Limosa* genus, about this big –' he gauged the size with his hands – 'there are three sub-species all with orange-russet head, neck and chest. In breeding plumage and winter colouration they are dull grey-brown, but they have a distinctive black-and-white wing bar at all times. It's amazing how far this bird can travel . . . to the ends of the earth, now can you imagine that? So, like most waders, it has a lengthy bill and a neck which can stretch and long legs and it breeds in fens, damp meadows, lake edges, bogs, almost any—'

'*Ja, ja*, I'm sure.' Naumann had had enough of this and cut him off as Von Bremen caught Cole's eye.

'So you draw them, do you?'

'*Ja*, Ernst, often. Why?'

Von Bremen pointed to the small suitcase containing the wireless lying on the car seat. 'I assume you have pencil and papers in there.'

Cole grinned. 'Correct, Ernst', and he opened the door of the Volkswagen and took out the crank and turned back to Naumann. 'I must get back to Apeldoorn. If you don't mind my asking, *brigadeführer*, what are you both doing out here, if you are not going for a walk like me?'

'We're on our way to Arnhem.'

'Really?' He moved around to the front of the engine. 'You're well out of your way. The main road is over there.' Cole pointed to the east.

A supercilious expression rode the extreme angles of Naumann's face but it was Von Bremen who answered, '*Brigadeführer* Naumann likes to travel on out-of-the-way back roads now and then. One never knows what one will find.'

Cole clicked his heels and raised his arm in perfect robot-like fashion and the two Germans replied in kind as he bent and put the crank in the crankshaft and started his engine.

'Must be arduous walking in the Veluwe with a cane,' Von Bremen observed and Cole shook his head.

'Not really, my knee improves all the time, the exercise is good for it.'

Keeping the two Germans in his vision, Cole slid into the driver's seat while they strode back towards their car and the soldiers with them mounted their BMW motorbikes.

Just as the Germans reached their vehicle, Naumann paused, turned and called, '*Standartenführer?*'

Cole's head swung round. '*Ja, brigadeführer?*'

'I'd like to see your drawings some time.'

'Of course you shall.' Cole lifted his hand in salute as he drove away.

When the two SS officers climbed into the back seat of the staff car, Von Bremen shook his head. 'I don't know Bayer intimately, but there was a short time in Hamburg when we mixed in the same circles and I saw quite a lot of him. I never heard him talk about blasted birds and nature before.'

'*Ja*, he was positively ardent. Must be something he got interested in recently since he was wounded on the Russian front.'

'*Ja*, must be. Birds, of all things? All I know about them is that I hate crows.' He frowned in thought. 'Yet Lucien Bayer seems very altered to me from the man I knew.'

'Really? What do you mean? This penchant he has for nature?'

354

'*Ja*, that and other things — for one, his hands seem different.'

The SS general grunted in surprise. 'His hands?'

'I could be wrong, but I seem to recall he had big, flat hands. They are not like that any more.' Von Bremen paused in contemplation before he added, 'And I'm damned if I don't think he's taller than he used to be.'

Brigadeführer Erich Naumann gave a shrill laugh as he leant back in the seat. 'Ernst, no, you must be wrong. Your memory plays tricks.'

Von Bremen's chiselled features became grim. 'Perhaps you are right, *brigadeführer*. Time can play tricks on us all.'

Chapter Fifty-six

22 October

The sun was starting to fade through the coloured-glass windows of the grey-stone restaurant on the edge of Apeldoorn which was for the exclusive use of the invaders' hierarchy. Cole and Letta sat at a white cloth-covered table and one other was occupied by a Wehrmacht captain drinking alone. Cole took up Letta's hand and spoke in an undertone. 'I hate this place but at least we can be alone.'

'I feel guilty eating well when everything is rationed and so many of my countrymen are hungry.'

'I know you do. Letta, I must get back to my office, I'm to meet Wimmer. He and Himmler have a plan to reopen Leiden University for Dutch collaborators from the army and the SS.'

The University of Leiden had been closed down in May 1942 when the patriotic majority of the faculty had resigned rather than be coerced into following German demands relating to the persecution of the Jews.

Letta nodded. 'I remember when many of the faculty were arrested. I knew one of the professors in law. He was a brave man.

I wonder if he is still alive?' She shook her head. 'How odd that you have to work with Wimmer on reopening it.'

'Not from choice and I won't be working too hard on it, I can tell you, but I do have to meet with him.'

Silence fell between them. Cole had noticed that Letta was not her usual self: on the surface she appeared to be but there were moments when her face fell into repose and her usual graceful features dropped into heavier lines of despondency. He had decided that it was because of his idea to explode the factory and that it was natural for her to be concerned about it. He lifted her hand to his lips and kissed it and she shivered.

'Darling, you're trembling.'

'Oh, I'm just cold, that's all; it's a little chillier this afternoon.' She removed her pale fingers from Cole's on the white tablecloth and, running her nail – a perfect ellipse shining in the light of the candle – across the skin on the back of his hand, murmured, 'Your hand is so brown compared to mine.' She turned her head and kissed his cheek. They rose and he wrapped the cape around her shoulders and they moved to the door. Outside the breeze dallied round them and her hair rippled gently on her shoulders as she walked, her heels making distinct clicks on the stone of the footpath. He could smell the faint sweet essence of her perfume, exotic like herself, wafting around him as they crossed to the staff car and the corporal opened the door for them to slide into the seat.

'Take me to my office and then return Fräulein de Witt to her home.'

It took only a few minutes to arrive at the town hall and as Cole stepped out of the vehicle Friedrich Wimmer's secretary came down the steps. 'Ah, *standartenführer*, I have caught you. Commissioner

Wimmer sends his compliments but he cannot meet with you, for he has been called to the Hague.'

As he got back into the car and told Letta that he could spend a few more hours with her, her spirits seemed to be back to normal, for she leant over to him and took his hand. 'That's wonderful.'

They were delayed on the road to her home by troop movements and it was almost dark when they entered the blue door of the house near the stream. Taking off their coats Cole found a lamp and lit it and soon they sat together in the parlour with curtains drawn, so that no light was revealed to the outside, and a small fire crackling in the grate.

'Letta,' Cole took up her hands in his, 'I did not tell you in the restaurant, but I now have the date to blow up the factory: the ninth of November, let's hope that's a propitious day for us. My superior in England has found operatives who have the ability to swim the river and they don't dare to leave it any longer because winter could set in and make it all impossible.'

Her hands slipped around her waist as she considered what he had said. 'Just three weeks. Then I . . . need to get over to the farm and see Piet.'

'You do. Now there are other things I want to discuss. Darling, earlier you seemed faraway and detached. Is something wrong?'

Letta shifted a little on the sofa as she replied, 'Well, I suppose I am thinking about all sorts of matters. *Ja*, about the factory, what needs to be done . . . I worry sometimes about a lot of things.'

He hugged her. 'Of course you do, I understand.' He looked into her eyes and tenderly touched the inky dot at the corner of her mouth. 'You're so beautiful, I don't want you to worry. Everything will be all right. But there is something I have decided I must tell you.'

She gazed at him and he hesitated for a few moments before he began: 'I have avoided telling you what I'm about to say and I want you to listen carefully. If I had not fallen in love with you it all would have been simpler for me. I would have come here and done what needed to be done and then disappeared – all as planned. But everything has altered.'

'Lucien, what are you talking about?'

'It is time to tell you what I've held from you. I've been organising to take you out of Holland with me.'

Her eyes opened wide in surprise. 'What do you mean?'

'As soon as we've exploded this blasted factory, my superiors in England want to bring me out of Holland and I want to take you along. I've told them about you in a wireless message and I've informed them that I'll be bringing you out with me.' He paused momentarily and with a fixed look at her said, 'Letta, I am not Lucien Bayer.'

She sat perfectly still, her eyes on his. 'You . . . are . . . not . . . Lucien Bayer?'

'I'm a British secret agent masquerading as Bayer. He looked very much like me so they made some adjustments to my face . . . to my body . . . I studied his life, everything about him that was known to us and I took his place. I've been living as Bayer.'

She closed her eyes. It had never dawned upon her that he was not German, nor a disillusioned Nazi, but now she saw it; of course, she acknowledged that this was it: this was what she had sensed all along. No wonder there had been something so incompatible with the Nazis she knew: he was . . . not . . . Bayer.

'Oh my God in heaven.' She shook her head. 'Where is the real Bayer?'

'Dead.'

He took her hands in his again as pinpoints of alarm stung in her throat. The fear that she had tried to hide from him tonight and had only partially succeeded in doing, flooded her mind.

Last week, when *he* had come here to her house and cast the shadow of dread over her, *he* had said the words: 'And since I've seen Bayer again, you know, it's odd, but even though he's been wounded, the man is just different somehow.'

Letta's throat hurt and her chest felt tight. *Oh God,* the shadow of dread *suspects something about you. He's cruel and evil and he suspects something.* Her voice caught in her throat. 'You're a British secret agent?'

'Yes. I'm here to gather as much intelligence as I can and then I'm returning to England. That's what I've been saying, I want to take you out with me when I go.'

Her lids closed and she felt as if her heart would break. She sat that way for some seconds before she opened her eyes. 'Who are you?'

'It's safer if you continue to call me Lucien, if you don't know my real name, for now.' He took up her hands and kissed them. 'If we can blow up this factory, I have two escape routes. Can you swim?'

Her eyes were wide as she shook her head. 'No.'

'Ah . . . that's all right, I have a way out that we can take without worrying about swimming. Darling, when can you go to the farm-house and talk to Piet? There will be three agents coming in and if it's possible for Piet to help you to meet them and to take them back to the farmhouse, then that will be ideal.'

Letta's blood coursed speedily through her veins. Lucien wanted to take her with him; he did truly love her. Yes, if they could explode this factory and get away together . . . get away from *him,* her *shadow of dread* . . . everything would work out, she knew it would. She could tell everything to this man who loved her then . . . when they were in England. He would understand, wouldn't he? Of course he would.

Three weeks? That was not long. Surely she could keep *the shadow of dread* at bay for three weeks. He had stood on her balcony in the wet, enveloping dusk, just days ago, with his callous gaze holding hers and told her, '*I shall let your little flirtation go on for the time being.*'

Surely the Lord God would help them get away. The thought of leaving with Lucien was all that mattered and it would guide her through the days to come.

'Letta? Letta?' Cole was speaking at her side. 'You're miles away.'

'Oh – I'm sorry, my *Lieveling*, I was thinking of how I could get over to the farmhouse and see Piet. What reason I can have for going.'

'I've told you before, I'll supply the reason. I'll get a permit for you to go to your farmhouse on the pretext of doing work for me in Doetinchem – gathering some information, like the number of farms still operating in a five-mile radius, or something. I'll get the permit out tomorrow.'

She stood and moved to the portrait of him. It was finished and dry and she lifted her hand and touched his on the canvas. She turned her head to look at him and she sighed. 'This is the best thing I've ever done.'

'You're prejudiced.'

'Perhaps. But I do believe it, for I painted it with love.'

He rose from the sofa and came over to hold her around the waist. He kissed her hair. 'It's undoubtedly me, but there's more in it than good, competent painting. It has some intangible quality which I suppose all fine art does. Perhaps it's the eyes. You are very

361

talented.' He kissed her and as they separated she took his hand in hers and led him back to the sofa.

Rain was spattering noisily on the window as the flickering firelight skipped across Letta's bare skin and she lifted her fingers to caress the scar at the side of Cole's eye.

He looked down at her; her naked body appeared golden in the fire-glow and Cole was reminded of the second time he had ever seen her — in the Rosengart by the canal when she had leant her head back and the evening sun had kissed her neck and the skin of her arms and chest.

'Do you remember the afternoon you came to me at Castle Trentaneborg and we went in your motorcar down by the canal and talked?'

She nodded. 'Of course. It was the day you told me what had happened to Rada.'

'Yes. I think that was when I realised how brave you really are.'

She gazed up at him from under her lids. 'No, I am simply a patriot. It is you who are more courageous than it is possible to imagine. What you have done is hardly credible.' Saying this reminded her of *the shadow of dread* and she shivered and sat up and reached out for her clothes to dress.

He watched her and kissed her bare shoulder as it began to disappear beneath the material of her blouse. 'To think that soon we'll leave together.'

She paused and gazed at him, a sick feeling sitting in her chest. 'Please be careful. You are in grave danger all the time.'

'Letta, I came here to the Netherlands knowing that.' He hesitated and stroked her hair. 'I would not have met you if I had not come.'

She closed her eyes to keep her tears inside her lids.

'So,' he said as he rose and took up his clothes from the rug before the fire, 'I shall organise the permit for you tomorrow and you can go over to your farmhouse the following day.'

Chapter Fifty-seven

Ernst Von Bremen stood at his office window in Apeldoorn looking down. In the bright glaze of noonday he could see a squad of soldiers drilling in front of the bust of Willem I, draped in its Nazi flag. He was about to turn away when his eyes dropped to the section of the square immediately below. His face tightened and he leant forward to the glass.

Cole stood there. He had exited the building with two of his aides and now spoke to them. Von Bremen's thumb and forefinger rose to his mouth to hold his bottom lip in thought until Cole strode away.

A few minutes afterwards, Von Bremen's gaze rested on the woman who was Cole's secretary.

'*Standartenführer* Bayer is out?'

'*Ja, Standartenführer* Von Bremen. I do not expect him back for some hours.'

Cole's secretary was a dainty blonde Dutch girl with whom Von Bremen had struck up an acquaintance the week prior when she and two girl friends had joined him and some other SS officers for drinks. He moved closer to her desk. 'So, Hendrika, I hear that *Standartenführer* Bayer is keeping company with a very good-looking woman.'

'Oh *ja*, a lot of men seem to think she is.'

He grinned. 'You don't like her?'

'Oh *mijnheer*, I don't like or dislike her. She comes from a wealthy family and wears fine clothes. I suppose it is easy for her to look attractive.'

'Ah, I know the type.' Von Bremen leant over the desk. 'It sounds as if she is not good enough for him.'

The girl paused before she said, '*Ja*, I think that's true, *mijnheer*.'

Von Bremen straightened up and moved from the desk. 'I will come back some time when the *standartenführer* is here.' He turned to walk away and halted at the door and looked back. 'Hendrika, you must come out again and meet with me for another drink. Perhaps this evening? I have an inspection of the aerodrome at seventeen hundred but will be back by nineteen hundred.'

The girl preened and, removing a lead pencil which sat in the plait wound neatly round her head, exclaimed, 'Oh, I would love to, *mijnheer*.'

That evening after a couple of glasses of Rhine wine, Ernst Von Bremen told Hendrika that she was easily as lovely as any woman he had seen in his life and after another glass of riesling he moved the conversation to *Standartenführer* Bayer. 'I think you like him.'

'Of course I do, he is my boss.'

Von Bremen laughed and patted her hand. 'I hear he goes out to visit his woman at her house in the countryside nearby.'

'*Ja*, often. And now he has her going south near the border to help him do a survey.' She sniffed in a way that left her disapproval plain. 'It means she gets petrol rations for her car.'

'Oh really? Well, I suppose she is just being helpful. We are all working for the Reich, you know.'

Hendrika nodded. 'Of course.'

'Exactly where in the countryside is she going?'

'Down near Doetinchem.'

'Ah, I wonder what the survey is that she is doing for him?'

'I don't know.'

He lifted her hand to his lips. 'Would you like another drink?'

She giggled. 'I don't think I should.'

'You have beautiful hair and a woman with beautiful hair should have another drink.'

She giggled again.

It was no coincidence that the following morning Von Bremen was in the administration department where he found out that Cole had indeed requested a permit for Fräulein de Witt to do a survey of all dairy farms still operating and producing milk within a ten-mile radius of the town of Doetinchem.

Ernst Von Bremen returned to his office and, taking a large map from his files, opened it and studied the Doetinchem area. He remained staring at it with his elbows on his desk and his chin in his hands while he tapped his top lip with his index finger.

After some minutes his steely eyes narrowed in recollection and a knowing expression twisted his mouth in silent affirmation as he reached across his desk with his pale blue-veined hand and picked up a red pencil. Marking an X upon a spot to the north-east of the small village of Zelham, he said aloud, 'Mmm . . . so, Laetitia, what is really going on?'

A few minutes later he made a telephone call to another part of Apeldoorn where the German Intelligence Service – the Sicherheitsdienst – commonly known as the SD, had their offices and half an hour later two men arrived in a Mercedes-Benz to see him.

The duo had been sent from the SD. They were Secret State Police – the Geheime Staatspolizei – more often called the Gestapo, a branch of the SD. The two men were shown into an anteroom and after five minutes they were taken to an interior room with desks and chairs, where they found *Standartenführer* Von Bremen standing in front of a wall map of Holland. He walked forward to them, the sound of his boots ringing on the stone floor.

At that instant a wild commotion began on the windowsill outside where two large crows banged their wings against the glass. It almost seemed as if they fluttered, screeched and cawed in some sort of weird protest against the three individuals in the room. Von Bremen hurried over and hit the glass with his hand to frighten them, but still they fought. He swore and banged it again and they flew away.

'Blasted crows.' He turned back to the arrivals. 'How I hate *Krähen*. They hang about on the ledges and make nuisances of themselves. I've asked the guards to shoot them.' He sniffed and walked over to the wall map. 'Now, *Kriminalkomissar* Ostermann, who is this you've brought?'

Ostermann, the Gestapo equal of a lieutenant in the SS, came to attention and introduced Shiffer, whose rank corresponded to that of a sergeant.

'Shiffer is a very good man and we are at your service, *standartenführer*.'

'*Gut*. I want you to watch a farmhouse for me. It is here, a few miles from the village of Zelhem north-east of Doetinchem.' He picked up a wooden pointer and tapped the spot. 'The farmhouse is owned by a very beautiful woman. Her name is Fräulein de Witt.

I want you to watch the property and report back to me who comes and goes from it and, if possible, what goes on there.'

'Do we approach any of those who enter?' Ostermann asked, adjusting his spectacles.

'No, but you will have your men follow them. I do not want Miss de Witt, or anyone else who might come to the farmhouse, to know that they are being watched. Just find out what you can.' He looked from Ostermann to Shiffer. 'Miss de Witt is *Vertrauensmanner* and she is doing something very special for me. She is not to be troubled, for she is acting a role and everything needs to appear quite normal, for her sake. I shall alert your superiors as to what I am doing but all this is to be secret and you are to report only to me.'

'*Jawohl!*' Ostermann and Shiffer momentarily closed their eyes and bowed their heads in understanding.

Chapter Fifty-eight

26 October 1943

The wind howled around Laetitia's farm not far from the German border. A small wood fire made from trees on the property burnt in the grate. The smell of kerosene emanated from the only other form of heating: a tiny portable tin stove on the kitchen table.

Letta was swathed in a thick cardigan and her feet were in boots. Opposite her sat Piet Lombard in an overcoat. He had arrived at the main farmhouse on his bicycle a few minutes earlier and now sat in the meagre warmth emanating from the tin stove in front of him.

The room smelt musty and the single lamp threw shadows across the kitchen as Piet smiled and the lines around his mouth melted into the multitude of creases on his face. Running his work-hardened hand back through his thinning hair, he made an affirmative sound. 'I understand everything you've told me, Miss Laetitia. We bring no one else in; we are doing this for a Resistance cell who are part of De Kern* and you and I will meet the British

* De Kern: see Author's End Notes, page 530

agents on our own, probably on the sixth or the seventh of next month, and we'll bring them here. As I said, I'll fix three of the old bicycles for us to ride and I'll fit makeshift second seats so we can double them. To guide the aircraft in we'll use three of my bicycle lamps set on sticks and I'll hold my torch; it still works well and you'll be able to supply me with batteries.'

Letta nodded and smiled. 'Yes, and I'll return to Apeldoorn before the curfew tonight and I'll come back here on the fifth of November in readiness for the arrival of the British operatives.'

'Good; I'll come over to see you that evening as dusk falls.'

'Yes, that's a good idea. All I hope is that the weather does not get too much colder, especially as they have to swim the river.'

Piet grinned. 'Now that's one thing I reckon I know a bit about; learnt it from my old mother, I did. She was a wonder at predicting the weather. You can tell weeks in advance by the evening light as the sun sets. You just have to know what to look for.' He pursed his lips and raised a gnarled finger in the air. 'And the way I see it, November will not be any worse than now. Yes, it will be cold, but not bad, and it will be fair. Wouldn't like to have to swim the Oude Ijssel myself, but for a young, fit fellow? Should be all right.' He rubbed his hands together. 'Now, do you mind if I smoke?'

'Go ahead.'

As he lit a cigarette he smiled again, showing stained teeth. 'This is one of the last smokes I have, but I thought to myself, "If Miss Laetitia is back here, it's something to celebrate."'

'Thank you, Piet.'

'I was thinking earlier about when you were little and how you used to run down to my cottage in the summer evenings laughing, with your mother's dogs jumping and barking all around you. You liked to listen to me playing the mouth-organ, remember?'

'I remember. Your wife made the best oatcakes in the world.' She sighed. 'Those were the days.'

'Yes, we were masters of our own fate, then, unlike now when the Boche have us under their heel.' His features became sombre. 'That's why we must do all we can to fight back.'

Letta stood up as she replied. 'Piet, you know I cannot tell you more. You must simply trust me.'

He nodded. 'Yes, I understand. That goes without saying.'

'We must be very careful.'

'Of course we must, Miss Laetitia. Aren't we always?'

2 November

In the compact Oranjepark in the middle of Apeldoorn, Cole waited, his eyes on a unit of jackbooted German soldiers marching along one of the side streets. He stood near the bandstand beneath the leafless mud-coloured branches, the garden beds in front of him devoid of flowers and the heavens a canopy in hues of grey.

Everything appeared dull and spiritless: sky, buildings, trees, human beings. There was no laughter in Holland; the very landscape of this occupied country was a patchwork of the melancholy of its citizens. Gloom pervaded the Netherlands. The country's coal, food stocks, grain, petrol, cattle and manufactured goods were stacked aboard freight trains and carried east across the border to *Duitsland*. After over three years of occupation by the Germans, the Dutch were finding it hard to exist with the strength of their work-force enslaved by, their food stocks depleted by, and energy taken by, the aggressor.

As Cole stood in the rising wind listening to the marching feet of the soldiers he compared the day to the heat of southern Queensland at this time of year . . . and there she was in his mind: Shelly Longford. He began to move restlessly back and forth as he recalled how they had often met in the tiny Memorial Park by the RSSAILA* building in Ipswich. He could see Shell in his mind's eye, smiling at him, and he could hear her say, 'I'll just pop round to the Viola Café and pick us up something to eat.'

He closed his eyes, visualising her and the warm grass beneath them and the sun on their backs, and a wistful expression softened his eyes. He had enjoyed those times with Shell and he could not help wondering how she was. This made him uncomfortable and he cleared his throat and opened his eyes to see a lone woman coming towards him. Even impeded by her overcoat she moved with a smooth, flowing movement that reminded him of a dancer. Letta was so recognisable.

He walked forward to meet her. Reaching him she took his arm. 'Did you hear from England?'

'Yes, they're sending in three agents just as I thought. They'll come in on the night of the seventh – well, early morning on the eighth, really. We know two of them.'

'What?'

'It's unorthodox, but it seems the controller of this operation decided on Dirk and Mako again; he wants to move in haste to ensure we blow the factory before the weather makes it impossible – and he has no time to train others – though the wireless operator is a new man, code name Tymen. He was born and grew up here not all that far from Doetinchem. That'll be helpful.'

Letta's eyes had widened in amazement and she stepped back

* RSSAILA: see Author's End Notes, page 530

from Cole, putting her hand to her head as if she had been hit. 'What?' Her voice was tight with tension. 'Dirk's coming back?'

'That's right.'

'Why? Why are they sending him?'

'Well, as I said, because it's impossible to find and train anyone else in the time. Oh, and he's a mighty swimmer, don't forget that. We need first-rate swimmers to cross the river after the barge heads into the factory.'

'Are you sure it'll be him?'

'Yes. Remember, his Dutch is perfect and his German is good, and he's one of the best. He's using the same code name.' Cole met her eyes. 'Why are you so concerned?' His tone registered slight sarcasm. 'I thought you liked him.'

She hesitated and met his eyes. 'I do *like* him. I'm just shocked that he's coming in again. I didn't expect it. As you said, it's highly irregular.'

'You're right, it is.' Cole watched her closely and spoke slowly. 'I don't need to be jealous of him, do I?'

She paused and frowned. 'For God's sake, no, you don't, not at all. It's not that. I never for a moment thought it would be Dirk or Mako.' Her eyes flicked back and forth. 'This is wrong; they know about you. Dear Lord, if they get caught they both know who you are.' There was patent fear in her face. 'Lucien, the Germans have no conscience. Torture, murder, it's all the same to them. God . . . Why did you agree for men you know to come in again?'

Cole's irritation sounded in his answer. 'Damn it, Letta, it's not for me to agree or disagree; this has been decided by others. Think about it – Dirk and Mako are perfect for this. I'm an agent, I do what they say, we all do. Once they agree on a mission, that's that.'

'Can't you tell Hans not to send them?'

'No, why the hell would I do that?'

'Because . . . because of what I've just said. They know who you are.'

He took her hand and pulled her forcefully across the grass and in behind a clump of thick tree trunks. 'Letta, stop this. Don't be silly. They won't get caught. And, in any case, I've been ordered to get out of here and I'm taking you with me.'

She looked blankly at him and he went on, 'Now listen to me. You're not making sense. You, Piet, Dirk, Mako and the wireless operator will all play your parts and everything will run according to plan. You have no need to worry . . . please . . .' He held her close and brought her chin up with his hand. 'You tell me I have nothing to be jealous about and I believe you. Dirk is coming and he'll blow the blasted place to high heaven and you and I will leave Holland – straight away, if you like. All right?'

She almost moaned as she answered, 'All right.'

'Good girl. Now I'll manage to get out to your house before you leave for your farm.

'Once the target's exploded, Dirk and the others will lie low for perhaps a week with you; you're approved of and are my woman, and no one will suspect your property to be the safe house, thank God. You'll be free of suspicion. And, as I said, we'll depart – even before them, if it makes you more at ease.'

A trembling sigh shook from Letta and Cole gazed into her eyes before he gave a swift glance around the empty park and kissed her firmly on the mouth.

Chapter Fifty-nine

With a blinking of his eyes and a sickening feeling in his stomach, Cole pushed a number of papers away from his sight. He had hand-copied the important ones and would take them back to England with him. Much of the *work* in front of him was related to the Jews: the deportation and disposing of them and the records of the depraved medical experiments being perpetrated on helpless Jewish captives where little or no anaesthetic was used to cut out bone and internal organs with a complete disrespect for any human dignity. All done in the name of *Nazi science*. Cole now believed that the pathological hatred the Nazis held for the Jews was merely a starting point: if they had their way, other races would follow.

Lately he was having trouble looking Rauter, Naumann and the others in the eyes in case his disgust and loathing were somehow revealed in his expression. He stood and moved to the window and opening it wide, took a deep, noisy breath as if it could cleanse him of such abominations.

It was only days until Tudor and the others would blow up the factory and swim the Oude Ijssel river. There were a mere forty German soldiers in Doetinchem and, to his knowledge, none in

Zelhem, so by the time the alarm was raised Tudor and the boys should be safely back at the farmhouse.

Once that was completed he and Letta would take their own escape route and be together. As an SS colonel he could move around Holland – and other occupied countries, for that matter – with ease and he had already received Rauter's agreement for him to start a week's leave on 12 November.

A noise at the door brought his gaze round to his secretary's face. 'Excuse me, *Standartenführer* Bayer, but I have *Standartenführer* Von Bremen here to see you.'

Before Cole had a chance to respond, Ernst Von Bremen pushed past Hendrika and entered, dismissing her with a gesture of his hand. 'Lucien, it's time we had a talk. The weeks are passing and we have not reminisced at all.'

Cole, who had turned from the window, replied casually. 'Ah, well, unfortunately not now. I have an afternoon filled with a dozen things. Firstly, I'm off to see General Christiansen, so perhaps the best thing is to meet one evening for a drink . . . shall we say one night next week?'

'But it is lunchtime. Don't tell me you aren't stopping for lunch?'

'Today I can't afford time to eat lunch.'

Von Bremen fixed him with a cool stare. 'You're very diligent these days, Lucien . . . a most conscientious SS officer.'

Cole ignored the slight mocking sound in the man's voice. '*Danke*. I would have thought you the same.' He picked up the papers on his desk, walked to his record-keeping cabinet, opened it, put them in and turned the key in the lock.

His visitor looked around the room. 'Where's your art case?'

Cole spoke from the wooden record cabinet. 'Art case?'

'*Ja*, the black leather one you keep your bird drawings in, I'd like to see a few.'

Cole turned slowly as he slipped the key into the pocket of his uniform. He delivered his visitor a supercilious grin. 'Really? Now? In the middle of the day when I'm due to meet with the Luftwaffe general? And you must be busy on a dozen matters yourself. You can't be serious, dear Ernst?'

The Nazi smiled in return. 'Then we must make sure we get together soon, as you say.'

Cole moved back to his desk and took up his briefcase and spoke as he walked to the door. 'So, shall we go?' He indicated with his free hand for his caller to depart and Von Bremen gazed around the room and strode past him to the outer office where Hendrika looked up at them.

Cole glanced at her. 'I'll be out for the afternoon.'

And as the girl nodded and smiled he turned back to Von Bremen. 'When did you become interested in birds, Ernst?'

'Amazingly enough, since I realised you were interested.'

'Very commendable of you. One can learn a lot from nature.'

Once in the corridor Cole nodded his head in goodbye and as he turned away Von Bremen asked another question. 'On the Russian front, wasn't your senior officer General Koehler?'

Cole knew this name was correct. He looked back and met the Nazi's eyes. '*Ja*, indeed.'

'Didn't he have a woman whom he used to take from battle to battle with him?'

Cole gave the Nazi a patronising gaze. 'Ernst? Let's save our trivial and idle talk for our next social meeting, to which I shall bring a number of my drawings as you show so much interest in them.' He smiled widely and spun away. He did, in fact, have about twenty bird drawings. He had asked Letta to produce them for him as a precaution after his surprise encounter in the Veluwe with Von Bremen and Naumann. Cole was aware the mental sparring would not last for ever. He thought he could hold Von Bremen off a little longer . . . but not for ever. As soon as that factory went up and the boys were back safely in the farmhouse, he and Letta would leave on the twelfth.

Chapter Sixty

5 November

Letta closed the door of the blue Rosengart. Her suitcase was in the back and food Lucien had supplied for the week to come was stacked beside it. Everything was ready for her departure to the farmhouse over near the German border north-east of the village of Zelhem.

She hurried back up the steps to the blue door and entered the house where, passing through to the kitchen, she locked the back door and paused.

She did not need to take anything else, for Piet Lombard was gathering all they would need and at twilight this evening he would come up the path from his cottage beyond the wood to her farmhouse and they would go through their plans again. He was a strong, capable man and his presence would be a comfort to her. Tomorrow evening, before dusk, the two of them would ride their bicycles to the field set in the middle of the uninhabited area some miles away from the farm and decide where to position the battery-operated bicycle lights for the following night's arrival of the men who would fly in to explode the factory.

Thinking of them brought apprehension. She did not want to see Dirk. Why, oh why, had they sent him? What a bad trick fate was playing upon her. She thought of all the foolish commitments she had made to him: the intimate things they had done and said to each other when he was in hiding. She gave a tiny shiver recalling the promises they had made in the dark of the hot, still night when he had departed for England in the motorboat.

It all seemed so rash and imprudent now; now that she was in love with Lucien. She felt guilt for her indulgent behaviour over the years. Perhaps, if she were completely honest, she did blame her mother for her own conduct; possibly, in truth, she always had blamed her without formulating the thought. Letta recognised how superficial and self-indulgent her mother had been and while she had loved her mother, she hated that she had grown just like her.

She prayed regularly now and surely, in the eyes of heaven, what she had done to fight the Germans would bring some grace.

And now *the shadow of dread* was back. She sat down in a chair and took deep breaths to calm herself. If she could keep *the shadow of dread* at bay, just for another week, she could leave with Lucien – go to England, get away. Yes, yes, she must. She would.

Thank God she was leaving Apeldoorn today.

With this reassuring thought Laetitia stood and picked up her small feathered hat and sat it firmly on her head. She reached for her black leather handbag and removed her overcoat from the back of a kitchen chair to hurry down the hall past the parlour where the portrait remained on the easel but, now, was covered with a blanket. Leaving the portrait behind when she left for England would be very hard to do, but she must, there was no alternative.

She would paint another . . . yes . . . even finer than this one. That made her feel better.

Lucien had said he would come to see her before she left this morning but he had not been. She frowned in deliberation: perhaps she should drive into the town now before departing and see him.

Crossing the front hall she stepped back out into the burgeoning morning light where she stopped suddenly as she saw the SS officer standing by her car. A moment later a broad, happy smile broke across her mouth as she recognised him and, locking her front door, hurried down the steps. She looked around the yard and there, inside the front gate parked near the first of the great oaks, was a waiting staff car.

'*Lieveling*,' she began, 'I thought I might not see you.'

Cole took her in his arms. 'I couldn't allow that.' He kissed her longingly on the mouth before he lifted her chin and gazed in her eyes. 'Letta, once the target is destroyed, Hans believes that Dirk and the others will depart the farmhouse within days, all being well. I've already requested leave from the twelfth. Rauter knows, so it's a formality.

'There's a small hotel called The Knights' Inn which is abandoned and boarded up and it's on the Zelhem Doetinchem road about three miles south of Zelhem. It will be simple for you to get there as you will be out and about doing your survey. Behind the building is an overgrown, covered terrace. I shall meet you there on the twelfth in the afternoon, between thirteen hundred and fifteen hundred. I cannot imagine anything will go wrong but if, for any reason, I do not come, return to the farm and go back to that terrace inn every day at the same time. I will come no matter what. We will leave Holland together.'

She did not speak as she hugged him close and hid her face in his chest while he kissed the top of her head. 'Now go, my brave girl, and tell Dirk I shall look forward to seeing him again.'

Releasing him at last she looked up into his eyes. He did not see the fear and desperation which were living in her soul; he saw only her enchanting face and he kissed her again. 'We'll be together soon. I'm only sorry I cannot take part: I'll be on tenterhooks waiting to hear on Wednesday morning. No doubt the SS will be alerted of the explosion pretty quickly.'

He cranked the engine of the Rosengart and it spluttered into life and settled into a steady whirring as Laetitia entered the vehicle and dropped her coat and bag on the leather seat. Remaining silent she watched while Cole slipped the crank on to the floor of the cabin and closed the door. He locked eyes with her and gave her an encouraging smile. 'Good luck, sweetheart.'

He had stepped away when she reached for his hand through the open window so he came forward and clasped her fingers. As their palms met she spoke at last. 'I will miss you until we meet at the inn.' She stared at him. 'Could you? Would you? Tell me your real name?'

He returned her stare, looking concentratedly into her eyes. He was highly aware of the smooth skin of her palm on his. It was dangerous for her to know his name, but then it was dangerous for her to know that he was masquerading as Bayer; everything they did was dangerous – every moment.

'I would like to know,' she added, 'so that while I am away from you now, I can think of you . . .' she paused, 'as the man you truly are.'

His gaze strayed to her mouth, to the dark spot at the side of her lips and down her unlined throat to the maroon buttons of her jacket which hid her sensual shape. He glanced away from her towards the stream beyond the broken fence before he brought his eyes back to the pert feathered hat and down to the face looking up at him from under it.

'It's Cole Wareing.'

He saw her silently mouth his name and her voice broke as she said, 'Thank you.'

They fell silent until she spoke again. 'Would you do something for me?'

'Anything.'

'Would you change the name on the photograph I gave you?'

'What do you mean?'

'On the back. I wrote *My Darling Lucien*. Please would you cross out *Lucien* and write *Cole*?'

He gave a short laugh as he released her palm. 'My dear, here, you can do that yourself.' And taking the photograph from his inside breast pocket, he handed it to her. 'I always carry it.'

She took the photograph and the pen he offered and altered the words.

As she handed them back he studied her. 'Satisfied?'

She nodded and smiled her entrancing smile and whispered, 'Cole', as she pushed the car into low gear and drove away.

He stood watching the vehicle disappear past the black German staff car waiting for him. Why the hell had he yielded to her request to tell his real name? He knew it was better if she did not know. He was a British secret operative; it was the one thing you never did; you never gave your true identity to anybody. But God, she was not anybody – she was Letta, and she had asked today . . . of all days . . . when so much was at stake and their emotions ran high.

Well, it was too late now. She knew. And hell, he had trusted her with everything, with his life, for heaven's sake, so why not his name? It was only right she should know who he really was. It was risky to keep this postcard now with the name *Cole* on it, but what the hell? He would. If anything untoward happened he would destroy it immediately.

He grunted as if in agreement with himself and began to limp towards the staff car, his gaze flicking to the thick boles of the oaks and the bracken nestling behind them. As he neared the Mercedes-Benz the SS corporal who waited for him came to attention by the open door and Cole bent into the back seat and sat down.

'Back to my office in Apeldoorn.'

As the car headed away at speed he sat back in the seat gazing out at the trees, now mostly bare, and suddenly his mouth tightened. Again Shelly had slipped into his thoughts and he felt ill at ease in the way he always did. It was inexplicable and it bothered him. She was lovely and had fallen for him from the start: he had always known that. But why would he think of her at this moment?

He was in love with Letta, she had captured him and yet the reflection on the girl so far away made him long for the days before the war.

He closed his eyes and for a minute his features slipped into repose. Shelly stood for calmness and sanity. She represented a time when the world was not insane and he did not have to live as a demoniac follower of the Third Reich. Musing on her brought peace to his overtaxed mind.

Yes. Of course, that was doubtlessly what brought Shelly to his thoughts: a continual yearning to be away from this hotbed of Nazis. Not necessarily in Australia, just away from this place, back somewhere sane like England – where, even though they were at war, they lived without the mind-numbing terror of those in an occupied country. Yes, that was it, that's why Shell slipped into his head now and then.

He opened his eyes and blinked and sat up straight while the Mercedes-Benz sped on and a frown reinstated itself in his brow as he turned his deliberations to the exploding of the factory and the planning of the escape.

He had copied hundreds of SS records in Apeldoorn and the Hague and he held endless intelligence on troop movements and build-ups throughout the occupied countries of Europe. There was a mass of intelligence to take back to Hans: much of it he had committed to memory. Yes, soon he and Letta would be on their way and Rauter, Von Bremen and the others of their kind could go to Hades where they belonged.

Chapter Sixty-one

Letta drove along in the November sunshine saying *his* name to herself. Sometimes she spoke aloud and at others she simply thought it. 'Cole Wareing, that's his name.' *It is a beautiful name, it sounds just right — the perfect name: Cole Wareing. Yes, it suits him so very well.*

Naturally Letta had become accustomed to the alias of 'Lucien' and even though she had decided 'Cole' was so suitable, so befitting to the man she knew, she found herself not thinking of him as Cole, but as his entire name, 'Cole Wareing', as she might of someone remote from her, someone she admired, but had never met.

The journey was uneventful: she halted at checkpoints and road controls and handed over her identity papers and the letter Cole had written for her. All ran smoothly even though she was detoured now and then when roads were closed. Once she was held up while a troop movement took place ahead of her.

When she was within a mile of the small village of Zelhem she entered a wood of beech trees where the autumn leaves made a carpet of golden brown on both sides of the road and there ahead was another road block. Letta slowed down and stopped the car at the barrier, glancing past a substantial stone hut which appeared to serve as a shelter, to where nine or ten soldiers gathered around an open fire, three of them sitting smoking on a fallen trunk. It surprised her that this number of German soldiers would be at a checkpoint for an insignificant community so close to the German border. Cole had informed her there was only one contingent of the occupying forces in the whole area.

The sentry on duty came forward and Letta was surprised again, for he was a *sturmmann*, a lance corporal in the Waffen SS, and she thought it odd that an SS unit would be stationed so near to Germany. Handing her papers through the window to him, he read them and opened the back door of the Rosengart, looked in at the suitcase and lifted the lid on the box of food. 'This is a great deal of food, Fräulein de Witt.'

'Oh, *ja*, my stay in this area might be longer than I originally thought, so *Standartenführer* Bayer has seen to it that I received more supplies. Here,' she took up another piece of paper and proffered it to him. 'I have the requisition order from the SS commissariat in Apeldoorn for it.'

He took it, smiled, and spoke deferentially. 'Just wait a moment.'

He walked inside the small building to the second room where Ernst Von Bremen's impassive eyes lifted from the papers on the desk in front of him and the soldier saluted and spoke.

'Fräulein de Witt is outside, *standartenführer*.' He handed over her papers and before he read them Von Bremen lifted his gaze to his companion who sat at a smaller desk in the corner.

'So, *Kriminalkomissar* Ostermann, my reliable Miss de Witt is here.'

Ostermann had, of course, believed everything Von Bremen had told him, including that Laetitia de Witt was a Nazi and working with them. The Gestapo officer stood and motioned to the door. '*Ja*, will you go out to her car to see her? Or shall I bring her in here to you, *Standartenführer* Von Bremen?'

'Neither. She knows I am here,' he lied. 'And I shall see her at the right time. We must make all this look as natural as it can for her.' He read the letter and the other papers. He gave a nod as he eyed the requisition order. *Enough supplies to last a number of people for a week or more.*

He handed them back to the soldier. 'Berlitz, you can return these to the lady. She can pass.'

The soldier clicked his heels. '*Jawohl, standartenführer.*'

When the *sturmmann* had closed the door, Von Bremen walked across to the window where he could see the back of the blue Rosengart. 'How many men do we have watching her farmhouse?'

'Four, *Standartenführer* Von Bremen, and I have a squad of soldiers near at hand.'

'*Gut*, continue giving me the regular reports.'

He watched *Sturmmann* Berlitz hand the papers back through the Rosengart window and he remained standing there as the barrier lifted and Letta drove on by. When the car disappeared into the continuing forest of beeches he smiled with satisfaction and sauntered back to his desk.

Chapter Sixty-two

Early morning, 8 November

In the chill which descended after midnight, Laetitia and Piet waited by the bicycle lights in the chosen field. It was, of course, better to have people to hold the bicycle lights, but because the mission was so secret and limited to just herself and Piet as the reception committee on the ground, Piet had mounted the lanterns on sticks which they had pushed into the earth. On the evening of the sixth, she and Piet had ridden here and decided exactly where they would place their lights to guide in the coming RAF aircraft.

Just being with Piet had reduced her nervous tension. He was so calm and competent and was a constant reminder of her girlhood when her world had been carefree. She had slept more soundly here than she had for some time but on waking her anxiety had returned.

And now, as the British Halifax aircraft came in low, Letta lifted her torch and flashed the prearranged signal: the Morse code for 'R' into the night sky.

The black matt aircraft came in to pass overhead and in the illumination of an almost full moon, three ebony figures left its belly to drift down suspended from three pale umbrella shapes and to touch down and plant their feet on Dutch soil.

Laetitia and Piet ran forward to greet them as the engines of the British bomber faded, leaving the feeling that the aircraft had never been here. The arrivals wore knapsacks strapped to their chests and two of them, Tudor and Mako, held light machine-guns.

Laetitia spoke to the figure she ran towards. 'Dirk? Mako?'

It was Tudor who answered. 'Yes, Laetitia . . . Dirk here.'

She ran up to Tudor who held his sten gun in his left hand and hugged her to him with his right. 'I'm back.' She felt the touch of him, rock-like, rugged, suddenly all familiar again. In the gloom he found her lips and gave her a swift kiss. She pulled quickly away from him as he removed his parachute and began to fold it.

They were soon all together and introduced and Letta spoke, looking around in the gloom. 'We've got three bicycles. Piet and I rode two in and Piet brought in the third holding its handlebars. He has rigged up second passenger seats on two of the bikes so we can all ride. I'll lead the way while you four follow me. It's a few miles to our destination.'

They finished gathering their parachutes as Tymen, the wireless operator, asked, 'Are there any soldiers around here?'

Piet replied, 'Very few over this way. There's a curfew so there's never anybody around. We expect an uneventful ride home.'

Letta could not see Tudor's face in the darkness but she felt his fingers on her arm and heard his low voice in her ear. 'I would have liked to ride back with you.'

She pulled from his touch and kept her torch pointed to the ground as it revealed the three bicycles leaning against a tree trunk. 'All right, mount up . . . and follow me.'

* * *

Laetitia led the way in the silent night, the hissing of the bicycle wheels the only noise.

Tudor watched her ebony shape ahead. When he had taken her in his arms in the field where they landed he had suddenly realised how badly he had missed this woman and the sweet aromatic smell of her helped to rekindle his old feelings.

In the few months he had been back in England he had thought of her often and recalled her touch with relish, but now that he was near her again he could not help but want her in his arms. He was reminded with clarity of their short love affair. Yet he was a professional secret agent; he had assented to come back to Holland simply because he was. You didn't analyse why the hell you were here: sure, you hated Hitler and the Nazis; sure, you craved something else that normal warfare didn't bring . . . but to come back to this jeopardy where one false move could have you tortured or dead – for a woman? No, never. Even though at this moment, sliding through the darkness on swishing wheels, he admitted that Laetitia de Witt was back under his skin.

As their black shadows pedalled across the landscape through heathland and woods and over waterways he thought of what had happened to bring him once more to Holland. When he had returned to England in early August he had finally met the man who went by the code of CD, the executive head of SOE: Major-General Colin McVean Gubbins, a wiry Scot who had been born in Japan and who had been decorated for gallantry in the Great War, and led the forerunners of the commandos in Norway against the German invasion in 1940.

Gubbins was a skilled linguist and the tireless force of SOE. He rarely met any of his operatives but he had been intrigued by the mission which had left a man in Holland masquerading as a

Nazi and he had wanted to meet Tudor to discuss the night in the Groningen inn when the changeover had been made. He had listened fascinated, nodding his head at intervals, occasionally lifting his forefinger to rub his military toothbrush moustache and asking questions with a penetrating gaze from under his bushy eyebrows. It was near the closing of this particular meeting that Gubbins complimented Tudor again. 'Wing Commander Harrington, this is one of the most daring undertakings in occupied territory I've ever heard about and it's congratulations to you and the others with you, for getting back here with the important intelligence you brought from Bayer.'

'Thank you, sir. The woman Laetitia de Witt was instrumental in our escape.'

'Yes, I'm aware from the cross-questioning sessions and the notes you made on your return. I believe a file has been opened on her. Hans Buckhout is receiving regular wireless messages from Lucien Bayer and so far this mission is going better than we possibly could have hoped. It's almost unbelievable that Bayer is doing this. It's a superb piece of trickery: I hope he makes it back.'

'Me too, sir, he's a real pal of mine. Great actor.'

'Mmm.' The chief smiled. 'He must be exceptional.'

Tudor put down the teacup he had been holding and they shook hands and Gubbins's secretary came in and took Tudor to see his Chief of Staff.

It was this officer who told Tudor that Hans Buckhout did not want to lose him back to French Section. 'Buckhout's requested that for a time you might become an STS. Would it interest you?' These letters stood for Special Training School where agents were trained. 'I know they're keen to have you as an instructor over at Ringway, if you are interested.'

392

So it was shortly afterwards that Tudor was seconded to STS 51, Ringway Airfield in Manchester, to train secret agents.

He had enjoyed the rigorous days and occasionally had seen Hans and been informed that his friend was still in Holland and sending vital intelligence back to England.

It was a few weeks ago that Hans had proposed Tudor's return into Holland. 'I'd like to blow this factory Lucien Bayer has found as soon as possible because it will help set the enemy's unmanned rocket testing programme back again and we must get it over before winter. But to do it fast I've no time to train anybody and I need exceptional swimmers . . . cuts down the choice considerably.

'You and your explosives expert, Mako Vanderbilt, are strong swimmers – I even tried to enrol Felix again – but he's caught pneumonia. Yet I've managed to find a young wireless operator who swims well and who grew up in Holland. He's actually familiar with the area involved, around Doetinchem. He's keen to go. If you and Mako consent, I can do it quickly, using him as the third; if you don't, I can't.'

And so here he was, riding a bicycle in the dead of night in the chilly air swirling across from the North Sea. The night was empty and the road laced like a black ribbon across the low land. Ahead of him Laetitia turned off and wove down a lane and up a long, gentle slope to pass in through an open gate. He followed her, past tall trees and on by what appeared to be a hedge, down a dirt road until they came to a large dwelling. Pedalling around the side of it, they halted at a shed where they lodged their bicycles. Letta led them by the moody shape of an outhouse and she entered the farmhouse closely followed by Tudor, to arrive in a utility room. There they took off their coats and boots and Letta lit a lamp and moved with it through to the kitchen.

'Wait . . .' Tudor caught up with her and took her free arm. 'You've hardly greeted me, Let.' He slid his other hand around her waist.

She pulled from him and put the lamp on the table. 'No, Dirk, this is foolish.'

'I've just realised how much I missed you.'

'Don't say that. It's not right.' She turned back hurriedly to where Piet and the others entered behind them.

Piet wore a smile. 'We have some real tea for you, I've been saving it.'

Mako and Tymen spoke in unison. 'That'll be good.'

Later, when Laetitia left the men and went briefly to her room, she found Tudor waiting at the bottom of the staircase when she descended.

As she went to pass by he caught her close and kissed the side of her forehead as she turned her face away. 'Have you been seeing much of Lucien Bayer?'

'You know I have. He's the one who found the factory.'

He continued to hold her, speaking in Dutch. 'You're as beautiful as ever.' She could feel the firm tautness of his body as he held her; the scent of him filled her nostrils, she remembered it, somehow musky, manly, virile.

He kissed the side of her mouth and down her neck. 'You can't like Bayer that much. Come on, Let. I'm still mad for you. This is a crazy war and fate's thrown us back together.'

She avoided looking into the blue lustres that were his eyes and her heart began to race. 'I . . . can't do this, Dirk, I can't. Don't you under—' he closed his lips over hers and she felt the overwhelming warmth of his mouth and his strong fingers

394

slipping down her spine, pressing the lower part of her torso into his.

Now he was whispering in her ear. 'It was so good between us, Let . . . for both of us. Remember? You said you loved me. Remember that night I left? I reckon you'll always be mine.' His hands were solidly against her backbone. 'Why are you resisting me? You didn't resist me then.'

They could hear the voices of the three men in the kitchen and she pulled away to go in their direction, but he still held her arm. Her eyes flashed. 'I wasn't expecting you to come here. I thought you were back in England for ever and that I'd never see you again. There's a war on, for God's sake, and you're a British agent. This is just wrong. Stop! God, Dirk, can't you see what you're doing to me? I'm in love with . . . Lucien.'

His tone was sarcastic. 'Oh, really? So what's the difference between the love you had for me and the love you have for him?'

She met his eyes. 'Dirk, I thought I'd never see you again. That you're here is not my doing.'

'How in hell can you change this much in just over three lousy months? Jesus, you were mad for me; I was mad for you.'

She looked at him a moment longer, sighed loudly and spun away to walk towards the kitchen.

Tudor waited until she disappeared before he followed in silence.

Chapter Sixty-three

Letta lay wide awake listening to the squeaking of a shutter outside her window as the wind chased the clouds across Holland's night sky. She was aware of a slight, not unpleasant, scent wafting in her bedroom, coming from the huge drapes which hung over the windows. She could not sleep: a myriad of thoughts hurtled around in her head.

Piet had remained while they all drank their tea and ate and talked. An hour later he left on his bicycle when the secret agents went to bed. He would return later to go through the details of the coming mission with them.

Seeing Dirk again had made everything so much worse. She was in love with Cole Wareing and yet her past was catching up with her. She rolled over, pulling the blanket up around her ears. Just as she did so she became aware of the door of her bedroom opening, and in the murky darkness she heard, 'Angel . . . it's me.'

She lifted herself. 'Dirk?'

He had begun calling her *Angel* in the final week before he had left Holland previously. She was startled to hear him use it again – and a groan broke from her as he approached her in the darkness.

She had been half expecting this. It was natural that a man you had slept with only months ago would expect you to do so again.

She moved to slip out of bed as he reached her. 'Don't get up, Angel. Please just talk to me. Listen, what about the words of love? Those promises you made . . . how could you forget me so quickly? I realise it's Lucien Bayer who's changed everything.' He held her shoulders to keep her from moving.

She pushed his hands away. 'Yes, promises made to you at midnight in the moonlight *mean nothing*.'

In the silence that followed his breathing was audible. When he spoke again it was no more than a whisper. 'I can't believe you're saying that. You promised to be mine always. That we'd find each other after the war.'

'I know what I said but, Dirk, please understand, things have altered for ever. I've altered. Though how can I expect you to believe that? It's not your fault, I led you on, I know.' She exhaled unhappily.

'You sure did.' He put out his hand and touched her cheek and she did not pull away as she spoke softly.

'I'm asking you to understand. Real love alters you, Dirk . . . completely. I'm not the woman I was when you saw me last. I'm different. Can you try to believe that?' She sighed. 'Don't you have a girl, Dirk? Isn't there someone else you care about?'

Tudor took a deep, disconsolate breath. Now Jane Morley was in his mind. 'I used to have,' he answered. The thought of Jane brought a multitude of considerations to his mind.

There was a long silence as his fingers slipped from her face to caress the side of her neck and to gently slide down to hold her shoulder. He sat that way for a few moments before he stood up. 'Lucien is my best friend. I'm wrong to do this. I just got carried away when I saw you again. You're so beautiful and mighty hard to resist, honey. But I won't bother you again, now I know you mean it.'

The black shape of him turned away. 'I'll see you in the morning.' The door squeaked again as it closed behind him.

Sun was stealing in between the drapes when she rose and washed and dressed. Entering the kitchen she found only Mako, and on the table in front of him sat the guns they had carried in with them: two Mark II 9mm Sten sub-machine-guns and Tymen's weapon, a Smith & Wesson .38 revolver. Not all agents carried weapons, some believed it was safer without, in case they were questioned and searched, but Tudor had requested the sub-machine-guns because of the nature of the operation. 'I'd prefer to fight my way out, if anything goes wrong.'

Mako's austere face smiled at Letta as she looked around and asked, 'Where are Dirk and Tymen?'

'They've gone with Piet on their bicycles to the river, to check where to go tomorrow tonight. Dirk thought that it was good for young Tymen to get a look at things.'

'But isn't it risky?'

Mako shook his head. 'You don't know the boss, he'll be mighty careful. He checks everything. The boss wants to study the trees so he's certain of just what's what.'

'I understand.' She pointed to the guns. 'They've gone unarmed?'

'No, boss's carrying two hand grenades.'

'When are they due back?'

'We only slept a few hours; they went at dawn, so pretty soon, I'd say. We'll go to bed early tonight and get a good rest. Tymen will contact our base in England and then we'll be set for tomorrow night.'

398

'Yes, of course. I'll have something to eat and then I'll bake a cake. What do you think?' She had been given the luxuries of flour, eggs and sugar by Cole as part of the food supplies and she wanted to make something special for the agents.

Mako grinned again. 'Too right. What a grand idea.'

'Good.' Letta shivered and pulled her cardigan more tightly around her middle as she turned away to the kitchen hearth, saying, 'Let's relight this fire, Mako, it's a bit cold in here.'

The cake had been a great success. The men had taken refreshment when they returned from the river and as the afternoon advanced Tudor had gone through the procedure for the next night with them once more. They had gone early to bed, as Mako had predicted, and the next day everybody cleaned their guns and seemed a little tense until mid-afternoon, when they drifted off, one by one, to their rooms to rest for a few hours.

Tudor slapped the others on their shoulders before they mounted the stairs to the bedrooms. 'Get some sleep. We'll leave early tonight to be in position in tons of time before that barge arrives.'

With the men all in their rooms, Letta was uneasy. The house was quiet and she assumed they were sleeping. She was too nervous about the coming night to rest or draw so she was soon pedalling her bicycle along the trail leading through the cluster of fir trees towards the entrance to the farm, the late afternoon sun dipping to the horizon and kissing the top of her hair. Halting about fifty yards from the front gate she leant her bicycle on the tree trunk of a maple and, with her hands well down in the pockets of her overcoat, strolled across an area dotted with more maples towards the wood of birch and red oaks which lay on one side of her property.

A walk would do her good; she must take her mind off the coming night.

She was nervous on behalf of the British agents but she knew Dirk and Mako were experienced and skilful and Piet was steady and reliable; the young Tymen was in expert company. Yes, she must settle down, all would go well; they would explode the factory and be back to her in the early morning hours. And after lying low for a time they would leave.

On the twelfth, Cole Wareing will come for me and we shall depart Holland for ever . . . and leave the shadow of dread *behind.*

As she neared the wood she passed close to her boundary fence where she could see through the trees to a section of the lane which ran by her property. All was still. The world was so quiet and peaceful here and she felt better than she had in the confines of the house. She had been walking for perhaps five or six minutes smelling the good, clean odours of the earth and the forest, when, ahead of her, Letta thought she heard the grunting of a boar. She halted in surprise for she had not believed there were any left in this part of the country: they could be dangerous creatures and were best avoided. Hence she turned sharply and hurried back the way she had come.

As she arrived at the edge of the wood where she could see the lane through the maple trees, she stopped dead for she thought she saw a man about a hundred yards away outside her property. The glimpse was only momentary and he vanished immediately into the dense forest behind him; but it unnerved her and she ran back to her bicycle and returned to the house.

When the men came out of their rooms and, once more, Tudor took them through the mission and they prepared for the night, she tried hard to forget the image of the figure in the lane, but it would not leave her and it was a tense Letta who, some two hours later, stood near the back door in a long cardigan, arms folded across her middle, to see off the riders. She had been in a quandary wondering whether or not to mention the figure she had seen. She did not want to appear alarmist and her companions had been so cheerful and animated before they left that she had decided to say nothing. After all, she concluded that it was probably some old woodsman; there were still a few around here.

When the moment for departure came, Piet hugged her in fatherly fashion while Mako doffed his brown cap and Tymen shook her hand.

Dirk was last to leave. He held her upper right arm firmly in his hand and kissed her fleetingly on the mouth and gave her a warm smile of encouragement. Studying her a moment with an intense expression, he asked softly, 'Are you all right, Angel? You seem a bit jittery.'

She had smiled and answered, '*Ja*, just a bit edgy, I suppose. Worrying about everything.'

'Now don't worry about us. We'll be back before you know it. And thanks for all you've done.' He looked earnestly at her and for a few seconds it appeared as if he wished to elaborate but abruptly, instead, he grinned and winked his sky blue eyes at her in the lamplight. 'We'll be seeing you in the early hours, Angel.'

And now they had gone: four ebony figures leaving silently in the cool of night, and she shivered again and held herself around her waist as the picture of the man in the lane came back to her.

Chapter Sixty-four

An hour later Letta had been up and down the stairs to her bedroom three times. A copy of Somerset Maugham's book in English, *The Painted Veil*, lay open on the kitchen table. She had begun to read it in recent weeks in an effort to improve her English now that she knew it was Cole Wareing's first language. Beside the open book lay her lead drawing pencil and some papers, but she had achieved nothing. Her mind was with the men who were out in the night.

She was walking again to the foot of the stairs when she paused and her brow furrowed. She heard a noise.

A car had entered the yard!

Her large eyes became balls of fright and a desperate choking feeling constricted her throat as she stood stock still and listened.

The engine stopped and as her heart began to race she crossed back into the kitchen to hear boots on the stone path to the door and the voice she knew so well called, '*Guten Abend*, Laetitia. Open the door.'

Letta was dumbfounded. She took an instinctive step backwards from the voice of *the shadow of dread* outside. She stood petrified for a second or two. Why was he here? But even as she asked herself the question she knew the answer and knew what the figure in the lane meant.

Oh God, Piet, Dirk . . . I've been duped. And you? . . . you will be caught.

She walked with leaden feet to the door and unlocked it. 'What are you doing here?' The words caught in her throat as Ernst Von Bremen beamed at her and stepped over the threshold.

'I have come specifically to see you, *mein Liebster*. Oh, I know I told you I was going to the Hague . . . ah, a little deceit, my beautiful creature, so that you went ahead with your plans.'

She used all her self-control to speak without alarm in her voice as she followed him to the kitchen. 'What do you want?'

'To make my intentions clear to you, dear Laetitia.'

She knew she was beginning to tremble involuntarily as he held out his hand to her and she came slowly forward to him.

'How long have you been watching me?'

'Ah . . . well, I alone? Just this evening, my beautiful. But others have been watching old Lombard ever since you came here two weeks ago and met with him: watching him restore bicycles and mend lamps and clean the bedrooms in here, in readiness for your friends.' He glanced around. 'So where is the wireless?'

She did not speak, she could not speak, she was staggered and bewildered but she knew it was useless to attempt to mislead, so pointed at the ceiling.

'Upstairs, yes, of course.' He stepped to her and drew her into his arms and kissed her hard on the mouth.

Her pulse drummed in her head. How could this be happening? But it was . . . and when he released her, he smoothed her hair back with his hand. 'Now, *Liebling*, get used to my kisses. I know that you are in some sort of an intimate liaison with Lucien Bayer, but that must cease now for many reasons. Firstly, you are mine, always have been, and secondly, I know that he was working with you on tonight's events. Otherwise, why would he have supplied you with your permits and your reason to be here? I have been suspicious of him since I came here; I've been studying him for weeks and now I'm sure he is a British agent . . . and an imposter! Oh, at first I could not believe it; it is unthinkable that he has been able to get away with it. You know, I can almost admire the insolent, audacious effrontery . . . *almost*.

'You have met with no one else except him and old Lombard in all the weeks I've been here . . . just your associates. And I know for certain old Lombard hasn't organised tonight's little scheme. Ah, *nein*, it was Bayer who developed it, whoever the bastard actually is. Oh yes, he planned whatever the saboteurs came to Holland to do.'

He looked at his watch. 'Speaking of the saboteurs: they will be at the river around now, down by the Oude Ijssel, where they will receive the perfect welcome.'

Letta's mind was numb and she could not think as he took hold of her again and pulled her close, pressing her breasts into his body as he looked down into her eyes. 'The only reason I did not have them arrested here in your presence was to save you from seeing it; you understand, *Liebchen*, I could have taken them in front of you but I knew you would not like to witness it. I am conscious of your sensitivities.'

Oh God, oh God, oh God!

'Now, I am sure you do not want to die. To have terrible pain inflicted on your glorious body and be shot as an enemy of the Reich. But worry not, for you will not be. Oh no. You will be under my protection and will do just as I say. *Ja, exactly* as I say. I know you and Bayer have been working for the British, my *Liebchen*, and I cannot have that.'

She said nothing, her face was frozen, inanimate.

'Things will be just like they were: you and me. Husbands and wives should be together, *mein Liebling*. It is only fit and proper. I have spoken to my superior, *Brigadeführer* Naumann, about you and he is happy about our reunion.'

She moved to the table and leant upon it in an automatic mechanical fashion, like the action of a marionette.

He appraised her. 'Once I saw you again, I realised what I've been missing all these years. I want the feel of you under me once more, my beautiful Laetitia. You are legally mine, nobody else's, and as long as you co-operate with me in *every* way, nothing will happen to you. I have already told the Gestapo who have been watching you that you are working with me. So you are safe, perfectly. If the surviving saboteurs speak out against you I will have them shot. These recent weeks I have wondered how on earth I could ever have let you leave me.' He shook his head. 'But then I didn't let you, did I? You absconded.' He sniffed and gave her an absurd understanding smile. 'Well, you're back where you belong.'

Through the dazed fog in her head she remembered the years with him: when she was young and impressionable . . . and spoilt, so that what she had wanted she must have – immediately. He had been an art historian from Stuttgart and she had met him in Switzerland when he was on a skiing holiday and she staying with her uncle. He had returned to his post at Stuttgart University and three months later, in early 1932, they married. They had spent their honeymoon in the Alpine village of Mittenwald, Germany where, in another quixotic mood, they had decided to stay and he had become a mountain guide and ski instructor.

She had spent idle days with long breakfasts by the boxes of yellow roses at the Alpenrose Hotel in the village and lazed and painted in the afternoons in the sitting room with the Bavarian Alps for her backdrop. In the evenings they would meet acquaintances and drink and talk and listen to music in the village taverns and, even then, they had occasionally quarrelled about Hitler and his rise to power and his Brown Shirt Storm Troopers.

When Hitler had been appointed Chancellor of Germany at the end of January 1933, Von Bremen had shocked Letta by immediately joining his German Nationalist Socialist Party. This had caused their arguments on ideology to become almost a daily occurrence and for the first time he had become violent. These bouts had been followed by Von Bremen's contriteness but Letta was no longer enamoured of him and her fear of him grew as his threats during their disagreements became more brutal. When he had been recruited to the Schutz Staffel, he had come to her and told her she must now live with him in Berlin. He had lifted his finger and proclaimed, 'Fortunately you are predominantly Dutch, my dear, and therefore of a Germanic people, so I believe I can have you classified Aryan. You will have to attend courses in domestic and ideological training, of course.' His callous gaze had held hers. 'Which will do you good, Laetitia; you will understand more and protest less. I am tiring of all that.'

He took her face between his taut, hard fingers and declared, 'You are my wife. I am a loyal follower of the Führer who will bring us to glory and you will do as I say.'

He had finished this speech with the Nazis' cry, 'Germany Awake! And we will.' Now terrified, Letta had agreed to all he said, and on their arrival in Berlin, she had taken her first opportunity to flee to Paris to her father. She had gone back to calling herself Laetitia de Witt and had believed him out of her life.

His voice grated in her ears as he pulled out a chair for her.

'Now, *meine Frau*, sit here while I go upstairs and bring the wireless down, then I will leave you here so that you can pack and prepare to come with me early tomorrow.'

She lifted her head and asked in a faraway voice, 'Where will we go?'

'Don't worry about any of that. I will take care of everything. You are back with me, Laetitia. The British agents will be in Doetinchem holding prison within an hour and you must get used to the idea that Lucien Bayer, whoever he is, is someone you will never see again.'

He bent down and kissed the top of her head.

Chapter Sixty-five

That same night

At the checkpoint on the south road into Apeldoorn in the jet-black night, the German staff car carrying Cole came to a halt behind the first of their miniature convoy. In the Mercedes-Benz in front travelled *Brigadeführer* Erich Naumann and an SS major. In the staff car behind were two SS captains. It was a happy coincidence that Cole travelled alone with his driver and could be at one with his thoughts. The SS officers were returning after a meeting in Utrecht with Anton Mussert[*], the German collaborator and head of the NSB – the National Socialist Movement of the Netherlands.

On their journey back to Apeldoorn, the going had been slow for there were road closures and they had come through the narrow roads of the nature lands of the Veluwe and had been held up again outside the little village of Beekbergen, where a German army exercise was taking place.

Cole watched Naumann's car ahead as two soldiers peered in the window, shining torches, and immediately stood to attention

[*] Anton Mussert: see Author's End Notes, page 530

on seeing the SS general. In the weak light at the road block the sentries looked unkempt and tired as they saluted with a '*Heil* Hitler' in unenthusiastic fashion and waved on the fleet of three Nazi staff cars and their motorbike escort.

Cole looked at his watch in the pale yellow glow of the torch he carried. In a few hours the three British agents and Piet Lombard would be on the barge and setting the explosives to blow up the factory.

Cole had never met Piet, Letta's caretaker and gamekeeper, and while he was quite cogniscent of the reasons for that, he felt somewhat uneasy not knowing the man. Still, he allayed this fear by reminding himself that Letta was certain of the man's trustworthiness.

He dipped his hand into his pocket and took out the two photographs which Letta had given him only weeks before. In the torchlight he looked at the Villa Thalberg; it certainly was imposing with its grand lines and row of linden trees and what he could see of the grounds appeared immaculate. Slipping it behind the other picture he studied the glamorous and enticing likeness of Letta with the lake view behind her. When she had revealed her desire for them to have a place to meet in Switzerland if things went wrong, he had not known what to think. She had asked him to memorise the address of her Uncle Glenro's villa, which he had done, to placate her. But his mind was set on their escape together.

He switched off the torch and leant back on the leather hearing it creak gently as he closed his eyes. Escape routes were created by immense and systematic organisation. The escape route out of Holland for Tudor, Mako and Tymen had been established by Hans: they carried fake work passes and papers to get them on trains to the town of Kampen, south of the reclaimed land in the Zuider Zee, and describing them as engineers required for the boatyard there on the River Ijssel. In the open land to the north they would be picked up by the RAF at prearranged co-ordinates.

His own way out of Holland had been set up to be two-pronged.

Before he left England Hans had instructed him that the Royal Navy would schedule a torpedo boat pick-up to be activated on Cole's request but these arrangements had never been put into action. The route he had decided to use was to head straight south to France by rail. As an SS colonel he could pass with impunity anywhere in occupied Europe: trains were at the disposal of the invaders. He would go on his leave and simply *leave*.

In the town of Dax in south-eastern France a man called Pierre Hension, a cobbler, whose shop was across the square from the cathedral, would smuggle Cole across the Pyrenees and the British Consulate staff in San Sebastian were on the alert to expect him.

As Cole's fondness for Letta had increased and he had discovered she could not swim, his decision was to utilise this route to enable him to take her along. He had already made sure her papers to travel with him were all in order.

The last time he contacted the Essex farmhouse Hans had transmitted that he wanted Cole out of Holland: that Cole had achieved enough and been at risk too long and that prior to, or as soon as, the factory was blown, he should escape. Cole had replied that as Letta was involved in the mission he would wait until it was complete and bring Letta out with him via Spain.

'We have arrived, *standartenführer*,' the driver informed him as he slowed to a halt and jumped out to open the door.

The cool air smacked Cole's face as he stepped out while the sentries near the red-brick town hall came to attention. Naumann and the others had gone on to Het Loo Palace; Cole had decided to come back to his office where he would not need to keep company with any of them. Tonight he was tense and worried about the factory mission and making Nazi small talk was not what he had in mind.

He strode forward and hesitated with his foot on the bottom step. His eyes flicked back and forth. It was a fine, clear night but getting colder by the minute and he was thinking about Tudor and the others having to swim the blasted Oude Ijssel tonight: thank God they were fit and healthy because that water would be pretty icy.

Taking no notice of the sound of a vehicle entering the small square behind him, he mounted the four steps in two strides to pass through the tall opening to the building when a voice shouted, '*Standartenführer* Bayer?'

He turned to see a Volkswagen pull up in the murky light and a man jump out and walk to the first sentry.

It was Major Zimmermann, one of Hanns Albin Rauter's aides and a passionate Nazi whom Cole particularly loathed, though obviously the object of Cole's disgust was unaware of it.

Cole came back towards him. 'Zimmermann, what is it?'

'*Standartenführer* Bayer, the general has sent me to inform you to get ready to leave. We depart Apeldoorn tonight.'

Tonight? No . . .

'He says to tell you that you have only time to grab some clean uniforms; we're going to the railway station within the hour.'

Cole managed to find his voice. 'Train? Where exactly are we going?'

'I've been told to give you this message.'

The aide handed it over and Cole nodded. 'Wait here, I'll read it.'

His pulse beat more rapidly as he walked into the dimly lit

interior of the town hall and closed the door behind him to show no light outside. The note made it clear that he was to accompany Rauter to a series of high-level meetings in Berlin. In fact, Naumann was joining them and a staff car would be outside the SS quarters to pick up Cole and Naumann at 2100 to transfer them to the station – in about fifty minutes.

There was a PS to the note in Rauter's own hand:

Lucien, I know that you are expecting a week's leave from the twelfth, but unfortunately I think it will be the eighteenth or later before we are back. Never mind, you can have an extra few days as compensation.

Cole stood in thought. *Jesus Christ! How could this have happened now, tonight of all nights?* Should he abandon everything? Get a car, drive to the farmhouse and find Letta and try to get away? For some moments he actually considered this scheme before logical reasoning took over and he knew it would be fatal for them all: Tudor and the boys included. He had no choice but to go to Germany and he had no way of informing Letta.

He walked quickly back out to Zimmermann. 'I'll be ready but I need to go up to my office first. Find someone to come and wait here to drive me to my quarters.'

'I can wait, *standartenführer*.'

Cole paused before he said, '*Nein*, I will be at least twenty minutes here, perhaps half an hour, collecting papers and organising; get another vehicle.'

'Certainly. *Sieg Heil*.'

Cole hurried away. He had arranged to meet Letta on the twelfth at the boarded-up Knights' Inn on the road south of Zelhem. He would be some days late but thank God he had mentioned that the possibility of a delay had to be considered and when he did not turn up on the arranged day she would keep coming to the appointed place as agreed.

He had no one to trust. Did he dare to take his radio with him into Germany and try to use it there and alert Hans in England to inform Tymen of what had occurred, and so to warn Letta that way? He decided that would not work as he had been into Germany on these trips with Rauter and with Christiansen before and he was never alone except to sleep.

The wireless and batteries were well hidden and a senior SS officer's rooms and office would never be searched; but he knew that Von Bremen suspected something about him. How much he suspected he was not sure. Would Von Bremen dare to break in and forage through them while he was in Germany? Yes, he was that sort of man. He must destroy the wireless now. But how? He had nowhere to bury it or to dump it and he had to be ready in about forty-five minutes. Perhaps he could dismantle it, break it up into small parts and throw some away and hide others. He might just have time for that. It meant he could never contact Hans again but it was a precaution he probably should take.

His priority was to keep his senses alert and concentrate: to listen and be aware; going into Germany was an opportunity to gain more knowledge, he must use all the tricks of his trade to see what he could discover which might be of value to London.

He rubbed his chin in thought as the Volkswagen drew up outside his quarters. As difficult as it was, he must put Letta and the boys out of his mind for now and organise his departure for Germany.

Chapter Sixty-six

The chill wind chased the bicycle riders through the night, but they were hot and sweating from the exertion when the company of four halted under a stand of oaks with the stars and the moon awarding a wan illumination to the night.

Tudor pointed across the flat field into the distance. 'Over there.'

'Yes, this is it,' concurred Piet. 'So we follow the path through the meadow to the point where we can easily walk in and reach the trees on the river bank.'

'Though it looks a little different at night,' added Tymen, and Piet grunted in agreement.

On the ride Tudor had thought fleetingly of Laetitia. She had been anxious when they departed the farmhouse but that was all natural enough for the one who had to stay behind. He accepted that she was in love with Cole. Yeah, well, he wished them luck, though he reckoned Cole might have taken on a greater challenge than he could handle with Angel, considering the way she slipped in and out of the cot. Anyway, this blasted war would probably put paid to anything lasting for them. It did that to all sorts of people.

'Shall we go?' Piet asked in a low voice beside him.

Tudor lifted his head and sniffed the nutty aroma of the trees around them. 'Okey doke,' he replied.

Along the path which snaked across to within a hundred yards of the river they followed Tudor and he came to another halt on the edge of a patch of tall grass where they all hopped off their bikes. 'We need to walk from here.' He glanced at the Dutchman beside him. 'Piet, you've got plenty of time to get our three bicycles from here to your position downstream. Soon as we leave the barge, I reckon we'll take about six minutes to swim across river and down to you on the other side. By that time the factory will have well and truly blown.' He looked around their faces in the night. 'Everybody hunky-dory?'

Tymen and Mako leant on their bikes; Mako carried the various sticks of dynamite and the fuses. They answered in unison, 'Too right.'

Mako patted the bandolier he wore which was filled with bullets for the Sten gun strapped to his back. Tudor lifted his arm. 'Then let's go.'

They pushed their bikes in single file and came to the edge of the trees where once more they stopped and Piet spoke softly. 'Drop your bicycles over there in the long grass so I can find them after I leave you on the bank.'

They set their bicycles down and Tymen handed the dry clothes they would put on later to Piet. Tudor took his Sten gun from his back, calling in a low voice, 'This way,' as he led the way followed by Mako, Tymen and Piet and they walked into the jet-black shadows of the trees.

They had not taken more than ten strides when the woods lit up like daylight. Mako yelled, 'Germans!' Beams from arc lights hit them and automatically Tudor replied with a burst of fire at the nearest bulb, knocking it out, as he hurled himself into a bunch

415

of shrubs. A rattle of bullets followed him as Mako, who had thrown himself behind a tree, fumbled for his Sten gun and Piet ripped the pin from a hand grenade and threw it just as he was hit by a hail of bullets causing him to crumple to the ground. As the barrage continued from both sides, Piet's grenade exploded followed by moans from soldiers who had been hit by the blast.

Another beam of intensely bright light revealed Tymen, who had spun round to run, but bullets spat across the ground lifting the dirt and taking him down with a wound in his back and his leg, as now a solid mass of German soldiers appeared from both sides and behind them.

A disembodied voice shouted in English, 'Stand fast, drop your weapons and raise your hands', but Tudor was still firing and another German soldier fell from his gunfire and a second doubled over. The soldiers nearest him walked forward, pumping volleys at the bushes hiding him and abruptly silence reigned and the battle ceased.

The sheer weight of numbers of German soldiers pressing forward blocked any thoughts of escape and Tymen and Mako were soon disarmed.

Moments later the small British contingent's unconscious leader was dragged out into the clearing. His left arm was covered in blood and there was blood on his face and neck.

Into a beam of light stepped a man in grey Gestapo uniform. His rage coloured his face to high pink; his eyes dilated with anger behind his spectacles. These devils had dared to put up a fight and he was furious.

His shape cast a shadow across Tudor on the ground as *Kriminalkommissar* Ostermann yelled in English with a strong German accent: 'You are all under arrest!'

Chapter Sixty-seven

Letta opened her eyes. It was still dark. The lamp remained alight and she looked down at her fully clothed body. She had finally fallen asleep on her bed wrapped in a blanket. There was an empty feeling in her stomach and she shivered as she rose. She glanced at the big wall clock in her bedroom. Soon dawn would be breaking: *breaking like my heart*. She took the blanket and wrapped it around her shoulders. The pieces of furniture appeared murky and formless in the exiguous light of the lamp as she stood staring, the ache in her chest swelling as if to burst through her bones. Finally she moved to the mirror and with a shaking hand automatically combed her hair before taking the lamp and walking through the still house and into the kitchen.

She halted just inside the door looking at the emptiness, remaining motionless as her gaze turned to the ladder-backed chair where only yesterday Tudor had stood with one foot upon it, his arm resting on his knee as he leant forward in the firelight, animated, self-assured, positive, going through the operation one last time. She saw Mako's sunken eyes alight with the excitement of the coming night and she pictured Tymen's youthful smile as he held the last piece of her cake in his hand and turned his head to watch the leader speaking. She trembled as she imagined Piet, arms folded on the far side of the table, his kind, wise eyes upon her.

She walked to the table and put down the lamp, standing holding herself around her middle to stop shaking. Her throat stung, and now her whole body ached.

Perhaps they are all dead.

Why did she not tell Dirk about the man in the lane? But even if she had, what could he have done? They were as good as captured when they landed in the field from the RAF aircraft.

Last night she had thought all sorts of wild things. She had fancied she could drive to Apeldoorn to warn Cole. But no one was allowed to drive after the curfew, even one holding her papers which allowed certain privileges. She would have been apprehended.

Perhaps she should leave at six this morning when the curfew was lifted? But she would never get to Apeldoorn through all the checkpoints and detours before Von Bremen was due here for her. And if he arrived to find her and her car gone, he would know immediately what she had done and would make telephone calls and she would be caught.

She walked to the window and eyed the darkness, her reflection ghost-like. Was it only yesterday that she had moved about this kitchen with fragile dreams of spending her life with Cole Wareing?

Suddenly she thought about going into Doetinchem, right now, to the German command with a concocted reason to telephone Cole: it was a risk but perhaps it could work. However, she swiftly abandoned that thought. Cole Wareing would not be in the SS offices until eight o'clock and Von Bremen would be here before then.

As a child might, she dropped her head, her mouth trembled,

and she began to weep as she whispered to the wooden floor at her feet, 'I'm sorry, oh, I'm so sorry.'

For a long time she stood by the window feeling desperate, tear marks dry on her cheeks, until she became aware of the first delicate illumination in the sky, and turning with heavy steps compelled herself to bathe and dress.

Her suitcase was standing beside her on the kitchen floor and she was in her overcoat and hat looking out the window thinking about how she must now deal with the devil incarnate, when a lone rabbit came into her vision and made its way over the grass in the frost. It proceeded stealthily into the wood beyond the sheds. How had it survived without being eaten? Her countrymen were living off anything they could find these days. She watched it disappear behind a tree trunk. The little rabbit had survived so far and that's all she could hope to do now . . . survive!

She remained where she was until she saw the arrival of the black car with the SS pennant on the bonnet and heard the knock she had been expecting on her back door.

Composing herself she walked to the utility room. All she could do was appear to co-operate with *the shadow of dread* who had come for her and hope to delay him from moving in on Cole until she might have a chance to warn him. She unlocked the door.

Holding his death's head cap under his arm and bowing from the neck in a precise action, he clicked the heels of his polished boots and stepped into the house. 'I know you will be most interested to hear that we have the British agents in the holding prison outside Doetinchem and, sadly, your caretaker is dead.'

She heard herself say, 'Dead? Piet is dead?'

'The bastards put up a fight, Laetitia, very annoying of them.

419

He and the youngest one are gone. I know Piet Lombard's death will upset you, but it is done and you must not dwell on it.'

Not dwell on it? He's deranged . . . Oh God! Piet and Tymen — but then, perhaps they are better off.

He strode on by into the kitchen.

Letta watched him: the self-important walk, the swagger as he turned, the chilling handsomeness of him and the conceit in his expression as he gazed at her indifferently. It had all attracted her years ago, when she was selfish and immature and less like a thinking, caring human being. She knew the only weapons she had against him were his own follies: his conceit, arrogance and vainglory.

He glanced down at her suitcase. '*Gut*, you are ready to leave?'

'*Ja.*' *Piet and Tymen are dead, and they have Dirk and Mako . . . Oh my God in heaven.*

He looked her up and down and clasped her in his arms. 'You look tired, tired but beautiful, Laetitia.' Taking her chin in his hands he kissed her a long time upon the mouth. When they separated he grunted in satisfaction. His voice grated in her ears. 'The house is all closed up, *meine Frau?*'

She detested him but she must show nothing: steeling herself, she found her voice. '*Ja.*'

'So we go.' He took up her suitcase and she followed him out through the back door and locked it behind her.

Chapter Sixty-eight

As they approached the black Mercedes-Benz, Letta hesitated and asked, 'Where are we going?'

Von Bremen paused at her side, appearing to weigh whether he would answer her or not before he replied in a matter-of-fact tone, 'First into Doetinchem to see the senior German officer in residence and then to a place called Villa Bouchina, where a batch of Jews were kept under the protection of Mussert for some months earlier this year. I have Reich business there.'

She dared not think what the business might be.

He gently urged her towards the car as he went on, 'This afternoon we will go to the holding prison outside Doetinchem where the British prisoners are.'

Tingles of alarm ran through her. 'Why are you taking me there?'

'Because I want to, *Liebchen*.'

What if he makes me see them? Oh no, I cannot bear it. To see Dirk, for him to look at me with this creature.

She gazed up at him, straight in the eye, and made herself draw closer. She did not try to be alluring, she simply attempted to look contrite. Her tone was respectful. 'When we go to the holding prison, I will not have to see the prisoners, will I?'

He surprised her by kissing her lightly on the nose. '*Nein, Liebchen*, you don't need to see them and I don't need to set eyes on them either. I only want to find out if they have talked yet.' He spoke in a dismissive manner. 'I am planning to send them to Amersfoort camp anyway, where we have all sorts of advanced methods to make them co-operate. We are not set up for interrogation here.'

Oh God, poor Dirk and Mako. And Piet, wherever you are. Forgive me . . . please forgive me.

He pointed for her to get into the car as the *rottenführer*, an SS corporal, opened the door. He spoke to her as if they were unified, as if she were indeed his fellow traveller. 'Laetitia, if by any chance the prisoners have already mentioned you, I will, as I said before, have them shot.'

They entered the car and drove away from the farm, Laetitia beside him in the back; in front of the vehicle rode three Waffen SS soldiers on motorcycles and a *scharführer*, an SS sergeant, followed in her Rosengart.

As they turned into the lane Letta shivered, for they drove by the spot where she had seen the figure standing in the trees watching. *If only I had told Dirk; perhaps by a miracle he could have escaped.*

They continued in silence while *the shadow of dread* studied numerous papers in folders and Letta watched the flatlands of passing trees, the gates of the fields, the windmills, and the men and women dressed in drab colours, walking or riding on bicycles.

Her mind reeled and her heart raced. But she was aware that this man beside her lusted for her once more, so yes, it seemed she was indeed safe – for a little while. And as long as she had enough time to warn Cole Wareing – that was what consumed her.

When Von Bremen had first arrived at her house near Apeldoorn he had frightened and intimidated her but he had only hinted at wanting her back permanently. She had lived in terror of him with his shadow hanging over her night and day, until Cole Wareing had revealed to her his desire to take her to England. Only then had she dared to believe that it just might be possible to humour Von Bremen until after the factory had exploded.

She had been encouraged in this view when he had visited her again one night in late October and told her he would be too busy to see her for a month as he must travel back and forth to the Hague on important business for his superior; but that they should have a serious talk on his return.

He had even said, '*Ja*, Laetitia, the Führer's work must come first so, even though I desire to visit you regularly, I cannot, so I must wait a month to see your beautiful face again.' He took her in his arms and kissed her that night and she had let him, her heart leaping at the thought that while he was away the British would come in and blow up the factory and she and Cole Wareing would be gone before he returned. But he had completely duped her.

She looked around at him as he read his papers and, feeling sick, turned back to the window and the passing trees. They were driving through a wood, the streaks of sunlight shimmering through the branches to enliven the dappled boles of the trees and the mounds of russet and gold mottled leaves upon the ground. Her eyes saw it but her brain did not register it.

When they stopped briefly at a checkpoint he put his arm around her shoulders and squeezed her to him before he went back to his reading. Mentally she shuddered. He had not seen her for a decade yet he was acting as if these weird performances going on between them were all quite normal; as if no time had elapsed since they had been together.

Her mind continued to race with ideas of how to warn the man she loved. She felt certain of the mode of action *the shadow of dread* would take. He would go to his superiors in the SS – Rauter and Naumann – and present them with the capture of the British secret agents and the foiling of their attempt to explode the factory. He would reveal to them that *Standartenfüher* Lucien Bayer was an imposter who had set up the plan to explode the factory and then he would want to confront his victim himself; to watch Cole Wareing's reaction to the denouncement and to see his face as Von Bremen revealed that she was his wife. It made her stomach turn to think of it. *Oh God, what if he makes me go with him? No, I'd rather be dead.*

She spent the day with hideous thoughts racing through her mind and she was thankful she was alone much of the time while he performed whatever grim business it was he had to conduct; though he always left a soldier nearby. It was past mid-afternoon when they reached the outskirts of Doetinchem to discover a delay at the boundary roadblock. A horse-drawn vehicle with a broken wheel was stopped in the middle of the road.

The convoy came to a halt and the soldiers on the motorbikes began yelling at the man with the horse. The corporal driving them in the Mercedes-Benz appeared to believe he could move matters along for he left the car and joined in and, a moment later, Von Bremen turned to Laetitia, a strange gleam in his eyes. He put his arm up on the back of the seat behind her. 'I had a telephone call this morning. I must return to Apeldoorn tonight . . . that is, *you and I* must return to Apeldoorn tonight. We will not arrive there until late but you can return to your house and reinstate yourself. My superior, *Brigadeführer* Naumann, has told me I can spend time with you when my duties permit.'

He is unbalanced. He must be. He really believes we are going to live as man and wife.

'The *polizeiführer* and my senior officer, *Brigadeführer* Naumann have gone into Germany for a time so I'm needed.' He paused before he added, 'Lucien Bayer has departed into Germany with them.'

She flinched and he smiled. 'That surprises you, *mein Liebchen*.' He kept his intense gaze upon her.

Letta dropped her eyes to her lap. 'Well, naturally it would, as I had no knowledge of it.'

'Ah well. No need for you to expend thoughts on that.' He pointed to the car door. 'We'll get out and walk a little, while this horse business is dealt with; come along.'

The corporal saw the rear door of the automobile open and he ran back to hold it for Von Bremen, then hurried around to Letta.

They ambled past a closed-down bakery to stand under an elm. He cleared his throat. 'You realise, Laetitia, that you are going to have to tell me all about it, don't you? All about *who* he really is, who he actually works for and what he was sent here to do. It's your duty.'

Her heart began to pound again, but she steadied herself and managed to make her voice solemn as she faced around to him. 'Ernst, I do not know who he is. I have never known. He has never told me. I was amazed when you said he is an imposter; that can't be. I have always believed he is *Standartenführer* Lucien Bayer doing whatever he is doing for his own reasons.'

She took a long silent breath. *Cole Wareing is in Germany.* The shadow of dread *wants the glory of exposing him; it gives me time, time to think, to work a miracle and warn him.* 'Ernst, you are a step ahead of me. You are completely aware of the role I played in all this and you are prepared to forgive me. I am truly blessed by such charity. Just give me time to come to terms with things. Perhaps until tomorrow . . . so that I feel a little better before we talk too much.'

425

Laetitia's eyes lifted to his and they opened wide, the expression soft and tender. In her gaze Von Bremen saw a vulnerability and read all sorts of offerings there. This remorsefulness of hers appealed to him. He felt powerful.

He said nothing but he put his arm around her and they turned and walked back to the car where the road had been cleared and they were soon on their way towards the prison.

Chapter Sixty-nine

Tudor's eyes opened. He remembered he had fallen asleep: blessed sleep. He lay on a cot against the wall and raised his gaze to a reflected pale light emanating from a barred window above and sniffed the air. The room smelt of mildew and something else – pungent; almost like the stale smell of beer. He ached all over and as he rose to a sitting position, pain shot through his left elbow which had been shattered in the rifle fire last night. It was loosely bandaged and as he moved, it hung inertly at his side. He remembered that when he had been brought here last night he had drifted in and out of consciousness for an hour or two but recalled that a man in a white coat had used some water to wash it and, afterwards, perfunctorily bandage it.

There were marks on the wooden wall of the cell in his eye line. He wondered momentarily what they were – probably the number of days some other poor bugger had spent here.

He had been interrogated this morning as soon as he was awake, the endless questions, on and on, to which he always gave the same answer: 'I don't know.'

'Tell us what is your real name?'

'We know you are a British secret agent. You might as well admit it.'

'We have all your false identity papers so we know your cover name. Dirk Hartog, you see, so it's no use lying. What is your code name?'

'What is your real name?'

'We know you were dropped in from an RAF aircraft. From what airfield did you leave England?'

'Where did you do your training?'

'What was your target? The factory on the river? Yes, we are certain it was, so why not admit it?'

'Who was your male contact on the ground other than Piet Lombard?'

On and on and on. And every now and then they would come back to, 'What is your code name?'

'If you tell us your code name you can have a nice hot breakfast. Bacon and eggs, yes, a nice British breakfast.'

'Your friends have already told us a great deal so you might as well answer me. We have all sorts of information from them.'

Tudor knew for sure when this was said, that it was a lie. Before he had been wounded himself in the short battle, he had seen Piet fall heavily to the ground, obviously badly wounded, and Tymen take bullets in his back; neither would be in any fit state to talk, even if they were still alive. Tudor had not seen Mako, Tymen or Piet since they had been brought here, though he could not help but suspect that Tymen and Piet were dead. And Tudor knew that the boy was fearful of torture and had told Tudor he would take his L pill if he were caught.

Tudor believed without a doubt that Mako would never talk, no matter what they did to him. Both he and Mako had decided at the last minute to leave their pills behind at the farmhouse – in a sort of superstition that if they did not have them they would not need them – well, so much for that!

In all the hours of interrogation never once had Laetitia been mentioned. It was the only circumstance which seemed odd to him; all the other questions he had expected: he had even expected the number of punches in the face which he had taken and the final kick in the stomach. He was sure it would get worse soon because his interrogators were getting frustrated with his unrelenting answer of 'I don't know.'

The questioning had taken place in another dank room with a *kriminalkomissar* – a lieutenant in the Gestapo – who had remained for about an hour before he was replaced by a wizened little bastard of about forty with a pock-marked face. His companion, in contrast, was a quite cherubic-looking young man in his mid-twenties whose squeaking voice reminded Tudor of Peter Lorre, the European actor who went to Hollywood. He was the one who had punched and kicked. Somewhere deep in Tudor's mind he had seen the amusing side of the younger one's resemblance to the Hollywood actor and the second time he had punched him, Tudor had actually deviated from 'I don't know' and declared, 'You're the perfect little sadist, *Peter!*'

He had received the kick for that.

Before they had brought him to this room *Wizened Face* had informed Tudor that, 'Tomorrow the people who will question you will not be as friendly as we have been.'

No doubt that threat was intended to give him a sleepless night.

Tudor assumed the prison was near Doetinchem for he had heard the guards who brought him to this room say they were going into that town to a tavern; though how far away from it they were he was uncertain. His captors had no idea he understood German. They were aware he spoke English, of course, and also Dutch, for that was obvious by the fact of his being here and, too, the information on his false identity papers which were in their keeping. The escape cover for all three of them had been as Dutch engineers transferred from Doetinchem to the shipyard in Kampen Port. His interrogators had spoken to him in English and when they had conversed with each other in German, Tudor had given no sign that he understood anything.

He stood up. His mouth was swollen and sore and he realised the afternoon must be advancing from the amount of light which came in at the window. Earlier he had been given one bowl of something that resembled soup and one piece of dry bread; the bread had been difficult to eat because of his bruised and tender mouth.

On his tiptoes he could see out. It was raining lightly. About a hundred yards away was a barbed-wire fence and beyond a forest.

This location was, in fact, a compound containing three build-ings which sat alone along an unsealed road four miles from Doetinchem in a dense wood. Before the war it had been built as a training camp for the Dutch Army. Its use by the invaders had been intermittent but it was the ideal place for them to incarcerate those in the area who came under their suspicion.

Tudor still had no idea who had informed, though he had ex-perienced all kinds of weird thoughts that it must have been Laetitia, especially as his questioners had not mentioned her, but then he would discard the notion as madness. For if that were the case, then Cole would be as good as dead too and she had professed with great sincerity to love him.

Tudor's mind had been playing games on him and at times he would imagine that Cole's impersonation of Bayer had been discov-ered and that it was Cole who, under torture, had informed on them. But he dismissed that as absurd as well.

And then he would come back to the fact that no one else in Holland was aware of this mission other than Cole and Laetitia, except for the dead Piet. Well . . . as far as he knew.

Tudor had only been to Holland twice and both times his operation had been sold down the river; quite literally *the river* this time.

The abrupt sound of a key scraping in the door brought Tudor's head round to see it swing in as a shiver of apprehension ran through his frame. The electric light in the corridor behind the man revealed his portly shape in silhouette and when he spoke Tudor did not recognise his voice. He spoke in Dutch. 'Bring your belongings and come with us.' A soldier moved behind him. 'You're being transferred this evening.'

The civilian stepped inside the cell to help the prisoner to his feet but Tudor shook his head, replying in Dutch, 'I don't need your bloody help and I've got no belongings, or hadn't you noticed, fatso?'

The man paused and waited until Tudor rose unaided and followed him out into the weakly lit corridor where the soldier stood. The civilian led the way and the soldier came behind as they walked past six doors with grills in them and turned left along an extensive corridor which ended in a locked door.

After passing through they entered a hallway which opened up into a sort of vestibule where two guards could be seen standing at an exit in the distance and three SS soldiers sat at a table playing cards. Crossing to the end of the area, the stout civilian unlocked a door with a key from his pocket and gestured for his captive to enter. Inside, in a long empty room, was a single chair and a glass of water on a table.

During the morning's questioning Tudor sang 'Dixie Land' in his head to take his mind away from what was being said. He knew his captors were all liars so the truth might be that he was not being transferred at all: that this was just the first form of a sick game. He was steeling himself for what was to come when the man with him, still speaking Dutch, stated, 'Wait in here. You can drink the glass of water if you wish.'

'How very kind of you.' Tudor's words dripped with sarcasm.

He moved forward down the room to the grubby pane of glass in the single window and looked out. It was late afternoon and an insect ran across in front of his eyes. 'You must be a hardy little devil to stand this place,' he said to it in English and his keeper asked as he moved to the door, 'What do you say?'

Tudor did not look round and replied in English, 'I'm talking to the insect, any conversation of his would be preferable to yours.' As the listener did not reply this was probably lost on him. The door closed behind him and Tudor heard the key turn.

He remained a few minutes at the window which overlooked a bleak, muddy courtyard where soldiers moved about and two lorries with canvas-covered rear bodies were parked. Fine rain still fell. Another wing of the building stood opposite and looking up he could see three balconies on the storey above and the bleak sky beyond.

Noting the vibration of boots passing outside in the vestibule Tudor moved away from the window, back down the room. There, he could hear the SS soldiers outside talking and as he came up to the door, their conversation became plain.

They were speaking German which, of course, he understood perfectly. The discussion was the food they had been given for lunch.

'That meatloaf would have been turned away by a pig.'

'You're so hard to please. I thought it was all right.'

432

'Ah, but that's you all over, Becker. What would you know about good food?'

'More than you; my mother's family employed a cook.'

Derisive laughter from the other two greeted this statement. 'That's what you tell us.'

After they had wearied of the conversation about food the subject turned to superior officers.

'What do you think of the *standartenführer*'s woman?'

'*Gott*, I've never seen anyone as good-looking as her. She's like a goddess. Oh, how I'd like to be inside her bones.'

'*Ja*, lucky bastard. Officers have all the beautiful women.'

'What did Berlitz say her name was?'

'Let me think.'

'How the hell did Berlitz know her name?'

'He was on duty at the roadblock outside Zelhem when she came through there about five days ago.'

'Hold on. Wasn't it de Witt?'

Tudor stood stock still.

'*Ja*, that's right. Funny first name, Li-eta or something.'

'*Nein*, Becker, you fool, it was Laetitia.'

'That's it.'

'I agree with you. Oh, to be between her legs . . . what a body for a cold night. The blankets would sizzle.'

They all laughed again.

'How come the *standartenführer* has brought her here today anyway?'

'To show her off to us poor unfortunates, of course.'

This was greeted with more amusement.

'They came especially. I heard Sergeant Fischer say she was instrumental in catching the British saboteurs.'

'Well, that one inside there now is to be transferred this afternoon, with the other survivor.'

'*Ja*, Fischer said the orders have come straight from the *standartenführer*.'

'Where are they being sent?'

'Kamp Amersfoort would be my guess.'

There was a murmur of agreement.

'*Ja*, that's where they'll go.'

'I think it's because the Gestapo are set up with better methods at Kamp Amersfoort. Anyway, they'll finish up in Germany, if they live.'

'*Ja*, they'll probably shoot them in the end. Shh, quiet! The sergeant is crossing the courtyard.'

There was a scuffle of movement and silence fell. Tudor's face was rigid, his bloodshot eyes were the only part of him that moved. His head spun and his mind felt numb. So . . . it had come to this. Laetitia de Witt and her *standartenführer* – Bayer, of course. *God, Cole, how did they suck you in?*

All revealed by serendipity to him here in this room. He could have been transferred to Amersfoort and died there, or in a death camp in Germany, and never have known the truth.

She had been agitated and uneasy when they rode away last night, of course she had! The lousy bitch. He felt sick at the thought of ever having touched her; of holding her close, of trusting her. Well, that bastard Wareing deserved her. *He's turned double agent, that's what's happened.* The two of them, sickening traitors together.

He moved slowly back down to the window where he stood holding the sill and staring outside. His face wore a tortured expression as his gaze drifted past the end of the section of building opposite. About seventy-five yards away he watched a door open and he started as a woman come out. It was Laetitia de Witt!

She hurried down the three stone steps and turned away and right on her heels came an SS officer wearing his cap. *Jesus, Wareing!* Tudor gave a spontaneous shudder. *So it is true, revoltingly true. At least if I die in a bloody German camp, I'll die knowing for certain what scum de Witt and Wareing turned out to be.*

A guard who crossed to the couple gave a Hitler salute and followed them as the *standartenführer* threw a greatcoat around Laetitia's shoulders and hugged her into his side as they hurried away with their backs to Tudor.

It's her and that goddam bastard Wareing. Tudor watched them disappear around the far end of the building.

He was still standing in the same place with his mind lurching from thought to thought when the door opened again.

'Come on, you . . . out.'

Chapter Seventy

Tudor and Mako sat on a fixed bench bumping along in the back of one of the Opel Blitz lorries that Tudor had seen in the prison courtyard. They were both in handcuffs: Mako's hands behind his back, Tudor's in front of him, only because the soldiers could not get his badly injured arm to bend. They had not spoken to each other as speaking was forbidden.

Mako's grim face was swollen, and when he had smiled on seeing his leader, he revealed a broken lateral incisor tooth. His hands were cut but he walked straight and looked the Germans in the eye.

Tudor was in torment. *How could I have trusted her? . . . and him? My good friend . . . Goddam, how? I swear I'll get them both. One day I'll get them both, no matter how long it takes or whatever I have to do. I must survive no matter what, to kill those two animals.*

The canvas flap at the rear of the truck was down and secured and a guard holding a rifle sat inside opposite them on the other fixed bench.

A driver with another soldier beside him occupied the front cabin and behind rode two escorting troops on motorbikes.

It had continued to rain as they were forced into the back of the lorry and Tudor had heard the driver say to their soldier escort that they needed to be in Doetinchem at the railway station by four o'clock. 'It's five miles, so we need to hurry.'

The truck was travelling at speed and Tudor reckoned they had come perhaps two and a half miles along the dirt road in the light rain when suddenly the brakes were jammed on and the vehicle skidded and slewed sharply sideways. The noise was horrendous as a motorcycle behind crashed straight into the back of the lorry and the other swerved to avoid it and ran head on into a tree trunk. The vehicle lifted in the air and smashed with another deafening sound into the forest as it shuddered, overturned and came to rest on its side.

Tudor regained consciousness first. He was on his back and the rods that held the canvas were bent and the canvas ripped asunder. Groans came from the front cabin which was wedged between two massive trees and had concertinaed in on top of the soldier and the driver. The back of the truck was free and Mako was half in and half out of it. The guard who had been with them was lying beside him unconscious, with blood on his head. Tudor reacted immediately and crawled out past Mako and the soldier, picking up the Mauser bolt-action rifle with his good hand even though his wrists were handcuffed.

One of the soldiers who had been riding behind lay inertly underneath his twisted motorbike, one wheel broken completely away. He could not see the other rider.

'Mako, Mako, wake up, pal.' Tudor glanced swiftly around. The dirt road was empty and fine rain continued to fall.

Mako moaned and opened his eyes. The big man had a cut on his arm which was bleeding through his torn shirt. 'Jesus, what happened?'

'I've no idea, but let's get out of here.'

Mako got to his feet. 'My back hurts a bit but I'm all right, boss.'

'Then come on.'

They moved away from the truck in the direction they had been heading, unaware of the huge, now dead boar which had emerged from the wood directly in front of the lorry and caused the accident. The two escapees had gone about sixty yards when a bullet whizzed by them, followed by a second one and as Mako hit the dirt, Tudor spun round to see one of the soldiers who had been on a motorcycle. He was wobbling in the middle of the road near the lorry, pointing a pistol at them.

Even in handcuffs Tudor's finger could reach the trigger of the rifle. He held it against his right side, aimed it at the swaying man, and fired a burst. The soldier fell face down. 'Come on, Mako', and the big man scrambled to his feet and off they moved as fast as they could.

'Where the hell are we going?' Mako asked. 'What if some bastard comes along?'

'That's unlikely, thank God.'

'That was a bloody miracle, boss, but they'll catch us sure as sure. We're handcuffed, for God's sake.'

'I know, but we must move, let's give ourselves a chance.' They hurried on for about five minutes and Tudor exclaimed, 'Look, there ahead is a track into the trees, we'll take it. Night's coming soon and that might help.'

Even though they had both been beaten by the secret police they were athletes and in peak physical condition and they were soon running on the track through the darkening forest. They had made about a mile when the light was fading quickly and they came abruptly out into a clearing and stopped dead. A middle-aged man on a bicycle had come hurtling out of the trees to the right and as he saw them he screeched to a halt. Tudor lifted the rifle and pointed it at him.

'Don't shoot. Who are you?' he asked.

There was little point in lying. Wearing handcuffs and in their injured dishevelled state they both looked exactly what they were. 'We're escaping from the Germans,' Tudor replied in perfect Dutch.

And that's when the second miracle occurred! The man smiled. 'You are lucky men to have found me. I can help you. But we must hurry for there are two others not too far behind me who are collaborators with the Germans.'

Andre Janssen was a Dutch patriot. He took them via a round-about route to his house on the far side of the woods and opened their handcuffs by doing exactly what Tudor and Mako told him to do to remove them. Opening any lock was elementary to SOE agents once they had a small, thin piece of metal.

Within half an hour they had bathed, had their wounds attended to and were wearing Andre's clothes. Within two minutes more they were on bicycles travelling in the dark with Andre towards the other Dutch patriots, who, each night, would pass them on from area to area. Until finally, after weeks of living in hay barns, garden sheds and out-of-the-way farms in Gelderland, Overijssel, Drenthe and Groningen, they were finally on the Dutch coast.

There they were hidden in an attic until the local Dutch loyalists organised to smuggle them aboard a fishing vessel and sail the two escapees across the Baltic Sea to reside with anti-German fishermen in Sweden until the end of the war.

Chapter Seventy-one

11 November

Wrapped in a dressing gown Laetitia stood in her parlour looking at her portrait of Cole. She had placed it back up on the easel and the early morning sunshine revealed him to her standing in an arbour with trees framing him, his right hand resting on the bole of a gnarled cedar tree. The chiaroscuro was masterful and trails of light fell through the leaves above to rest on his face and to illuminate his right hand and the narcissuses growing at his feet. Though she formed no thoughts of how well she had painted it; she merely leant her head against it and touched his replica fingers with her own, her eyes wet and her body trembling with emotion.

Von Bremen had left the house half an hour previously and she had washed and rewashed herself since he had gone.

She felt vile and mean and low. The light in her appealing eyes had gone and she moved as a marionette would move. She did not know how long she could endure existing with Erich Von Bremen.

After their hour at the holding prison and their late arrival here the previous night, he had been interested only in bedding her, not in questioning her. She thanked God for that. This morning he had hurried to leave but before he did he said to her, 'I will write a deposition for you today. It should be sufficient to ensure you do not need to be questioned by anyone other than me.'

'What will the deposition say?'

He had come to her and held her chin in his hand. 'Laetitia, we are now together again, husband and wife. It will denounce Bayer, obviously. It will save you from torture and death, *mein Liebling*.' He dropped his hand to her shoulders and caressed them as he gazed in her eyes. 'It will state that you acted under my orders — and in the interests of our ultimate victory you became intimate with him and feigned a disloyalty to the Reich to gain his confidence.'

He pulled on his boots as he explained further. 'It will recount the arrival of the saboteurs and how you led them to *Kriminalkommissar* Ostermann.

'This evening you can tell me about Bayer and the prisoners and I will add any detail necessary. Once you have signed it, I'll take it to the High Commissioner; there will be enough evidence to arrest Bayer.'

The man is not only evil, he has truly lost his senses.

Using all her self-control she asked calmly, 'You mean to arrest him while he is away in Germany?'

He stood up and turned to the mirror, running a comb through his black hair. 'I'll talk it over with the High Commissioner. It would be enjoyable, of course, to wait for him to return here and to confront him.' He brought his hands together in a loud slapping noise and Letta flinched.

Bursting into laughter he took her arm and pulled her round to him and kissed her on the mouth before he strode to the door throwing his words lightly over his shoulder. 'You should begin a painting today, Laetitia . . . perhaps another of me; the previous one you did was so long ago, of the younger man.' He frowned and turned round in the doorway. 'By the way, where is it?'

He actually believes I would have kept it? She had destroyed it long ago but she answered thoughtfully, 'Ah, I believe it is at my uncle's in Switzerland. We shall have to redeem it.'

'*Jawohl.* I shall see you tonight, *meine Liebe.*' His footsteps echoed on the wooden flooring as he walked swiftly away to the top of the stairs.

Letta leant her head on the painting of the man she wanted to save. All she lived for was to warn him so he would not get caught. Her body shook with the intensity of her thoughts.

Cole Wareing was safe until *the shadow of dread* acted. He held Dirk and Mako prisoners and he had her exactly where he wanted her.

She moved from the painting and sat in the parlour for a long time, her gaze trained on nothing, staring ahead. At last she roused herself and dressed in the blue frock Cole had always liked: in her anxious state of mind she felt somehow strangely comforted to be wearing it. A few minutes later, covering the dress with her overcoat, slipping on gloves and wearing a knitted beret over her hair, she walked out into the chill daylight, down the pebbled path to the gate and out to the stream. Holding herself around her middle in habitual manner she passed along the bank to her secret arbour and sat on her flat rock looking at the water.

Many of the trees had lost their leaves and there were no summer swallows to sweep along the stream and skip carelessly along the branches. She thought of her life and wiped the tears from her eyes with her gloved hand. She knew she had been wilful, foolish, living for the moment and had made many mistakes. Who was she really? She believed she was a Dutch patriot. She had done her best to fight the Nazi aggressors and was succeeding until *the shadow of dread* had returned into her life.

He was the symbol of ugliness, of a stupid transgression that she had made in her days of vanity and self-indulgence. How she despised him and all his kind who had raped her country and battered her people into submission.

She looked down at the grass around her feet, soon to be clothed in winter snow, and she shivered, mouthing a silent prayer, her hands palms together, as she had worshipped in childhood.

Finally, she decided what to do.

She did not know what she would find once she got there but she would go into Apeldoorn to Cole's secretary, Hendrika. She knew the girl did not care for her but she was loyal to Cole. Perhaps Hendrika could tell her something; perhaps she even had a way to send a message to him. Von Bremen was stationed at the Het Loo Palace so he would not know and, to be inconspicuous, she would ride her bicycle.

Within minutes she had returned along the stream and, tense and fearful, but with a fierce determination now manifesting in her eyes, she rode her bicycle by the great oaks down to her front gate and away from the house by the stream.

Chapter Seventy-two

Standartenführer Ernst Von Bremen sauntered with a skip in his step up the flight of stone steps, past the guards to the front doors of the Dutch baroque Het Loo Palace in the woods on the northern edge of Apeldoorn. It was this property that the Royal Dutch House of Orange had called home for three centuries and it was here Queen Wilhelmina, who had escaped to England, had resided prior to her departure. The magnificent symmetrical building had been commandeered by the invaders as the headquarters of the German High Command in the area. He entered the building and halted: coming down the staircase towards him was an aide to his superior, Erich Naumann.

'Ah, Huber, I will need you and Krupps to help me later this morning. With *Brigadeführer* Naumann away I have much to do, handling work for the Hague.'

'But he's not away, *standartenführer*.'

'What? I was informed he went into Germany with the *politzeiführer* and *Standartenführer* Bayer?'

'They came back yesterday. Well, they certainly left here on the train the night before last, but insurgents had blown up the railway line not far from the border with the Fatherland.' He made a

clucking sound. 'The reprisals for such acts are not severe enough
. . . I know they spent the night in a village over there for they did
not have enough coal to come back on the train. They were supposed
to obtain more for the onward journey once across the border.
They returned here yesterday from Amelo in military vehicles. The
polizeiführer was furious and so was General Naumann. They remained
briefly and their plans must have altered, for about two hours later
they left for the Hague.'

Von Bremen shook his head. 'So *Standartenführer* Bayer went to
the Hague with them?'

'*Nein.*'

'What?'

'My understanding is that he remained in Deventer . . . something
he's handling for the *polizeiführer*, to do with our police training
school in Schalkhaar. I think he'll be there all day.'

Von Bremen hesitated. 'Ah, I see. You can go, Huber.'

The junior officer clicked his heels. 'What time do you want
me?'

Von Bremen directed his pale eyes to him. 'Hmm? What did
you say?'

'The time you want me later this morning?'

He paused. 'I'll let you know.'

Huber clicked his heels again, gave the Hitler salute and departed
as Ernst Von Bremen walked on with a furrow of concentration
forming between his eyes.

He had reached his office door when it opened in front of him
and his adjutant, *Hauptsturmführer* Kaufmann, greeted him with the
words, '*Standartenführer*, I was coming to find you, there is an urgent
telephone call for you.'

Von Bremen hurried by into his office and picked up the receiver.

As he listened, the crease in his forehead deepened and his eyes closed. 'The incompetent fools!' he screamed, a high colour flooding to his cheeks. 'Put those who are still alive on charges and continue combing the area. They must be found, you hear, they must be found.'

He knocked a pile of papers to the floor as he stood from his desk and hurried to the door in a rage. He burst into the next room yelling, 'Kaufmann, come with me and arrange for a vehicle to await me at the front door!' His secretary and the junior officer leapt from their desks to do his bidding.

Minutes later, in another wing of the palace, Ernst Von Bremen's eyes gleamed with intensity as he and Kaufmann searched Cole's rooms. Cole's personal servant had protested but the authority of an SS colonel had prevailed.

'What are we searching for, *standartenführer*?'

'A wireless.'

Kaufmann's expression was one of amazement.

Yet as the minutes passed and they found nothing, finally thwarted, Von Bremen strode out, followed by his adjutant, and made his way to the front door where a Kübelwagen waited.

'To the town hall!'

Once there they hastened up the steps into the building and on up the inner stairs and along the corridor to where Hendrika rose to her feet in amazement as the two Germans entered her office. 'We are here to search this office; stand still and you won't get hurt.'

'But . . . but *Standartenführer* Bayer does not—'

She tried to block the door to Cole's office but was slammed aside into the wall by Von Bremen who yelled, 'Out of the way!'

The petrified girl stood dumbfounded while the intruders opened all the cupboards and the locked cabinets and flung drawers to the floor. Von Bremen's wrath burgeoned even more when again he could find nothing incriminating.

He had turned to depart when his eye caught something under the cabinet nearest the door. He bent to retrieve it and his expression altered as he made a satisfied high-pitched sound. 'Aaah! What does this look like to you, Kaufmann?'

The aide studied it. 'It appears to be a knob of some kind.'

'Like one on a wireless set?'

'*Ja*, true, like one on a wireless set.'

'I must speak with *Brigadeführer* Naumann in the Hague immediately. Get him!'

And Kaufmann hurried to do his bidding.

But he was to be disappointed. The *brigadeführer* was busy in a high-level meeting; so it was over half an hour before they spoke and, meanwhile, he had returned to Het Loo Palace. The telephone conversation lasted many minutes. Twice the connection was lost and twice they were re-linked. Von Bremen's final words to Naumann were, '*Ja, brigadeführer*, I knew you would be astounded, even though I had mentioned to you previously certain conclusions of mine about Bayer. As I said, my estranged wife was suspicious of him for months and when I arrived here in Holland we worked together on this. I shall go to Schalkhaar immediately and arrest him myself. And as we have now agreed, my wife will sign the affidavit as soon as I return with the prisoner.

'Also worry not, we will catch the escaped saboteurs if it's the last thing I do.'

Chapter Seventy-three

Hendrika sat at her desk, sunlight from the window glinting on her flaxen hair, her lead pencil tucked through the plait above her ear. She was still bemused by the morning's events with *Standartenführer* Bayer. She had eaten lunch and a cup of ersatz coffee was near her hand when she received her second surprise of the day.

Hearing a knock on her office door she looked up to see it open and a soldier stood aside to allow Laetitia de Witt to enter.

'Fräulein de Witt requires to speak with you and the lieutenant has agreed she can see you.'

Hendrika's mouth opened and closed as she stood. 'Oh? Come in.'

The soldier departed and Letta came forward to the secretary holding her hands together as if in supplication. 'Hendrika, I know you aren't fond of me, but I believe you are loyal to *Standartenführer* Bayer.'

Hendrika lifted herself to her full height which was not inconsiderable. Her answer was guarded for she was remembering the visit of Von Bremen and the way he had treated her, and the mess she had needed to clean up after he had searched the inner office. 'I work for *Standartenführer* Bayer and have always done what was required of me.' The girl noticed her visitor's troubled expression and agitated manner and suddenly felt a little sorry for the woman she had always envied, the woman who dressed so elegantly and was so beautiful: even in her obvious distress she wore a modish knitted beret and a smart overcoat on top of what appeared to be a blue frock with a white collar. 'What is it you want?'

'Nothing for myself. I just need to know how long *Standartenführer* Bayer will be in Germany and if you have any way of sending a message to him? Anything . . . a telephone number . . . anything?'

'But he is not in Germany.'

'Not . . . in . . . Germany?'

'No, the train he was upon did not get through.'

'Where is he? For God's sake, where?'

Hendrika had worked with the Germans now since they had taken over her country. She was fearful of them and had co-operated with them to have an easy time and to earn money, but in her heart she felt more and more apprehensive. She saw many things happen that upset her equilibrium and she was not as enamoured with the invaders as once she had been. She did not care for this woman in front of her, but she felt close to *Standartenführer* Bayer, for he was more caring and very different from the other SS officers.

She suspected now that *Standartenführer* Von Bremen's personal attention to her had been to gain information. He had thumped her hard against the wall this morning without a second thought and hurt her shoulder badly; whereas Lucien Bayer had treated her always with respect, and even kindness. She recalled when she had been ill and he had insisted on her going home and not coming back until she was well – a small deed – but other secretaries were not treated like that; they were expected to work no matter what.

So all this engendered her willingness to answer Letta's question.

'He is in Schalkhaar at the police school, I do not know for how long, but—'

A frantic look came into Laetitia's eyes. 'But what?'

And the girl heard herself answer, 'Another officer – *Standartenführer* Von Bremen – was here.'

'In this office? Why?'

'He . . . he searched it.' She pointed to Cole's office.

'Oh no!' Letta's eyes became wild with fear and Hendrika suddenly decided to tell all she knew.

'He found something, under this cupboard.' She walked to the inner door and opened it, pointing to the floor. 'I was standing here so I could see. It was a knob of some kind, Von Bremen said it was from a wireless. He has gone there, to Schalkhaar. He closed this door and made a telephone call to the Hague from here in *Standartenführer* Bayer's office. I did not hear what he said but as he rushed out by me he ordered the officer with him to get six soldiers and a truck to meet them over at Het Loo Palace. I am afraid for *Standartenführer* Bayer.'

'Oh my God in heaven. When was Von Bremen here?'

'Perhaps an hour ago.'

'Oh no . . . that long . . . he will be in Schalkhaar easily by now.'

'Please don't say I told you.'

Letta managed to utter, 'No I won't. Thank you . . .' before she turned and dashed out of the office, down the stairs and out of the building into the square. She ran past the guards and picked up her bicycle and rode away.

As she pedalled through the streets and out into the woods and along the lanes, her confused thoughts tumbled over one another: *Von Bremen found a knob on the floor, a wireless knob. Von Bremen knows everything. He will arrest Cole Wareing . . . oh no . . . he will have arrested him already; it does not take long to get to Schalkhaar. It's too late . . . all too late. It's all over!*

Oh God, he will bring me the affidavit: he will force me to sign it. Cole will die. I cannot sign. I will not sign. Cole might already be dead and all because of me. Dirk will die because of me. Mako will die because of me . . . all my fault. Rada is dead. Piet is dead. Tymen is dead . . . and now the man I love will die. All because I am married to the shadow of dread, all because of me . . .

By the time she reached the house by the stream and ran up the steps to the blue door she had decided what was the one thing left to do.

Through to her back room she ran and searched the shelves, fumbling to open boxes and dropping them to the floor and climbing the small ladder to reach the higher shelves.

Not discovering what she looked for, she ran through to the room where she stored her canvases and again she searched, shelf by shelf, and there she found it! It was lying in a cardboard box. With trembling fingers she took out her father's Great War Chamelot-Delvigne revolver and stood looking at it in her hands. Slowly she removed the bullets from the bottom of the box and loaded the weapon.

Chapter Seventy-four

Cole limped through the doorway of the Schalkhaar police training school and climbed into the Horch V8 engine staff car and was driven away. It was not a vehicle favoured by high-ranking Nazis but often used by Wehrmacht officers. This one had been borrowed from the Wehrmacht to transport Cole when he had remained in Deventer after Rauter and Naumann had proceeded to Apeldoorn.

Yesterday, when he had been left here, Cole had made a telephone call to Wimmer in Apeldoorn and had gently pumped him to see if the Nazi commissioner had heard anything about the factory being exploded the preceding night. But when nothing was forthcoming Cole began to be concerned. He had spoken again to Wimmer early this morning, hoping that by now word of the explosion would have filtered through to Apeldoorn, but still there was no news. Cole's concern increased.

As he drove away from the tiny village he was relieved to depart from the confines of a 'school' where young Dutch recruits were indoctrinated with Nazi ideology and taught how to use terror and brutality against their own countrymen. Each day Cole became more and more desperate to quit Nazi-held Holland and his surroundings. When Rauter's party had been forced to leave the train the night before last due to the blowing up of the railway lines ahead by the Dutch Resistance, he had been grateful to have his trip into Germany aborted.

Yet now, since he had heard nothing through the Nazi grapevine, he was becoming hourly more anxious about Letta, Tudor and the others and he was impatient to get back to Apeldoorn as soon as possible. He knew he had been psychologically ready for this mission when he arrived, but now, each twenty-four hours that went by brought greater apprehension. He managed to pass these feelings off with the knowledge that he had been trained for all this; that he was a professional secret agent; that he was immersed in the persona of Lucien Bayer and that as long as he retained his nerve, all would be well.

He told himself all this now, as he travelled the two miles from the village of Schalkhaar to the historic centre of Deventer where he was to meet with the senior officer of the local Wehrmacht before returning to Apeldoorn.

He stepped out of the car in the town, arrogance in every move-ment, wearing his grey uniform, Iron Cross at his throat, the blue and gold Order for Merit gleaming on his left breast and leaning on his ebony and ivory cane. There, where many of the buildings dated back to medieval times, he was greeted by a Wehrmacht lieutenant who clicked his heels, bringing them together with a formal 'Sieg heil' and telling him, 'The industrial area was bombed last night and Major Zimmermann is discussing the events with his staff in a villa near the Bergkerk.'

Cole nodded. 'Ja, I heard the explosions in Schalkhaar.' He left the lieutenant and drove to the imposing villa situated not far from the Bergkerk – the Church of St Nicholas. There he was informed by a lieutenant that Major Zimmermann had gone, some time previously, to the industrial area but was expected back any minute. Again with a clicking of heels and bowing of shoulders, Cole was asked, 'Would you care to wait, *Herr standartenführer*? We have a waiting room. As I said, he should be back any minute.'

'All right, I'll wait briefly.'

With a deferential bow from his shoulders the lieutenant showed Cole into a spacious room on the ground floor. 'Could I bring you something to drink?'

'*Nein.*'

Left alone, Cole studied the room. He stood on a huge plush rug under a tall ceiling with half-columns of the Doric order at intervals along the walls between long windows. A chill breeze came in at an open window on his left and he walked over to it and looked out on to a narrow stone balcony. He was on the side of the villa nearest the *Bergkerk* and he could see its towering spires as he glanced along the lane to where the engine of his Horch staff car jutted out, the remainder of it hidden by the building.

He waited perhaps four minutes and moved away from the window to observe more closely a walnut writing desk with an inlaid floral design of maple and pear, when the door he had entered opened opposite him and he glanced up.

Erich Von Bremen strode in holding his Sauer pistol. 'Ah, *Standartenführer* Bayer, or should I use your real name? I would, if only I knew it.' He smiled. 'But never mind, I will . . . I will.'

'What are you talking about?' Cole concealed his surprise and came forward to him as Von Bremen kicked the door closed behind him.

Von Bremen shook the gun. 'Stop there, no closer or I'll blow your imposter's head off.'

'What game are you playing, Von Bremen?'

'I play no game but *your* game *is up*. We know you are a British agent.'

Cole met his gaze. 'Really?'

'I am here to arrest you.'

'On whose authority are you acting?'

Von Bremen's cold eyes flashed with anger. 'On *my* authority as a loyal officer of the Führer! *Brigadeführer* Naumann is aware of your deception and *Polizeiführer* Rauter and the High Commissioner will know all about you by now.'

Cole took a half-step nearer and Von Bremen backed away towards a window, lifted the pistol and aimed it at Cole's head. 'Do not move again or I will kill without hesitation.'

Cole remained still.

'Your friends who were here to blow up our factory were caught the night before last.'

Von Bremen saw the sudden minute change in Cole's expression, fleeting though it was. 'Ah, you dislike that piece of information, I see. But you will dislike even more the other news I have yet to impart.' Von Bremen was enjoying himself and his smile widened. 'Now you will stand there and listen quietly. My next surprise is that I have soldiers waiting outside this room who are ready to do my bidding and to remove you to prison, unless, of course, I shoot you first.'

Cole was calculating the distance between himself and the Nazi. It was about six feet. 'No, that does not surprise me — cowards always bring a cohort.'

Von Bremen could barely contain his fury at that and he pushed the pistol out towards Cole as he declared, 'And the one piece of information you will dislike most of all, the shock which I have come here especially to give you, is that the woman you have been consorting with for the past months, the woman you appear to be exceedingly fond of, shared *my* bed last night.'

Cole's eyes blinked and he felt a sting of emotion but he showed nothing as he steadily replied, 'You're mad, that's absurd.'

A strange-sounding, high-pitched peal of laughter broke from the German. 'Ah, but I'm not mad and it's true – absolutely. You poor fool.' He laughed again and wagged the revolver at Cole's head. 'You see, whoever you are, Laetitia de Witt . . . is my wife.'

Cole did not move a muscle but he could not hold the murmur of disbelief which broke from his lips.

Von Bremen savoured these moments. He tilted his head to the side and gave a small, knowing grunt. '*Ja*, indeed, Laetitia and I have been married for many years. We married in Germany, and afterward we lived in a charming Alpine village; happily, I might add. Ah, those days and nights with her . . .' he smiled again, 'especially the nights, eh? We revelled in each other, you might say, in our house in Mittenwald where the violins played beneath our bedroom windows.'

Mittenwald! As if his blood had turned to ice, the listener stood frozen, but a tell-tale clenching and unclenching of his jaw gave Von Bremen immense satisfaction. Cole was remembering a conversation with Letta months ago. It all came flooding back into his mind in seconds.

She had been painting a picture in her parlour and chatting to him and her tinkling-bell laughter had charmed him. '*I once lived for a time in the village of Mittenwald in Germany . . .' she hesitated . . . looked away, and making a sudden annoyed sound, dipped her brush in the open tin of turpentine on the covered table. 'Oh, I don't have much of this left either. Everything is so difficult in wartime.'*

'You were saying?'

'What was I saying?'

'About living in Germany.'

'Oh, nothing, really . . . my mother was there . . . taking singing lessons, can you believe it? She was enamoured of a . . . er . . . music teacher — had met him in Switzerland, I think.'

Yes, this degenerate was telling the truth! She had slipped up by mentioning Mittenwald and quickly lied about the music lessons. No wonder she had been so interested to learn about this bastard when he had arrived in Apeldoorn . . . It was all patently clear. Jesus, dear Jesus, Laetitia was married to him!

Von Bremen sighed as, once more, he wagged the pistol at Cole's head. '*My wife* has been instrumental in helping me to catch your little band of secret agents who came all the way from England to fall into my trap.' Now he sniffed in satisfaction as his tone became cool, matter-of-fact. 'I have reclaimed my wife and she has not resisted. In fact, she has come very willingly to my bed. You see, she is prepared to let you die to save herself. Ah . . . that's a woman for you.' He paused and angled his head to the side again, still smiling. 'Have you anything to say?'

Von Bremen moved a little closer to the window and at that exact moment the black body of a crow cast a passing shadow across the speaker as it flapped on to the outside sill near the man, striking the glass with its wings. He started, and for a fraction of a second looked towards the bird. In that instant Cole moved faster than Von Bremen believed possible. He leapt forward, and, using the unarmed combat training he had received from Andy McClure on the cold western coast of Scotland overlooked by rocky Creag Mhor, he kicked the pistol from Von Bremen's hand. As it fell to the rug, Cole brought all his force to bear and, closing with the man, smashed the hard rocklike base of his right palm up into his

457

enemy's nose, pushing splintered bone into his brain and snapping his neck violently backwards, killing him instantly.

The last thing that registered in Von Bremen's brain as he groaned in death and before he slipped into eternal darkness, was his fervent life-long detestation of crows . . . *How I hate those birds* . . .

Cole caught the man as he crumpled and brought him silently to the carpet while his mind raced and his eyes flicked to the door – no key – someone could enter any time. *Move, Cole, move!*

Picking up his cane and hastening over the rug to the open window Cole stepped through it on to the ground-floor balcony. He was soon over the balustrade and in the lane and hurrying towards his car.

His driver stood waiting by the vehicle and jumped to attention as Cole emerged from the side lane and limped to the car. The two motorcycle soldiers who had accompanied the staff car also sprang to attention as Cole raised one palm to them. 'You two wait here. I'm coming back. I just need the car for a short time.'

One of them protested mildly. 'But we are not supposed to leave you, *Standartenführer* Bayer.'

Cole laughed. 'I said I'll be back soon. Wait here.' He turned away and climbed into the back of the Horch as the two soldiers shrugged their shoulders and accepted the situation.

Once the vehicle pulled away Cole leant forward. 'To Apeldoorn. And hurry, I must get there quickly.'

'But, *standartenführer* . . .'

'Are you arguing with me?'

'*Nein, nein,* of course not.'

'Then hurry as requested.'

'*Jawohl, standartenführer.*'

458

Chapter Seventy-five

In the villa near the *Bergkerk* SS Captain Kaufmann waited outside the room which contained the two SS colonels. Beside him stood the four troops who had come from Apeldoorn with him. A few minutes had passed since Von Bremen had entered and closed the door. Kaufmann heard *Standartenführer* Von Bremen's laugh more than once and occasionally the sound of a raised voice reached him. The *standartenführer* had told him not to enter until he knocked on the inside of the door. 'For that will be the signal that I have arrested him and you can enter.'

After a time no sounds reached him but Kaufmann thought perhaps they had dropped their voices and, in any case, he was loath to disturb his superior, for Von Bremen was not a man who liked his orders countermanded. He waited and more time passed. A crease of concern began to form between Kaufmann's eyes when only silence continued from the other side of the ornately carved, gold-inlaid door.

His misgivings increased and when he guessed it was perhaps nine or ten minutes since Von Bremen had gone in, he began to feel decidedly uneasy.

Finally his concern made him bold and he knocked tentatively on the door.

No reply.

'*Standartenführer* Von Bremen!'

No reply.

He rapped loudly and when he was greeted by continuing silence he turned the handle and gently opened the door.

All appeared still.

He entered and glanced around the empty room in bewilderment. Suddenly he noticed the body half hidden by a bureau and with a shrill cry to the soldiers outside he ran to it.

Men stormed through the doorway as Kaufmann stood aghast. 'Oh no, *Standartenführer* Von Bremen is . . .' the angle of the head and neck told him how to complete his sentence – 'dead.'

When Cole judged that the staff car was halfway between Deventer and Apeldoorn he ordered the corporal driving to pull it over to the side of the road. The man did so near a field high with yellow grass where two windmills sat with their sails spinning in the rising wind.

'Adler, we need to get out.'

'Out? Here?'

'*Ja.*'

Once the corporal was outside the vehicle Cole slid past him into the driver's seat and drove away, while Adler stood with his back to the long grass watching in stupefaction.

Cole calculated his next move: he must find Letta.

She was married to Von Bremen! Of all the bizarre tricks of chance the universe could play upon him that was the worst. That the woman he had decided to marry was already married to that Nazi degenerate. It made him feel physically sick. He had loved her, wanted her, had told her he would take her to England with him.

When was she going to tell me? When? Never?

He felt numb. Von Bremen's words kept repeating in his head. '. . . *Laetitia and I have been married for many years*' . . . *many years* . . . *many years*. He had to get away from Holland now as fast as possible; had to escape from this lunacy he had been living. As Von Bremen had said, the game was up indeed.

He felt certain he would find Letta in her house by the stream. Von Bremen would never have taken her to his rooms in the wing of Het Loo Palace. Cole could not be sure of the verity of all that the Nazi had said, but the one thing he knew to be true was the one thing he wished were not.

Could he ever come to accept that his woman, his Letta, his love, had been married to Von Bremen? He could not answer that now; he was still in consternation, still in shock.

Yet he knew the first thing to do was to find her and to make a bid to escape with her. The rest he would think about in time. He would not analyse it now. If he tried to, it would send him mad.

He had promised to take Letta to England and he intended to try, albeit that everything between them was different now and the added complication was that they were on the run.

There was only one checkpoint on the road he was taking to Apeldoorn and after he had passed it he could go by back roads to the house by the stream. At the roadblock the soldiers would probably recognise him for they would be troops from Apeldoorn, and they knew he often drove a vehicle alone even though it remained customary to have an armed escort. He had a reputation for breaking the rule and driving around by himself. Only after he and Letta travelled out of the environs of Apeldoorn would it become tricky to explain a lack of military protection.

461

With a little luck, whoever found Von Bremen might not realise Cole would make for Apeldoorn first; it depended how much Von Bremen had confided in those accompanying him. Eventually, whoever chased Cole would know about Letta and where she lived, but it might not happen quickly.

Fortunately, he had his briefcase and suitcase of belongings with him for the failed mission into Germany, so he would simply present himself as an SS officer on leave to begin with, which had always been part of his escape plan.

He and Letta would have to abandon the car somewhere but he was feeling sure that they could travel for some hours before messages would have gone out to all checkpoints. It would be somewhat complicated for whoever found Von Bremen to get in touch with officers of a rank high enough to give orders to stop and arrest Cole, a *standartenführer* in the SS. Cole suspected that Von Bremen, wanting the glory, would not have brought many into his confidence about his masquerade.

Of course, once the general order to arrest them went out, the danger would multiply. But he believed he had some hours before such a circumstance prevailed.

Cole decided he would have no discussion whatever with Letta now. All that would come later. He would simply impress upon her the urgency of their escape and she could grab a few possessions and they would speedily get on their way.

They would make for the town of Hasselt in Belgium; about ninety miles away. The first contact on his escape route lived there: a retired school teacher called Daniel Poncheau whose name and address he had learnt by heart from Hans Buckhout all those months ago . . . months that seemed like years.

His gaze lifted to the sky where clouds were developing and he exhaled noisily as he calculated how much longer it would be before he reached Letta.

In the house with the blue door which sat by the stream, Letta held the pistol in her right hand and walked through to the parlour to stand in front of Cole's portrait and smile at him. She lifted her hand to his face and stroked the tips of her fingers across his mouth.

Tears ran from her eyes but her voice was calm . . . too calm. 'Nothing matters now, Cole Wareing. You see, my darling, I am married to him, that ugly vile *shadow of dread*. I have lived a life which I deeply regret – I have done many things I ought not to have done. Good men like Dirk have been trapped by evil men and you are doomed . . . all because of me.

'You made me so very happy for a little while, here in the midst of all this hate and horror and madness, and yet, perhaps all the time . . . from the very first . . . I knew I could not have you. I am so sorry.

'You will die and so that means I must die too, for I will not let *the shadow of dread* make me sign the paper.'

Slowly, with her eyes upon the portrait, she aimed the pistol at her right temple. And giving a small, infinitely sad murmur . . . pulled the trigger.

Laetitia de Witt fell to the carpet, blood spurting from her head.

Chapter Seventy-six

Cole knelt beside Letta. She was lying on the floor in front of his portrait, her head was in a pool of blood which had run from the hole, dark with congealed blood, in her right temple. She wore the blue dress which had always been his favourite and its white collar was soaked crimson. In her right hand she held an old revolver. For some seconds he was immobile with disbelief.

He felt her pulse.

Nothing.

Her face blurred before his eyes and an extended moan escaped from his lips. 'Why, Letta, why?'

Slowly and tenderly he removed the pistol from her limp hand and, lifting her in his arms, he carried her to the sofa. He did not believe she had been dead very long for she was not cold. Ah, but he was: chilled to the core, as he placed her gently down and folded her arms across her body and stood looking at her while the seconds passed. *If only I had been here perhaps ten minutes earlier this would not have happened. Why did you feel the need to kill yourself? Were you truly false? Did you give me away to Von Bremen?*

He answered his own question aloud. 'No, I don't believe that.

The bastard was always suspicious of me . . . it was not you. I knew the you who was fine and good.'

He stood looking down at her, unaware of time passing, his eyes clouded with tears. Finally he wiped his hand across his eyelids and he lifted his gaze – glancing past his replica on the easel, out the window, through the avenue of sturdy oaks . . . and suddenly he flinched.

Down at the open front gate motorcycles were rolling into the yard followed by a black car.

Soldiers!

His mind raced. He had parked his car at the rear of the house to be hidden from the road. He was aware there was a back way out: a track led through a thicket of trees to a fence near the brook and a rusty gate opened out on to a dirt road. These men would probably be coming to Letta simply to ascertain from her whether she had seen him or not.

He had very little time before they arrived at the door. He took a precious moment to touch Letta tenderly on the lips before he spun round and charged through the house, unclipping his holster and pulling the pistol out as he reached the back door where he leapt down the steps to the staff car. It was facing in the wrong direction to take the track and by the time he had started the engine and begun to turn the vehicle, two soldiers and an SS officer appeared around the side of the house.

Cole swung the wheel and the car screwed around as he pushed his foot down on the accelerator and the SS officer began screaming and pointing at him and the soldiers raised their rifles to fire. As bullets struck the side of the windscreen Cole drove straight at them, firing his pistol out the window. One soldier toppled sideways, blood spurting from his neck to spatter his superior as the

465

officer jumped out of the way and the Horch rammed the second soldier just as he pulled the trigger. The man's legs broke instantly and he collapsed across the bonnet and slid into the wall of the house, his bullets going wide and missing the escaping car as Cole sped by on to the track. As he accelerated even more, careering and swinging over the holes and bumps and disappearing through the trees, a bullet whizzed by his head and a second one hit the back window. Reaching the gate he drove straight through it, the Horch lifting the barrier from its hinges and knocking it towards the stream.

Glancing in the rear-view mirror he saw no one but he knew it would only be moments before his pursuers followed.

Indeed, the principal hunter who was now issuing commands behind Cole was the blood-spattered *Hauptsturmführer* Kaufmann who had been in Von Bremen's confidence since early that morning when they had searched Cole's office. 'Mount up!' he shouted to the military escort as he ran through the grass near the shed where the pebbled path led to the gate in the broken fence. The morning sun revealed the high shine on his black boots, his face under his death's head cap flushed with fury and his hands flailing the air. 'You, *scharführer*,' he pointed to the house, 'see if Frau Von Bremen is in there. If she is – stay with her.'

Von Bremen had told Kaufmann of his certainty that Bayer was an imposter and of Bayer's link with the British saboteurs whom he had arrested. He had said that *his wife* had feigned love for Bayer for the good of the Reich and that she was going to sign a deposition revealing all.

When Kaufmann found the dead *standartenführer* in the villa in Deventer he had immediately, and correctly, concluded that Bayer would head to Laetitia.

Kaufmann continued yelling as he threw himself into the back seat of the black Mercedes-Benz behind the driver and an SS soldier. 'Let's go! Let's go!' and the depleted military convoy accelerated forward through the trees and, traversing the trail, proceeded out past the twisted iron gate.

Cole was holding the wheel with such force that his knuckles gleamed white. *Letta is dead . . . Letta is dead.* The words filled his head as if to consume all other thought. He had been going to make a run for it with her; try to get them to Belgium and then, with luck, into France and finally to Spain.

But now he was in flight alone and Letta was lying in her own blood on the sofa in her parlour. He would never see her again. She was gone from this planet into endless time: her tinkling-bell laugh, the grace of her movements and the smile that stretched to the tiny beauty spot at the corner of her mouth; the dusky eyes . . . gone, all gone. And searing into his mind returned the words: *'Laetitia and I have been married for many years . . .'*

What else had that degenerate said? *'My wife has been instrumental in helping me to catch your band of secret agents . . . she has come willingly to my bed . . . she is prepared to let you die to save herself.'*

No! He must forget all that now. That would only bewilder him. He must think clearly: make the right decisions – and quickly.

He glanced into the rear-view mirror and there in the distance were two motorbikes and the black car. He was heading south and knew this area of the Veluwe well; he and Letta had driven over it many times. It was mostly forest with a lone farm or two. He came to a turn and took it as sharply as he could, recalling the route he needed to take. He was now on a back road that wound in the shape of a U round a farm about a quarter of a mile ahead.

When he reached the farm he accelerated past it to the bottom of the U and skidding slightly, swung the Horch into the curve to speed along the other side. The convoy chasing had now gained the first side of the U and the distance between him and his hunters across the field was not much more than a hundred yards. Cole glimpsed a light machine-gun pointing out of the front window of the Mercedes-Benz and as he arrived opposite the vehicle the soldier holding it opened fire; bullets sprayed across the top of his bonnet and he was knocked sideways as he felt the impact in his left upper arm. Momentarily his hands lifted from the wheel and the car swerved but he rallied and straightened it.

'Bugger, that's all I need, a bullet in the arm.'

The pellet was lodged in his flesh and he could feel the blood escaping. Thank heaven he had a clean uniform in the suitcase he had been taking to Germany and if ever he could shake off his pursuers he would bind his wound.

He was now back in the wood beyond the farm and, being familiar with it, he knew that after about a mile the road made a sharp right turn and ran through a thicket of ancient beech trees where it forked.

Blood was seeping down inside his sleeve as he came to the fork in the road and giving a swift look into the rear-view mirror, there in the distance he saw his hunters. Like a witch's familiar, on came the black car . . . What if they caught up to him? He considered the L pill that he carried habitually in his inside pocket. He had thought to offer it to Letta in case they were caught, but now he was alone.

He feared being captured by his enemies; he always had, even with all his confidence, nerve and self-assurance. Even though he had never admitted it until now. He had begun this masquerade thriving on tricking the Nazis; it had been like a risky, dangerous, spell-binding game, but he no longer considered it that way: being here all these months had altered him. Arrest was a prospect every operative had to consider even though it lived shrouded in the recesses of the mind where a secret agent chose not to look; but perhaps it was time. He took a deep breath and as he dared to accelerate a little more on the loose dirt road, he growled, 'I'll cross that bloody bridge when I come to it.'

Blood stained the entire arm of his jacket as Cole gained the copse of beech trees and pushed the Horch to top speed along past their massive moss-laden trunks. As he swung the vehicle into the right fork of the narrow road to hurtle down a gradual, winding incline, he suddenly recalled that there was a track ahead, somewhat hidden and overgrown, but wide enough for the passage of a vehicle.

Half a mile later he reached it and swerved sharply into the entrance, automatically bending his head as the overhanging branches scraped the roof. Holding the veering car steady, Cole prayed that his pursuers would race past the entrance to this escape route, for he had now formulated the rest of his plan. This trail meandered on until it led to a ford over a stream and finally returned him to a sealed road which ran south to Arnhem and north to Apeldoorn.

Even if they found the track and came out on to the Apeldoorn Road behind him, he hoped they would make the mistake of turning south towards Arnhem – for the one place he believed the Germans would be certain he would not go was back to Apeldoorn.

He clenched the wheel and urged the car onwards.

Chapter Seventy-seven

On the Apeldoorn Road Cole had covered close to two miles and had passed only locals on bicycles and two military trucks heading south so he felt certain he was not being followed. Recollecting an area where he could leave the road, he drove in behind a cluster of ancient pines and juniper bushes to a rocky watercourse where a windmill sat in the distance. The wound was bleeding badly and opening his suitcase with his right hand, he took out clean clothes and his SS ceremonial dagger, removing it by its black handle from its ebony enamelled scabbard. For a moment he eyed the motto on the blade: *Meine Ehre heißt Treue – My honour is loyalty* – and murmured in disgust before he used it to slash a shirt into strips for bandages.

Taking off his badly stained jacket and shirt he bathed his wound in the running brook and attempted to stem the blood flow. Finally binding his wound, he tied the knot with his right hand and his teeth before he put on his clean shirt and jacket and hid his blood-stained clothing in the junipers and undergrowth. His arm had begun to ache but he was still able to use his fingers.

As he slid into the Horch he looked up to the sound of aircraft overhead but could see nothing, for the bright morning sun had given way to a deal of rolling cloud. He hoped they were a British squadron making a daylight raid.

He knew that as time passed the bullet in his arm would slow him down. This meant he had to move rapidly: to make moves which his hunters would not at first suspect. Taking his planned escape route to the south was out.

Abruptly, it came to him! There was a way he might just be able to escape immediately from Holland: but it had to be carried out audaciously and with supreme confidence.

Cole headed into Apeldoorn.

When he came to the checkpoint on the outskirts of the town he knew the soldiers on duty by sight. They were quite aware that *Standartenführer* Bayer often took vehicles out on his own, and they simply met him with a Hitler salute and waved him onward. Cole drove through the built-up area without stopping and out past the checkpoint on the far boundary with the same consequence.

He saw a Heinkel aircraft touching down as he approached Apeldoorn Teuge Luftwaffe Airfield and as he slowed down to a halt at the military barrier on the boundary, he tried to ignore the gnawing pain in his arm. Recognising one of the two Wehrmacht guards on duty he called him over.

The man gave a quick Hitler salute and Cole replied in kind. 'I am here well ahead of General Rauter and his aides. My staff are following. We are all to take off for Germany this morning.'

The soldier knew nothing about this. Neither the *politzeiführer* nor *Standartenführer* Bayer were on his register of those to expect for the day, but he decided not to question a colonel in the SS. He simply let him through and closed the barbed-wire gate on to the airfield behind him.

Cole took the Horch along the dirt road past the air-raid shelters up to the cluster of camouflaged sheds on the edge of the field near a wood of white-barked birches, the ground dotted with fading autumn leaves.

Beyond the furthest construction, which was the administration block, sat two Junkers Ju 88 bombers with ground crew working on them, and the Heinkel He 111 which had just landed rolled in towards a small group of pilots lounging in deck chairs in the near distance. An aircraft flew overhead and a 'stuka' – a Junkers Ju 87 dive bomber – was in the process of touching down. The closest aircraft was a Messerschmitt, a Bf 108B, a four-seater trainer and transport which was free of ground crew, and standing by it was an *unterfeldwebel* – a sergeant in the Luftwaffe – the lone man of any rank whom Cole could see close at hand. Cole brought the Horch to a rest near the single wooden hut where it was usual to wait before a flight.

The increasing clouds were being pushed by a light breeze as Cole exited the vehicle and held his briefcase under his good right arm and carried his compact black suitcase in his right hand. He gritted his teeth to carry his cane in his left as he limped into the hut. It was empty.

The need for haste was paramount and he returned outside and called the sergeant over. The man reacted in sprightly fashion and ran to him. As he neared, a look of recognition passed over his face. He had seen *Standartenführer* Bayer twice before. The last time had been with General Christiansen and they had flown into Germany. The man came to attention. 'We were not expecting you, *Standartenführer* Bayer.'

'Perhaps not. It is a special flight I am taking along with the *politzeiführer*. I am very early, the carrier is coming in from the Fatherland.'

'*Ja*, of course. Would you like to wait inside and I shall inform the *oberstleutnant* of your arrival?' The *oberstleutnant* was the commanding officer and equal to a wing commander.

Cole shook his head. '*Nein*, do not bother him yet as I am so early. While I'm waiting I would like to have a look at that four-seater Messerschmitt over there. I remember flying in one just before the war.'

The man smiled. 'Certainly.' *Standartenführer* Bayer had previously shown interest in aircraft and he was keen to accompany the senior officer. 'Do you wish to leave your cases here in the hut?'

'*Nein*, they contain important documents . . . I don't want them out of my sight. But here, you carry them.'

The man was pleased to do so and they walked over the airfield to the Messerschmitt where Cole wandered around the aeroplane. This aircraft had no armaments but it was no time to be choosy. Suddenly he gave a laugh. 'I think I should like to sit in this craft and perhaps even start it and feel it purr for old times' sake.'

'Of course, *Herr standartenführer*, just as you like.'

Cole stepped up on the portside wing and opened the cockpit canopy. In this model it was hinged on the side and swung forward so he pushed it out with his good right hand, before turning and asking the *unterfeldwebel* for his two cases. The man frowned, looking momentarily uncertain, but lifted them up to Cole, who bent down and took both, one by one, and dropped them inside on the rear seats. Suddenly he felt unsteady and he shot out his left hand to hold the side of the windscreen. Pain seared down his arm to his fingers as he became dizzy and light-headed. *Don't faint, Cole, for Christ's sake, and don't stagger. Come on, get in the cockpit, damn it, control yourself.*

He lifted his right leg and stepped in just as a shout sounded in the distance behind him and he turned to see a *leutnant* – a pilot officer — hurrying towards them. Cole ignored him and sat down, taking stock of the instrument panel and the throttle. *Jesus . . . just stay calm . . . you can fly any aircraft built.*

The pilot officer now broke into a run and as he drew near he waved his arms at them. 'What the hell's going on here, *unterfeldwebel?* Who is that in the cockpit of this aircraft?'

Cole was studying the instruments and gauges but before the sergeant could answer he turned his head to look down at the newcomer and the Luftwaffe junior officer stopped dead as he noted the imperious expression in the eyes aimed at him. He took in the death's head cap; the Iron Cross at the man's throat and the gleam of the silver bullion oak on his collar tab which showed just above the body of the machine.

The pilot officer immediately came to attention, clicking his heels and bowing from the shoulders as he apologised. 'Oh, *standartenführer . . . Ich bettle Ihre Verzeihung.*'

Cole gave a sharp nod and as a result felt odd again, but he spoke with unquestionable authority. 'I wish to enjoy the feel of the aircraft.'

The *leutnant* bowed from the neck again. *'Jawohl,* of course.'

Cole had already turned on the fuel supply and the battery switch while the sergeant offered an explanation to the new arrival. *'Standartenführer* Bayer flew this model of Messerschmitt before the war; he is an enthusiast.'

Cole was now using the fuel pump to pressurise the fuel lines as the junior officer gave a co-operative smile.

'Ah, I see, I understand.'

Cole looked once more to the *leutnant.* 'On take-off I understand the aircraft is tail heavy.'

'Ja, that is so, *Herr standartenführer,* but holding it level on the

474

main wheels and making sure there is plenty of flying speed before lifting gently is all that's needed.'

Cole knew Messerschmitts did not start without the canopy closed hence he smiled down at his two companions on the ground. 'I shall just start the engine now.'

Both men were bewildered but neither raised an objection and as Cole closed the canopy with his left hand and grunted while his entire arm throbbed, the two men on the ground watched in mystification as the *leutenant* declared, '*Guter Gott*, I think the *standartenführer* actually intends to fly it. Perhaps I'd better go up with him.' And taking the initiative he jumped up on the wing calling, '*Standartenführer* Bayer, you are not going to fly it surely?' But by now the master ignition switch was turned on and the starter switch engaged, and moments later the engine began.

The German was crouching on the wing and to his utter consternation he now saw a large dark stain on the upper arm of the officer's jacket. He began tapping the canopy. '*Standartenführer*, what are you doing? Stop!'

Cole braced himself and looked around at the shouting man and there, beyond his shoulder, he saw a stationary black Mercedes-Benz and two soldiers on motorbikes over at the administration block.

His trackers had arrived.

'Bugger!' *Come on, Cole, move!*

The aeroplane began rolling forward. He had flown a Spitfire more than once but in this craft the top of his head just cleared the inside of the canopy. He was feeling a bit dizzy again and the man outside was now hitting the canopy with force. 'Stop! I shall come with you,' he called, but Cole yelled, 'Get off the wing.'

The sergeant on the ground was now running after the

Messerschmitt and waving but Cole's eyes were on *Hauptsturmführer* Kaufmann and his men who now sprinted out of the administration block back to the ebony car and climbed into it. Cole saw it head at full speed towards him in a line which would take the Mercedes-Benz right across the aircraft's path.

Cole's whole being was now willing the aircraft along the field, his hand on the rudder, as the automobile raced inexorably towards him with an armed soldier leaning out of the front window aiming at him.

As the senior officer's intention became undeniably clear to the junior officer clinging to the aircraft gaining speed, he decided that if he wished to survive he had better retreat. To that end he leapt off the wing, hitting the ground hard but rolling over and rising to his knees to watch the continuing spectacle.

Inside the cockpit the revolutions per minute were rising and Cole's heart was pumping as the seconds passed until he let out a wheeze of relief, knowing he had gained enough power. 'Come on!' he shouted. 'Lift, baby, lift!' He pushed the stick full forward and to the right, and like the miracle he needed, the machine responded and rose into the air as a rattle of bullets emanated from the black car speeding by beneath.

'You little ripper!'

His left arm ached, the pain extending through his shoulder and into his neck, but he must concentrate and stay awake. He could not take the aircraft high without oxygen, so he must remain at low altitudes, but he was heading for safety at last: only two hundred miles to the coast of England.

He must not black out; he must not think of Letta; he must not think of anything but making it to dear old Blighty!

* * *

It was over an hour later and he was slipping into long moments of semi-consciousness when he saw the coast of England. The blessing of flying in and out of low cloud had saved the Messerschmitt from being sighted by a British aircraft as he crossed the sea. And now as he passed over the Norfolk coast, his vision was beginning to blur when he realised he was being shot at from a battery on the ground.

'I'm one of you, mate – miss me!'

Abruptly the engine started to cough and falter. He had been hit and the rudder was not responding. He sped across the beach and over a cluster of flint cottages, a road, more cottages and a wood. His altitude was dropping swiftly and he was only perhaps seventy feet above the ground when the last thing he saw before he blacked out was a woman in a field angrily waving a pitchfork at him.

Cole woke in a military hospital in Great Yarmouth with a military guard around him who were amazed when he began to speak to them in perfect English.

It was not until he convinced the captain in the local branch of the Home Guard* to phone the number Cole gave him, that it resulted in a visit by Hans Buckhout and Andy McClure – and the astonished Home Guard officer realised that Cole was not 'a Nazi bastard' after all.

* Home Guard: see Author's End Notes, page 531

THE PEACE

Chapter Seventy-eight

28 December 1947

After the rain-soaked night when Cole and Edward Shackleton had arrived at the door of Myrtle Shackleton's house, dawn revealed a drier morning with sunshine appearing through wispy cloud. Shack insisted that Cole rest his leg for the day and the patient succumbed to that command, during which time he sat thinking with his leg up on a footstool in his aunt's lounge. It was easy to be comfortable in his aunt's house surrounded by her cosy gentlewoman's trappings of chintz curtains and cushions, soft rugs and numerous Royal Doulton porcelain figurines.

After breakfast, Edward made a run back to the Castle Hotel and learnt that a man had come searching for him around midnight under the pretext of knowing him and wanting a room, but when he learnt that Dr Shackleton was not in residence, he had left, having signed the register as King George VI.

Cole nodded knowingly at that news. Over breakfast he had revealed in brief to his friend the circumstances which had brought him to Taunton. 'So the sooner I get to Laetitia de Witt the better.' He held his chin in his hands in thought. 'Once I heard that she was calling herself "Thalberg", I knew in truth that Laetitia was alive. As I told you, it's her uncle's surname, and one she would quite naturally assume: we need to get to him in Switzerland. It's three months since she was sighted in Alexandria with *an elderly man* and Glenro Thalberg would be well into his seventies. There's a chance she might even be in Switzerland with him now and if not, at least we should be able to find some sort of lead to her whereabouts. That's if her uncle still lives there and I'm guessing he probably does. How strange to be heading to *Villa Thalberg*. I remember the day she asked me to commit the address to memory.' He leant back and murmured softly, 'And I did.'

Shack regarded him sympathetically. 'I know you're still struggling to find it credible that she's alive, my boy.'

'You can say that again.'

Cole closed his eyelids and in the hiatus which followed Shack read *The Daily Telegraph* until the younger man opened his eyes and stared at the winter countryside beyond Myrtle's window while the minutes continued to pass. When, in due course, the older man folded the newspaper, Cole spoke. 'Shack, I feel sure Tudor and the others will go back to see Andy in Bath; might have already. And that means they, too, will learn about Letta. Tudor's been searching for me for years but he holds the grudge against her as well. So once they know about her, they could well give up on seeking me out and work on trying to find her because they'll reckon – and they'll be right – that I'll head straight to her.'

'Yes, my boy, I think that's all pretty logical.'

Cole's eyes narrowed in deliberation. 'I wonder where Tudor, Mako and Felix are right now?'

✻   ✻   ✻

482

At that precise moment the three friends were walking along the platform of Paddington Station in London.

Handing their tickets to the collector at the gate, Tudor spoke brightly. 'You know, I really should drop into my club over in the city. I haven't been in since before we went to Australia. We can all stay the night there.' He gave a tender smile. 'Might be a letter from my sister waiting as well.'

Mako grinned. 'Yeah, from the photographs you had, she's a good-looking girl, that sister of yours.'

'She's married,' Felix retorted as they reached a rank of taxis and Tudor spoke to the driver. 'To Bedford Row, the Kitchener Club.' As the taxi gathered speed he shook his head in recollection. 'You know, boys, Wareing was one of the guys who nominated me for membership of this club during the war. It's a bit of an irony, that.'

The rebuilding of London, which would take decades in all, had begun after the enormous devastation of the German bombing during the Blitz and as a result of the V-I and V-2 rockets which had been Hitler's last attempt at subduing the undying spirit of the people of London. So it was by an indirect route which avoided closed streets and blocked-off areas of reconstruction that the cab took its passengers to Bedford Row in Holborn in the City of London.

They were nearing their destination when Tudor suddenly smiled.

'You look like a cat that swallowed the cream, boss,' Felix commented with a grin.

'Do I? Well, it's because finally I've recalled where I heard the name Thalberg before. *She* said it to me.'

'You don't say?'

'I do. One night in Groningen when we were in hiding: it's the name of some villa a blasted relative of de Witt's owns. I think she said it was in Switzerland . . . Now, was it Lake Geneva?'

Mako's gaunt face creased with interest. 'Heck, does that mean we might go to Switzerland?'

Tudor nodded. 'Well, Holland first, I reckon, but yes, I think we might.'

They alighted in the street as dark clouds hovered in the escalating breeze outside the Kitchener Club: an all-military services' club. Passing by the newly planted trees in the wide thoroughfare, the three men climbed the short flight of stairs and entered the neat front hall. It was clad in brand-new mahogany wood panelling, for a V-I had, in the latter part of the war, demolished much of the front section of the structure.

As they crossed the Axminster entry rug, Milton, the club's resident tabby cat, leapt off the polished countertop as Baines, the hall porter, stood up from behind it. He granted Tudor a wide grin from under his handlebar moustache while he brought his hand up in a salute. 'Wing Commander Harrington, how wonderful to see you. Must be six or seven months since I laid eyes upon you, sir.'

'Yes, Baines, must be.'

Baines lifted his index finger high in the air as a thought came to him. 'Ah, yes, that reminds me, I've a small batch of letters waiting for you; had no idea where to send them on, sir, you left no forwarding address.' He hurried over to his desk and came back with a number of envelopes tied with string.

'Thanks, Baines. My friends and I will go through to the bar. We'll have lunch in there. Oh, and we'll need three rooms for the night.' They handed across the cases they carried and the porter nodded.

'Certainly, Wing Commander.'

In the bar, where a painting by Winston Churchill of the beach at Deal in Kent hung behind him, the barman greeted Tudor warmly. 'Wing Commander Harrington, haven't seen you for ages. Where have you been, sir?'

'All sorts of places, Carstairs. Now, we'll all have a whisky, right, boys?'

Mako and Felix acquiesced.

They seated themselves in capacious leather chairs while the bar began to fill up with various men in uniform and mufti and as they waited for their drinks, Tudor sifted through the letters. 'As I thought, one from my sister, Lorraine.' He continued flicking through them and hesitated, holding up a long grey envelope as a crease formed between his eyes. His mouth twisted in an odd way as he tore open the letter. Both his companions noticed this reaction and watched as he read the contents.

'Jesus H Christ,' he whispered as the colour drained from his face.

'What is it, boss?' asked Felix, leaning forward in his chair.

Tudor stared at the page. 'This can't be,' he spoke *sotto voce* and a tiny muscle beneath his eye twitched involuntarily.

Mako and Felix glanced at one another and Mako reached out to Tudor's arm. 'What can't be? What's happened? You've turned pale.'

At that moment a clap of thunder sounded, followed by a spattering of rain on the window at the end of the bar as a storm began and Tudor, in a measured way, slowly folded the pages and placed them back in the grey envelope as he lifted his troubled eyes to his friends.

'Storm or no storm, we need to abandon lunch and catch a train to Dover this afternoon and the night ferry to Calais. I know exactly where Laetitia de Witt is. This letter is from her and it changes everything.'

Felix whistled through his teeth and Mako grunted in astonishment asking, 'What? How is it possible to receive a letter from her, boss? She only knew you as Dirk Hartog, not by your real name.'

Tudor tapped the envelope. He answered in a preoccupied way, his voice low and subdued. 'I'm goddam dumbfounded and finding what I've just read hard to comprehend . . . but she says she found out my real identity accidentally through some Canadian Intelligence officers who were working with British Intelligence in Groningen . . . she spent the final part of the war there.'

'Gawd, it defies imagination,' commented Mako as Felix shook his head.

'Apparently there was a search out for you and me, Mako, throughout Holland after D-Day.' Tudor was blinking in consternation and still staring at the envelope. 'There's a lot more here, boys. This alters everything. We've got to get to her in Switzerland.'

'So she *is* in Switzerland! Is she at that villa?'

'Uh huh.' He took a long, deep breath as he slipped the letter into his inside pocket and stood. 'We'll be OK going back through France and our identity papers should get us across the Swiss border . . . come on, let's move, I'll tell you all about it as we go.'

Chapter Seventy-nine

After Cole's twenty-four hours of rest, Edward Shackleton insisted on accompanying him to Europe: 'You will need someone with you who has only your interests at heart, my boy. This will not be an easy pilgrimage for you to make alone. I must come along.'

On the various railway journeys which took them from Taunton to London to Paris, Cole was not talkative. When they were alone in a compartment, he sat with his injured leg up on the seat opposite. He continued struggling to find it credible that Laetitia was, in fact, alive. Having lived in the belief that she had been dead since 11 November 1943, to be told indisputably at the end of December 1947 that she was not dead, had been a bombshell.

They arrived in Paris on the evening of the thirtieth to find that the French communist railway workers were striking and a number of lines were closed, including the one between Paris and Lyon which was the route they needed to take. The station master walked up and down wringing his hands and people milled about in utter confusion. Only weeks prior the Paris–Tourcoing Express train had been derailed by communist strikers and over twenty people killed. European communism was on the rise and France had been crippled by communist strikes all year, so hold-ups were not unexpected; but it was frustrating for the two travellers who had to remain in Paris until New Year's Day 1948. Cole used the time to see Hans Buckhout in his residence at 16 Rue d'Anjou to find that Tudor had visited him only days earlier. The Dutchman enlightened Cole of Tudor's purported reason for the visit and was very helpful with a permit for Shack to cross the border into Switzerland.

It was by a devious route that the two men consequently travelled to Lyon and it took the second and third days of the new year to make the odyssey. They arrived late at night and were completely exasperated to learn that no trains to Switzerland were running the following day.

'The commos seem to have a stranglehold on this country,' Shack opined.

Cole agreed. 'Indeed. Two and a half years since the war and the economic devastation from it remains catastrophic for Europeans. These nations are still dispersed and suffering. It's only natural that bloody communism is on the rise. What with the Soviet Union's armies still in occupation in so many countries here, old Stalin is laughing in Moscow. He's the next monster the West has to deal with.' He halted suddenly in the insipid electric light of the railway station and put his hands in his pockets. 'However . . . our dilemma is how to get to Geneva tomorrow, and I've decided we abandon train travel and find a driver.'

They finally paid a ransom-like amount to a baker who bought petrol on the black market and carried them through a landscape of snow in his delivery van the sixty-odd miles to the village of Soral, just inside the Swiss border. Knowing a deal of Cole's story now, Shack was content to let the younger man live with his thoughts as the hours passed quietly. In the darkening chill of early evening they arrived in Soral where the baker went into a huddle with the young Swiss officer on duty and the result was that Cole handed over a British five-pound note and the officer gave a cursory glance to Cole's and Shack's papers before he waved the van on along the road to Geneva.

When at last they rolled by the waterfront of Lake Geneva, Cole's hand strayed to the knot in his tie as he pulled on it to loosen it slightly and turned his eyes to Edward who sat next to the driver. 'I'm not enamoured with Switzerland . . . this country was far too helpful to Germany for my liking. It only pretended to be bloody neutral! There's a lot of Nazi-stolen gold from poor murdered buggers sitting in Swiss banks right now. I know Rauter, for one, had a bank account here. And while other Europeans starve, the Swiss get fat. So as soon as I find out where Laetitia is, I want to get out of this rotten place fast.'

Shack nodded. 'Of course, my boy.'

They paid their deliverer and took rooms in the luxurious Beau Rivage Hotel overlooking the lake and Shack arranged with the concierge for a man to drive them out to Villa Thalberg in the area of Promenthoux the following morning. By their calculations the destination was some fourteen to sixteen miles along the lake.

When they were installed in their rooms, Cole walked to the windows and stood looking out at the dying day and the various hues of grey in his vision around the frozen lake.

'Shack, I want to tell you something.'

His friend bestowed upon him a sympathetic smile and came over to him. 'Go ahead, my boy.'

Cole did not begin to speak immediately and his gaze drifted out the window again so that the older man thought perhaps his boy had decided not to tell him anything after all. But, ultimately,

Cole drew in a loud breath and leant forward with his hands on the sill. 'Those last days in Holland were surreal.'

'Yes, my boy, I realise that.'

'When I crash-landed in the Messerschmitt in Norfolk and woke up in that military hospital, it all seemed to have been a bizarre sort of dream, as if I'd been hallucinating for months on end.' He paused and spoke with his eyes on the darkening sky. 'I remember I spent an awful lot of time thinking about Letta and Von Bremen. I kept seeing her dead body. And then I'd start wondering just when she was finally intending to come clean and tell me she was married to that swine.' He gave a short, hard laugh and raising his hand in a dismissive wave and making a negative sound, he fell again into silence.

Shack remained studying him and after a minute Cole moved and began toying with the tassel on the plaited red cord which tied the huge blue drapes back. He remained like that for ten seconds or so until he turned to face his friend and raised his hand to rub the scar at the side of his mouth, delivering a scornful, mocking laugh. 'To think that, outwardly, I still resemble Bayer – how grotesque is that?'

'You shouldn't reflect on such things, my boy, they aren't good for you.'

'Ah, but I do. It's almost worth seeking out those two who did the work on me: old Doctor Campbell and Durst, the orthodontist – get them to operate and turn me back to what I was.' He laughed again, a grating, unhappy, unnatural sound.

'Stop! My dear boy, please. Don't talk like this. I know you well and my sense is that the thought of seeing Laetitia de Witt and opening up all that was closed, is making you reminisce about matters you've suppressed; matters that should remain in the blasted past where they can do no damage. And one thing I'm positive about – it would be best for you to completely forget about Bayer. You're Cole Wareing, nobody else. And, personally, I think you look more handsome than ever. You turn heads, my boy.'

'Thank you for attempting to cheer me.' Cole granted him a weak smile. 'I remember Shell asked me once how it was my teeth were different to the way they were before the war. I told her the German guards threw hand grenades at us during our escape from the POW camp and along with my facial wounds, my front teeth were broken, so I had porcelain crowns put over them. She believed me.' He shook his head and momentarily closed his eyes. 'All the lies I told her . . . all the lies, lies, lies, bloody stinking lies. How many times I wanted to tell Shell the truth.' His voice hardened. 'Jesus Christ, how many times.'

His head dropped to his chest and his companion put his hand out and touched Cole's hair in a fatherly, loving gesture. 'Surely if you had told her, she would have understood?'

Cole's eyes flashed as he lifted his gaze. 'God, Shack, understood? How in hell could she have understood? Yes, I could have told her about being in SOE. That part would have been easy. People *were* secret agents and she would have realised that. But . . . having your face and body operated upon to make scars; altering your mouth and your teeth; impersonating an SS officer for five solid months; every day witnessing discussions on how to exterminate the Jewish race and standing impotently by while you saw innocent men, women and children tortured and shunted off to death camps. Having an intense affair with a woman whom, to this day, you are in conflict about . . . and then, into the bargain, telling your wife that she was living with a man who had the prospect of his one-time best friend turning up at any hour of the day or night to kill him because the friend believes that he was a traitor and betrayed him to the German secret police? No, Shack, I wasn't prepared to ask Shell to understand that.'

Shack said nothing, he simply nodded his head.

Two hours later they sat at dinner in the hotel dining room where Cole ate little and a frown of concern settled on his companion's brow.

'Cole, my boy?'

Cole raised his eyes.

'You're not eating.'

'I'm thinking, I suppose.' He lifted his right hand to rub his chin. 'I'm here to see Laetitia's uncle, Glenro Thalberg, right?'

'Yes, my boy, that's right.'

'In the belief that he will know the whereabouts of his niece. Correct?'

'Yes, correct.'

'And if he does?'

'I gather we go and see her to squeeze the truth out of her.'

Cole grunted. 'To squeeze the truth out of her, huh? But what if there is no truth? What if she knows nothing? What if she knows no reason why Tudor would want to kill me? Then I've seen her and . . .' He fell into a deep absorption, staring in the substantial gilt mirror which was fixed to the wall behind his companion.

Edward Shackleton leant forward across the white tablecloth and placed his palm over the hand of his companion. 'My boy, from all you've told me, you have no other lead to go on. Laetitia de Witt is the only avenue you have. She will know something – or nothing. Either way you must find out.' Shack now patted Cole's hand. 'And if you're having second thoughts about finding this woman, I'll understand. I appreciate that the idea of seeing her again is all very strange and challenging for you, but you've come all this way . . .' He paused and the younger man did not reply, so he added, 'And if that's the case, and you decide not to go out to Villa Thalberg, you'll have to stay on the run from Tudor.'

Cole made no reply to that either. He simply studied his friend with a pensive expression and picked up his knife and fork.

Shack spoke cheerfully. 'That's it, my dear boy, eat something and have a glass of wine. We'll sleep on it all.'

Chapter Eighty

On that very same night Shelly and her newly found French friend Yvonne Gavare, sat on the railway platform in the Torino station in Italy for four hours in the middle of the night hugging each other to stop the bitter cold seeping through their overcoats. They were heading towards Switzerland after a week's travel from Toulon.

The seas in the Mediterranean had been so rough that they had been forced to hole up in the little fishing port of Villefranche-sur-mer for four days before they could venture out again.

So, ultimately, Pierre Gavare and his partner had delivered Shelly and Yvonne to Cap d'Ail where Pierre's cousin Antoinne lived in a cottage on the cliff two miles west of the principality of Monaco. The following morning Antoinne delivered the women to 63 Avenue de la Costa in Monte Carlo: the address stamped on the reverse side of the picture postcards Shelly carried.

Under a lowering canopy of cloud and a brisk wind, Shelly stood facing a boarded-up shop and appeared about to burst into tears, but she held herself together. 'All this way and there is no such place as Printemps and Co photographers.'

Momentarily she leant defeatedly on the wood nailed across the window. 'What do we do now?'

'Ask next door.'

Shelly rallied, stood up and set her shoulders. 'Of course. Let's go.'

Not only did they ask next door but at every house and building in the long avenue: people remembered the photographer but they had no idea where he had gone. At last, in a small, dark café past a vacant lot, a waiter gave them hope.

'Monsieur Bonnet might know something. He delivered the post before the war.'

They found the ex-postman in one of the houses behind St Nicholas Cathedral and he clearly remembered the gent who had run the photography business. 'Yes, old Deville lives with his daughter now out in Eze.'

The corners of Yvonne's mouth creased with optimism. 'That's close to where we're staying; we can go there easily.'

A few hours later, Monsieur Charles Deville the retired photographer, greeted them swathed in greatcoat and blanket and smoking a pipe in front of a fire in a stone cottage in the walled village of Eze which rested atop a rocky peak high above the Mediterranean Sea.

A Briard Sheepdog, which had barked at the visitors' arrival, lay at the photographer's feet as he examined the postcards. 'Mmm, ah, indeed, these are my pictures.' His pale brown eyes lifted to the women in front of him. 'Why do you want to know about them?'

Yvonne explained that they were searching for the woman in the picture for she might hold a clue to the whereabouts of her friend's husband.

He looked Shelly up and down. 'So you have lost your husband?'

'*Oui*, in a way, I suppose I have.'

He tapped the picture of Laetitia. 'To this woman?'

Shelly answered slowly in French. 'Ah, monsieur, that's what I'd like to know. I would prefer not to go into detail, if you would excuse me.'

'Mmm.' He drew his mouth down. 'I don't need any detail, that's your business. Because of the war there are millions of people who don't know where their loved ones are; you are not unique.'

Shelly nodded her head in sombre agreement.

'You see,' Yvonne spoke up trying to hurry things along, 'we hope you can recall where the pictures were taken.'

His mouth drew down in affront. 'Of course I can recall where I took them. What do you think I am? A tyro?'

'Oh dear no, not at all, forgive me.'

This appeased him and he revealed the location: 'Switzerland, 1938. I remember these photographs were a commission. I took many likenesses of the beautiful girl you seek.' He tapped Laetitia's picture. 'This one was in the colonnade. I think she was the niece of the owner of the villa. Her mother was there. I—'

'Yes, monsieur, we understand,' Yvonne broke in, 'please excuse me, but what lake was it and do you still have the owner's name and address?'

'What lake was it? The well-known one, Geneva, of course. Come along, I have my records in my room.'

They accompanied him to his bedroom where he discovered the rest of the details in his meticulously kept files. Holding up a blue card with satisfaction he read: 'Monsieur Glenro Thalberg, Villa Thalberg, Promenthoux, via Prangins.'

With hopeful steps the two women left him standing with his daughter at the door and he drew small smiles from them as he winked at them both before they hurried away into the bleak afternoon.

Chapter Eighty-one

5 January 1948

Cole was again quiet at breakfast but he did eat two eggs and some toast so Shack was pleased about that.

He had cleaned the stitches in Cole's calf with antiseptic and wrapped a bandage around the leg for support and Cole walked out to the Citroën saloon car without limping. Dawn was lightening the sky and the snow from the overnight fall piled a few inches on the windowsills as they climbed into the back seat outside the Beau Rivage Hotel. Shack smiled encouragingly to 'his boy' and commented, 'The sky looks clear; perhaps it will be a decent morning, if a little cold.'

The vehicle had been custom altered and there was a sliding panel between them and the driver so they could converse privately. From time to time as they travelled, Shack commented on the scenery and Cole responded in succinct fashion until they drew close to their destination and over the treetops the shape of the Château de Prangins came into view, standing on its elevated position above the lake. 'It was built two hundred years ago and I believe it's set in formal English gardens,' Shack commented, but the younger man did not acknowledge the statement, instead he brought his serious gaze round to his friend.

'Shack?'

'Yes, my boy?'

'I've been thinking a great deal about everything.'

'Well, of course you have.'

Cole's brooding eyes caught the early morning light as he exhaled noisily. 'If talking to Thalberg does, in fact, lead us to Letta . . .' He wiped his hand across his brow. 'Seeing her again will be . . .' He hesitated, fell silent and shook his head.

Shack waited quietly until Cole spoke again. 'Bloody hell, she's been dead to me since the eleventh of November 1943. She was lifeless. Lying in her own blood, still holding the weapon in her hand, a hole in her temple.' Fleetingly he shut his eyes and turned his face to the window. 'How in God's name can she be alive? Unless there was a bloody miracle.'

The older man turned in the leather seat and the planes of his face settled into a meditative expression. 'Cole, I haven't said this to you before but I've experienced this once in my life. It was on the front in the Somme Valley in 1917. The Germans had come at us pretty heavily that morning. Your dad's battalion lost a lot of men. In the regimental aid post, I tended a fellow in the Lancashire Fusiliers who was shot through the temple and the bullet completely missed his brain and went out cleanly through the top of his head. We sent him out of the line and later we found out that he lived. Had bad scars, but he lived. Being a medical doctor, I know it *is* possible – highly unlikely and almost incredible, but possible.'

'But I felt her pulse. There was none.'

'Well, you see, that's possible too. In those circumstances, the body in shock like that . . . her pulse would have dropped to where it was not distinguishable by feeling her wrist or her neck. To all outward signs she would appear dead. I believe this is what must have happened to Laetitia de Witt.'

Cole dwelt on this counsel while the car climbed a long hill and as it reached the crest, he murmured, 'I see.' His hand slipped inside his overcoat and into his jacket pocket and he withdrew the photograph of Laetitia that Andy had given him. He looked at it pensively, emitting an affirmative sound. 'Yes, her hair is different. It covers her right temple. There could be a hidden scar.'

He returned the picture to his pocket. 'Anyway, the fact is that Laetitia is alive and so what you describe *must* have taken place.' He grunted and looked down.

Shack reached out and covered Cole's left hand with his own and the younger man gave a wan smile. 'I was a pretty confused bloke back in those days after Holland, but time passes as it always does, eh? I found some peace, solace, normalcy for a while, until now, my dear friend, when here I am running, trying to stay ahead of Tudor; trying to find out what it is he holds against me . . .' He paused as he caught sight of the white structure which was appearing in the distance through the naked trees.

The sun that had attempted to cheer the January morning an hour previously, had disappeared and with the grey lake behind it and the leafless trees around it, the pale building standing on the promontory in acres of snow radiated a majestic bleakness.

Shack edged forward on his seat for a better view as the car rounded a bend and slowed down.

The expression in Cole's eyes was indecipherable. *So fate has inevitably brought me to Villa Thalberg.*

Chapter Eighty-two

In bone-chilling cold, Shelly and Yvonne stepped out on to Cornavin Station early on the morning of 5 January carrying one suitcase between them. The day before they had spent gaining a permit to enter Switzerland via a friend of Antoinne's who worked for Prince Louis at the palace of Monaco, and in travelling by train via western Italy where they spent the hours around midnight waiting in Torino.

On the railway journey they had passed many a transit camp for Eastern Europeans.

Europe was to remain a maelstrom of displaced persons for a decade and Shelly had long since appreciated how fortunate Australia and the United States had been to avoid the horror of being invaded or badly bombed.

Every day she had been in Europe she had seen something to evoke sympathy for the plight of those forced from their homes in Europe and as the train had passed a camp for Hungarians and Ukranians, a small barefooted waif waved to the carriage. Tears of pathos had risen to her eyes as a great sadness for the child welled in her heart because all she could do was return the wave.

As they exited Cornavin Station in Geneva tired but keyed up with the prospect of what might be to come, Shelly confided to her friend: 'Yvonne, I'm not a fool, so I realise that there's an awful lot I don't know about what my husband did during the war. I've thought about it all now for weeks on end. We know he must have been a spy or in a secret service of some kind because of the strange items I discovered in his service trunk but the Nazi medals and paraphernalia still have me at a loss . . . Why he held things back from me, I have no idea, but one thing I've always known is that Cole is not naturally deceitful. It's obvious from the inscription on the postcard that he and Laetitia de Witt were close, probably lovers. But Yvonne, he wasn't honour bound to tell me about her, because he'd written to me during the war telling me not to wait for him; so he wasn't unfaithful to me.'

She shivered and slipped her arm through her friend's as they headed to the Station Hotel. 'I don't think I'm being blind. Sometimes I think perhaps he felt I could never understand what he had to tell me, so he simply kept it all to himself. He was badly wrong, if that's what he thought, for I'm stronger than that; but whatever it was, I feel in my heart, that he made the decision to keep it from me out of care for my feelings, not simply to hide a wartime romance.' She trembled again adding, 'Yet she is so beautiful. I know I can't hold a candle to her . . .'

'What?' Yvonne broke in and stopped walking so that Shelly halted at her side. 'That's not true. Yes, she's beautiful, but so are you.'

'Please, Yvonne, I know how I look.'

'Then stop being silly. Your figure is better than almost any woman's I've ever seen and you are radiant. Your skin, your eyes, there's a quality about you . . .'

'Stop trying to bolster me up. I know exactly what you're doing, in case I have to face her.'

The French woman groaned in frustration and urged Shelly forward as she kept talking, 'Yvonne, this whole journey is to learn something to help us find Cole. Laetitia de Witt knew him during the war. Tudor Harrington knew him during the war. It's simply my intuition which has always led me in her direction . . . just intuition.' She yawned.

Yvonne pulled Shelly in through the door of the hotel. '*Oui, ma chérie*, that's why we're here shivering . . . your intuition.'

As they registered, Yvonne asked about buses. 'Do any go out to Prangins?'

'*Oui*, of course,' the hotel clerk answered. 'Twice a week at ten in the morning: Monday and Thursday.'

Yvonne's mouth dropped open. 'Oh my goodness, today's Monday.'

Chapter Eighty-three

As the Citroën approached closer to Villa Thalberg the occupants noticed recent vehicle tracks running from a side road and leading along towards the property. They slowed and travelled along the stone wall surrounding the estate.

The tyre tracks led to the tall iron gates which stood open and afforded a view of four cars standing parked to the side of a flight of imposing balustraded steps.

Cole studied the scene, and made a strange melancholy sound in his throat.

Shack frowned with concern and opened his mouth to speak when the glass panel between the front and back seat slid open. 'Shall I drive in through the gateway, sir?'

Cole answered, 'Yes, drive in.' And he made ready to exit from the vehicle.

As the car halted Cole exited into the wind whipping up from the lake. He pulled his overcoat about him as the tails flapped around his legs and he made his way across the gravel and began to mount the marble steps.

Edward Shackleton jumped out of the vehicle and hurried up behind him.

As Cole reached the huge front doors he rapped the polished brass knocker. Eight seconds later the door opened and a man in his seventies of medium height with heavy brows and dark eyes behind spectacles said in English with a strong French accent, 'Please come in, Monsieur Wareing, we have been expecting you.'

An expression of suspicion crossed Cole's face as he hesitated with Edward Shackleton at his elbow. 'Expecting me? Why?' He glanced past the man to the interior of the house, swiftly taking in the wide hallway and sweeping staircase, large ornate mirrors and sofas of various descriptions resting on Persian rugs.

At that second a door opened to the side of the foot of the staircase and a small boy of about three ran out towards them followed hurriedly by a wiry, diminutive middle-aged woman in a black dress calling, 'Drake, *mon petit choux.*'

The man who had opened the front door turned and the child came running straight across the hall to him while the woman in black rushed forward, talking very fast in French and picking up the little one.

The man faced back to his visitors. 'I am Glenro Thalberg, please come in.' But Cole remained exactly where he was, fixed in place on the doorstep, staring in fascination at the small boy in the arms of the woman in black.

The child had brilliant sky-blue eyes and fair hair and there was not a vestige of doubt in Cole's mind who the father was. It was patently evident that this child belonged to Tudor Harrington!

Chapter Eighty-four

A strange silence fell in the lofty hall. Shack, Glenro Thalberg, the woman holding the child and Cole stood in static tableau with the wind coursing in through the open front door as Cole gazed in wonder at the little boy. It was Glenro who spoke first. 'Monsieur Wareing, I see you are interested in little Drake.'

Cole gave a supercilious grunt. 'Yes, you might say so, he has a startling resemblance to a bloke I know.'

The older man nodded. '*Oui*, of course he does, for he is indeed the child of your old friend Tudor Harrington.'

Shack murmured in amazement behind Cole as he replied in an icy, phlegmatic tone. 'He hasn't been a friend of mine for some time.'

Glenro acknowledged that statement: 'I know', and reached out and took hold of Cole's arm to draw him into the hall. 'This is a sad house you have come into, monsieur.'

The woman in black began to weep as Glenro moved to the door and closed it while he continued speaking. 'I know exactly who you are. My niece revealed much of her wartime experiences to me. It would seem that fate has brought you here in time to say goodbye to her. You have arrived on the day of Laetitia's funeral. In an hour or so we leave to bury her.'

'What?' Cole almost whispered the word. He did not move even though he felt he had been struck by a bullet.

'*Oui* . . . My niece died six days ago on the eve of this new year. She was ill for many months.'

Letta died six days ago? This is all madness. She was dead and she was alive again . . . and now she's dead?

Glenro's aging eyes blinked with emotion. 'Medical science could do nothing for her. We saw dozens of doctors; even travelled to Egypt to a clinic where they gave her some hope for a short time, but it was no use. Her heart was not strong.' He walked over and kissed the child in the sobbing woman's arms. 'This is her little boy.'

'Her little boy . . .' Cole echoed it, controlling himself so that there was no outward sign of his true feelings.

He was still staring at the child as the door in the far wall opened and Tudor walked out and advanced across the black-and-white marble flooring holding up his good hand in the action of surrender. 'Cole, I'm completely aware it was a God awful mistake I made about you and about Let . . . Laetitia. If it's possible, please forgive me . . . forgive us.'

Cole took a step backwards as his own right hand slipped automatically into his greatcoat pocket to feel for his gun. He said nothing as Tudor added, 'We figured that you would turn up here sooner or later and have been watching out for you.'

Cole remained where he was as Felix and Mako, looking contrite, appeared behind Tudor who came right up to within two yards of his former friend and halted. 'Suffice it to be said now that I mistook a Nazi called Von Bremen for you . . .' He nodded. 'Yes, I'm now aware of who he was . . . It all happened when I was in the Gestapo prison. Mako and I understand just how goddam wrong we were.'

'We sure do,' Mako agreed.

Cole's finger was on the trigger of the Walther as he analysed what he had just been told. *Von Bremen? In the Gestapo prison Tudor thought Von Bremen was me?*

Cole's face continued to remain impassive while inside he fought to stay calm. *So Tudor and Letta slept together after all! Another secret. Oh hell, none of it matters. Letta is really dead!*

Tudor shrugged his shoulders and began to speak again: 'Cole, there's so much to tell you. So much you need to learn. I arrived here just in time to talk with Laetitia. Mako, Felix and I are now aware of all that we did not know. She revealed everything to me. Goddam, man, we're so sorry. I can explain the entire bizarre mess to you.'

The newcomer made no move and no reply, he simply stared at his erstwhile friend who recommenced appealing to him, 'How can I make expiation to you? I badly need a pardon from you, Cole. I made the worst possible goddam misjudgement of you and I influenced Mako and Felix against you as well.'

In a corner of Cole's mind in a half-formed thought he felt sorry for the man who had been so physically perfect and now had lost the use of his left arm. He gazed steadily around at the people in the hall as they all waited for him to react, still keeping his hand on the pistol in his pocket. While he had been startled by the revelations of the last few minutes, the logical mind of Cole Wareing was calculating all he had heard and seen.

Finally he spoke in a voice that sounded foreign to his own ears. 'Now Letta's dead? After being dead . . . and then miraculously alive again . . . And so, while we believed her alive we all headed here to her for explanation of many things, only to find that she's dead – again.'

No one commented though they all looked around at one another.

Cole maintained his examination of Tudor with enigmatic eyes. 'You managed to get here in time for her to reveal everything, you said.' He shook his head and repeated – a tenor of great sadness slipping into the word – 'Everything.'

Tudor's lips tightened in a grim expression. 'Yes, Cole, and it's all been a revelation to me. We have to leave in an hour or so . . . for the funeral. In the meantime, I'd like to relate to you what Laetitia told me, if you'll be kind enough to listen.'

Cole did not move. With his hand remaining on the trigger of the pistol in his pocket he watched as Glenro Thalberg put his arm around the woman in black before he gestured to a nearby door. 'Madame Fourchet and I will take the little one away now.' He glanced to Tudor and pointed to another ornate door not far from the staircase. 'Please use my study to converse, messieurs. You will be comfortable there. I shall send in refreshment.'

Cole still did not stir and Tudor politely requested again, 'Please, Cole, come with me. There's so much I need to resolve with you and so much that needs to be made clear to you.'

Cole's gaze followed the retreating backs of Glenro, the woman and the child and as they departed Tudor inclined his head towards the little boy. 'Yes, he's mine. Dear little guy – Cole, please hear this – conceived *before* Laetitia fell in love with you. Please be clear about that. She wanted you to know that particularly.'

Cole shrugged as his eyes left the child and returned to Tudor who continued to explain, 'Glenro Thalberg and his legal representatives worked through some private detective type and traced me to my London club at Laetitia's request. She wrote to me about the baby when she knew she had the heart disease and a limited time left.' He grunted sadly. 'The letter sat waiting for months for me. As soon as I read it, I rushed here with the boys.'

Cole was obviously still wary and disinclined to co-operate until Shack put his hand on his arm and spoke gently. 'My dear boy, I truly think it is best if you do allow Tudor to fully explain matters to you. You came here for answers, that was the whole reason for this trek; it would be such a waste to disallow them to be revealed to you.' And giving Cole's arm a squeeze and delivering an encouraging smile, he added, 'I'll wait here for you.'

'We'll stay with you,' Felix piped up in friendly fashion.

'Yes, we'll keep you company,' agreed Mako. 'We'll get you a hot drink.'

And as Shack responded, 'Thank you', in acceptance of the offer, Cole at last released the trigger of the Nazi Walther in his pocket and spoke. 'So, Tudor, it was you who got here in time to see Letta.'

'Yes, Cole, it was me.'

Cole let out a weary-sounding breath before he glanced towards Shack who gave him another heartening smile, and he stepped out and followed Tudor Harrington into Glenro Thalberg's study.

Chapter Eighty-five

Tudor, Mako and Felix had travelled in haste from London and arrived at Villa Thalberg just before dawn at 0730 in the morning on 30 December after avoiding communist strikes and managing to catch trains through France which, surprisingly, ran almost on time.

Glenro, who was still in his dressing gown, was so relieved to meet Tudor that tears formed in his eyes. 'Monsieur Harrington, I had given up all hope of your arrival. Do you wish to see your son?'

Tudor answered that he preferred to see his mother first. 'Though, Monsieur Thalberg, I want you to understand clearly that if, as Laetitia's letter claims, I am the father of the child, then I accept my responsibility completely.'

'As you will note when you see him, his parentage is in no doubt. Laetitia has always said he is a replica of you.' He stared earnestly into Tudor's blue eyes. 'And I now realise he is.'

'I see.'

The elderly man motioned for them to follow as he revealed the situation to them. 'Laetitia is mortally ill. We do not believe she will live more than another day or two, so the Lord has brought you just in time.' He sighed so deeply that his chest rose and fell. 'She is not yet awake so perhaps it is best you do come and meet your son.'

In the nursery, Tudor stood silently gazing at the child he had fathered without knowing, before he hesitantly spoke to him, but the little boy was more interested in playing with Glenro's spectacles than in relating to the new arrival.

Toast, tea and coffee arrived and was consumed by them all as Tudor waited impatiently for news that Laetitia was awake. His fervent hope was that she would remain strong enough to be able to speak with him.

Forty minutes later, as snow began to drift down upon the patchwork of ivory and grey outside the windows, they were informed that Laetitia had been roused and Tudor kissed his child and Glenro guided him through the house and up the stairs.

The letter that Tudor had read in his London club on 28 December and which Laetitia had written to him in July 1947, had informed him she had delivered his son in early May 1944 and that she was not expected to live longer than six months from the date of writing. She had advised Tudor that if he wanted his son he should come to Switzerland and claim the boy. She wrote that they had been trying to trace Tudor ever since her illness was diagnosed for she believed that if he could not be raised by his mother then her little boy should be with his natural father – providing that Tudor wanted him.

On the landing outside Laetitia's room Glenro stood by Tudor and, touching the newcomer's arm to hearten him, opened the solid cedar door. 'My dear, Tudor Harrington is here.' He motioned for the man to enter. Tentatively he did so and crossed the carpet to discover Laetitia lying propped up on pillows under her canopied bedhead.

Her bed faced the east and French doors led to a balcony with a view of the lake. From where she lay Letta could see the morning was burgeoning but because of the snow drifting down, the whole iced-up lake was in hiding and so, too, was the opposite bank in the distance.

She thought of summer when the pink and white room was filled with flowers and the sun reflected from the water and danced on the pale oak furniture and floral curtains and striped wallpaper. Her inky eyes lifted to her visitor's over-bright blue ones as he moved quietly to the side of her bed and sat on the vacant chair. She turned her head slightly more and her hair fell away from her face on to the pillow, allowing him to catch sight of the substantial scar on her temple even though make-up had been applied to cover it. Her hair was still thick and lustrous, but no doubt there was a hidden, second scar where the bullet had come out. Tudor had known since his return from Sweden in '45 that Laetitia had shot herself and he could not help but consider the irony of it all; for now, when she wished to live, she was going to die. Involuntarily he emitted a subdued, sad sound as she spoke.

'At last you've come, I had given up hope; but now I should call you Tudor, yes?'

He nodded and tried to smile. 'Yes.'

She shivered.

'Are you cold?'

'No, I was just thinking that in the summer this place is so beautiful, whereas now it's bleak. I shall never see another summer, Tudor.'

He shook his head and raised her hand to his lips and tried hard to smile again as she asserted in a weak voice, 'I'm very pleased to see you.'

'I'm so very pleased to see you too, Angel.' He unconsciously used the pet name he had called her in Holland.

512

'Angel,' she closed her eyes briefly, 'I do not think I am going to be one.' She managed a fragile expression of amusement and met his gaze. 'I've always supposed that you blame me for your capture that night, Tudor, but you are wrong.'

'Am I? It doesn't seem to matter quite so much any more. I've held a bad grudge, Let. It consumed me for years, but now . . .' He sighed and hesitated.

'You blame me and you blame Cole Wareing.'

He started and his eyes widened. 'You know his real name?'

'Yes. He told me.'

'Goddam, he must have loved you.'

She gave another wan smile but did not comment as she tried to lift herself a little on the pillow and he helped her.

And so the December morning passed by in the pink room while Laetitia talked and Tudor listened. She would fall silent for long periods during which Tudor simply sat and held her hand and now and then Glenro came in and smoothed her hair and the nurse arrived with liquids and Letta would drink with her eyes closed.

She revealed to him all that he had not known: her marriage to Von Bremen and the way he had used her to trap him and the others.

He was astounded. 'You were married to a Nazi?'

Letta closed her eyes. 'Many years before . . . left him when he joined Hitler's national . . . socialist party . . . but he came back . . . came back . . . and ruined it all.'

At times she spoke so softly he had to lean forward to understand her and at others her voice became stronger so that he could understand her clearly.

When she disclosed that it was her husband, *Standartenführer* Ernst Von Bremen, who had taken her to the prison near Doetinchem on the day Mako and he were being transferred – the day that they escaped from the back of the lorry – the listener had felt physically sick. 'Oh my God, he was the one who brought you there? It was *Standartenführer* Von Bremen and not *Standartenführer* Bayer?'

'Yes.'

'Goddam, Let, I heard the guards outside the room where I was confined talking about the *standartenführer* showing you off to the men and I made the God awful mistake of presuming it was Cole.' He shook his head and his mouth tensed in a tight remorseful line as his head bent forward to his chest with guilt. 'I lived all those years in hatred of you and sought deadly revenge against Cole. Laetitia, I thought I saw you with Cole hurrying away in the rain.'

She attempted to lift her hand to him and he took it and held it as he sat shaking his head, his eyes clouded with sorrow.

'Yes,' she spoke gently, 'you could have mistaken them from a distance . . . I suppose. It seems you have some . . . apologising to do, Tudor?'

'Yes, it does.'

When Letta told him that she had attempted suicide because she believed that Cole and Tudor were both taken by Von Bremen, Tudor gently kissed her hand again and whispered, 'Forgive me for doubting you.'

'It was afterwards . . . when I was in the hospital recovering that I found out you and Mako had escaped.'

She bestowed upon him a tired smile. 'I have been wrong many times in my life and I regret a great deal. I was wrong to make love to you, Tudor; though my misconduct has brought into this world a most beautiful child and that surely is a good thing?'

He nodded tenderly. 'Of course it is. Let, please listen to me, don't have any regrets. You were brave, so very courageous, a freedom fighter. You did nothing wrong, please don't say you did.' His gaze slipped to the colonnade down by the grey lake and back to her pallid face as he added, 'What we did together we did because there was a war on; we could have been killed any time. We lived for the moment. We were justified. We had our reasons.'

She murmured and closed her eyelids. 'Thank you for being kind and perhaps what you say is true. But when you returned to England from Holland in August 1943, I had no idea . . . about the baby. Yet all the time I was in love with Cole Wareing I carried your son.' She stopped speaking for a long time at that point and he sat there silently until she gave a weak cough and began again, 'You see, I had been told when I was very young that I would not be able to bear children, so it never occurred to me . . . and . . . I was . . . one of those women whose monthly cycle was not regular – I thought nothing of it, even as time passed.'

She breathed a long sigh and he tenderly patted her hand. 'When the Nazis took me to their hospital after I'd shot myself, the doctor informed me that I was having a baby. The bullet had missed my brain and gone cleanly out of the top of my head. It's a miracle my son survived.' She paused. 'My little miracle must grow up happy and carefree.' She took a trembling breath. 'That is why . . . I wanted him to be . . . with you, his father. He will be the heir to all this.' She motioned weakly with the hand he was not holding. 'Uncle Glenro has no one but me to leave it to and now he will leave it to little Drake. I gave him an English name, I always liked it . . . the dashing seafarer Francis Drake . . .' She faltered and did not speak for an extended time while he sat just holding her long fingers, his eyes on her perfectly shaped nails. Finally, she said, eyes closed, 'You must guide him, Tudor, and be a . . . good father.'

'My dear, dear Laetitia, of course I will. I promise you.'

When her breathing altered and came in short, fast gasps, Tudor needed to bend down towards her and to remain there to understand. 'Once I realised that Cole Wareing had escaped, I said nothing. The Nazis treated me as a heroine – assuming that Cole Wareing had shot me, not that I had shot myself. Something always told me . . . the baby was yours . . . even though perhaps at one time I wished otherwise; but when I saw baby Drake, there was no doubt – and now? I would have it no other way. So I lived quietly with my little one up north in Groningen until the end of the war . . . and then . . . I changed my name for I wanted to be free of all that had gone before.'

She gave an insipid smile as a stab of fire shot back into her dark, elegant eyes and her voice gained strength. 'I talked a Canadian officer into giving me passes to escape here to Switzerland.'

Tudor leant forward to her ear. 'You could always charm anybody, Angel . . . anybody at all.'

That pleased her and she managed another frail smile. 'He was the intelligence officer who mentioned you in front of me, not believing that I could possibly know any British secret agents. That's how I learnt your real name . . . strange that . . . life and its . . . serendipity . . .'

She trembled and he pulled the sheet and blanket up around her shoulders just as the nurse came in and said he should not stay any longer; but Letta opened her eyes and flashed them again. 'No, he must stay.'

'Let, we owe you so much. I'm the one who had it all so shockingly wrong. Absurdly, madly wrong. Forgive me, please.' He made a disgusted sound in his throat. 'Thank God I didn't catch up with Cole. All the things I blamed you both for . . . all wrong.'

She lifted her head and flicked her hand in a negating action.

'None of that matters now.' Her eyes locked with his. 'Look after our son.'

'Oh, Angel . . .' Again he unknowingly called her the name he had used in Holland. 'Angel, of course I will.'

And falling silent, he sat watching her until he added softly, 'I am expecting Cole to turn up here any time – you see, he's here in Europe. I was chasing him. I know for certain he heard about you, Let, I reckon he'll come here.'

Her eyes remained on his and with the oddest faraway look she shook her head and fell into silence.

After many minutes during which Tudor watched the view from the windows and the snow and sleet ceased to fall, Letta opened her eyes. The wind continued to howl around the many turrets and corners of the extensive villa by the lake as she said, 'Tell Cole Wareing we conceived Drake before I . . . fell in love with him.'

'Of course I will.'

'Did he ever – is he married?'

'Yes.'

She closed her eyes and took a long, deep breath and seemed to fall to sleep.

After a few minutes Glenro entered noiselessly again with the nurse behind him and seeing that Letta was sleeping, he signalled for Tudor to come away.

Tudor gently slipped his hand out of Laetitia's and was surprised when she spoke again.

She did not open her eyes but her voice was stronger and more forceful than it had been all morning. 'Dirk, please tell Lucien Bayer . . . that . . . I'm so very glad he killed *the shadow of dread.*'

Chapter Eighty-six

Tudor lifted his eyes to Cole who sat opposite. 'And those were the final words Laetitia said to me.' The two men were in green wing-backed leather chairs and empty cups rested on a decorative inlaid table standing between them.

'Cole, I'm guessing that you know what that last statement of hers meant?'

Cole had not uttered a word since Tudor had begun to speak and now he finally made a sound, a dismal noise deep in his throat. He leant his head back on the leather of the chair and closed his eyes. 'Oh yes, I know what she meant. I was the one who killed Von Bremen . . . before I escaped. No doubt, in her mind, he was *the shadow of dread*.'

'Ah, I see. And I thought it very odd that at the end she called me Dirk and you Lucien.'

Cole's eyelids opened and he sat up and rested his elbows on his knees. 'Perhaps she was back in Holland in her mind . . . or perhaps she simply preferred to remember us that way . . . as Dirk and Lucien.'

The wind shook the shutters and the two men, noticing the fire in the grate had died, rose together as Cole addressed his one-time friend. 'I think Laetitia would have approved of your rendition of her story.'

'Thanks. I sincerely hope she would.'

They exited Glenro Thalberg's study and there in the front hall, polishing his spectacles with his handkerchief, they found the mature gentleman waiting for them. He beckoned Cole to him, and as Tudor moved away he asked, 'You understand the past now?'

'Yes. Much more than I did before.'

'Good. That is good. To live not understanding how the past affected you has a way of engendering anxiety in the soul.'

Cole was not about to argue. 'You might be right.'

'There is one thing I should tell you.'

His listener waited while the elderly man wiped his arthritic hands across his chin as he spoke. 'There is part of a painting . . .'

Cole frowned.

'Of you, which my niece saved and brought with her to this house – it is of your face . . . just your face. She obviously could not carry the entire painting with her on her flight from Holland to Switzerland with a child. It's a very good likeness. I have no idea where the rest of the portrait is, but if you want it . . .?' He looked questioningly.

Cole did not speak immediately. He paused as down in the penetralia of his mind he heard her say, '*This is the best thing I've ever done.*'

He met the intelligent, aging eyes watching him keenly and giving a kind smile he shook his head. 'Keep it or give it away, monsieur, I don't mind.'

Glenro Thalberg greeted this reply with a slow nod of his hoary head. 'I will keep it,' he answered. 'To remember you by.' And a moment later he asked, 'Are you coming to my niece's funeral?'

When Cole did not immediately reply Glenro bestowed upon him a knowing, sympathetic look. 'I see you are not coming, my son.'

'Your niece would understand that I cannot come. You see, she died for me on the eleventh of November 1943.'

'Yes, I understand that, my son. I truly do.' He held out his hand. 'I shall alert your friend Monsieur Shackleton that you are ready to leave.'

Chapter Eighty-seven

While Cole conversed with Glenro, Tudor had stood waiting for him.

He was thinking how he would explain to little Drake as he grew up that his mother was a brave Dutch patriot who was in the Resistance. Yes, he would make the little guy proud of his mother.

And suddenly he knew just where he would take the boy. To Jane in Sussex, his land girl.

He would stay here a few weeks and get to know the child and when little Drake was comfortable with him, he would bring him home to Jane, wonderful Jane, with her big heart and her compassion. She would love the little boy; he just knew for certain that she would and he would love her. Hadn't Jane's mother said she'd carried a torch for him all these years? And in time the two of them, together, would tell Drake about his real mother, his beautiful, amazing real mother.

Yes, they would be a family. Angel would be pleased about that.

He needed to send a telegram to Jane. Goddam, he would tell her he was in love with her! That he would be back in a few weeks.

He took a deep breath and strode across the rug to intercept Cole as his former friend left Glenro and made for the front door of the villa, across the black-and-white marble floor.

Tudor cleared his throat. 'You're leaving?'

'Yes.'

'Not going to the cemetery?'

'No.'

'I understand.'

'Do you?'

'Yes, Cole, I reckon I do.' He moved from one foot to the other. 'Goddam, I'm so repentant. I feel such remorse. I'm so very sorry.'

Cole locked eyes with him. 'Yes, I guess you are.'

Tudor opened his mouth to speak, stopped, closed it and gazed at his old ally for a few moments before he said, 'Look, I apologise as deeply as it's possible . . . I hope you can accept that now. But I won't blame you if you don't.'

Cole shrugged his shoulders and Tudor felt the need to go on, 'And I'm uncertain what to say about little Drake – it's been as much a shock to me as it is to you.'

A supercilious expression rose in Cole's eyes. 'You wanted to kill me until a few days ago, so please don't pretend you care about my feelings.'

Tudor grunted in acquiescence to that.

'Well, anyway,' Tudor declared confidently, 'I'll take good care of the little fella.'

'Yes, Tudor. I reckon you will.' Cole paused and decided to be charitable. 'I hope he brings you happiness.'

'Thanks. I'll let him know his mother was a patriot.'

'Yes, you must do that.'

They lapsed into silence, standing looking at one another while the sound of the wind rose and fell outside, until a wistful expression crossed the younger man's face. 'I'll probably never see you again after today, Cole.'

'I expect that's true. What will become of Felix and Mako now that you don't have to chase me around the world?'

'Guess they'll end up living with me. In the few days we've been here, Drake's already taken to them both.'

Cole glanced across the hall to where the two men hovered, waiting. 'They're loyal. That's for certain.' And as he lifted his hand to them they came over.

Mako's raw-boned features formed remorseful lines as he blinked at Cole. 'Ah, please accept our apology, we made a terrible blunder.' He turned to Felix who was of the same mind.

'Gosh yeah, Cole, we really regret this bloody awful mistake – you can keep my Fairburn-Sykes . . .'

Cole saw the amusing side of such contrition and negated any further display. 'Right, Felix, Mako. I understand.' He looked steadily at Mako and back to Felix, holding each man's eyes a few seconds before he added, 'All water under the bridge now.'

'Heck, thanks, Cole.'

He shook their hands and they retreated together as Cole turned back to his erstwhile comrade who held out his good right hand. As their palms met, their eyes met and they both recalled, for a nostalgic moment, their strong intimacy of long ago. Cole could not help but think of how this man had been like his younger brother.

'Good luck, Cole.'

'Good luck, Tudor.'

At that moment Shack appeared and joined them as Tudor hesitated and added tentatively, 'I might just come out to Australia again one day and visit you.'

Cole's mouth edged back in the semblance of a smile. 'Well, for God's sake don't come at midnight.'

Chapter Eighty-eight

Cole and Shack hurried down the wide front steps to the waiting Citroën. They did not speak until they entered the car when Shack could no longer refrain from asking the question he had desired to ask for days but had contained. 'My dear boy, I'm deeply worried about you. Am I to understand that you are heart-broken? That you are still in love with the dead Laetitia de Witt?'

Cole's gaze slowly came round to his companion and a puzzled expression rose in his eyes. 'What? Still love Letta? Do you think that? Have you been thinking that?'

'Yes. You've been so quiet, so introspective all the time . . . and now that you've heard what Tudor had to tell you . . .'.

'Of course I was quiet, Shack. It was a threat for me to meet Letta again. I was afraid to come here. Not because I loved her, but because I no longer loved her.'

'Ah, my boy, I didn't understand. All I kept thinking was that your passion for her was still alive.'

'Shack, my dear Shack, the great passion I felt during the war for her was for a phantom Letta; a Letta of my own making. Just as she loved a man of her own making. She loved *my portrayal* of Lucien Bayer.'

He met his companion's concerned gaze. 'To find out today that she bore Tudor's child was a shock, but not a painful one. I have long since accepted that Laetitia de Witt had secrets. A myriad of secrets were always lying unrevealed between us. I know some of them now, but the others she has taken with her.'

He fleetingly shut his eyes before he grasped his companion's arm in an affectionate action. 'What I feel today for Letta is a deep sadness knowing that she is *truly* gone from this world. She was so beautiful, enchanting, mysterious and gifted; she deserved to live.

'And I cannot stay for a funeral which took place in my mind years ago.'

The older man nodded and patted his boy's hand, comprehending all that he had not known before.

'Ah, my dear friend . . . I love my wife. The woman I married. I love Shell. Somehow she always remained with me. In the war she used to come into my mind at the oddest times. After a sickening day with the Nazis there she would be in my thoughts: I would picture her with her hair blowing in the wind or see her looking at me with her darling eyes . . . it somehow soothed me.

'Letta was an enigma to me. What I felt for her was a magnificent illusion; what I feel for my wife is real, it was born out of her beauty and her strength and the honesty and enduring quality of her love for me. It belongs to the real world and will last for ever.

'I can't wait to walk with my arm around Shell as the sun sets over Apple—' The muscles in his face tensed and he leant forward in his seat, his index finger lifting. 'My God . . . look . . . that woman walking towards us in the snow.'

Shack slid forward on the seat. 'Where?'

'That's Shelly . . . there, on the roadside.'

'But it can't be!'

'It is. How in the Lord's name can she be here?' He rammed the glass panel aside and called to the driver. 'Stop! Beside these women – here – stop.' His fingers reached for the handle and he threw open the door and leapt out.

Shelly and Yvonne had disembarked from the bus into the icy wind and the snow-covered landscape and walked from the main Lausanne highway about five hundred yards gently winding downhill.

They paused as they heard an engine ahead and moved to the roadside into deeper snow to let the car pass. As it appeared through the trees and came closer they realised it was slowing down to a halt beside them and they both stepped away in confusion as the back door swung open and a man leapt out shouting, 'Shell? How on earth can you be here?'

Shelly was astonished as her husband swept her into his arms. 'My darling Shell, you're here? How can you be? God, how much I've missed you . . . how much I have to tell you. Oh Jesus, Shell . . . There's so much I'm aware of now. I should have told you before – forgive me, I love you so, I've missed you so.' He took a breath. 'Shelly, darling, what in heaven's name *are* you doing here?'

Extemporaneously his wife attempted explanation: 'I came searching for you. I followed you . . . caught a ship and followed you . . . I found a postcard, given to you by Laetitia de Witt. I found all sorts of things in your trunk in the attic. This is my friend Yvonne, she's helped me – I was so very worried about you . . . Oh Cole, I wanted to very badly to help you . . .' The tears welled in her eyes.

He stood gazing with pride and amazement at her. 'You followed me across the world to help me? Oh my God, how did I ever deserve to get you?' And pulling her to him he kissed her longingly on the mouth and when they separated he smiled. 'Everything's all right now, there's nothing more to be worried about.'

Shelly looked up into the eyes she loved, tears of joy on her cheeks. 'But Tudor Harrington . . . the men who came in the night?'

'All over, Shell, I'll explain everything.'

'They're not after you?'

'No.'

'The woman in the postcard?' She paused a long moment. 'She meant a lot to you, didn't she?'

'Yes, Shell,' he answered quietly, looking intently at his wife. 'In a different world – for an important time – she meant a hell of a lot to me.'

He caught her to him and hugged her close, his face in her hair. 'But it's you I want for all time, Shell. You're the one I want and need for *all time*.'

'Oh heaven, Cole, then can we go home? Home to Apple Gate?'

'God, Shell, yes, we can. Just you and me, that's what I need.'

Shelly smiled. 'That's all I ever needed, Cole.'

And as her husband continued to hug her to him, Shack and Yvonne broke into wide smiles of satisfaction while Cole kept kissing Shelly's hair, her forehead, her eyes.

And mysteriously – for the universe is mysterious – the bitter wind abruptly died down, a white bird dipped from the sky above and sailed just feet above their heads and the sun came out in brilliance from behind the clouds to gleam on the small gold heart hanging around Shelly's throat.

Author's End Notes

Page 141   Arthur Seyss-Inquart: born Austria, 22 July 1892, was German Reich Commissioner of the German occupied Netherlands. He instigated a policy of which he said, 'We demand everything that is of use to the Reich and suppress everything which may harm the Reich.' He expropriated works of art, deported Dutch Jews in massive numbers to slave and death camps in Germany and waged a savage war against any resistance. He sent five million men to work as labourers for Hitler and the Third Reich. He was hanged as a war criminal in Nuremberg, 16 October 1946. Before he was hanged he accused Hitler of ruining Germany.

Page 142   Hanns Baptist Albin Rauter: born Austria, 4 February 1895, was a Nazi general and the Higher SS and Police Leaser of the German occupied Netherlands. He participated in the detention, deportation and murder of over 100,000 Dutch Jews, seized Dutch citizens for deportation to slave labour projects in Germany, shot to death hostages and waged a relentless war on any resistance. He was executed as a war criminal by firing squad near the Hague, 24 March 1949.

Page 246   Commissioner Fritz Schmidt did, in fact, disappear off a train on an official trip to France on 26 June 1943. It has been generally accepted to have been either suicide or murder by Higher SS and Police Leader Rauter's SS.

Page 270   Mr James Minnis: was a chemist and Mayor of Ipswich, Queensland, from 1939–1949.

Page 303   Erich Naumann: born Saxony, Germany, 29 April 1905, was a Nazi SS General of the Einsatzgruppen mobile killing units which were responsible for the murder of hundreds of thousands of Jews, gypsies and communists. In 1943 he was sent to Holland as a Commander of the Security Police to assist Police Leader Rauter. He never repented and was found guilty of war crimes against humanity in the Nuremberg Trials and was executed 7 June 1951.

Page 369   De Kern, 'the nucleus', was a committee formed in early 1943 of leaders of certain Dutch Resistance organisations who were finally co-ordinating their activities in a once a week meeting in Amsterdam in the height of secrecy.

Page 372   RSSAILA: Returned Sailors', Soldiers' and Airmen's Imperial League of Australia.

Page 408   Anton Adriaan Mussert: born in 1894 and in 1931 founded the NSB: Nationaal Socialistische Beweging: the Dutch National Socialist Movement. After the German invasion and the disbanding of the other political parties in 1941, this was the only political party allowed existence by the Nazis in Holland. Mussert co-operated with Hitler and the Nazis for the extent of the German occupation. He was executed as a war criminal on 7 May 1946.

Page 477

The Home Guard were volunteers in Great Britain who, in the event of an invasion by Germany, were expected to defend the coastline and to hold the enemy at bay until the regular troops could arrive. Usually these men were not in the military forces because their daytime jobs were necessary to keep the country running, or they were too old or too young to join the forces. Originally called Local Defence Volunteers, these men were given military training and when the anticipated German invasion never occurred their contingents guarded key targets like factories and airfields and patrolled beaches and sea fronts, etc. as well as taking prisoner German airmen whose aircraft had been shot down.

Bibliography

Chambers, John H., *Everyone's History*, Xlibris Corporation USA, 2008

Churchill, Winston S., *The Second World War*, Vols. 1–6, Folio Society, London, 1952

Foot, M.R.D., *The Special Operations Executive 1940–1946*, Pimlico, London, 1999

Foot, M.R.D., *Holland at War Against Hitler: Anglo–Dutch Relations 1940–1945*, Routledge, London, 1990

Hirschfield, Gerhard, *Nazi Rule and Dutch Collaboration*, Berg Publishers Ltd, 1988

Lozowick, Yaacov, *Hitler's Bureaucrats: The Nazi Security Police and the Banality of Evil*, Continuum, London & New York, 2000

Pattison, Juliette, *Secret War: A Record of the Special Operations Executive*, Caxton Editions, London, 2001

Rigden, Denis, *SOE Syllabus: Lessons in Ungentlemanly Warfare, World War II*, Public Record Office, Crown Copyright, Surrey, 2001

Seaman, Mark, *Special Operations Executive: A New Instrument of War*, Routledge, New York, 2006

Van Der Zee, Henri A., *The Hunger Winter: Occupied Holland 1944–1945*, Bison Books, USA, 1998

Warmbrunn, Werner, *The Dutch Under German Occupation 1940–1945*, Stamford University Press, California, 1963

Numerous bona fide Internet sites